For permissions or enquiries, please contact: **Info@Moguhl.com**

ISBNs:
Paperback: 978-1-9192245-2-7
Audiobook: 978-1-9192245-5-8
Library: 978-1-9192245-6-5

Author Attribution

Author:
Heath KM Groves
Primary author of The Silence We Hide. Creator of the Moorside House: The Series of Silence saga and principal architect of its characters, plot, and vision.

Co-Author:
Eden EM Groves
Collaborative writer whose narrative contributions, character development support, and thematic insight were instrumental throughout the manuscript.

Co-Author:
Kelly-Ann Groves
Responsible for providing structural and narrative feedback as well as regional and historical accuracy throughout development.

Co-Author:
Jericho M Groves
Responsible for providing imaginative input and conceptual depth throughout development.

Editor:
Ged Henderson
Responsible for the editorial refinement of the manuscript, including structural feedback, narrative clarity, and line editing.

Content Warning

This book contains scenes of graphic violence, drug abuse, adult language, home invasion, graphic war sequences, depictions of trauma and violence and child bereavement that some readers may find disturbing. Reader discretion is advised.

It is intended for mature audiences only (18+).

While inspired by certain real-life settings and experiences, this is a work of fiction. Any resemblance to actual people, living or dead, or actual events is purely coincidental.

Moorside House: The Series of Silence

Welcome to Book Two
The Silence We Share, which is the Second
in the Series of Silence.

The Series of Silence is a crafted work that spans 10 novels, broken into three trilogies and a final book that span three different eras and follow three interconnected families that have occupied the same house.

Trilogy One
The House of Overaugh (2025) - Where the Silence is Faced

Book One: The Silence We Hide
Book Two: The Silence We Share
Book Three: The Silence We Reveal

Trilogy Two
The House of Hawthorn (1940s) - Where the Silence Awakens

Book Four: The Silence We Awaken
Book Five: The Silence We Suffer
Book Six: The Silence We Bury

Trilogy Three
The House of Becker (1880s) - Where the Silence Begins

Book Seven: The Silence We Create
Book Eight: The Silence We Fight
Book Nine: The Silence We Become

Book Ten: The Dark Quarters - Where the Silence Ends

Acknowledgements

Welcome back to Moorside House: The Series of Silence
First and foremost, thank you! By picking up The Silence We Share, you have chosen to continue this journey with us, and for that, we are incredibly grateful.

When we released The Silence We Hide, we were absolutely blown away by the reception. Watching readers connect with the Overaugh family, debate their choices, and immerse themselves in the mystery has been a humbling experience for our entire team. It reaffirmed exactly why we embarked on this ten-year passion project in the first place.

We do this for one simple reason: so that you can enjoy a good story. We believe in the power of fiction to transport, to challenge, and to entertain. We write to create a world you can lose yourself in, even when - perhaps especially when - that world becomes a dangerous place to be.

We promised that the silence would deepen, and we meant it. We have poured everything into this second instalment to ensure the stakes are higher, the shadows are longer, and the secrets are darker. We are confident that The Silence We Share will not disappoint.

Thank you for trusting us with your time and your imagination. We hope you enjoy reading this book as much as we loved writing it.

The Moguhl Team

THE SILENCE WE SHARE

THE HOUSE OF OVERAUGH

The Series of Silence - Book 2

Prologue

Wednesday, 29th January 2025

7 weeks before 'The Incident'

The frost had turned the canal path into a ribbon of cracked glass, each footstep crunching in the half-light. The water itself was a sluggish black, a skin of ice breaking where it lapped at the bank.

Two mildew-stained tents sagged under the weight of frozen condensation, pitched on the patch of scrubland where the canal met the railway embankment. The ground was a mixture of frozen mud, crushed beer cans, and discarded needles. A charred fire pit sat in the middle, filled with wet ash and the stink of burned plastic.

Moxy unzipped his tent with a sound like tearing fabric. He emerged wearing the same grey hoodie he'd been sleeping in for weeks its, cuffs black with grime. His breath steamed in the air as he lit the first cigarette of the day, holding it between finger and thumb as though even nicotine owed him money.

"Fucking Baltic," he muttered, eyes narrowing against the

smoke. "Swear down, Skeggs, one more night of this and I'm moving into the bus station in town. At least it's got a roof."

From the second tent came a groan and the sound of something being knocked over. Skeggs crawled out, bleary-eyed, scratching his stomach through a stained T-shirt that had once been white. His hair stuck up in damp spikes and his face looked like it had been carved out of a raw potato.

"You'd last ten minutes in that bus station before some smackhead shanked you," Skeggs said, wiping his nose with the back of his hand. "Oh wait - that's us, innit?"

Moxy grinned without humour, revealing the teeth of a man who last saw a dentist in primary school. "We're the top of the fucking food chain, mate. Apex predators."

Skeggs squatted by the fire pit, flipping over a dented spoon. "Speaking of which..." he said, pulling a small wrap of brown powder from his pocket.

They worked in silence, Moxy cupping his hand around a lighter to melt the heroin, Skeggs drawing it up with the precision of a twenty-three-year-old who'd done this every day for years. Their age was one thing they had in common – apart from their chemical dependency of course. They didn't talk about the cold, or the fact that the only people who would still spend time with them were each other. They didn't need to.

"That's the ticket," Skeggs sighed after the hit, swaying slightly. "Better than a full English that is."

Moxy wiped his nose with his sleeve. "Still can't believe that Blackburn job. Four hours of graft for a laptop and a telly some old slag probably bought from Cash Generator. Fifty quid, split two ways. Waste of our fucking time."

"Burglary's not what it used to be," Skeggs replied. "Too much CCTV, too many nosy bastards all wanting to be heroes... need something easier."

"Yeah," Moxy said slowly. "Something steady. A nice little pension pot. Like… we find some mug who's already got the goods, and we just… collect."

Skeggs smirked. "Yeah, like protection money?"

"Call it what you want. I call it smart. Let some other idiot take the risks and we skim the cream."

The wind rushed in off the water, rattling the tents. Neither man flinched. They were already thinking about the next score, not about the ruin they'd leave behind, or who they'd have to bleed to get it.

"Need someone gullible," Moxy said, flicking his cigarette butt into the canal. "Someone soft. Someone who thinks we're the mutt's nuts!"

They both grinned, eyes narrowed against the morning glare, already walking away from their camp and towards town. Behind them, the tents slouched in the frost, surrounded by the carpet of litter. Squalor was an understatement.

They cut along the towpath into town, past shuttered shopfronts and boarded windows. The streets were empty apart from the odd early riser shuffling to the bus stop.

Halfway down Manchester Road they saw her.

An old woman, no more than five feet tall, looked to be in her seventies, bundled in a navy wool coat with a tartan scarf wound tightly around her neck.

A handbag on her arm, heavy enough to swing with each step

she walked slowly, deliberately, like she'd been navigating the same route for decades.

Moxy's eyes lit up. "Easy pickings."

Skeggs grinned. "She'll fold in one... no doubt."

They didn't run at first, just lengthened their stride, drifting in from the side, like they always did. Moxy moved in and grabbed for the strap, giving it a sharp tug.

But the old woman didn't let go. Her hands were knotted with arthritis, but she held on like her life depended on it.

"Oi! You cheeky little sod!"

She didn't get to finish. Skeggs's fist came in sideways, fast and hard, connecting with a sickening crack that echoed off the shopfronts. The woman went down like a dropped coat, her head hitting the pavement with a dull thud. Blood was already running from her eye as the socket swelled grotesquely.

Moxy wrenched the bag free. "Told you mate. Easy!"

They ran, boots pounding on the icy pavement, cutting down a side alley before anyone could react. By the time they reached the covered market they were breathless, grinning like schoolboys who'd got away with a prank. Skeggs re-enacting his blow-by-blow prowess of punching the old lady in the face and Moxy giggling along.

Skeggs rifled through the bag, tossing aside tissues, receipts, and a half-empty packet of mints. His hand closed on a battered purse. "Thirty quid," he said with mock disappointment, then grinned. "Better than nothing."

Moxy laughed, shoving the notes into his pocket. "It's a start. Next one'll be bigger. Always is."

They vanished into the warren of back streets, the stolen bag abandoned in an overflowing bin, already thinking about the next score. Behind them, the old woman lay curled on the icy pavement, blood seeping into her scarf, the morning light catching in her broken glasses as she slipped into unconsciousness.

Act V

The Grooming

Chapter One

Saturday, 1st February 2025 – 11:45

The Mall Shopping Centre, Blackburn

Brendan Hughes was in Game Exchange, scanning the rows of cases like a prospector panning for gold. He lingered at the Nintendo Switch section, eyes flicking over the bright, cartoonish covers, but his heart wasn't in it.

The Switch was fine for killing time, but the lack of adult content drove him mad. There was nothing more satisfying than unloading a digital clip into a swarm of enemies on the PS5, watching them scatter in showers of pixels and ragdoll physics.

He was about to drift over to the PlayStation section when raised voices cut across the low hum of the store. It wasn't the usual Saturday chatter of kids haggling over trade-ins. This had teeth.

At the counter, Lee Moxon - Moxy to his friends - was in full swing, leaning in on the young assistant, voice loud enough to carry across the aisles. He had a PS5 under his arm, the box scuffed and taped like it had been dragged out of a skip. "It's worth more than that, you fucking mug!" he snapped, jabbing a nicotine-stained finger at the clerk. "Don't try and shaft me. I know what this is worth."

While the argument rumbled on, Steven Skegg - Skeggs to his friends - was already moving down the shelves, casual as you like, plucking boxed toys and items from the racks and sliding them into his coat. Brendan watched him in the reflection of a display case, lips curling into a faint smile.

The clerk threatened to call security. Moxy spat on the counter in reply, a wet, deliberate gesture, then turned and stormed out. Skeggs followed, but not before catching Brendan's eye and giving him a slow, deliberate wink.

They were gone before anyone moved to stop them, their laughter echoing back through the automatic doors.

Brendan lingered by the racks a moment longer, pretending to flip through cases, but watching the doors they'd disappeared through. There was something about the way they moved. No hesitation, no second-guessing, no fear of who might be watching.

They were lawless, untethered, like the rules everyone else lived by didn't even apply to them. Most people spent their lives worrying about jobs, rent, bills, making sure they stayed in their lane. Moxy and Skeggs didn't have lanes, they just cut across the grass, trampling whatever got in the way.

It was reckless, Brendan knew they were the kind of blokes your mum told you to stay away from. But there was a part of him, a restless, impatient part, that envied how free they seemed. Free to take what they wanted. Free to laugh in a shopkeeper's face and walk away without a care in the world. Free from everything that made his own life feel small.

Brendan left the store twenty minutes later, a carrier bag swinging at his side with a second-hand game that he didn't really want. The February air slapped him cold the moment the sliding doors closed behind him, the brightness of the mall replaced with the grey of a Blackburn Saturday.

He pulled his hood up and was about to cut towards the bus stop when a voice cut through the noise of the street.

"Oi. You!"

Brendan turned. Skeggs was leaning against the wall beside the cash machine, a half-smoked roll-up hanging from his lips. Moxy was a few feet away, crouched over, flicking a lighter at something cupped in his hands.

"You were in the shop," Skeggs said, pushing himself off the wall. His eyes were sharp, measuring. "Saw you clocking us."

Brendan shrugged. "Yeah."

"You didn't say nothing."

"Nope."

A slow grin spread across Skeggs's face. "Appreciate that. Most punters would've run to the staff, playing hero. You didn't."

"Not my business, pal." Brendan said.

Moxy looked up from whatever he was lighting. "Exactly. Not your business. That's the kind of mature thinking I like." He stood, exhaling a thin stream of smoke, the sweet, earthy tang of it drifting over. "How old are you kid? You smoke?"

Brendan hesitated, then nodded. "I'm eighteen."

"Good lad, don't want to be leading no minors astray, now

do we." Moxy said, handing him the joint. "First one's on us."

Brendan took a drag, coughing at the harshness, eyes watering. Skeggs laughed.

"You'll get used to it," Skeggs said. "Thing is, we don't let anyone tell us what to do. No boss, no landlord, no bills, no bollocks. If we want something, we take it. Simple."

"Too many mugs living life in a straight line," Moxy added, taking up the theme. "School, job, mortgage, grave. Nah. We live on our own terms. No one owns us."

Brendan exhaled slowly, the buzz creeping in warm at the edges. "Must be… liberating."

"It's the only way to live," Skeggs declared, stepping closer. "Everyone else's problem is they're scared. Scared of getting caught, scared of what people think. We're not scared of anyone. That's why we always win."

Moxy chuckled. "Winning's just grabbing what's there for the taking. Doesn't matter if it's a PS5 or a bag of cash. World's full of stuff. Most people are too polite to nick it."

Brendan found himself smiling. There was something intoxicating about the certainty in their voices, the way they spoke like the rest of the world was asleep and they were the only ones awake.

"Stick with us, lad," Skeggs said, clapping him on the shoulder. "We look after our own. You don't grass, you're alright in our book."

Moxy flicked the roach into the gutter, grinding it out with his boot. "Come on, let's go find something to do that's not boring as shit."

"Here you might as well have this, no one's going to buy it, and we don't even have a fucking telly to plug it into!"
He thrust the PS5 into Brendan's greatly accepting hands.
Brendan followed without thinking, the first quiet step away from his old life and towards theirs.

Chapter Two

Friday, 14th February 2025 – 18:32

Scrubland, Altham

Three weeks had passed since Brendan first crossed paths with Moxy and Skeggs. What had started as the occasional smoke and bit of banter had turned into whole afternoons spent hanging around with them. Loitering by the canal, killing hours in the bus station arcade, and drifting through Burnley and Blackburn's backstreets like they had nowhere to be.

He'd learnt their rhythm quickly. Moxy was the mouth; always talking, always scheming, half his sentences beginning with what if. Skeggs was quieter, but sharper in ways Brendan couldn't always put his finger on. Skeggs was the one who noticed things - the bloke counting the till in the corner shop, the delivery van left running outside the takeaway, the CCTV blind spots on the high street.

Brendan stuck to weed when they passed it round, ignoring

the little foil wraps that sometimes appeared in Moxy's hand or the syringe marks on Skeggs's arms. He told himself it was fine. He was just there for the craic, for the easy laughs and the way they seemed to carry themselves like the rules didn't apply.

This evening, they were sitting on a low wall by the railway arches, the frost from earlier that morning already turning to dirty slush underfoot. Moxy was rolling a joint, the paper crinkling in his nicotine-stained fingers.

"We need a good gig," Moxy said, licking the edge of the paper and sealing it with a snap of his fingers. "None of this piss-about fifty-quid nonsense. I'm talking proper."

Skeggs leaned back, hands shoved deep in his coat pockets. "One decent job and we could be set for months. None of this scraping by. None of this 'what's in the till' bullshit. A lump sum, enough to breathe and live a little."

Brendan took the joint when Moxy passed it to him. "And what, you're just gonna magic that out of nowhere?" he asked.

"Not magic," Moxy said, grinning. "Opportunity. It's everywhere lad, you've just gotta see it. Most people walk right past it because they're scared or stupid. That's where we come in."

Skeggs nodded towards Brendan. "See, you're smart. You've kept your head down these last few weeks, but you've got the eyes for it. You notice stuff. Like when you clocked me in that shop, you knew to keep your mouth shut. That's instinct."

Brendan shrugged, exhaling smoke into the air.

"Wasn't my problem."
"Exactly," Moxy said. "That's the mindset. You just need to start thinking bigger. One big score, you can do what you like. No boss, no bills, no one breathing down your neck. That's freedom, that is."
"Freedom," Skeggs echoed. "And the buzz. Don't forget the buzz."
Brendan said nothing, but the words lodged somewhere in the back of his mind. The way they said it made it sound easy... like all he had to do was take one step and he'd be out of the grey, plodding life he'd been stuck in.
Moxy flicked the roach into the weeds, his grin widening. And just like that, the seed was planted.
They walked down the towpath to see if anything was brewing. Brendan peeled off at the lights, heading for the bus stop with his hood up against the drizzle. Moxy watched him go, hands buried in the pouch of his hoodie, a faint smirk on his face.
Skeggs shifted his weight, pulling a crumpled pouch of tobacco from his pocket. "I don't gerrit, mate," he said, rolling with quick, impatient fingers. "We've been dragging him round for weeks. He barely buys owt, barely talks, won't touch the gear. What's the point?"
Moxy lit a cigarette from the stub of another, the flame briefly catching in his narrow eyes. "It's called playing the long game, lad."
Skeggs snorted. "Long game? We're skint now. I'm not looking for some apprentice."
"You're looking for your next fix," Moxy said flatly. "That's

the difference. I'm thinking about how to make it easier down the line."

Skeggs glanced in the direction Brendan had gone. "He's green, soft, doesn't know shit about anything."

Moxy exhaled a thin stream of smoke, leaning back against the wall. "Exactly. Soft's good. Soft means he's pliable. He's got a family with money... I can smell it. Might not know it yet, but he'll lead us somewhere worth going."

"And if he doesn't?" Moxy shrugged. "Then we get him on the hard stuff. Once he's chasing that, he'll graft for us just to keep himself straight. I'd rather have someone else doing the legwork while we sit back."

Skeggs grinned, a slow, nasty curve of his mouth. "So, he's paying in, one way or another."

"Now you're getting it." Moxy flicked his cigarette butt into the gutter. "Sometimes you don't have to nick a wallet straight away. Sometimes you just fatten the calf first."

The two of them stood in silence for a moment, the rain pattering on their hoods, each picturing Brendan's face and what they might wring out of him before they were done.

Chapter Three

Saturday, 1st March 2025 – 10:10

Scrubland, Altham

The sky was a washed-out grey, low clouds hanging heavy enough to touch. The scrubland at the end of the canal was slick with last night's rain, the ground a patchwork of mud and crushed grass. The two battered tents slouched in the middle of it, flanked by the skeletal remains of a pallet fire and a scattering of cans, bottles, and discarded wrappers.

Brendan was buzzing. Practically bouncing as he cut across the wet ground ignoring the squelch of his trainers, the cold, the smell. "Moxy! Skeggs!" he yelled, voice cutting through the stillness. "Oi! Get up, you lazy bastards!"

From the nearer tent came a muffled groan. The zip rasped halfway before a pale, scowling face appeared. Moxy's eyes were bloodshot slits, his hair sticking out in damp clumps.

"What the fuck's with the foghorn lad?" Moxy croaked. "It's… what time is it?"

"Ten past ten," Brendan said, grinning. "And you're gonna want to be awake for this."

Skeggs's head appeared from the other tent, his hair flattened on one side, a cigarette already hanging from his lips unlit. "If you've come to tell us Asda's out of doughnuts, I swear..."

Brendan cut in, almost dancing on the spot. "It's big. Like… properly big."

Moxy rubbed at his face, yawning. "Go on then, soft lad. You've got my attention."

Brendan crouched down between them, lowering his voice as if the scrubland had ears. "I was round at my mate Jonah's last night. His dad was banging on about renewing the contents insurance. Guess what's up for renewal?"

"His Netflix?" Skeggs muttered.

"No," Brendan said, eyes bright. "His watches. All of them. Proper posh ones, too. I've seen them out on the table before. Omega, Rolex, that Tag one. Looked like a bloody jeweller's shop. Jonah says they're worth twenty, maybe thirty grand easy."

Moxy's expression sharpened instantly. "And the policy's up for renewal?"

Brendan nodded. "End of this month. Seth's been putting it off because the premium's going up. Jonah said if anything happened to them before then… well, they're not covered."

Skeggs scratched at the stubble on his jaw, finally sparking his cigarette. "So, you're saying… if they went missing before the paperwork's done, it's a total loss?"

"Exactly." Brendan's grin widened. "Which means they'll be pissed, yeah, but they could claim if he renewed, and he said he was renewing this week. So, if they go missing it's a victimless crime!"

Moxy sat up fully now, the lazy morning slouch gone. "That's not bad, lad. Not bad at all. No harm, no foul, they get paid out."

"I knew you'd like it," Brendan said, riding the thrill of their attention. "And I know Jonah. He won't kick up a fuss. If we cut him in for, say… two and a half grand, he'll keep his mouth shut. Let's face it he doesn't need to know how much we can get for them."

Skeggs gave a short laugh. "Two and a half? For a thirty grand haul? Harsh."

Brendan shrugged. "He's a wet blanket. Always skint, always moaning. Two and a half in his hand and he'll think it's Christmas. He's my mate. I'm not gonna stitch him up entirely just, I can spend the money in much better ways."

"Mate or not," Moxy said, leaning forward, "you've got the right idea. Keep him sweet, keep him quiet. But the main thing is shifting the gear."

Brendan frowned. "You think you can get rid of them?"

Moxy smirked. "Course I can. I know a bloke in Preston, works the antique and pawn circuit. Fences high-end watches all the time. He'll take the lot in one go, no questions, no receipts. We're talking twenty grand clean, maybe a bit more if he's feeling generous."

Brendan's grin faltered slightly. "Twenty? Thought you said thirty."

"That's retail," Moxy said, as if explaining to a child. "Fences don't pay retail. You're paying for speed and silence. Twenty grand is good money for something that could land you in jail for five years."

Skeggs exhaled smoke through his nose. "And once we've got it, we split it three ways, yeah?" Brendan nodded. "Course."

"Four ways," Moxy corrected smoothly. "Your mate Jonah gets his two and a half. What's left, we divide proper."

Skeggs gave Moxy a look. "You're playing this straight?" he whispered.

"For now," Moxy said, eyes flicking back to Brendan. "The important thing is keeping everyone happy until it's done. We don't want this Jonah getting twitchy before we've even started."

Brendan leaned in, lowering his voice further. "We'd have to be careful. His dad Seth's got cameras all over the place, and he's a big guy."

"Cameras can be avoided," Skeggs said. "You just don't go where they're pointing."

"And you don't go in yourself," Moxy added. "You've got connections to the house, so if your face shows up anywhere, you're finished. Leave it to someone who knows what they're doing."

"Meaning you?" Brendan asked.

"No, Skeggs, this is more your cup of tea."

Skeggs grinned around his cigarette. "Damn right."

Brendan sat back on his heels, the excitement still bubbling in his chest. "So, what do we do first?"

Moxy held up a hand. "First, nothing. We sit on it. We let you keep being Jonah's mate. Keep your ears open. You find out if those watches ever leave the house and if that Seth

bloke's still dragging his feet on the renewal."
"We need the perfect window. They're less likely to go nuclear on the police reports if they're covered."
"And if there's no window?" Brendan asked. "There's always a window," Moxy replied, a slow smile spreading across his face. "It's just a matter of spotting it."
Skeggs tapped ash onto the ground. "I like it. Feels clean. In and out. No drama."
Brendan couldn't help laughing. "You two don't do anything without drama."
"That's half the fun," Skeggs said, standing and stretching. "But if this goes right, we're set for months. No more chasing scraps. No more freezing our bollocks off waiting for some pisshead to walk past so we can liberate their loose change."
Moxy pointed a finger at Brendan, his tone turning serious. "Just remember, this is a team thing now. You keep it between us. No one else. Not your mum, not your mates, not some bird you're trying to impress."
"One slip and it's all gone. Keep our names out of Jonah's head, he doesn't know about us, right?"
Brendan nodded quickly. "I'm not that stupid." Moxy smirked. "No. You're not. That's why you're here. As far as Jonah will know, you're doing the deed, okay?"
They sat for a while longer, tossing around ideas - timing, entry points, how to move without drawing suspicion. Moxy kept steering the talk back to the fence, to the payout, to how easy life could be when you weren't scraping for the next fix or flipping cheap stolen gear for pennies.
By the time Brendan stood to leave there wasn't yet a plan,

just a bright, glittering possibility. But it was lodged in his head now, he could feel it growing, taking shape with every step back down the towpath.

Moxy watched him go, leaning into Skeggs. "Told you, long game. We've just hit the jackpot."

Skeggs smirked. "As long as he doesn't bottle it."

"Nah, he won't." Moxy said with quiet certainty. "One way or another he's gonna pay out. Just you wait."

"You really thinking a three-way split?" Skeggs asked.

Moxy laughed. "Like fuck, he's getting fuck all, and if he pipes up then he's going in the canal." They both chuckled.

Chapter Four

Saturday, 15th March 2025 – 00:06

Industrial Estate, Altham

As Brendan crossed the bridge he reached into his pocket and pulled out the cheap Android burner that Moxy had given him and started to text Skeggs's number:

'We're on.'

From the trees to his left, a harsh whisper cut through the night.

"No phones!"

Skeggs stepped out of the shadows, moving with a purposeful swagger that Brendan hadn't seen before. It wasn't the lazy, half-bent shuffle he wore in town. This was tight, controlled, dangerous. Even his silhouette felt different, like he'd put on a skin he only wore for certain jobs.

"Right, mate," Brendan said, more out of confirmation than warmth. Skeggs ignored it. "Just been scoping them out, they've gone to bed. You got the balaclava?"

Brendan handed over the black wool mask and the cheap pair of gloves he'd been keeping in his hoodie pocket. Skeggs snatched them without thanks, pulling the mask down over his face and flexing his gloved fingers.

"You know the layout. We've been through it over and over. Has anything changed?" Skeggs muttered.

"No. Front's lit, cameras all over," Brendan said. "Granny flat door at the side's unwired. That's your way in. Don't hang about in the kitchen. Straight through to the main hall into the alcove. That's where they keep the good stuff."

"Good lad," Skeggs murmured. He reached into his inside pocket and pulled out a tiny twist of clingfilm. Peeling it open with practised fingers, he dipped into the white powder and brought it to his nostril, snorting hard. He pinched his nose and sniffed twice more, eyes blinking rapidly.

Brendan frowned. "You serious? Now?" Skeggs grinned behind the mask. "Keeps me sharp. Don't worry lad. I've done more jobs wired than sober."

Skeggs jerked his chin toward the house. "You just keep your head down and your mouth shut. I'll be in and out before you've stopped shaking."

He moved off into the darkness, cutting along the treeline with the low, silent steps of someone who'd done this far too many times before.

The night was crisp but damp, the kind of air that stuck to your clothes. Skeggs kept to the shadows, eyes flicking constantly, not because he was nervous, but because habit had drilled him to see everything. The cocaine was already kicking in sharpening the edges of the world, making the house in the distance seem almost too clear with every light and shadow distinct.

When he reached the edge of the property, he crouched low behind a hedge, peering through. The house loomed against the dark sky, big and self-important. Every lit window an insult to people like him. He could see the glare of a security light near the front door, the faint red blink of a camera above it.

Skeggs's lip curled under the balaclava. Amateurs. You didn't protect a house like this with a couple of cameras and an alarm box stuck to the wall.

He slipped along the side fence, feeling for the spots Brendan had told him were blind to CCTV. A portly tuxedo cat bolted from under a bush, and he froze, letting the darkness settle again before moving on. Even the bloody cats were fat here, he chuckled inwardly.

The side door to the granny flat was exactly where Brendan said it would be - tucked under a shallow overhang, paint peeling on the frame.

Skeggs tried the handle; it opened just as planned. He slipped inwards and left the door open, always the best option to ensure no obstructions if a quick getaway was needed.

The atmosphere was still. He paused, letting his eyes adjust. The granny flat kitchenette was small, cluttered with mugs and cereal boxes. He moved through it without touching anything, his boots silent on the flooring.

Through the next doorway, he entered the main house. The air changed. A bigger space, colder somehow, the faint scent of polished wood and something floral mixed with pizza. His breathing slowed. He was in.

Skeggs padded down the hallway; every nerve tuned to the sound of the house. Floorboards creaked faintly above, but there was no rhythm to it - probably just the building settling. He slipped past a darkened alcove, glimpsing the heavy furniture in the moonlight spilling through the skylight.

The staircase rose ahead of him, broad and carpeted. He took the steps slowly, feeling for each one, keeping his weight even to stop the fabric crunching underfoot. Halfway up, he glanced back over his shoulder. Nothing but shadow and silence behind him.

At the top, the landing stretched out, wide enough to drive a car along. A thick rug muffled his steps. He was careful not to stand on the wood either side of it. Doors lined both sides, but it wasn't the rooms that caught his attention.

It was the thing on the right-hand sideboard.

A blue hue coming from one of the bedrooms, its door not fully closed, cast a faint light into the hallway. Even in the dim light, the statue drew the eye. Black basalt, tall, and wrong. Its surface seemed to swallow the light, its lines sharp but somehow alive. Two handles jutted from its sides like something built to be held, and for a strange moment, he thought it was watching him.

Skeggs stopped dead, pulse ticking faster; not from fear, but from the electric rush of the coke and the unsettling weight of the thing's presence. The job, the watches, all of it slipped a little in his mind as he stared at it.

Then he shook his head, muttering under his breath. "Weird bit of posh tat."

He started forward again, the soundless tread of a man with work to do, but the weight of the statue's gaze - real or imagined -seemed to follow him down the landing towards the alcove door at the far end.

Brendan moved quickly along the back edge of the garden, keeping low as he skirted the fence line. The night was cloudless, the starlight sharp enough to pick out the edges of the lawn and the pale gravel path that curved toward the terrace.

He kept to the shadows until he reached the overgrown bushes near the far corner. The same spot he'd picked out earlier as the perfect hiding place.

From here, he had a clear sightline through the rear windows, past the sweep of the staircase to the main landing above. The glass reflected fragments of moonlight, but he could still make out shapes inside. The high walls washed in dim light from somewhere deeper in the house. He crouched lower, pushing branches gently aside until he found the gap he wanted.

Reaching into his pocket, he pulled out the cheap Android burner Moxy had given him. It felt light, almost flimsy, but that was the point... disposable. Flipping it over in his hands, he unlocked it with a clumsy swipe and opened the camera app. He tapped the record icon then stopped it again, checking the playback.

The tiny screen lit his face in the dark as he squinted at the grainy image. It was rubbish quality, sure, but it worked. He could see the faint glow of the landing in the test clip and enough of his own face to know that it was good enough for his purposes. The railing's shadow stretched across the carpet.

That was enough.

He smiled to himself, but not for the reason anyone would think. Sure, it'd be a nice little reminder of the night, something to brag about in his head later; but that wasn't the whole game. This was leverage. Insurance.

Skeggs and Moxy thought they were the clever ones, pulling the strings, but Brendan wasn't stupid. If they ever tried to turn him over, pin it all on him or rob him blind, this footage would be his way to collect. Proof of who was really in the house, doing the job.

"Not as daft as you think, lads," he muttered under his breath.

He hit record again, this time letting it run, the cold seeping into his legs as he settled in to watch. And to make sure that if things ever went sideways, he'd have the upper hand.

Chapter Five

Saturday, 15th March 2025 – 00:23

A faint sound broke the stillness – soft, irregular, and close enough to turn every nerve in Skeggs' body taut. He froze mid-step, head cocked, listening past the rush of blood in his ears. It wasn't the settling groan of timber or the distant hum of the fridge. This was lighter, human… a shift of weight on carpet, somewhere along the landing.

He eased himself back, every movement measured and slipped into the narrow alcove beside the bathroom door. The space was scented with soap and something floral. A toilet sat just inside, the half-open door shielding most of him from view.

Holding his breath, he let the coke-fuelled edge sharpen his senses. A faint creak answered from down the hall, followed by the almost imperceptible hush of bare feet moving on carpet. He tightened his grip on the gloves around his fingers, muscles coiled.

From this spot, he could see the corner of the landing where a blue LED light bled faintly from an open bedroom door. Any second now whatever, or whoever, was moving would appear.

He pressed himself further into the alcove's shadow - the hard edge of the sink at his back - and waited.

Then he heard it. Soft. Slow. Bare feet on carpet. Moving towards him.

He leaned as far back into the shadows as he could, adjusting his stance so he could move fast if he needed to. The half-open bathroom door shielded most of him. But from the angle he could still see the far end of the landing where the glow from the bedroom spilled a pale rectangle onto the carpet.

The sound drew closer. Then she stepped out. A young girl, slight frame, long hair mussed from sleep, jumper pulled tight around her. Shit. Must be the daughter, Skeggs told himself. She padded out of the room, her head turned briefly, then she started towards the bathroom.

Towards him. Fuck!

Skeggs stepped out before she had the chance to see him fully. He moved like he was stepping out of a black wall. Sudden, solid, close enough that she stopped dead.

Her eyes met his through the slit in the balaclava. Wide, startled. He could see the flicker of recognition. Not of him, but of danger and then absolute fear!

He liked that.

She opened her mouth to scream, and that was it... no more messing about. He clamped a gloved hand around her throat, hard, forcing her back into the wall. Her shoulder blades hit first, then her lower back smacked into a sideboard. His other hand went over her mouth, cutting the sound before it got anywhere.

She kicked, tried to twist, nails scraping at his wrist, but he leaned his weight in, pinning her like he'd done a hundred times before. His breath came out hot and sour in the mask, filling the space between them.

A dull thud on the floor made him glance down slightly. The posh bit of tat from the sideboard. It rolled once and settled in the middle of the hallway. He ignored it.

"Don't say a fucking word, you little bitch," he hissed into her face, voice low and deliberate. He could feel her pulse hammering against his fingers.

Then, out of nowhere, a snarl ripped through the air. Low and vicious, building into a full-on attack bark. A blur of fur and teeth hit his leg, jaws clamping down just above his ankle.

"Fucking dog!" he cursed, trying to shake it off, but the thing was latched on like it had been born for this. Pain shot up his calf, sharp and hot. He kicked, but it only bit harder, teeth sinking through the fabric and into flesh.

The girl made a strangled sound... half choke... half scream. He shifted his grip on her neck, forcing her head sideways to shut her up. The movement was pure instinct. Control the situation, stop the noise.

Light flared at the far end of the corridor. A door slammed open.

A woman appeared in the frame. Hair wild, eyes blazing, already moving toward him.

"What the FUCK..." She was charging. Her foot slipped on

something on the rug, but she kept coming at him, faster now.

He braced, yanking the girl tight to his chest as the woman hit him. A finger jabbed into his eye, her shoulder slamming into his ribs. She was smaller than him but fought like she meant to take him apart; sharp, targeted strikes, not flailing. He'd tangled with enough people to know the difference. This one had training, and she was fierce.

He tried to shove her off, but she wrenched the girl sideways, breaking her free. Pain tore at his leg again as the dog renewed its assault, teeth gnawing at the same bloody spot.

For a moment, it was chaos. The woman hammering at him, the dog gnawing, the girl gasping for air on the floor. He managed to slam the woman back into the wall, pinning her by the throat. He used his reach, extending his left arm to keep her away.

The movement was automatic, finishing it with one clean hit. This wasn't a simple break-in anymore. It was full on aggravated burglary, likely to carry ten-plus years inside if he was caught.

In for a penny, in for a pound, he thought, the coke humming in his skull. I'll put these bitches down, hard… and maybe have a bit of fun before I'm done.

The thought aroused him.

It had been a while.

He brought his right fist back for a clean shot to her face, maybe across the jaw. He wanted to keep her pretty. It was never any fun raping a bleeding woman. Then, just briefly, out of the corner of his eye, he saw something…

Chapter Six

Saturday, 15th March 2025 – 00:25

CRACK!

The right side of Skeggs' skull felt like it had been hit with a cinderblock. Heat burst into his face, and his right eye went black.

The world went sideways and white at the same time. Cheekbone screaming, eye exploding into liquid fire. He couldn't see... couldn't see out the right side. Something was running down his cheek, warm, salty... wrong.

His shoulder and head smacked into the wall hard enough to rattle his teeth. A hollow sound rang in his ears, as if he was inside a drum. He tried to stay upright but his legs were folding. Stupid useless legs. He couldn't tell where the floor was.

Air. He needed air. He was making an animalistic nasal sound through broken sinuses.

Hands... where are my hands? he thought - arms moving but

slow, syrup-slow, like he was underwater. Then something yanked the back of his collar, and he was flying, weightless for a breath, before his back slammed into the floor.
Air punched out of him. His spine jolted. Panic. Pain. Air... he needed air!
He tried to put his arms up, anything between him and whatever this was but they weren't listening.
Through the one good eye that was partially covered by the balaclava he could see something above him. A foot, a bare foot above his head. Then it came down like a jackhammer.

CRUNCH!

His face caved in on itself. Pressure behind his eyes exploding. His whole body went rigid, arms snapping straight, legs kicking without him telling them to. Lightning in his skull. Then black fuzz trying to pull him under as he was about enter what MMA fighters call 'the shadow realm'.
No. No. Stay awake.
Blink... Blink... The shadow still over him. Something in his hand now... dark, heavy, wrong. Skeggs' head wouldn't turn but he could feel it in the air above, like the air itself was braced for it.
Then, impact. Solid and dense, driving his skull into the floor beneath. Sound gone. Only pressure. Only pain. No air.
Somewhere far away, he realised his own body twitching, and then everything went still.
For a moment, there was nothing. No pain. No weight. Just… quiet.

Could he see? Could he not see?
Could he hear? Could he not hear?
What was happening?
Skeggs hovered somewhere above the ruin of his own body, a drifting scrap of thought clinging to the scene below. He should have seen Seth there, looming over him, statue raised high. But this Seth person was gone.
In his place was something else.
Tall, rigid with a face swallowed by the shadow beneath a wide-brimmed hat. A long black coat hung from its frame, heavy yet shifting in a wind that seemed to move only for it. The air around it was dense, thick as if the room itself was holding its breath.
It made no sound. No footsteps. No breath. Only presence; ancient and immovable, as though it had stood in that hallway for centuries, waiting for this moment.
The folds of its coat swelled as unseen arms lifted, raising the blunt weight clasped within. It came down in a single, deliberate arc striking the lifeless form on the floor. The floorboards groaned. Again, it rose. Again, it fell.
It was screaming, "Zdychaj, ty skurwysynu!"
The statue his attacker had seized upon was no longer just cold basalt. It seemed alive and trembling with a dreadful power. From its surface, waves of light began to pour forth. Not clean, straight shafts but warped, wavering streams. Like heat rising from scorched stone.
They writhed as though seeking out their prey, finding each soul in the hallway.
A pale-grey beam lanced into the young girl, clinging to her

like a shroud of fear.

A deep-blue current flowed inexorably into the woman wrapping her in the crushing weight of sorrow.

The apparition the raging figure that rained blow after blow upon his weakening body was drowned in a crimson haze. The very air around it trembled with rage.

And from the heart of the statue, a final wave tore upwards and backwards, bursting through the roof into the night sky. A sickly green twisting column that seemed to pierce heaven itself.

The scene was grotesque, unreal, a theatre of madness painted in colours no mortal should ever see. For a moment Skeggs wondered if this was the coke playing tricks on him if the powder he'd racked up had tipped him into some waking nightmare. Yet the pain, the weight, the fury all of it was too real.

It was an ecstasy of horror, and as his physical, lucid thoughts slipped away he could only wonder what infernal gear he had sniffed to conjure such a vision.

With each blow, the hallway seemed to shrink, the edges of Skeggs' awareness closing in, the world narrowing to the silent, relentless figure and the cold certainty that it would still be there long after all else was gone.

The air crackled, thick with the stench of iron and ozone. The whole hallway seemed to shudder. For a heartbeat Skeggs thought the coke had torn him into madness - that this nightmare tableau was nothing more than poisoned imagination.

Then the sound came. A detonation without fire, a

concussive bang that shook through the walls of his reality. Darkness swarmed his vision, a depthless, eternal black. And in that void, cold and close, came the voice.

A whisper, yet thunder. A presence that filled every inch of whatever he had become.

"You're mine now!"

The words coiled around what was left of him, branding themselves deeper than flesh. His final thought was not of resistance, but of falling endlessly into a place that had been waiting for him all along.

The dream came fast.

Skeggs came to with a lurching sensation, as though he had fallen too far and landed nowhere. The world around him was neither light nor dark, but a shifting void of shadow and muted colour like the inside of smoke. The air was thick, pressing at his chest, but it was not air at all. It was presence, heavy and suffocating.

And there, before him, was a figure.

Tall and thin, dressed in the dark coat of another age, his beard ragged but his eyes sharp with a feverish light. He carried himself with the unmistakable crooked dignity of a man who had known filth and madness yet exalted in both.

Skeggs staggered, though he felt no body beneath him. "What the fuck is this place? Am I… am I in Hell?"

The man laughed a low, mirthless chuckle that carried no warmth. "Hell?" he repeated, savouring the word like wine on his tongue. "No, no, no. Hell will not have me. They will not take I. That is very good for me… but I fear, very ill indeed for you."

From the shadows at his side, a smaller shape emerged. A girl no older than eight with golden blonde hair, her pale form subdued, her eyes hollowed by years beyond imagining. She did not speak, but her presence was accusation enough.

"This here..." the man said, laying a skeletal hand upon the girl's shoulder, "is Charlotte Hawthorn. Though I dare say she goes by Lottie in the whispers of her kin. She has been with me for…" He narrowed his eyes as though tallying a conundrum. "Eighty-three years. Yes. From the year of our Lord 1942 until now."

Skeggs swallowed, his throat dry, though he had no throat. "Eighty-three?"

"Yes," the man said, his grin wider. "And let me tell you, for the first thirty years, it was diverting sport. To torment an innocent child, to watch her weep, to taste her terror. Ah, it was a banquet to a man such as I. But after thirty years… after fifty… after threescore years…"

He gave a little sigh, almost wistful. "The pleasures grow thin. A child's innocence cannot be despoiled forever. It dwindles, it fades, and one tires of the same cries in the same voice. It is a stale game. Certainly, when the child never really deserved to be here in the first place."

He turned his eyes back to Skeggs, and their gleam hardened. "But you, Steven..." he lingered on the name with mocking precision, "...you are different. You are no innocent. You are corrupt, venal, and violent. You are meat already spoiled, and to carve upon such meat is a greater delight altogether."

"I shall flay your soul until there is nothing left but rags. And then I shall begin anew, for there is no death here, only my hand, and my will... and your endless screams."

Skeggs tried to back away but the void had no space for retreat. The shadows seemed to cling to him, pulling him towards man and girl.

The figure's voice softened almost tenderly as he looked back at Lottie. "You may go now, child. You have suffered your fill. I have no more use for you. Go to whatever body parts you may have left."

The girl looked up at him, hollow-eyed, as though not believing. For the first time in decades, a light seemed to kindle around her - a burst of brightness that cracked the dark like glass. She lifted, her form dissolving into radiance, and with one final look of longing toward something beyond, she whispered 'Merry', and she was gone.

His smile followed her ascent, but when he turned back to Skeggs it was transformed, a grin so sinister it twisted his face into something not quite human. His eyes glowed faintly, reflecting some inner fire, and his voice was silk stretched over knives.

"So, Steven," he said, enunciating each syllable with relish. "Let us get acquainted."

He stepped forward, his shadow spilling across the nothingness crawling over Skeggs like oil. "I have an eternity to make an art of your undoing. You shall scream, and I shall savour."

"And when you think the end has come, when you believe yourself emptied, I shall begin again, and again, and again...

until time itself has forgotten you."

Skeggs tried to speak, but no words came, only a strangled rasp. The void around him pulsed in time with his terror, the shadows dragging him down, deeper and deeper.

The figure tilted its head, studying him with some delight. "You are mine now, resident in my dominion. In it you shall serve as my amusement, my canvas, my unending sport."

The grin widened, teeth flashing like the edge of a blade.

"Welcome," the figure said, his voice dry as dust yet cutting through the gloom. "Welcome to my Dark Quarters."

"Now… let us begin."

Chapter Seven

Saturday, 15th March 2025 – 00:24

The bushes at the back of the garden climbed up the embankment, so by the time Brendan crouched low among them he was almost level with the first floor of the house. From here he had a clear vantage point of the wide star-light window some five metres tall, stretching from the rise of the staircase to the long landing that cut across the upper hall.

His breath came ragged in the night air, the condensation drifting into the branches like smoke. He clutched the burner phone so tightly his knuckles ached, the tiny red recording dot blinking in the corner of the screen.

He couldn't believe what he was seeing.

The Overaughs' house was Grade II listed, its windows nothing more than old single-paned glass. That thin sheet did little to mute the chaos inside. Every sound travelled through the night air and into Brendan's ears. The sudden crash of ornaments, the deep bark of the dog, the scream caught halfway in a throat.

The sounds made the fight inside feel closer, like he was not outside in the garden at all but pressed up against it all, a silent witness with no power to intervene.
Fear came over him in waves. His stomach tightened, threatening to heave and yet he couldn't drag his eyes away from the flickering shapes through the glass.
He could see Izzy, a blur of pale limbs thrashing against a black shape. Then Natalia wild and furious, hurtling into the fray.
It was chaos with bodies smashing against walls, the old timbers of Moorside groaning under the weight of violence.
Brendan felt torn. One part of him wanted to run and bolt up the embankment, over the canal bridge, and never look back. He could feel the adrenaline pooling in his legs, screaming at him to move.
But the other part of him was rooted to the soil: compelled to watch, compelled to record. The tiny phone in his hand had become his anchor, the screen's dim glow casting his face in pale light. This is proof, he told himself. This is insurance.
But another voice cut through, shriller and rawer. What if he kills them? What if he kills her?
His breath caught as the black-masked figure slammed Izzy against the wall. Brendan's gut lurched he should shout, he should do something, anything. Terror glued his tongue to the roof of his mouth, his pulse hammered so loud he was certain they'd hear it inside.
The recording wobbled in his grip as his hands trembled. The image shook, warped, but still caught the moment that Natalia came tearing into the landing, her body colliding with

the intruder like a storm. Brendan's heart surged into his throat. He wanted to scream, to beg them to get out. But he did nothing.

He crouched lower, branches clawing at his cheeks, bile burning in the back of his throat. He had never felt so powerless, so utterly paralysed by fear. The fight before him was no video game, no film. It was blood and breath; he was watching it unfold in real time.

"Jesus Christ," he whispered to himself, the words steaming into the leaves. His voice sounded alien, a thin croak lost in the night.

He tightened his grip on the phone and tried to steady his breathing, but his chest heaved as though he'd run miles. Panic warred with instinct. If he stayed silent, he lived and could prove he didn't touch them. If he made a sound, he risked everything. But if he did nothing and one of them died, wasn't that blood on his hands too?

The phone screen flickered catching another crash inside, Brendan's whole body shuddered. He felt as though something inside was staring back at him through the glass recognising him.

Panic boiled over. He gagged, clapped a hand over his mouth, fought the urge to vomit into the bushes. He couldn't move. He couldn't speak. He couldn't do anything but sit in the cold dirt, the brambles biting into his legs while watching through that old glass as the Overaughs' world was torn apart.

Then another figure burst into view...

Seth.

He came out of the far doorway in nothing but his vest and

boxers - eyes wild, hair sticking up like he'd been yanked out of a nightmare. For a second Brendan didn't even recognise him. This wasn't the calm, controlled Seth who always had an answer for everything. This was something primal.

Through the window Brendan saw the moment just before Seth lunged. It was raw, uncalculated, and almost animalistic, yet ruthlessly professional and swift. The punch was devastating.

Brendan flinched. The phone slipped in his sweaty hands again as he scrambled to keep it level, catching flashes of limbs thrashing, the glint of Natalia's hair as she clawed her way free - Izzy curled against the wall gasping, clutching her throat.

Then Seth again... his face contorted, teeth bared, not shouting words but a guttural roar that made Brendan's stomach clench.

"Christ almighty," Brendan whispered. His whole body trembled.

This wasn't defence anymore. This wasn't about survival. Seth had gone past that. His fists hammered down repeatedly each blow shaking the old timbers. He had something in his hand and was raining blows down with a furious intent that Brendan had never witnessed before.

Brendan's insides churned again, part of him wanted to look away to shut his eyes and bury his face in the dirt, but the other part couldn't. This was the Overaughs stripped bare, not the tidy family at the dinner table, his friends with the jokes or the school-run smiles.

This was them in blood and violence, tearing a man apart on their landing.

He could hear Seth's voice now ragged and hoarse, words spilling out between grunts and blows. Brendan couldn't catch them all through the glass, but the rhythm was unmistakeable, curses and raw hatred spat like venom. Natalia's voice joined, sharper, like flint striking iron, and Izzy's sobs bled into it all.

The noise and the sight of it pressed down on Brendan like a massive weight. His legs cramped, and his fingers shook so badly the recording lurched in jolts, the picture breaking into jerks of movement and light. He felt sick, torn between the terror of being caught and the dawning realisation of what he held in his hands.

Because this wasn't just proof anymore.

This was evidence.

Evidence of murder unfolding in real time.

And Brendan Hughes, hidden in the bushes, had captured every second.

Chapter Eight

Saturday, 15th March 2025 – 01:05

Brendan was shell-shocked.

He had stopped recording and was just kneeling, gently rocking backwards and forwards trying to process what he had just witnessed. The screen of the burner phone went dark in his hand, the tiny red recording light gone, leaving him alone with nothing but the night air and the pounding in his skull.

His breath came in short bursts. He could still hear the chaos inside, the bark of the dog, the crash of something breaking, the faint echoes of shouts that had cut straight through the glass. He'd seen shapes, movements, shadows flailing in the starlit window. And then... silence.

Not peace. Not calm. Just the wrong kind of silence.

Brendan crouched lower into the branches, twigs scraping his hoodie, damp earth soaking through the knees of his joggers. He kept waiting for the obvious blue lights, sirens, neighbours flicking on lamps, doors slamming open. Someone must have heard. Someone must have called.

But the estate stayed still, the only light was from the windows showing yellow squares against the black sky. The only sound was his own ragged breath and the distant hum of the bypass.

Minutes bled together. The phone told him it was gone one, then closer to two. No flashing lights, no raised voices outside, no police. With every minute that passed, the dread shifted into something else.

They weren't calling it in.

They weren't asking for help.

They were covering it up.

He wiped at his mouth with the back of his hand. Whatever had happened in that house and whatever had happened to Skeggs inside, Seth wasn't phoning anyone. Natalia wasn't. Izzy sure as hell wasn't.

They were making it disappear.

The thought dug in sharp and cold.

He pressed himself tighter into the hedge straining to see, but the angle gave him nothing now but the side wall and the landing window black again and silent. He shifted, branches cracking, and realised he'd have to move if he wanted to know more.

Staying put was no use.

Slowly, carefully, Brendan slithered backwards out of the undergrowth, crouching low as he worked his way along the embankment and towards the front of the house. Every rustle of dead leaves sounded like a shout, every snap of a twig made him freeze, listening intently certain that Seth would be there, torch beam cutting through the dark.

But nothing came.

He edged round to the gravel front, pressing himself against the low hedge that marked the drive. From here, the view opened and was still a CCTV dead spot. The green front door, the carriage lamps, the broad sweep of windows on the ground floor glowing faintly. He stayed crouched, heart still hammering.

Then the latch clicked. The door opened, spilling a thin wedge of yellow light across the gravel.

And Seth stepped out.

Brendan ducked lower, barely breathing.

Seth's silhouette filled the doorway. His shoulders hunched, his coat thrown on, and his boots unlaced. He looked both larger and older in that moment.

He didn't move for a while. He just stood there, surveying the night, one hand braced against the doorframe as though steadying himself.

Then he descended the single step - slow and deliberate.

Brendan's chest tightened. He had no idea what Seth was carrying, no idea where he was going, but he knew with a horrible clarity that whatever was happening here wasn't panic anymore. It was purpose.

This wasn't a family in shock. This was a family cleaning house.

Brendan slid lower into the hedge clutching the burner phone to his chest, his mind spinning with a single thought: if Seth saw him now, he wouldn't walk away. He'd likely receive the same fate as Skeggs.

He pressed deeper into the shadows as Seth moved back and forth between the shed and the fire pit, a spade glinting under his arm. The scrape of metal against soil carried through the night. Seth started to dig, and Brendan, trembling, lifted the burner phone again and hit record.

After a while Natalia came outside, her torch beam cutting through the dark. She stood close directing the light, her face set and cold. Brendan's stomach tightened. This was being run like some kind of military operation, precise, methodical.

Then the earth gave way to something else. Brendan's breath caught as he realised that they weren't just digging down, they were pulling something up, an old box?

Were they looking for something?

For a fleeting second his heart lifted. Maybe he'd been wrong all along. Maybe this wasn't what he thought.

But then Seth and Natalia went back inside. Moments later they re-emerged, struggling under the weight of what looked like a rolled carpet. Brendan's chest hollowed, it wasn't carpet. It was Skeggs.

His heart sank like a stone. He hadn't been wrong; this was a cover-up.

They unwrapped the body and pushed it into the hole. Brendan's throat closed, but then something shifted. Seth wasn't finished. He strode back to the shed and returned with something long and heavy in his grip. The torchlight caught it.

A saw.

"No," Brendan whispered, stomach turning. He realised he was about to watch Seth Overaugh cut a man into pieces.

The front door opened again, and Izzy appeared. The dog burst out beside her prancing in her usual eager way, tongue lolling. She barked once, then broke into a trot... straight toward Brendan's hiding spot.

Fuck!

Brendan fumbled through his pocket, fingers scrabbling, finally pulling free the dog chew. Lydia skidded to a stop in front of him, tail wagging furiously. He thanked the Lord that the bushes hid them both. He stroked her head, shoved the chew into her mouth. She wagged once more satisfied and bounded back toward the house, crunching happily.

"Izzy," Seth called softly, stepping forward quickly. "Go back inside."

"No," she hissed, her voice shaking, stepping closer. Her eyes fixed on the fire pit, on the pale, twisted shape half-covered by soil. "No… you can't, what are you doing?"

Natalia reached for her, voice taut with desperation. "Izzy, you shouldn't be here. Please, just go back inside."

Seth shifted to block her view, but the move dragged him fully into the torch beam. Brendan's camera caught everything - dirt-streaked face, boots thick with mud, the saw hung in one hand.

Izzy's eyes widened. Her breath hitched, she doubled over retching violently into the grass.

"Izzy," Seth pleaded, dropping the saw, moving to steady her. "Please... you have to understand-"

"Understand what?" she screamed, snapping her head up, tears streaking her cheeks. "That you're cutting him up? You're sick! Both of you! This isn't right. This isn't us!"

"Sweetheart..." Natalia tried again voice cracking, reaching gently.

"Don't touch me!" Izzy recoiled, eyes blazing. "You said we were good people. But this? This is insane! I want nothing to do with it!"

"TOUGH!" Seth roared, his voice shaking the air.

"This little bastard tried to harm you, he laid hands on your mother, he broke into our home, came upstairs into our space, and for sorting him out we're the bad ones? I don't fucking think so. Life is not bubble-gum and wishes, Izzy!"

Izzy staggered backward stunned, her expression twisting in disbelief. Then she turned, her footsteps quickened to a run. The slam of the front door echoed through the night.

Brendan's hands shook so badly he almost dropped the phone. His camera caught Natalia's face, pale and stricken, her voice barely more than a whisper. "We must finish this now."

Seth bent and retrieved the saw, together they turned back to the pit. The torch beam cut across them as they set about their macabre task.

Brendan kept recording, his breath ragged, until terror finally tipped him over. Hot urine spread through his joggers, and with a shuddering gasp as Seth raised a severed arm above his head to stack the parts properly, he fainted, crumpling into the undergrowth.

Chapter Nine

Saturday, 15th March 2025 – 03:27

Brendan came to with a sharp intake of breath, as though he'd been drowning and had just broken the surface.

His hoodie was damp, his joggers clammy and reeking. Cold mud on his palms. His head throbbed with a dull, nauseous ache. The branches above him shivered in the faint breeze, their skeletal tips rattling together like bones. For a moment, he couldn't remember where he was.

Then the smell hit him.

Earth. Bleach. Something metallic that hit the back of his throat.

And then he remembered.

His chest seized, panic flooding back in a hot rush. He'd seen it, he'd recorded it. Seth in the torchlight, boots caked with soil, saw in his hand. Natalia directing the beam her face locked in grim focus. Izzy's scream. The body in the pit. The pieces.

"Fuck," Brendan whispered, clutching his head. "Fuck,

fuck, fuck."

He rocked forward onto his knees. His hands shook so hard he nearly dropped the burner phone. The red recording light was off now, but he knew it was there... everything. All of it, his only proof, his only weapon.

But also, the reason that they'd kill him if they ever knew he had it.

His breath came in sharp gasps, fogging in the cold night air. His mind spun in endless circles.

Do I go to the police? No, they'll know I was here. I'll be dragged into it, blamed, stitched up.

Do I delete it? No, it's my insurance. But if they catch me with it… Jesus Christ, what if Seth comes looking?

He clawed at the hedge, pulling himself upright. His legs were weak, jelly-like, but adrenaline carried him. He couldn't stay here, not a second longer.

He staggered backwards, retracing his steps, snapping branches underfoot. Each sound cracked like a gunshot in the stillness. He froze with every rustle, certain Seth's silhouette would emerge from the doorway, torch beam cutting across the lawn, soil-stained, saw glinting. But the house stayed quiet. The only movement was Lydia, briefly visible near the side hedge, padding back inside.

Brendan's pulse thumped in his ears. He half-crawled, half-stumbled back along the embankment, the same way he had come hours earlier. Branches whipped at his face, catching his skin. His hoodie snagged on a thorn bush, and he tore it free without looking back.

As he broke away from the garden and up toward the slope

that led to the towpath, his trainers slipped on the damp grass nearly pitching him face-first into the earth. He righted himself, gulping for air, the dark water of the canal glinting faintly ahead.

Finally, he hit the towpath. The gravel crunched beneath him too loud in the silence. He staggered forward, sucking in deep breaths - the canal to his left, the looming black shape of Moorside House behind him. He didn't dare look back.

His mind raced, get back to the garage, delete the footage? No, keep it. Tell Jonah? No, don't tell him. Police? No, they'll lock me up. Shit, shit, shit...

The burner phone felt heavy in his hand. He clenched it tighter, every nerve screaming at him to run faster, to put as much distance between himself and that house as possible.

So he did.

He broke into a shaky jog, hoodie flapping, his shadow darting along the path in the glow of the distant streetlights. His chest burned, lungs aching, but he didn't stop. Not until the bulk of Moorside disappeared behind the trees and the sound of his ragged footsteps was the only proof he was still alive.

After what felt like a life time the tents came into view.

He pressed the burner phone tight against his chest, terrified to even look at it. He knew what was on there. He knew he couldn't ever unsee it.

The tents sagged ahead of him, mould-dark and damp. The place stank of smoke, sweat, and dog shit. It felt like home and hell all at once.

"Mox," he croaked, his voice raw. "Oi… Mox!"

There was a shuffle from the nearest tent, a muffled groan. The zip rasped open, and Moxy stuck his head out, eyes puffed red, a stub of roll-up stuck to his lip.

"Jesus Christ, Bren," he muttered, squinting. "You look like death. Where've you been? How did it go?"

Brendan staggered closer, fell to his knees in the mud outside the flap. His hands shook so badly he could barely hold himself up. "I saw it, Mox. I saw the whole fucking thing. He's dead. They killed him, Skeggs is gone."

Moxy frowned, rubbing his eyes. "Slow down, who's dead?"

"Skeggs!" Brendan spat, half sob, half shout. "He went in and got caught, they... fuck... they used a saw, Mox. A saw. Seth cut him into pieces. Nat was holding the torch, and Izzy saw it too."

Moxy blinked, baffled. "Wait… what are you even talking about? You saying you watched your mate's old man chop Skeggs' up? You off your tits?"

Brendan grabbed his hoodie by the chest, shaking him. "I've got it on video! Right here!" He held up the phone like a holy relic. "I recorded the lot, him digging, Nat dragging. The pit, the saw, it's all here."

Moxy froze, the smirk sliding from his face. For a moment he just stared at the phone, then back at Brendan's wide, wild eyes.

Moxy could smell opportunity, real opportunity here. He had to play this cool.

"Jesus, lad," he whispered. "If that's true, you're fucked. They see you with that, you'll be next."

Brendan's breath came in short, ragged bursts. "What do I do

Mox? Tell the cops? Delete it? Keep it? I can't.... I can't think straight."

Moxy shoved him back lightly, steadying his own nerves. "First, stop screaming the place down. Second… you keep your gob shut; you hear me? This is way above your pay grade now. You take that to the police, you're not a witness, Bren - you're an accessory. You were there, you filmed it, they'll drag you under with them."

Brendan shook his head violently. "No, I didn't go in, I didn't touch nothing, I was just watching!"

"Doesn't matter," Moxy said flatly, finally stepping out of the tent. His hoodie was stained with old ash, his trainers caked with mud, but his eyes were sharper now. "Doesn't matter what you think. To the cops, you're part of it and to Seth? You're a loose end, and by the sounds of it that guy doesn't fuck about."

Brendan gripped the phone tighter his nails digging into the plastic, his whole body trembled. "Then what? What the fuck do I do, Mox?"

Moxy lit the stub of his roll-up, inhaled deep, then exhaled smoke through his nose. He looked at Brendan with something like pity.

"Let me see it."

Moxy started to watch the grainy video with more intensity than he had in years. His mind whirring with the possibilities this could bring, he just had to keep his poker face in place.

Brendan's stomach dropped, bile rising in his throat. He rocked back on his heels, eyes wide, whispering like a prayer as he listened to the muffled audio.

"I'm dead, Mox. I'm already dead."
"No pal, you just need to calm down a little."
Moxy leaned back on his heels, watching Brendan unravel like a frayed thread. The kid's face was pale and blotchy, his hands trembling so violently he looked close to convulsing. The phone shook in his grip like it was burning him.
"Here, you can stay in Skeggs' tent till we figure this out, it's not like he's going to need it. Moxy opened the flap and ushered Brendan inside with Moxy close behind.
"Listen, Bren," Moxy said softly, a calmness in his voice that he rarely bothered with. "You've just seen something no one your age should ever have seen, it's rattled you, I get it. You're strung out, your head's screaming at you, you need to take the edge off."
Brendan looked up at him with wild eyes. "I don't, weed's enough, Mox. I can't..."
Moxy put a hand on his shoulder, squeezing just hard enough to ground him. "Weed ain't going to touch this, lad. You've just watched a bloke get chopped into bits. Trust me, no spliff in the world is going to make that picture leave your head. What you need… is calm. Sleep... Something stronger... just this once."
Brendan shook his head, mumbling something about not being "that kind of person." But his voice lacked conviction. His eyes kept darting back to the phone, the fear surging each time he remembered what it held.
Moxy rifled through Skeggs' stash and lit the match gently, cupping it against the wind as he pulled a bit of foil from his pocket. He was always ready... always. He tapped out a line

of brown powder, folded the foil into a shallow boat, and set it above the flame. The familiar sweet, acrid smell filled the air as the smoke began to rise.

"Here," Moxy said, pushing a makeshift tube toward Brendan. "You don't need to inject. Don't even think about that, it's just smoke. Nice and easy, in... out... let it do its job. It'll slow your head down, just a one-off to get you through tonight."

Brendan hesitated, lip trembling. His stomach twisted, but exhaustion and panic overrode resistance. He leaned in, drew the smoke, coughed hard then took another drag, desperate to believe Moxy's words. Within minutes, the tightness in his chest eased, his eyes grew heavy, and his frantic rocking slowed.

"That's it," Moxy murmured. "That's better, isn't it? Just let it carry you one night Bren, that's all. Tomorrow you'll laugh about it."

Brendan slumped on the rancid sleeping bag of a dead man, eyelids sinking as the warmth seeped through his veins. His head lolled sideways, he mumbled something. "Not me... not me..." before slipping under completely.

Moxy watched him for a long moment, a sly grin creeping across his face. He reached down and pulled the burner phone from Brendan's limp grasp, checking it quickly, making sure the pin still opened it. Bren had used his birthday: rookie mistake.

Skeggs had always been a liability, too wired, too erratic, too fond of stabbing first and thinking never. But Brendan... Brendan was different. A posh lad, soft around the edges with just enough desperation and just enough secrets to make him malleable. He could be groomed, bent, reshaped into something profitable.

Moxy waited until Brendan's breathing deepened into the slow rhythm of heavy sleep.

From his pocket, Moxy pulled a small wrap and a used syringe he'd stashed earlier. He worked quickly, practised hands drawing up the dose. He didn't need to kill the kid. Not even close, just enough to make sure that by morning, Brendan's brain had tasted what real dependence felt like.

"Sorry, lad," Moxy whispered, crouching over him. "But you're too good an opportunity to waste."

He slid the needle into the crook of Brendan's arm and depressed the plunger, watching the brown liquid disappearing into the vein. Brendan didn't stir, didn't flinch, lost in the fog of the smoke he'd already inhaled.

Moxy capped the syringe, tucked it away, and sat back on his haunches, eyes glinting in the dim light.

Skeggs had been unreliable. But Brendan Hughes? Brendan was a jackpot. A middle-class boy with shaky morals, a video full of leverage, and now the makings of a habit.

A pension plan in the flesh.

Moxy pulled the flap of the tent closed, lit himself another roll-up, and smirked into the dark.

"Welcome to the family business, Bren."

Chapter Ten

Saturday, 15th March 2025 – 09:27

Brendan woke to the sensation of his own skin crawling.

At first, he thought he was still dreaming, caught in some looping nightmare. But the ache in his bones and the sour taste in his mouth told him he was awake, his hoodie stuck damp to his chest, his joggers heavy with sweat, the sleeping bag twisted around him like a shroud. A sharp chill ran across his skin though the air inside the tent was stale and warm.

His head throbbed in pulses, his stomach clenched, twisting like rope. He swallowed hard, then gagged into the corner of the mat, dry heaves tearing through him until his ribs ached.

And then the memories came.

The fight, the hallway, Izzy gasping for air, Natalia clawing at the man in black, and Seth with his face contorted, his fists hammering down, the saw glinting under torchlight. The pit, the body, the pieces.

The images tumbled together, jagged and bloody, crashing against each other in his skull. His chest seized, panic pouring

back into him once again like acid.
"No," Brendan whispered, clutching his head. "No, no, no..."
But he remembered, he remembered everything. And the worst part he had recorded it all. On the burner that was now gone.
His body shook with a strange duality: one half drenched in fear, the other consumed by a hollow, clawing need he didn't understand. His muscles twitched, his skin itched, his stomach cramped again. He tried to convince himself it was shock, trauma, lack of sleep. But some deeper part of him knew it wasn't.
This was something else.
He curled into himself rocking gently on the foul sleeping bag, breath shallow and uneven. Every fibre of his body screamed for relief, though he couldn't name from what. He only knew that the warmth he'd felt last night, that fogged calm, that sweet drowning silence, was gone, ripped away leaving him raw and empty.
A voice whispered at the back of his mind, just one more to settle your head.
Brendan pressed his palms into his eyes until stars burst against the black, but the whisper didn't leave. It burrowed deeper, fusing with the memory of Seth's voice, ragged and furious,
"Life is not bubble-gum and wishes, Izzy!"
The words rang out in his head, jarring against his own whispered plea, I can't… I can't…
He wasn't sure if he was shaking from fear, from the sickness in his gut, or from the yawning chasm of need pulling him

back toward the smoke. All he knew was that his mind was breaking under the weight of it all.

Brendan Hughes was no longer just a witness, he was marked. And he could feel it.

He rubbed at his arm. A small, sharp ache lingered in the crook of his elbow, a bruise rising faintly under the skin. Panic flared. What the fuck…?

He yanked at the zip of the tent and crawled out into the cold morning air. The scrubland was grey and damp, a thin smoke curling from the makeshift fire Moxy had built out of broken pallets and rubbish. Moxy crouched low squinting at the burner phone in his hand, the screen casting his gaunt face in pale blue.

Brendan staggered closer, throat dry. "Mox… what the fuck did you do to me?"

Moxy didn't look up straight away. He tapped the ash off his roll-up, let the phone rest on his knee, then finally raised his eyes. Calm, too calm.

"You were gone last night, lad," he said evenly. "Proper gone, shaking, crying, begging, me to make it stop. You don't remember?"

Brendan shook his head violently. "No. I smoked a bit yeah, but my arm hurts. It feels like... like you injected me!"

Moxy exhaled smoke slowly through his nose his expression unreadable. "Aye you were begging, proper pleading. You wanted something stronger, kept saying you couldn't take it anymore. I weren't about to let you spiral, not after what you'd seen so yeah, I gave you a little jab. Just enough to calm you down, nothing major."

Brendan backed a step, panic fizzing under his skin. "You - NO, I wouldn't..."
"You did." Moxy's tone sharpened, just a touch. "Don't go calling me a liar, you were on your knees mate. I only helped you out and look you're still here, aren't you? Didn't kill you. Didn't even knock you proper out, just steadied you."
Brendan's chest heaved, eyes darting between the phone and the syringe bruise in his arm. "This isn't me, Mox. I'm not..."
Moxy cut him off, voice dropping back into a low, soothing drawl. "Listen, one little shot, that don't mean nothing. You don't get hooked off that, not if you keep it steady. What you need now is just a smoke, just a little bit to straighten yourself up, take the edge off. Then you'll feel fine."
Brendan shook his head weakly. "I don't… I can't…"
"You can," Moxy said leaning closer, lowering his voice like he was sharing a secret. "It's not about being a junkie, it's about surviving. You saw things last night that would fuck most blokes for life, you think your head's going to just forget that? You'll go, mad. Or…" He tapped his pocket where the foil crinkled. "…you take a little pull, breathe easy, and keep your head straight."
Brendan stared at the fire, the crackling wood spitting embers. His stomach churned, his skin itched, his mind rattled with images of Seth's fists and the saw glinting under torchlight. The ache in his arm pulsed, hot and accusing.
"You promise it won't…" His voice cracked. "…it won't get me hooked?"

Moxy smiled thinly, patting Brendan's shoulder like an older brother. "Course not, you're not Skeggs, lad. You're better than that. One little smoke, that's all. Set you right after the night you've had, you deserve it."

Brendan swallowed hard, throat burning. His body screamed at him for relief, for escape, for something to silence the chaos tearing his mind apart. Slowly, almost against his will he nodded.

"Alright," he whispered. "Just one."

"That's my boy," Moxy murmured, already pulling the foil from his pocket, eyes gleaming in the smoke-hazed light.

The smoke hit Brendan like a tide rolling in.

At first it was harsh, scratching the back of his throat, making his eyes water. Then the warmth came slow, creeping, wrapping itself around his chest, and seeping into his limbs. His stomach stopped its violent twisting, his heart slowed from a gallop to a heavy, steady beat. The shaking in his hands eased.

For the first time since the night before he wasn't drowning. He slumped back against the damp canvas of the tent wall, eyes half-lidded, his whole body buzzing with a strange, heavy calm. A sigh rattled out of him long and low, like air escaping a punctured tyre.

"Better, isn't it?" Moxy said crouching across from him, feeding another scrap of wood onto the fire. His grin was faint, but his eyes were sharp, watching every flicker of Brendan's expression.

Brendan nodded slowly. "Yeah… yeah, it's… it's quiet. In my head, I mean."

"That's the ticket." Moxy leaned in, dropping his voice to that reassuring, almost brotherly tone he used when he wanted to get inside someone's ear. "Now, we've got to think. What's next?"

Brendan blinked, the world moving sluggishly. "Jonah…" he muttered. "He was waiting in the car, he'll be wondering, he'll… he'll think I just bailed on him."

Moxy shook his head. "Jonah ain't wondering anything lad. If he's clever, he's lying low right now praying no one ties him to what happened. You go strolling home and what do you think happens? His mum calls yours, or yours calls his, word gets around you were together. Next thing, you're both on the hook."

Brendan's face tightened, panic flickering under the fog. "But I'll have to go back eventually. They'll… they'll notice."

"Not yet," Moxy cut in sharply, then softened his tone again. "Listen, right now nobody knows what happened to Skeggs. Far as anyone's concerned, you're the one who went missing last night, and no one has a clue who Skeggs was or that he's even connected to you or Jonah. You've been out here, that means Jonah, your mum, his mum, they might already think you're the one who got done in." Moxy liked that, he could feel a plan forming.

Brendan stared at him, the words seeping through the haze like ink in water. "They… they might think I'm dead?"

Moxy leaned back, rolling the stub of his smoke between his fingers. "Exactly, which buys you time. If they think you're gone, nobody's looking at you, nobody's asking questions."

"You stroll home now, all wide-eyed, and you are part of it. Maybe even the fall guy. But if you stay here with me…" He tapped his temple. "…we figure this out. We plan, and when you do go back, you go back clean as a whistle with your story straight."

Brendan rubbed his arm, eyes darting to the burner phone lying on the ground beside him. "I don't… I don't know, Mox. My head's all over the place."

"Course it is," Moxy said smoothly. "You saw something no kid should see, and you did the smart thing, you came here. You brought it to me that shows you've got brains, Bren. You don't just walk back into the lion's den after what you've seen. You'll get devoured instantly."

Brendan exhaled, a tremor running through his chest despite the haze dulling his nerves. "So, what do I do? Just… stay? Hide out here like nothing happened?"

"For now," Moxy said. "We sit tight, you get some sleep, clear your head, plan. Nobody knows you're here. Nobody even knows Skeggs is gone yet. That phone of yours, that's our ace, our pension. With that, we've got leverage, and leverage means money."

Brendan swallowed, throat dry again. "Money?"

Moxy's grin widened, sly and hungry. "Trust me lad, the Overaughs will pay through their teeth to keep what's on that phone buried. But that's tomorrow's job, for today you stay put. You're safe here, safer than you've ever been."

Brendan closed his eyes falling back into the tent, falling onto the sleeping bag. The warmth spread deeper, dulling the edge of panic.

Part of him wanted to believe Moxy, to believe he was safe, hidden. That someone else would take the thinking out of his hands.

But the bruise on his arm pulsed faintly reminding him of what he'd already given up, somewhere in the fog, a tiny voice whispered that he was already too far in to climb out.

Act VI

The Plan

Chapter Eleven

Sunday, 16th March 2025 – 15:01

"Right then, let's plan this out."

Moxy crouched by the dying fire, flicking at the half-burned wood with a stick as if strategy itself could be summoned from the embers. The air around the camp was fog, smoke, and chemical sweetness hung low clinging to everything it touched. Brendan sat opposite, hunched in Skeggs' old camping chair with the thin plastic cutting into the backs of his legs. His head throbbed from the lingering taste of the morning's hit.

He felt like a hollow version of himself: tired, raw, mind fogged but oddly light. Every part of him hurt except the part that should have been scared. That part was gone, thank God!

Moxy's voice cut through the quiet. "You, my lad, are gonna sit tight, no heroics, no grand gestures. You stay put here until next Thursday, you don't go into town, you don't show your face, and you defo don't contact that family of yours. You're invisible, a ghost. Got it?"

Brendan rubbed at his face. "Till next week? Out here?"

"Yeah." Moxy said, without looking up. "That's the beauty of it, by the time you show up again at the back end of the week the heat will have cooled, and the cops will be getting ready for the weekend. Everyone'll be desperate to see you safe, not to blame you. You stroll into your house on Thursday evening and give them the story nice and clean."

He sat back on his haunches, grinning. "You tell 'em you went wild camping, say you needed head space, bit of a digital detox. You'd been feeling low, wanted quiet. Maybe mention the stress of college. A good old mental health excuse, they lap that stuff up all empathy and understanding. That card's untouchable these days."

Brendan frowned, eyes bloodshot. "And Jonah? He's my mate, Mox, he's probably losing his head right now. He'll think I've -"

"Stop," Moxy said sharply, jabbing the stick at him. "This isn't about Jonah, that posh lad'll be fine. He's got mummy and daddy to mop up whatever mess he's in. You, though… " He leaned forward, the grin fading. "You're the one who was there, you're the one who saw what you saw. You open your gob to anyone even Jonah, and you're done, you're a full-on accomplice. Understand?"

Brendan swallowed, the back of his throat dry. "He wouldn't grass me up."

"You sure about that? He was the one sat in the car while you were supposed to do all the graft, some friend that." Moxy tilted his head, watching Brendan the way a cat watches a mouse it's already half-eaten.

"He's soft, you said it yourself. Sooner or later, he'll start talking, all guilt and tears, then what? You think he'll keep your name out of it? You think that family will risk their cosy life for the likes of you?"

Brendan looked down at his hands. His nails were black with dirt. "He's not like that."

"Everyone's like that when the coppers start poking around. You want loyalty? Get a dog," Moxy said, liking his own phrase and mildly enjoying the comparison to Brendan, his very own little new vein that was going to do whatever he wanted, when he wanted it. If he played this right.

The smoke twisted in the air between them, Brendan tried to steady his breathing, but his chest felt tight. He wanted to argue, to tell Moxy he was wrong, but the words tangled somewhere in the fog that had settled behind his eyes. Everything felt slowed down as if he was wading through glue.

Moxy smiled faintly, seeing the doubt fade. "Good lad. You're starting to get it. It's not about friends, it's about survival. Eleven days, then you go home. You give 'em the wild-camping sob story, you look tired and harmless, you promise never to do anything so silly again. They'll pat you on the head, maybe give you a cup of tea, and that's that. You'll be a free man while the rest of them are still choking on questions."

Brendan rubbed his temples. "And the video?"

"Forget it for now," Moxy said, his tone dropping into something almost fatherly. "We've got it safe on that phone, I'm going to chop it up for some juicy bits, that's our lifeline and if they don't play ball, we use it. They'll pay to keep it quiet. But you keep your mouth shut about it, you hear me? You and me, we're the only ones who know what really happened, and that's valuable."

He reached over and clapped Brendan on the shoulder. "Now, don't overthink it. You'll only wind yourself up. Smoke if you need to. Sleep when you can. Next Thursday comes; you walk into your house like nothing ever happened. Your parents will be so relieved the questions will disappear, then we take our time and make sure we get some real money out of this venture."

Brendan nodded slowly, the rhythm of Moxy's words sinking deep. It made a kind of twisted sense. Every time he tried to push back, the thought dissolved under the haze that wrapped around his mind. Moxy made it sound easy - logical, even.

Moxy leaned back, lighting another roll-up. "See? I told you. You're learning. Just keep that head straight and listen to me. Do that, and we'll both come out ahead."

Brendan didn't reply. He watched the smoke curl upwards, thin and grey against the dimming sky. For a moment, he imagined Jonah's face - the confusion, the worry then it slipped away, replaced by the calm lull of the high creeping in. Moxy was right, what right did Jonah have to anything? He did virtually none of the graft.

He told himself Moxy was right. That it was just eleven days. That he'd go home, tell his story, and everything would settle. But deep down, buried under the numbness, he already knew that once you started listening to Moxy, you never really stopped.

The days that followed slid together like melted wax. Brendan barely moved from the tent except to relieve himself or to cough the smoke out of his lungs. Moxy kept him fed, if crisps and tinned beans counted, but most of the time he didn't ask for food anyway. Just the foil, the lighter, and that look... wide-eyed, needy, already hooked. Perfect!

Moxy was flying. The gear was good, better than he'd seen in years, and now he had two stashes to dip into: Skeggs' hidden wraps, wedged in the lining of his tent, and his own private stock tucked down the front of his sleeping bag. Two paydays, two lifelines, and a new pupil who only needed less than half a burn to float away. The new vein took barely anything, a dusting, a taste, and the rest was his. Happy days.

He did the legwork while Brendan slept through the afternoons, his head buried under the musty sleeping bag, twitching and muttering in dreams. Moxy made runs to town, fenced a few bits of scrap, blagged kebabs off a takeaway delivery lad who owed him, and even picked up a battery pack for the burner. He'd sit at the edge of the canal afterwards, legs dangling, watching the black water move slow and steady, and think about how good it felt to have order again. Purpose.

Skeggs had been a drain, too loud, twitchy, always one mistake away from landing them both in a cell. But Brendan was clean, polite, easy to shape. A soft lad from a good house with too much guilt and too much to lose. He would pay all this back tenfold once you got the leash round his neck.

Moxy smiled at the thought. Whilst the Overaughs were being drained dry to keep their little family secret safe, he'd steer Brendan towards the secondary prize - a quiet raid on mummy and daddy's jewellery drawer. A proper inside job. He could already picture the payoff: a few grands' worth, maybe more, enough to keep him floating for months. A nice little bump on top of the pension that he would be getting off the Overaughs.

By Wednesday, he felt sharper, lighter, better than he had in five years. The aches had gone, the shakes had eased, and the future, for once, looked wide open. The death of his so-called mate didn't even register as a thought. Skeggs was just another body that had stopped being useful.

Chapter Twelve

Wednesday, 26th March 2025 – 13:58

They sat close to the fire that barely deserved the name in the damp air. Brendan's hands trembled where they folded round a battered tin mug. His pupils were wide, the whites rimmed with red. He looked smaller than the chair - thin, taut, frayed at the edges. The high had taken the edges off his fear and left him jittery and compliant, like a dog waiting for the next command.

Moxy watched him with a hungry approval. He liked the new shape Brendan made - pliant, eager, useful. He loved the way the lad's mouth worked when he tried to form the set of lies they needed. There was a satisfaction in shaping someone, making them into the right kind of instrument for your own personal use.

"So," Moxy said, hands warm with smoke, "we run it clean. Proper clean. You go home after tonight, yeah? Wait till most of the coppers are off shift after seven, stroll up like you've been atoning for your sins, and tell your folks exactly what we've practised. Jonah dropped you off. Wild camping. Digital detox. Mental health. Say you needed space. Don't improvise. Don't embellish."

Brendan nodded, voice thin. "After seven. Right." He swallowed like it hurt. "What if my Mum goes mental? Dad, he'll kick off for sure."

"Let them," Moxy said, as if the idea pleased him. "Let them shout. Let them make a show of it. It helps the story. You come in trembling; everyone gets distracted by the noise. They'll ring the cops themselves, desperate to show they did the responsible thing. That's when we slip the story in. You told them you'd been away to clear your head, you were home now, and if the police want to talk to you that's fine. Simple."

Brendan blinked fast. "They'll interview me, won't they?" The question came out breathy and small. He was dimly aware that the police shadows were already lengthening from the news feeds they'd watched the night before. People had linked him to the Overaughs, speculated, made a theatre of it online. That had spooked him but also given the plan a perverse gleam.

"Of course they will," Moxy said, pleased. "They'll come round for a check, maybe a proper interview. That's fine. You stick to the line. You say you wandered off, no phones, no socials, you needed to be alone. Mental health. They eat it up. The best bit is this - if anyone asks about Jonah, you make him the dodgy witness. Say he dropped you off then legged it. Make him sound flaky. If he contradicts you later, we laugh. That's how you survive, Bren. You make him the liar, not you."

Brendan's jaw worked. "Jonah's my mate." The words were a protest, feeble and half-formed. The junk had drained the edge from his loyalty and left the word as a thin echo. "He won't..."

"He will if he's scared," Moxy interrupted, sharp as a knife. "And if he doesn't? Fine. You keep your story. You look like the murdered child of circumstance and sorrow. He looks like a boy trying to wriggle free of the mess he sat in."

Moxy's praise was almost audible. "You came up with that. Proper clever." He tipped his head, letting the compliment settle. "You keep the tale clean and consistent; if you must go for interview you walk in and out of that police station, and no one bothers you. Everyone'll be too busy watching Jonah or looking for drama. You let them spend their breath on the wrong things."

Brendan let out a sound that might have been a laugh, might have been a sob. His fingers toyed with the rim of the mug as if it had a seam he could unpick. "And the Overaughs?" he asked. "What do we say to them?"

"Nothing, keeping them at distance is necessary, but if you do have to interact with them, use the same story," Moxy replied. "We tip them off beforehand. Let them hear it from us first so they aren't surprised when you turn up on the telly or in the local rag. They'll calm down if they think you're a harmless daft kid who needed a breather. If they don't - if they push - you cling harder to the story. Make Jonah look shifty. Make him the one who planned the trip, he left you out to dry."

He spat the last bit out. "And once the dust settles, maybe a

week, maybe two, we roll up to their house. We offer a nice attractive payment plan, yeah? Keep it small at first, something that looks like good faith. They take that, they shut up. If they don't, we make it unpleasant. But we don't need to be violent. We just need to convince them it's cheaper to buy the silence we share rather than make it public - especially the police!" Moxy flashed a sneer: this was brilliant!
Brendan's hands went slack. "And Jonah? If he talks…"
"Then you keep to the script and let him hang himself," Moxy said, practised and cold. "You're the victim of your own poor decisions. He's the dodgy lad who drove off. Who would they rather believe? The posh boy or the kid with the knackered trainers?" He grinned, the look of a man who'd done the sums and found them in his favour. "Trust me. People prefer tidy stories. And stop worrying about Jonah; he's not your friend anymore and never will be again."
The glow from the embers licked their faces and threw their features into shallow relief. For a moment Brendan let himself imagine the scene: the front door banging open, his mother's hands flapping, his father shouting, the loud domestic chaos that, in Moxy's telling, would be an asset. It felt like walking a tightrope with someone else holding the net.
"You sure you can pull off tipping off the Overaughs?" Brendan asked. His voice was small but edged with a spark he didn't fully understand.
Moxy rolled the cigarette between his fingers and flicked ash into the grass. "Course I can. I know people. I got ears. You leave that to me. You just get home, play the part, and keep your mouth shut. The rest is logistics. All you need to do is

get me their daughter's mobile number, and I'll use a new burner to tip them off on Snapchat." He paused, softer. "You do this right, Bren, and we both eat for months."

Brendan's head lolled, the muscles around his mouth slackening. The fog eased for a moment, and with it came relief - false and poisonous, but real enough to sink into. "After the week," he murmured, more to himself than to Moxy, "we go see them. They pay up. We shut up."

"Exactly." Moxy's grin was quick, pleased. "And if they're stupid, if they think they can hold out, then we can re-edit the video and pop it on the internet for the world to see."

They fell into a silence that had the weight of agreement. Brendan's breathing evened out a touch, and his hands stopped shaking as much. Moxy watched the sky collecting its grey, and for a moment he allowed himself the small, private satisfaction of a plan falling into place.

Skeggs' name drifted through his head for the barest of beats then was gone. It was an absence that had some teeth, but Moxy had no time for it. The world had provided him with a cleaner, younger ledger. He rubbed his palms together, already tasting the figures in his head, the warm arithmetic of profit earned by leverage.

Outside the tent the canal whispered slowly past, indifferent. Inside, by the feeble light, they polished the lie until it shone, never really truly understanding who they were about to try and blackmail.

Chapter Thirteen

Thursday, 27th March 2025 – 13:09

The day had dragged like wet rope. Every hour bled into the next - slow, heavy, thick with the weight of what was coming. Brendan had barely slept. He'd sat outside the tent most of the morning, staring across the canal, the water dark and sluggish under a Lancashire pewter sky. His clothes were stiff with grime, and the cold bit through every layer. Moxy had been in good spirits though, pacing about, whistling tunelessly, feeding off the power of his own vibe.

"Tonight's the night, lad," he'd said around noon, slapping Brendan on the back hard enough to make him flinch. "You walk in, keep your chin up, stick to the story, and you'll be golden. No crying, no confessions - just calm, steady, polite. They'll be so glad to see you alive they won't think to question it."

He'd grinned that wolfish grin of his, the one that said he'd already moved ten steps ahead. "Here," he added, tossing Brendan a tiny wrap of brown powder. "For the nerves. Just a taste before you knock on the door. Keeps you level. You don't want to go back shaking in front of the Old Bill or your mum."

Brendan had turned the foil over in his palm, heart pounding. "You sure this won't mess me up?"

Moxy had laughed. "You're already messed up, Bren. This'll just stop you looking it."

By late afternoon, Brendan had scrubbed himself down in the canal. The water was icy and stank of rot, but he forced himself through it - rubbing his arms raw, dunking his head, even swilling out his mouth until his teeth hurt. He came out shaking, gooseflesh crawling up his skin, hair plastered flat. He'd tried to wring the worst of the smell from his hoodie, but all he managed was to trade the sour reek of smoke and sweat for something colder, muddied, metallic.

When he'd caught his reflection in the water afterwards, it startled him - pale, hollow-eyed, with a thin red scratch down one cheek where a branch had caught him. He looked older and younger all at once.

Moxy had watched him from the bank, cigarette dangling from his lips. "Perfect," he'd said. "You look knackered - authentic. That's what sells it. They'll think you've been sleeping rough. Poor, damaged lad who just needed a break from the noise."

As the light faded, Brendan packed what little he had - the hoodie still damp, a pair of cracked trainers, and the burner phone with Moxy's number stored under M. Moxy tightened the straps on his own bag, humming under his breath.

"You remember what to say?" he asked.

Brendan nodded, voice thin. "Jonah dropped me off… went wild camping to clear my head… digital detox."
"And?"
"If they ask, Jonah didn't do anything wrong," Brendan said automatically.
Moxy smirked. "Not exactly. You make him sound flaky, right? Not a villain, just useless. That's the trick. It's believable, and don't forget to text me the daughter's number when you get to your phone – and make sure you delete the text afterwards!"
Hours later, Brendan stood on the cracked paving stones outside his house. The porch light was on - yellow, steady, and warm. It made his chest hurt - home! He could see the shadows moving inside: his mum pacing the hallway, his father slouched in the armchair, TV flickering blue across his face.
His fingers itched toward the foil in his pocket. The thought of stepping through that door sober made his stomach twist. He ducked behind the hedge, unwrapped the smallest pinch, and chased it off the back of a cigarette paper. The taste hit him sharp and bitter. The rush came a few seconds later, thin and silver through his veins.
The edge softened. The panic dulled.
He wiped his nose on his sleeve, took a deep breath, and looked up at the door. It was strange how ordinary it seemed. The brass handle glinted under the porch light, same as always. The doormat still had the faded words 'Home Sweet Home' even though it had never felt less true.
Moxy's voice echoed in his head: Walk in. Stick to the story.

Smile if you can manage it. Let them make the noise.
Brendan swallowed, squared his shoulders, and stepped forward. The cold metal of the handle met his palm. For the briefest moment, he hesitated - a flicker of memory: Jonah's grin, the hum of the car radio, the canal path under the moon. Then it was gone, smothered under the weight of smoke and fear and Moxy's voice.

He turned the handle.
The latch clicked.
Inside, the world was about to start spinning again.

Chapter Fourteen

Thursday, 27th March 2025 – 19:23

Jane Hughes paced the hallway for what felt like the hundredth time that evening, one hand hovering between the house phone and the kettle. The mug on the counter still steamed - the fourth cup she'd made and abandoned - milk cooling to a pale skin. Every few minutes she glanced at the front window, as though the missing piece of her life might just walk up the drive.

The house felt hollow, stretched too thin by the silence. Upstairs, Brendan's bedroom door stood ajar, exactly as the police had left it after their search: bed unmade, drawers half-open, trainers kicked under the chair. It wasn't mess so much as absence, and she couldn't bear to go in again.

From the living room came the low, constant drone of the television. Her husband Alan sat slumped in his chair, his work boots still on, the high-vis jacket draped over the armrest. His shift at the double-glazing factory had finished hours ago, but he'd gone straight home, too tired and too numb to speak. The flicker of blue light rolled across his face, making him look older, worn down to the grain. If it wasn't for work, he would go insane.

Jane paused in the doorway. "You've not eaten," she said softly.

Alan grunted without looking up. "Not hungry."

"You've got to eat something."

He didn't answer. The news had been looping the same footage for days. Brendan's school photo, the canal search, Jonah Overaugh's arrest. Now it was just static in his mind, white noise filling the hours until sleep.

Jane rubbed her arms, the kitchen light sharp against her tired eyes. "They should've found something by now," she murmured, more to herself than to him. "A lead, a sighting… anything."

Alan's hand twitched toward the remote, then dropped again. "They will," he said, but his voice carried no conviction. "It just takes time. It's what they find that concerns me."

She turned back to the kettle, the hum of it barely masking the ache in her chest. She'd called everyone - friends, cousins, even the vicar - all saying the same hollow things. He'll come home, luv. He's a good lad. He'll turn up.

But good lads vanished too.

She stared at the phone, wondering if she should ring the station again, just to feel like she was doing something. The detective, McIntyre, had told her not to worry about phoning unless there was news. But not worrying had stopped being an option a long time ago. The worry, as any parent knows, starts the moment their child is born; it's just the degrees of

worry that vary.
The kettle clicked off. The silence that followed seemed to swallow the house.
Then the door handle turned.
Jane froze.
For a heartbeat she thought she'd imagined it... just the house creaking, a trick of nerves. But then came the unmistakable sound of the door opening, slowly and carefully.
"Alan?" she whispered, not daring to move.
From the living room he stirred. "What?"
She turned, eyes wide. "The door."
There was a shuffle, a faint creak of the hinges, and then -
"Hi, Mum."
Jane's breath caught.
For half a second, the world narrowed to that single voice. Familiar, cracked, hesitant. Then she saw him.
Brendan stood in the doorway, half-shadowed by the porch light. His hoodie hung loose and damp, his jeans caked in dried mud, his hair dark with grease and rain. He looked thinner, older - but it was him. Her boy.
She screamed. Not out of fear, but from the sheer violent relief of it, a sound that tore through the hallway and made Alan jolt upright.
"Brendan!"
She was moving before she knew it, the mug clattering to the floor, tea splashing across the tiles. She crossed the hall in three strides and threw her arms around him, clutching him so hard he wheezed. He smelled of cold, some kind of rot, and smoke, but she didn't care. She buried her face in his

shoulder, sobbing into the damp fabric.
“Oh my God… oh my God, where have you been?!”
Brendan stood stiffly at first, then his arms came up in a slow, mechanical hug. “I’m fine, Mum. Honest. I’m fine.”
Alan appeared in the doorway, blinking as though the scene couldn’t be real. His mouth opened, closed, then opened again. “Jesus Christ, Bren…” He took a step forward, his face hardening. “Where the bloody hell have you been?”
Brendan swallowed, his voice barely a whisper. “I just… needed to clear my head.”
Jane pulled back just enough to look at him, her hands still gripping his shoulders. “You vanished, Brendan! The police have been everywhere, everyone’s been looking for you, we thought...” She couldn’t finish the sentence.
Alan’s voice cracked through the air. “Days, lad! You’ve been gone for nearly two bloody weeks! You had everyone thinking you were in the canal! What were you thinking?”
“I’m sorry,” Brendan said, the words quiet, rehearsed. “I just needed space. No phone, no people. Just… quiet.”
Jane’s sob turned into a laugh, ragged and half-hysterical. “You’re here, that’s all that matters. You’re here.” She hugged him again, holding on like she’d never let go.
Alan stood back, arms folded, trying to swallow his anger. The smell coming off Brendan made his stomach turn. Canal water, sweat, and something sour he couldn’t place. But he said nothing. Not yet.
“Come on,” Jane said, brushing Brendan’s hair from his face with shaking fingers. “We’ll get you cleaned up, love. Get you something warm. I’ll call the police and let them know

you're home."

Brendan's stomach tightened at that. "You don't have to."

"I do," she said, already reaching for the phone. "They'll want to know you're safe."

He nodded, forcing a weak smile. "Yeah. Safe."

Alan watched him, eyes narrowing just slightly, but said nothing more. He picked up the remote, turned off the TV, and muttered, "Welcome home, son."

Brendan stood there in the hallway, drenched in warmth and guilt, his mother's arms still clinging to him, the smell of home cutting through the rot on his skin.

And under it all, buried deep, Moxy's voice whispered like a curse.

Stick to the story.

Chapter Fifteen

Friday, 28th March 2025 – 08:03 – Blackburn CID

The morning light coming through the frosted panes of Blackburn CID was the colour of cold tea. DC Sarah McIntyre pushed through the double doors. As always, the sharp scent of disinfectant and instant coffee meeting her like an old adversary.

The night shift had left the place half-alive: phones blinking unanswered, two empty takeaway cups on the duty desk and the low hum of computers still logged in under borrowed passwords.

She slung her satchel onto her desk, shrugged off her coat and booted up her terminal. The machine groaned, fans wheezing, as if protesting the hour. Her coffee hadn't even cooled enough to sip before her inbox began to fill with new overnight incident logs, internal memos, press updates and the usual scatter of admin nonsense and mandatory online training requests.

Then she saw it.

MISPER – Brendan Hughes (18) – RETURNED HOME.

Call received 19:42, 27/03/25. Jane Hughes reports son home safe and well. Confirmed ID and welfare via phone. No officer attendance recorded.

McIntyre blinked at the screen, reading it twice before it sank in. "You have got to be joking."

She scrolled down to the clerk's note at the bottom - the bland, bureaucratic footnote that carried the weight of sleepless days:

Message left for OIC. Please review on return to duty.

Sarah pushed her chair back and exhaled through gritted teeth. "Brilliant."

Thirteen days of searches. Thirteen days of interviews, press conferences, and sleepless families. Jonah Overaugh's life in pieces. And now the boy they'd been tearing Lancashire apart to find had just… wandered home. What a total waste of time.

She jabbed at the keyboard, pulling up the case log. The file still sat marked active - no closure report, no welfare verification. The word LIVE flashed beside Brendan's name like an accusation.

"Morning, Mac."

She didn't look up. "Mark, tell me you knew about this."

DS Mark Hargreaves strolled in, shrugging out of his coat, steaming coffee in one hand, half-eaten croissant in the other. "Knew about what?"

She spun the monitor toward him. "This. Brendan Hughes.

Home since last night. Alive. Unharmed. Nobody thought to call us."

He leaned over the screen, eyebrows rising. "Christ. When did this come in?"

"Last night, nineteen-forty-two," she said. "Jane Hughes rang the out-of-hours line. The clerk logged it and filed it under update pending. Nobody attended. Nobody followed up. The duty inspector didn't even mark it urgent."

Mark whistled under his breath. "That's a hell of a way to start a Friday."

Sarah gave a short, humourless laugh. "Thirteen bloody days this kid's been missing. We've got Jonah Overaugh charged and remanded on the basis that Brendan might be dead, and it turns out he's been home since teatime yesterday."

Mark took a long sip of coffee. "You can't make this shit up."

"No," she said flatly. "You can't, but I have a strange feeling somebody has been."

She clicked through to the internal procedures tab, pulling up the safeguarding template out of habit before closing it again. He's eighteen, she reminded herself, so no social services required, no guardian. Just a straight voluntary interview under caution when the time came. At least that part of the paperwork wouldn't bite her.

Hargreaves dropped into the chair opposite, setting down his cup. "Alright, what's the move? You want to go out there?"

"Damn straight, I'll go now," Sarah said, already locking her terminal. "We need eyes on him and a welfare statement on record before his parents start rewriting history for him. If he's home and talking, I want the story from his mouth before

anyone else colours it."
"You reckon it's genuine?"
"I reckon," she said, standing, "that nobody disappears for thirteen days and walks in smiling without help. And if he's spinning a line, I'll know it before the kettle finishes boiling."
Mark smirked faintly. "You always do. Want backup?"
She shook her head, slipping into her coat. "No. I'll take one of the uniforms for the formality, but this needs to be quiet. No circus. We've already looked like idiots once this week, so I'll just do the subject seen as safe report as a cover to get eyes on him, before we haul in for the formal, probably next week now."
As she reached the door, Hargreaves called after her. "If he's really back, what does that mean for the Overaugh boy?"
Sarah paused, hand on the frame. "If Brendan's alive and well, we can justify Jonah's bail review today. If he's lying…" She met his eyes, calm but cold. "…then we've got a bigger mess than before."
Mark leaned back in his chair, the springs creaking under his weight. "Alright," he said, rubbing at the back of his neck. "That gives us grounds to shift Jonah's status. No sense keeping him sat in Wetherby if the lad he supposedly helped disappear is home eating toast."
He reached for his coffee, took another slow sip, and grimaced. "I'll start spinning up the paperwork for his release. We'll need a clean trail for CPS. No one wants to be accused of cutting corners once the press catch wind. I'll loop in the custody sergeant and get Wetherby notified; that'll trigger their bail prep."

Sarah nodded, half-turned towards the corridor.

"Make sure it reads tight," she said. "Last thing we need is some solicitor shouting procedural breach."

Mark gave a crooked grin. "You know me. I'll wrap it in red tape and make it look like the King himself signed it, not that Cartwright would ever notice."

"Good," she said, already moving. "I'll call you once I've spoken to the Hughes lad. Something doesn't seem right here."

He lifted his coffee in a mock salute as she was disappearing through the doorway. "Go on then, Mac. Let's see which one of our boys remembers how to tell the truth."

She left the office with brisk strides, the sound of her shoes echoing down the corridor. Outside, the grey morning spread low over Blackburn - dull, wet and unwelcoming. She pulled her coat tighter and headed for the carpool, the chill seeping through her sleeves.

It was 08:14 by the time she signed out a pool Astra and started the engine. The wipers groaned across the windscreen, clearing a thin mist of rain.

In the passenger seat, her notebook sat open, the case number scrawled at the top of the page:

MISPER-0325-BH. Brendan Hughes. Age 18. Returned. Statement pending.

She stared at it for a long moment before pulling out onto the road.

"OK Brendan, let's hear what bullshit you have to offer."

Chapter Sixteen

Friday, 28th March 2025 – 08:47

The Hughes residence, Blackburn

By the time Sarah McIntyre turned into the quiet crescent, the drizzle had thickened into a slow, steady fall that dulled everything to a shine. The row of semi-detached houses looked identical - same pebbledash, same cracked drives, same satellite dishes jutting from the brickwork like growths.

She parked at the kerb and checked her reflection in the mirror. Hair tied back, collar straight, notebook ready. When she stepped out, the cold bit through her coat. A uniformed PC was already waiting by the gate, his hat dark with rain.

"Morning, ma'am," he said, straightening. "PC Dalton. I reckon Mrs Hughes will be expecting us."

"Yep, I'd certainly hope so. Keep it informal," Sarah replied. "No need for the neighbours to start speculating and definitely don't want to spook him - not yet at least."

They walked up the short path. Before she could knock, the

door opened.

Jane Hughes stood there, pale and puffy-eyed, her hair scraped back in a messy knot. She looked like she hadn't slept properly in a week - which, Sarah supposed, was true.

"Oh, thank God," Jane said, stepping aside. "You must be here about Brendan. Come in, please."

The house smelled faintly of toast, clinging to places trying to erase worry and heartache. The hallway was cluttered with damp shoes, unopened post, and the ghost of normal life.

Sarah gave a polite nod. "Mrs Hughes, I'm DC Sarah McIntyre. We've spoken before, this is PC Dalton. We just need a quick chat for our records, to make sure everything's alright with your son and to close off the missing-person report."

Jane waved toward the living room. "He's in there. Still a bit shaken, poor thing."

The "poor thing" was slumped on the sofa, a blanket around his shoulders. Brendan Hughes looked like he'd been dragged out of a ditch - because, Sarah thought, he probably more or less had been. His skin was sallow, eyes ringed in grey, pupils too wide. He stank faintly of damp, smoke, and something metallic underneath.

He looked up when they entered, a slow, deliberate motion, like it took thought to raise his head.

"Morning, Brendan," Sarah said evenly. "Mind if I sit?"

He shrugged. "Sure."

She perched on the edge of an armchair opposite him, notebook open but pen capped. "I know you've probably told your mum already, but I just need a quick rundown of what happened. Where you've been since last Friday, why you didn't contact anyone. Nothing formal yet. This is just to confirm you're safe and sound."

Brendan nodded, swallowing. "Yeah. I'm fine. Just needed space, y'know?"

Sarah's pen clicked once, a small, soft sound. "Space? And no, I don't know. Please elaborate."

"Yeah." He rubbed his hands together, eyes darting between her and the floor. "Everything got… loud. Home, college, just life. So, I switched my phone off and left it here, took the tent, went camping. Near the canal, up toward Padiham. Digital detox, sort of thing. I didn't mean to cause all this, I didn't think anybody would notice."

Jane, hovering in the doorway, sniffed. "He's always been like that. Sensitive. I told him, you can't just vanish, love. You had us half-dead with worry."

Brendan gave a weak smile that didn't touch his eyes. "I know Mum, I'm sorry."

Sarah watched him a moment longer. His leg twitched restlessly, fingers fidgeting with a thread on the blanket. She knew that twitch. Not nerves, not trauma. Something deeper, chemical.

"You camped the whole time?" she asked.

"Yeah. Mostly."

"Alone?"

He nodded. "Yeah."

"Did anyone help you? Give you food, lifts, anything?"

"No. I was on my own. I took snacks."

The answers came too quickly, too clean. Over a week in the

cold and rain, with no serious supplies, and he still looked… wired. Not weary but wired. Sarah noted it silently, pen moving at a steady pace.

"Alright," she said finally, closing the notebook. "I'll keep this short. You're eighteen, so there's no safeguarding referral needed. I just need you to confirm for the record that you are home of your own free will, no one's forcing you to stay, and you don't feel at risk from anyone?"

Brendan hesitated, then nodded. "Yeah. I'm fine. Promise."

She looked at him a moment longer, then nodded back. "Good. That's all I need for now."

Jane exhaled, some of the tension leaking out of her shoulders. "So that's it, then? He's not in trouble?"

"Not at this stage," Sarah said. "We'll be closing the missing-person log, but we may need to speak with Brendan again as part of the wider investigation. Nothing to worry about right now."

Dalton handed Jane a printed slip with the case number on it. "If he feels unwell, or if anything changes, just ring the number there. It'll go straight through to the station."

"Thank you, officer."

Sarah stood. Brendan looked up at her, his pupils still blown wide. "Is… Jonah alright?" he asked suddenly.

She paused, surprised by the question. "He's safe. Don't worry about Jonah right now. You just focus on getting some rest."

He nodded again, too quickly.

Sarah glanced at Jane. "He'll need fluids, rest, maybe a check-up if he's not eating. And keep him off social media for a bit. There's already talk going round."

Jane's eyes widened. "People online?"
Sarah gave a small, tired smile. "There always are." She nodded toward Brendan. "I'll be in touch if we need anything further."
Outside, the rain continued its steady fall. Dalton fell into step beside her as they headed back to the car.
"You buying that story, ma'am?" he asked quietly.
Sarah didn't answer immediately. She opened her door, glanced once back at the house - at the thin shadow of Brendan in the window, rubbing his hands like he couldn't get warm - and shut it again.
"No," she said finally, starting the engine. "Not for a second."

Act VII

The Leverage

Chapter Seventeen

Monday, 31st March 2025 – 12:46

Moorside House, Kitchen

"…then who did we kill?"

Seth could not hide his concern. The words hung in the air, heavier than truth, heavier than guilt.

The kitchen felt smaller somehow - the muted tick of the clock, the hum of the fridge, the four of them caught in the middle of a silence that no one wanted to break, fearful of getting caught in a verbal crossfire.

Natalia leaned against the counter, arms folded, eyes fixed on the floor. "Whoever's behind this isn't finished," she said quietly. "That message. It wasn't the police. It was bait. Someone's pulling strings, and they're not doing it for justice."

Izzy sat at the table, pale and tight jawed. "So, we're being played? Like some game?"

"Exactly," Natalia replied. "We've been reacting since that

night - every move, every word, controlled. We're under threat from someone we know nothing about yet."

Seth turned from the window, his reflection fractured by the panes. "They'll show themselves eventually," he said, voice low but sure. "People like that always do. They can't resist the reveal."

Izzy's fingers twisted the cord of her hoodie, eyes darting between them. "I don't like being prey."

Seth's mouth hardened. "Good," he said. "Overaughs are not mindless sheep, we are not built to react, we are built to hunt."

Natalia straightened, her tone turning cold, steady. "Then it's decided."

Seth nodded once, eyes on his family - his wife, his children, his reason to fight. "If someone wants a war," he said, voice like flint, "they'll get one."

"Does that include the statue?" Izzy asked.

"Damn straight! It's time your mother and I taught you how to protect yourselves." Seth snapped.

They began that afternoon.

At first it was practical: clearing clutter, tightening routines, stripping every comfort down to purpose. But soon the rhythm changed. What had started as order became discipline, a quiet, relentless conditioning. They moved like soldiers sharing the same unspoken pulse.

In the garage, Seth set a tyre iron across his knees and showed Jonah how to dismantle a door hinge without waking the street. His movements were slow, exact. "If we ever end up in prison," he said, "you keep busy. You keep your mind sharp.

Routine keeps you human."

Natalia took charge of the kitchen. She turned meal prep into drill, chopping vegetables into uniform squares, teaching Izzy how to ration food by the gram. "We eat to last," she said, "not to linger." The cupboards became storage for things that mattered: bottled water, batteries, candles, and folded maps. Comfort was replaced by readiness.

Izzy started running. She looped the driveway until her lungs burned, timing each lap against her watch. Her playlist pulsed like a metronome: four beats in, six out. She learned to calm herself in rhythm, to let the panic pass through instead of owning it. Natalia always joined her at dawn, both silent except for the crunch of gravel beneath their feet, building cardio capacity as if their lives depended on it. Because for all they knew, it did.

Seth and Jonah trained in the garden. No theatrics, just the blunt, efficient lessons Seth had carried home from a younger, darker life. "Control, not force," he told him, demonstrating how to break a grip or disarm a shove. "You win by ending it fast." Jonah bruised easily but never complained. His silence became its own language.

Phones were the next to go. Seth wiped them clean, bought pay-as-you-go burners, and taught the others the rules: no photos, no location, no emotion in messages. Names became initials. Every text under twenty words. Every call under thirty seconds. The family that had once lived on chatter now lived on codes.

Natalia drew a map of Altham on the back of a legal pad, marking every exit route and blind corner. Red circles for camera dead zones, blue for fallback points: the church, the school, a friend's cottage out by Whalley. She kept a second copy folded into the cutlery drawer. Izzy memorised it like scripture.

At night, they rehearsed. Seth quizzed them from the living-room table, voice steady, tone clipped.

"What do you say if questioned?"

"Nothing without counsel."

"And if separated?"

"Stay calm. Don't volunteer."

"What if one of us is taken?"

"We wait for contact, not panic."

Sometimes he stood at the window afterwards, watching the lights along the canal, and wondered which of them would be strong enough when it truly came. Because it was coming. He felt it in his bones.

They also trained the mind. Natalia ran breathing drills, teaching them to focus through exhaustion. Izzy practised lying in front of the mirror, retelling small stories until her eyes stopped giving her away. Jonah learned to keep his tone even, to speak without revealing emotion. Seth called it "building the armour".

By mid-week, Moorside House felt transformed. Not fortified exactly, but awake. Alert. Ready to defend.

The house creaked at night as though it was listening.

On Thursday, Seth lined them up at the kitchen table. His eyes moved from one face to the next: Natalia's calm resolve, Jonah's quiet shame, Izzy's burning fear that was slowly becoming focus.

"Listen," he said. "We don't know who's behind this, or why. But we do know what we are... a family. Whatever comes next, we face it together. We stay fit, we stay clear, we stay disciplined."

"If the worst happens, if the law turns on us, or if the intruder's lackeys come to finish what he started, we survive it with our heads high. Prison, death, exile - it doesn't matter. We meet it standing on feet, not cowering in a corner."

Natalia reached across the table and rested her hand over his. "It's been a while since we've been this sharp."

Seth nodded. "From now on, we prepare for both outcomes. The fight or the fall. And when the enemy finally shows themselves…"

He looked at each of them in turn, his voice a promise.

"They'll wish they hadn't."

Izzy tipped her head. "Yeah... about these Army careers you two had. Since when did we keep a field manual in the cutlery drawer? 'Positions', 'rally point', 'exit bravo'. Were you intelligence or secret ninjas?"

Natalia's mouth twitched. "Intelligence Corps. Less Rambo, more reading rooms, though some of those rooms had doors no one else used."

Seth allowed himself half a smile. "And the odd bit of green kit. We weren't exactly your average soldiers."

Izzy blinked. "Translation: nerds with a licence to vanish."

Jonah nodded at the corkboard. "Explains the laminated checklists."

"Checklists win wars," Seth said.

"And stop teenagers losing their keys," Natalia added, sharing a knowing look with him.

Izzy huffed, reassured despite herself. “I’m both comforted and mildly terrified.”

“Good,” Seth said, the smile gone but the warmth of it still there. “Boots in five.”

Inside, the Overaughs continued to prepare themselves for war.

Chapter Eighteen

Friday, 4th April 2025 – 18:21

Moorside House, Kitchen

The air was thick with the smell of melted cheese and pepperoni.

For the first time in weeks, the kitchen felt almost ordinary: four paper plates, a box of lukewarm pizza in the middle of the table, the faint hum of the extractor fan filling the pauses between bites. Outside, early dusk was clinging to the windows like a film of ash, the light dimming minute by minute.

Jonah chewed slowly, eyes on the table. Izzy scrolled through nothing on her phone, the screen dark. Natalia tore the cheese stuffed crusts from her slice, stacking the edges in a neat little pile beside her plate. Ready to dispense it into the ever-watchful Lydia to fulfil the dog owners' cheese tax. The only one who seemed entirely present was Seth.

He swallowed, wiped his hands on a napkin, and looked at

each of them in turn.

"It's Friday," he said simply.

The words hung there, heavy and deliberate.

Izzy's fingers froze on the phone. Natalia met his gaze. Jonah pushed his plate away. They all knew what he meant.

"Another week," Natalia murmured. "Another dream."

Seth nodded. "We can assume it'll happen again. Same time, same way. Every Friday night since… that night. Like clockwork." He paused, his tone calm but tight. "We've been reacting to it, trying to forget, hoping it'll fade. But it's not going anywhere. So, we stop hiding from it. We start understanding it and start using it."

Jonah frowned. "Using it?"

Seth leaned forward. "We know what we can see in the dream. The field. The van. The girl. The women and the dark figure. But we still don't know what WE can do. If this thing is showing itself to us, we need to start pushing back, testing the limits or at least understanding the parameters of capability when we are having the dream."

Izzy looked uneasy. "You're saying… you want us to control it?"

"I'm saying," Seth replied evenly, "that the only power we've got left is how we respond. We treat it like reconnaissance. A hostile environment with familiar terrain. Every time we're there, we take a step forward."

Natalia's eyes narrowed in thought. "Parameters," she said softly. "Set them before we sleep. Define the objective."

"Exactly." Seth nodded. "Tonight, if it comes again, we each take a task. No running, no panic. Observe, record, test."

Jonah shifted in his chair. "What kind of tasks?"
Seth looked to each of them in turn. "I'll focus on the man, statue and weaponry. I want to know if it's fixed, or if it's aware of us being there. And if we can pull down things like branches. Can we pick up objects, throw them, use them?
"Natalia, you track the girl, see how close you can get before she disappears. Can you get to her? Can you get your hands on her? Is she solid? Is she real? Can she answer questions?
"Jonah, your job is to move. Test distance. See if there's a boundary. I want you to run up towards the back entrance to the house, see if you can get into it, who or what else is there. And Izzy…" He paused, softening slightly. "You see if you can talk to the women. Get in their way. Do they walk through you? Can they see you? Can they hear you?"
Izzy's eyes widened. "Ask them something?"
"Yes, we need to see if we can interact with them, if they can see or hear us. We can see and hear them, but we haven't tried to interact with them yet."
Natalia reached across the table and squeezed his hand. "And if it's not just a dream?"
Seth's gaze didn't waver. "This whole thing is terrifying, and that figure has had us watching him in the dream for weeks. He seems to like mental torture. I think it's a message. And whoever's sending it clearly wants to be heard. We need to find out if we can hurt him."
The pizza was cold now. The last of the daylight slid off the windows, leaving only the low amber glow of the kitchen lamp. Izzy exhaled slowly, nodding.
"Fine," she said. "I'll try and get to the women."

Jonah gave a small, humourless laugh. "What if we're all saying the same thing to the same person?"

"Then we might finally get an answer," Natalia said.

Seth leaned back, the chair creaking under his weight. "We go to bed at the same time. Phones off, no light, no talking once we're under. The moment it starts, focus on your task. If we're split up or don't spawn in the same place, make your way to the lane where we usually appear. We all join up first; confirm we are there and then we go about our business. Don't think about fear, don't think about what it means. Just observe."

"And when we wake?" Izzy asked.

"Kitchen, straight afterwards." Seth said. "Otherwise, its zero six hundred hours sharp, as usual. We compare notes. No matter what. It's vital that we write down everything we experience straight away. We can always review in the morning if we need to, but getting those fresh memories down on to a page is vital."

The wind rattled the windows then, a sharp, quick tap that made them all glance up.

For a heartbeat, no one spoke.

Seth smiled faintly, though there was no humour in it. "Looks like we're already being reminded."

He stood as Natalia switched off the light above the cooker. Jonah pushed his chair in. Izzy lingered, her reflection caught in the glass of the window. Pale, uncertain, but steadying.

"Same time as always," she whispered.

"Same time," Seth confirmed.

As the house settled into its night-time hush, the Overaughs went their separate ways: disciplined, resolute, and quietly afraid.

Each of them would drift into sleep with their assignment fixed like a commandment.

And if the dream came again, they would be ready to meet it on their own terms.

Chapter Nineteen

Saturday, 5th April 2025 – 00:24

The dream did not come fast.

It crept. The statue was clearly taking its time with them. Folding them in, one by one.

It took them.

One moment they were in their own rooms, the house settling, the slow drift of sleep beginning.

The next, they were standing together. Seth, Natalia, Izzy, and Jonah: side by side in the moonlit field beneath the black sky, just like the week before.

The grass was tall and wet with dew, cold against their bare feet.

They didn't question it. They didn't speak.

They all knew.

They were back.

Jonah looked down at his hands, flexed his fingers, felt the grain of damp earth between his toes.

"We're all here," Natalia whispered.

Izzy's eyes were fixed on the house. "Is it task time?"

Seth nodded. "Let's get to it."

He turned towards the nearest tree and began tugging on a low branch. The wood resisted, fibres straining, until with a dry crack it snapped free in his hands.

"I can feel it," he said. "There's resistance. It's real."

The others stared at him, uncertain. Seth gave a small shrug, then, with a grin that cut through the tension, whipped the branch against Natalia's backside.

"Ow!" she snapped, scowling.

"Right," Seth said, triumphant. "So, we can feel. That's one thing boxed off."

Izzy's voice came tight and low. "If we can feel… then he can too." She raised her arm, pointing towards the far edge of the ha-ha where the darkness was thickest. "We don't have much time. Move!"

Seth started running for the boundary where the figure always appeared.

Izzy peeled off towards the house, her nightshirt fluttering in the wind.

Natalia turned and headed for the place where the child first emerged.

Jonah hesitated, only for a moment, before bolting towards the rear of the house, his silhouette flickering in the half-light as he passed the van.

From the trees, the little girl burst into view. White nightdress, blonde hair wild in the wind, running with the frantic, full-bodied terror of someone who already knew no help was coming.

"Lottie!" Natalia shouted. She was barely four feet away. The girl didn't even glance back. Natalia lunged, diving forward...

And went straight through her.

"No!" she cried, scrambling up, her palms slick with dew. The child kept running, the figure already moving in pursuit.

Then-Bang!

The green front door of Moorside House slammed open with a crack that echoed across the field.

Izzy was nearly there. The two women - the mother and the matron figure - completely oblivious to her presence.

"LOTTIE!" the woman screamed, voice ripping through the night.

Izzy ran hard, closing the distance to less than six feet at which point she let out the loudest scream she could muster.

No reaction.

Nothing.

It was as though she didn't exist. Both women simply carried on with their charade.

Seth, hearing Izzy's scream, turned his head mid-stride. Just long enough to lose focus.

The figure was almost on top of him.

And then passed him.

Seth stumbled, cold tearing through his chest. He twisted; branch raised and gave chase. The figure moved fast, inhuman, the black coat dragging behind him like smoke.

He reached the girl first. She went down hard in the grass. The figure crouched over her, just as he always did, movements deliberate, ritualistic.

Then he turned his head - slowly, impossibly - until his gaze met Seth's.

"You're mine now," it said.

Seth swung the branch with both hands.

The wood connected.

A jolt ran through his arms. The figure was solid.

The blow threw it sideways. It rolled once, landing hard in the grass. The girl was gone.

Seth's heart hammered. He stepped forward, branch poised for another strike. The dark figure looked up at him, its face twisting into something almost human as it rose slowly to its feet.

A rasping laugh crawled from its throat.

"You're a clever little maggot, aren't you?"

And in that instant, the world shattered.

All four of them awoke at once. Gasping, bolt upright in their separate beds.

Lights flicked on in sequence across the house. First Jonah's room, then Izzy's, then Seth and Natalia's.

No one spoke. They didn't need to.

Within seconds they were moving. Doors opening, footsteps quick and sure down the landing, converging once more on the kitchen.

The clock on the wall read 00:28.

Outside, the wind moaned across the fields.

Inside, the Overaughs stood in the amber light, every breath tight with the same thought:

The dream had changed.

And now it felt more real than ever.

Chapter Twenty

Saturday, 5th April 2025 – 00:31

Moorside House, Kitchen

Steam from the kettle rose into the amber light above the table where the Overaughs sat, still half in shock, their eyes hollow with the residue of sleep and fear. The dream clung to them like static.

Seth leaned forward, elbows on the table, palms flat. His hands were trembling faintly. "Alright," he said, his voice low but steady. "Let's debrief. Start from the top. Every detail matters."

No one spoke at first. The clock ticked softly. The wind scraped along the back of the house.

Natalia broke the silence. "The girl isn't real," she said, her voice thin, analytical. "She's an apparition of some sort. She didn't see me. I ran straight through her; she didn't even flinch. Like she was made of light."

Izzy nodded slowly. "Same with the women. They were right

in front of me, close enough to touch. I screamed at them. Nothing. No sound carried. No reaction. It was like… watching ghosts act out a scene that doesn't care you're there."

Jonah rubbed his palms together, frowning. "That's not what happened with me. I got to the back of the house, right up to the kitchen door. I could feel the handle. Cold metal. I was about to open it, and then..." he stopped, glancing at his father. "Then it just ended. Like someone cut the power."

Seth's eyes flicked to him. "And nothing was waiting for you?"

"Nothing," Jonah said. "No sound, no figure, no girl. Just empty. But it felt… wrong. Like something was inside, watching through the glass."

Seth nodded, processing. His voice came slower now, thoughtful. "Alright. So, Natalia and Izzy, you both interacted with ghosts, light fragments or apparitions, whatever we want to call them. Jonah, you reached the edge, touched the boundary of the kitchen door handle. And me..." he hesitated, staring at his hands. "...I hit it."

Izzy blinked. "Hit what?"

"The figure," Seth said. "With the branch. It was solid. I felt it connect." He tapped his wrist where the impact still echoed through his bones. "It went down, rolled and then rose again. That's when it looked at me, properly looked, and spoke. Not like before. It called me a clever little maggot."

Jonah's chair creaked as he leaned forward. "So, you hit something that shouldn't exist. And it spoke back."

"Exactly." Seth's gaze fixed on the centre of the table, eyes narrowing in thought. "If we can touch nothing else in that world: not the child, not the women... but we can touch the figure, and the branches and the door handle… then it must be some kind of memory, playing on a loop."

Izzy frowned. "A memory of what? What dictates the loop?"

"The past," Seth said. "That girl. The mother. The house. It's a recording of something that's already happened... looping over and over again, like a broken tape. But that figure…" he exhaled slowly. "That's the anomaly. The only other moving solid element in the dream so far other than us. It doesn't belong to the past. It's here. Now."

The room went still.

Natalia's fingers drummed on the table. "If that's true, then what happens in there isn't harmless."

Seth looked up, puzzled. "What do you mean?"

Without a word, Natalia stood, turned slightly, lifted the hem of her pyjama top and pulled her pants down slightly.

A welt cut across the top of her buttocks. A raw, horizontal mark. The exact shape of the branch that Seth had tested on her.

Izzy gasped. Jonah swore under his breath.

Seth's mouth dropped open. "Jesus, Nat…"

"That's from you," she said quietly. "When you hit me in the dream."

He stared, unable to answer.

"It didn't hurt at first," Natalia went on. "Not until I woke up. Then it started burning." She straightened, lowering the fabric. "So, whatever happens there, certainly anything to do with harm against us, translates physically here."

Seth sat back slowly, the chair creaking beneath him. "If that's true, then we're not just remembering something anymore.

We're crossing over into something that has some kind of mental recording playing on a loop."
Jonah shook his head. "Crossing into what? Another world?"
"No, I don't think so." Seth said, his voice tightening. "The same one. Just maybe a different layer of it, or something inside of it."
Natalia's expression hardened. "This means if we can touch him there, then he can hurt us…"
"Correct, but why hasn't he tried so far?" Seth finished.
The kettle, which was becoming the most used appliance in the household, clicked off but no one moved to pour it.
For a long moment, the only sound was the slow, steady tick of the kitchen clock.
Then Izzy whispered, "Maybe he didn't know until now? He did call you a clever little maggot. Maybe you're the first to try."
Seth looked up, the lines in his face carved deep by the dim light. "That does track. We need to adapt. We have vital intel, but maybe so does he. We treat the dream as a battlefield. We document everything. Patterns. Times. Reactions. If it's real enough to leave a mark, then it's real enough to fight, but fighting goes both ways."
Natalia met his eyes. "And if he's waiting for us?"
He didn't hesitate. "Then we hit him harder. This isn't some silly movie where we get picked off. Next time all four of us make sure we stay within line of sight of each other. We make sure we get tooled up straight away with branches and whatever we can lay our hands on, protection is vital... then we see what damage we can do!"

Chapter Twenty-One

Saturday, 5th April 2025 – 07:56

Russian Hill, San Francisco

Charlotte Richardson liked mornings best when the city had not yet made up its mind.

Fog clung to the crowns of the Telegraph Hill pines, the cable car bell on Hyde Street lifting and falling as if underwater. From her kitchen window she could see a scissored strip of the Bay, dull pewter under low cloud. Alcatraz, a darker thumbprint beyond it.

The flat was an Edwardian survivor, with stubbornly original windows and a thin run of built-in bookcases. Half the shelves held catalogues, monographs, and field notes. The other half was devoted to what her clients loftily called 'reference objects' and she stubbornly called 'teaching pieces'. On the bench by the window - a narrow conservation table she'd coaxed up the stairs in 2003 with the help of two patient neighbours - lay the tools that had a way of calming her.

Linen gloves, a 10× Hastings triplet loupe magnifier, UV torch, soft sable brushes, pH test strips, a calliper, a box of cotton buds, and the battered black ledger that still made her throat tighten when she opened it:

Apotropaics: European Notes 1800–1920 (Rage/Containment)

She measured the room without thinking - humidity 48%, temperature 19°C. The portable dehumidifier in the corner hummed, keeping pace.

The appointment card on the dresser read:

09:00 - Private appointment (J. Halberd, Palo Alto).

Object: Late-19th-century North German apotropaic guardian figure (bog oak), iron inclusions, cavity sealed with resin; documented 1905 (L. Heiden, Berlin Folklore Survey); Wolfskehl estate 1934; export U.S. 1958 (S. Löwy); Butterfield & Butterfield 1997; Richardson 2025 (consignment from S. Löwy estate).

Notes: XRF iron content consistent with hand-forged nails c. 1860–1890; resin analysis pending (Dogpatch lab). Provenance clean; funerary context unproven - discuss ethics.

She dressed in the same functional elegance she brought to her work: navy blazer, charcoal trousers, white shirt and low boots that could do a Jackson Square morning and a Highway 1 sprint without complaint. Her silver hair and jewellery were pinned, the habit of a woman who understood the risks of sleeves catching on fragile surfaces.

Coffee in a small, chipped mug. Two sips standing; one slow glance at the ledger; a hand on the bench as if greeting an old friend. She zipped the field case and slid in the day's kit:

gloves, torch, loupe, microfibre cloths, a thin roll of acid-free tissue, two spare tamper seals.

The flat smelled faintly of beeswax, old paper, and a citrus cleaner she favoured because it didn't fight with the past. She locked up with two turns of the key, tested the knob - muscle memory from a hundred house calls and a thousand careful exits - then descended the narrow stairs, case in hand.

The Volvo waited at the kerb; the practical choice she'd made the year her father Luke had died; when everything became about reliability. Engine on; heater ticking into life; wipers clearing a crescent in the mist. She took Hyde down in first, respectful of the gradient, stopped at Pacific for a delivery lorry and a pair of runners holding coffees like talismans. She could have taken the cable car and walked the last few blocks, but she would be on the road south by noon. Russian Hill to Jackson Square by car felt faintly indulgent. It also cut an hour off the drive to Carmel.

She caught Lombard's wriggle on her left and turned down into the old brick grid where the city still felt like a nineteenth-century argument. Jackson Square was waking now. A florist hosed the pavement, a gallery owner dragged a crate into the light, a man in a hat checked his watch and then the sky, as if both were likely to answer back.

Her door was the discreet sort that reassured trustees and made fraudsters flinch: frosted glass, brass buzzer, a small, engraved plate that read RICHARDSON OCCULT ANTIQUARIAN. No frontage full of curios, no theatrical signage. Appointment only. Research by arrangement. Vault on site.

She disarmed the alarm, switched the lights to their shy morning level, then crossed the tiled floor to the vault and checked its gauges out of habit: temperature and humidity steady, seals intact. The guardian figure, the bog-oak carving with iron threaded through its chest like a blackened starburst, sat in its foam cradle like a patient. She checked it the way a doctor might check a pulse. Glance, breath, a single nod. No movement, no disturbances. Clean.

She had built something here, against the grain of a city that liked its stories fast and its fashion faster. A small office to the left with a reference library (Folklore Studies Quarterly bound in green; a run of Folklore journal; The Witch-Bottle Catalogue by Hedges; a tatty copy of Spirit Photography & Its Discontents), a conservation bench in the back room, a climate-controlled vault with a lock that made most people respectful.

Clients came by invitation. Museums sent registrars with lists. Private collectors arrived with careful smiles. Once, a movie studio sent a production designer to ask what sort of "ritual technology" would make a scene plausible. She had taken a breath, named three examples, and made them promise to credit the archivist who'd taught her the language of this work. Then she had gone home and made a note of how easily people asked for peril when they could not feel its teeth.

She set out the day's tray: nitrile gloves, loupe, UV torch, her catalogue sheet. The guardian's cavity was sealed with a resin plug she hadn't yet tested. Not a witch bottle, not a reliquary either - something intended to draw in, hold, and quiet. The iron was thick and hammered. The bog oak had taken a polish that suggested care, not rush work. Whoever had made it had set out to contain a thing. It made a certain kind of sense to her.

Emotion vessels. She'd written the phrase in the margin of an article once, then winced at its softness. The better ones didn't shout. They simply did their job.

She smiled to herself, a small, private thing, turned off the vault light, and headed back to the car. Jackson Square to Carmel was a long morning in the best of traffic. With luck, the appointment would keep to the hour.

By the time she pulled onto Sansome and took the soft left to Broadway, her phone had connected to the car. She was half a block from the Embarcadero when the hands-free chimed. EMMA - CARMEL lit on the dash.

"Emma, good morning." She kept her voice level, pleased. "You're meant to be off at seven."

The night nurse always sounded like she was speaking in a room with the curtains open. Kindness without fuss. "Morning, Charlotte. I'm just heading home. Your mother asked me to call you again before I left."

Charlotte's fingers tightened on the wheel. "Is she alright?"

"She's lucid. A little… urgent. She wants to speak to you as soon as you can. It's about the Friday night dream again."

A beat.

"She didn't have it again."

Charlotte exhaled. The words landed the way they had previously, in the precise place between worry and relief. "So that makes three Fridays now."

"Since mid-March," Emma said softly. "She says it matters

that you know why, and that you come. She asked me to tell you that exactly."

Charlotte took a moment, eased into the outside lane, and watched the Ferry Building slide by on her right. "Thank you for calling. I've an appointment at nine. I'll be on the road straight after. I can be there early afternoon."

"That'll mean the world to her."

"It's why I chose Russian Hill," Charlotte said, almost to herself. "Under three hours down Highway 1 if the traffic behaves. Tell her I'll make it for two."

"She'll be ready," Emma said. A smile in her voice. "Drive safely, love."

"Thank you, Emma. And get some sleep."

The call clicked off. The city breathed around her: a cyclist in a yellow jacket, a delivery van that couldn't quite decide what to do, the grey mouth of the Financial District yawning into its morning. She took the right turn that would loop her back to Jackson Square, the Volvo's indicators making their patient metronome.

She thought of her mother - ninety-one, still keen when it mattered - and of Friday nights that had stacked like weights across decades. She thought of how a silence could be worse than a storm. She thought of the description she had always been given by her mother. Hannibal sobbing, Elias frantic, Lydia defiant.

Charlotte found a space on Jackson Street, opposite the old brick warehouse that housed a dealer in maritime charts. She sat a moment, her hands quiet on the wheel, the day separating into its two clean halves: the appointment, then the road. Work first, as it had always been. Then care, as it had always needed to be.

She picked up her case, checked the time, and looked once more towards the Bay, the fog lifting off it in bands like something being folded away. When she spoke, it was to the car, or the morning, or perhaps to the ledger resting under her bench.

"Right," she said. "Let's get this right."

She crossed the street to her door, the brass plate catching what little light there was, and keyed in the code. The lock acknowledged her with its familiar, precise click and the day began.

Chapter Twenty-Two

Saturday, 5th April 2025 – 14:02

Carmel-by-the-Sea, California, Seaview Care

Emma met Charlotte at the front desk with a cardigan over her scrubs and the tired smile of someone who had volunteered for too many back-to-back shifts.

“She’s been watching the clock,” Emma said, keeping her voice low as they walked the short corridor. “Slept in this morning. Woke calm... No tremor. She asked if you were already on the road.”

“I was,” Charlotte said. “Thank you for calling.”

Emma squeezed her arm. “You always come.”

Meredith’s door was ajar. Charlotte knocked once, then slipped in.

Her mother was at the window, cardigan wrongly buttoned, a blanket over her knees, the afternoon light washed thin across her face. The room held the usual troop of careful comforts: family photographs; a small watercolour of the

Carmel Mission; a vase with eucalyptus that Emma must have pilfered from reception. On the shelf sat the stack of paperbacks Charlotte kept replacing as Meredith forgot the endings and found them new again.

“You came,” Meredith said, turning, relief breaking through the worry. “I told Emma you would.”

Charlotte bent to kiss her, breathing in the familiar scent of soap and the rose hand-cream she’d used for thirty years. “Always.”

They sat. Charlotte laid her coat over the chair, field case by her foot. For a moment neither of them spoke. They’d had this conversation so many times it had worn a groove in them both.

“No dream,” Meredith said at last. “Third Friday now.”

Charlotte nodded. “Emma told me.”

“It isn’t peace,” Meredith said, too quickly. “Don’t think it is. It’s… absence. I laid there waiting for it like a fool and all I could hear was the staff radio and the bloody clock. Then morning came like it had been hiding behind the curtain.”

Charlotte folded her hands. “What did you expect to see?”

“The same thing I’ve seen since I was a girl,” Meredith said, voice softening with the old ache. “The field. Hannibal. The… man, Elias frantic.” She swallowed and pinched the blanket. “Only it didn’t come. The silence, it feels wrong.”

Charlotte let the quiet move between them. “What do you think it means?”

Meredith’s gaze drifted past her, to the strip of Pacific visible through the gap in the pines. “Either it’s finished,” she said, “or it’s changed. And I don’t believe in finished. Not with that house."

"Do you think Lottie has been found?" The question left Charlotte before she could frame it better.

Her mother looked at her hands. "Not by me and not by you."

They sat in it, the old pain, the years of Friday nights stacked like plates in a cupboard.

Charlotte reached for her mother's hand. "I had a good appointment this morning," she said, because saying it steadied them both. "I'll drive back now, sort two things for Monday, then I'll come down again tomorrow. If you like, I'll stay the night."

"You have a life," Meredith said, a mild protest she had never meant. "You chose that hill because you can be here quickly."

"I chose that hill," Charlotte said, smiling, "because the parking is better and because I can be here in under three hours, that bit is true."

That won a small huff of laughter. Meredith squeezed her fingers, then let go. "Bring me a mochi from that place you like in Pacific Grove," she said. "The green one."

"Done."

Emma popped her head round the door with the ease of someone invited everywhere. "Do you need anything before I go, love?"

"We're fine," Charlotte said. "Thank you."

"Your mum's dinner is at five," Emma said to both. "I'll tell the late shift you'll be back tomorrow."

Charlotte stood, kissed her mother again, and lingered a second longer than necessary. "If the silence comes tonight, write it down. Even if it's only one line, I want to know if these dreams are in a hiatus or if the pattern has been replaced by a new one."

"I will," Meredith said. "Drive safe."

Charlotte collected her coat and case and stepped back into the corridor. The sea light followed her to the car park.

Saturday, 5th April 2025 – 17:41

Jackson Square, San Francisco, Richardson Occult Antiquarian

The city had shrugged off the morning fog by the time Charlotte let herself back into the gallery. Jackson Street's bricks glowed low and warm. Someone in the next building laughed, and the sound ran like a wire along the lane.

She disarmed the alarm and stood a moment, listening to the room settle - the soft breath of the HVAC, the faint tick of the regulator clock by the office door. She crossed to the vault and keyed in the code. The lock once again gave its private approving click.

She didn't touch the guardian figure. Not yet. Instead, she went to the back shelf, past the tidy ranks of bankers' boxes and the labelled binders (Apparitions; Spirit Photography; Wards, Bottles & Traps), to a ledger she hadn't taken down in years. Olive buckram. Tape-repaired corners. Her own hand on the spine, written long ago: APOTROPAICS: LANCASHIRE NOTES.

The leather cracked softly as she opened it. The smell rose

up... dust, old gum, a ghost of coal. She turned the first few leaves; past the contents page she'd laid out in a neat grid with an archivist's ambition: Parishes | Objects | Heraldry | Press. Her pencil travelled automatically to the margin, underlining dates and small forgotten decisions.

Halfway through, a tracing-paper flyleaf. A pencil sketch she had made while in her twenties and then embarrassed herself by inking. A quartered shield; a stylised boar; a sheaf; a narrow banner with a motto she hadn't been able to confirm and so had left blank. Next to it, in smaller script: Becker (Altham). Beneath that: Moorside.

She didn't smile. She didn't flinch either. She only turned the page.

The section on Altham was thicker than she remembered. Typed notes taped in; photocopies trimmed to fit; a handful of unhelpful press clippings with headlines that told everything and nothing.

MISSING CHILD in a font that made her jaw tighten. LOCAL MAN HONOURED. LOCAL MAN FOUND DEAD. ESTATE SALE LIST. In the margin, one item she had written years ago. 'Probate packet - try Preston Archives' - circled twice.

She read three lines, then closed the book gently.

There was no sudden revelation to be had. Just the patient fact of a trail she had followed once and could pick up again. A crest. A name. A house. A pattern of harm that had taught a child to be afraid of Friday nights.

In the vault light, the guardian figure sat in its cradle, iron showing dark under UV when she swung the torch across it.

The resin plugs in its chest caught the beam and threw it back in a dull bloom.

"Containment," she said aloud, testing the word against the room. "Or translation."

She slipped the ledger into a clear sleeve, left it on the bench, and wrote a short list on a card:

Preston archives - probate (Becker, Moorside)

Altham parish press register - 1880-1945

Heraldry cross-check - motto variants (B-?)

Contact - Bancroft/Mechanics' Institute (night lecture notes)

National Archive - Papers of Lydia Becker (Available online)

She put the card in her pocket, turned off the vault light, and locked up.

Outside, the evening had cooled. She stood for a moment in the smell of wet brick and jasmine and thought about the curve of Highway 1, the turnoff at Ocean Avenue, and the way her mother always sat up straighter when she walked in. Then she thought about a crest inked in a ledger in a hand that hadn't known yet what it was trying to find, and about a house that she'd never even set foot in that had shaped her family's entire life.

"Moorside, I think it's time we got acquainted," she said, as if practising, and let the door click shut behind her.

Chapter Twenty-Three

Thursday, 10th April 2025 – 17:49

Moorside House, Kitchen

As April started to creep in, the nights had started to become lighter. That meant more time for fires and more time for readiness.

Life had returned to a somewhat normal state, with Seth returning to work and the kids getting back into their college routines. They had a lot to catch up on, and the added benefit of getting ready for an impending war against an unknown adversary saw their discipline make short shrift of outstanding home and course work.

Steam feathered from the kettle and haloed the kitchen window, turning the car port beyond into a smudge of green and ash-blue sky. The house smelt faintly of bleach that never quite left the skirting boards, and smoke clung to the air like a story clings to a mouth that doesn't want to tell it.

Seth set his laptop bag on the bench seat and rolled his

shoulders till they clicked. He'd worn a shirt today, sleeves shoved to the elbow, lanyard still looped in his pocket out of habit. Work had been careful with him: voices soft on calls, the odd message that read like a handshake. Dave had texted just before lunch - 'All good, mate. Backlog clean. Shout if you need cover next week' - and Seth had stared at the screen a little longer than he meant to, relief and suspicion warring like brothers.

He pulled a Tupperware container from the fridge, lifted the lid, and sniffed. Pasta bake. Garlic heavy. Natalia's way of insisting how they lived.

"Timetable check," Natalia said, sliding the tray back into the oven. Her hair was tied with a rubber band she'd found on the side, the type that snapped if you breathed too hard. "Izzy -deadlines this week?"

Izzy sat at the island with her laptop open, nails chipped, pen tucked behind one ear. "Media on Tuesday, English on Thursday, the big portfolio hand-in next Friday, if I don't get an extension, which I'm not asking for, so Friday." She gave a small shrug that tried to look casual. "Told college I was off last week. Back in, no drama."

"Good," Natalia said. "No flare-ups?"

"Couple of muppets asked if I'd brought my alibi to college." Izzy replied flatly. "I told them to bring a brain next time they start a rumour. My tutor's decent. Says he'll mark me on work, not gossip." She glanced at her phone, then slid it face down. "No contact. I'm sticking to the rules."

Seth nodded once. Bail conditions weren't just words on a piece of paper; they were a fence line. "Jonah?"

"Was on site nine till four," Jonah said, leaning in the doorway with his rucksack still on. He'd grown leaner since Wetherby, everything harder-edged, but his voice was softer. "Sat in the far corner and kept my gob shut. I move before lunch bell, I don't cut across the canal, and I don't answer unknowns. Student Services said if anyone bothers me, I go straight to them. No sign of Brendan." He swallowed. "I didn't really look though."

"Good," Seth said again, the word carrying more weight than it ought. "We keep it boring. Boring is safe."

Jonah dropped the rucksack to the tiles, and the sound made all three of them flinch. No one mentioned it. Outside, a blackbird tried a bar of song then thought better of it.

They'd kept to their rituals. Kitchen, six on the dot, every morning. Phones off at night in the biscuit tin on the dresser. A laminated checklist pinned to the corkboard: tasks, bags, the map with route options scrawled in pencil.

The second shared dream had changed the tone of the house, made everything taut but purposeful. Seth had snapped a branch in that field and felt the sting in his palm when he woke. He spoke less about fear now, more about variables. Natalia tracked the girl in her head as if she could catch her by repetition. Izzy had shouted in the woman's face that never turned.

"Fire tonight?" Jonah asked, already knowing the answer.

"Brief one," Seth said. "Damp wood for smoke discipline, not a bonfire. Then the drills."

Natalia slid a tray of glasses across the counter and began to fill them. "We don't need to prove anything to anyone outside of this house," she said, half to herself. "We do what we said we'd do, and we do it well."

Izzy's gaze snagged on the shed through the window, its new brass padlock catching the last of the light. "Feels quieter with it out there," she said.

"No one opens that door alone," Seth replied. "Not even to look." He didn't say the word statue. None of them had for days. They feared that speaking about it might call it back inside. He'd put a new hasp on the shed and run the spare key onto a separate ring that lived in the drawer with the fuses. Even so, sometimes at night he felt the padlock in his palm, cold as a coin.

He crossed to the dresser and opened the tin. Four burner phones lay inside like patient beetles. He checked charge and signal, then put them back in the order they always used. The family mobiles stayed on the far end of the counter, stacked with their screens facing down. They were learning to live inside rules they'd written for themselves. There was a strange relief in it, a comfort in routine.

"Work decent?" Natalia asked, softer now.

Seth flexed his hands, knuckles pale. "Teams. Jira. The usual relief of nothing. I closed tickets, updated customers. Dave had covered the worst of it last week. I archived screenshots to the secure folder at lunch." He didn't add, 'The same way I did for the hate messages.' He didn't need to. "No one asked the wrong questions."

Natalia set a glass in front of him, water bright as ice. "No one will," she said. "You look like a man who knows how to say, 'no comment' in six languages."

Izzy snorted. Jonah smiled.

"Right," Seth said. "Fifteen minutes, then boots on."

They ate standing up, the way they had since the incident made chairs feel like a luxury. The conversation moved in quick, practical beats. Laundry loads. A form Izzy needed printing. Jonah's passport that had already gone where passports go when courts stop trusting you. The CCTV set on a 24-hour loop. Legacy recordings no longer existed, drives long since fractured into glittering nothing and handed to the earth at a tip no one remembers you at. There were still UV-cleaned lines of carpet you could only see if the light hit at the wrong angle. They pretended not to notice, but Seth knew sooner rather than later a full re-carpeting would be in order.

"College called at eleven," Natalia said. "Wanted to confirm I was back on email and reachable. I am."

Seth tipped his chin. "Keep every message."

"Already in the folder," she said.

They moved as a unit once they stepped outside. The air was damp enough to make the flagstones darken underfoot and the fire pit was ready, new ash sifted from old in a tidy ring. Seth stacked two logs crosswise and a third as a cap, no tinder flare, just a coaxed, modest bloom. Smoke took the hedge and climbed into the evening, like a secret up a sleeve.

Jonah hefted the canvas bag they'd prepared since the second dream and set it by the bench: torches, first-aid, paracord, a pack of chalk. Nothing that would trouble a conscience yet.

"Same pattern as last Friday," Seth ordered. "We gather. Natalia tracks the girl. Izzy runs interference on the women.

If they can't see you, you still get in the way see if they pass through you.
"Jonah tests the boundary at the back entrance and tries to get into the house. We meet centre of the field if one of us loses sight of each other. Observe, don't interpret." He paused. "And we meet in the kitchen at six. No matter what."
Jonah nodded, jaw tight. "Aye."
"The key test this time is if that bag is available in the dream. If it is, then it's game on. If not, then we must make sure we can scrounge enough weaponry in the dream to be useful."
The fire hiccupped and settled, the glow low and obedient. Seth watched the flame, saw a landing carpet in the flicker and had to look away. He walked the perimeter of the terrace instead, hand skimming the stone balustrade, counting fixings, feeling the old habit of checks returning like muscle memory from a different life. Corporate IT taught you the same thing soldiering and fatherhood did. You risk lives in the obvious places that you overlook when you're tired.
"After drills," he said, "ten minutes on breathwork, then bed. No screens. Alarms at zero five fifty hours. We're not giving that thing sloppy brains to play with."
Izzy almost laughed. "Sloppy brains. Nice."
Natalia touched Jonah's arm as he stepped past her. "You're doing well."
He glanced at her, then to the shed, then away. "I'm trying."
"Trying is the whole job," she said.
A breeze reached them and set the ash to whispering. From somewhere down the lane a dog barked twice and fell quiet. Seth checked his watch, not superstition, just marking the

hour, and flicked his eyes to the burners, then the back door. He'd set new locks on everything, replaced two screws that didn't need replacing, and changed the keypad code on the side gate because it made his hands feel useful. He'd told Dave he'd be online early on Monday, then deleted the message and retyped it with one fewer full stop.

"Positions," he said.

They lined up in the exact same places that they had been appearing in the dream.

"Take everything in, what is different here to what is different there. Time yourselves to your positions. We need to make sure we shave as much time off each one as possible. Every second counts in the dream, and the more we can discover the better prepared we will be."

"What's the end goal here Seth?" Natalia quizzed.

"Right now, it's about gaining as much intelligence as we can. This thing isn't going anywhere soon, and I'd rather spend my Friday nights battering him, than running from him."

"Damn straight!" Jonah concurred.

Seth went on. "No one is coming to save us Nat. Whoever or whatever this thing is, we need to deal with it and to do that we need to understand it."

Natalia nodded, the best form of defence was attack and she was done cowering. Yes, her children could be in danger, but she'd take mortal danger with a fighting chance over permanent misery any day.

Seth blew the whistle, and they shot off on their various test paths, timing, monitoring and observing everything as they went.

Thursday, 10th April 2025 – 18:35

Moorside House, Kitchen

They came in on a breeze of damp air and sweat.
Chalk lay in soft crescents along their palms where they'd marked split points and corners.
Timing was everything. If they could map the distances and the seconds, they'd know what the dream allowed and what it refused. For now, it was pure reconnaissance; soon they could pull the notes into a plan and, with any luck, break the cycle for good.
Natalia set the stopwatch on the island. Izzy propped the back door with her heel and shook the gravel from her trainers. Jonah leaned on the doorframe, head bowed, breath steadying. Seth switched the kettle on and reached for the laminated checklist with a ballpoint.
"Times," he said.
Izzy slid her phone across the counter, stopwatch still running as if it didn't trust them. "Lane to the birch; twenty-seven seconds. Was thirty-two on Monday."
"Birch to the mother and return?" Natalia asked.
"Forty-one," Izzy said. "I didn't clip the dip this time."
"Back entrance loop and return," Jonah said, rolling his shoulders. "One minute twelve first pass; fifty-eight on the second. Boots off would shave more, but..."
"Boots stay on," Seth said. "Dream is barefoot; reality isn't. We don't invite rusty nails."
He wrote the figures down - tidy columns under the day's

date - and pinned the sheet back on the board. Natalia poured four waters and slid them along the island with precision.

"Notes," Seth continued. "Obstacles."

"The slate by the front door is still slick," Natalia said. "That's twice now. We sand it or we learn to flow over it."

"Copy that," Seth said, then let the pen fall and leaned into the edge of the counter, looking at each of them in turn. "Right. Mini-debrief."

They stood closer without meaning to. Routine had a way of making them a small army of four and Natalia was quietly impressed with the maturity her offspring demonstrated.

"Dream tasks stay as briefed," he said. "Natalia tracks the girl; distance and intersect points. Izzy attempts interference with the women. If they pass through, you still map the crossing point. Jonah tests the rear boundary, handles, glazing, any change. I'll engage the figure again. 'Three and out' still stands; if any of us loses sight, we rally centre of the field. The only loss of direct sight with someone will be when Jonah goes round the back. We have no idea what's there so no heroics. Just observe and then report pal."

Jonah nodded. "Aye."

Izzy's jaw worked once, then settled. "We go in as a pack."

"As a pack... with line of sight at all times." Seth echoed. He set the water down and let the calm settle before he added, "And remember, this isn't just one fight."

They looked up as he continued. "In the dream, we are aware of the enemy now. He's solid. He reacts. We can move him, and we must assume he can move us. That's one front."

He lifted his hand and ticked a finger down. "But daylight

has its own enemy, and it hasn't shown its face yet. The snap to Izzy. The fake alibi that arrived and vanished. Someone is pulling strings out here and we can't let our guard down."

Natalia's gaze flicked to the kitchen drawer where the knives slept. "They will show themselves soon."

"Exactly," Seth said. "I'd assume he, her, them or they are watching to see how we behave so they can make their move. We must always assume eyes are on us." He ticked the next finger. "This is a war on two fronts. One front we currently know about. One we don't. We don't get to choose which one comes first."

Jonah pushed a knuckle into the small of his back where an ache had made a home. "So, we hold the routines."

"We hold the routines," Seth reiterated. "Operational security stays tight. Household stays boring. No loose talk on the family phones. Burners only when necessary and only for the prescribed actions. We keep doors locked, no one opens the shed alone, and we don't deviate from routine, because routine is how we see patterns and noise appear. Things that are outside of a routine are much easier to spot."

Izzy's eyes had gone to the window without her permission. The brass padlock on the shed had caught the last strip of light and held it like a coin. "When do you think they'll show?" she asked.

"I have a feeling it will be this week," Seth replied. There was no theatre in it, only measure. "People who pull strings either want applause or panic. Both require an audience. So, we stay vigilant and we deny them both. No applause and no panic."

Natalia exhaled slowly and flattened the day's sheet with her palm. “Practical vigilance,” she said. “Watch rota tonight?”

Seth nodded. “Half hour float before bed. I’ll take the lane with a torch sweep at twenty-thirty. Jonah, boundary at the back door. Natalia, spot-check the fuse drawer. Izzy, cameras and drive. No gaps.”

“Roger,” they said, almost together.

The overused kettle clicked off. Seth poured, slid mugs into hands, and let the quiet do the rest.

“Two fronts,” he said finally, as if fixing it in all their heads. “One we meet in the dream. One we meet at the door. We keep our heads. We keep each other grounded. When the second enemy shows itself your first instinct will be panic, remember the breathing exercises. When the hidden one steps out of the curtain, observe, take in as much information as possible and don’t flinch.”

Izzy lifted her mug. “We won’t.”

“Good,” Seth said, and for a heartbeat something like a smile moved through the room and was gone.

Chapter Twenty-Four

Thursday, 10th April 2025 – 19:53

Scrubland, Altham

Moxy was positively bristling!

He had the new burner balanced on his knee and a roll-up stuck to his lip, cap pulled low against the light drizzle. The battery icon glowed full, with a fresh SIM sat warm in its tray. On the screen, the CapCut video editing app showed a timeline trimmed down to twenty seconds of pure poison.

He hit play again, because it felt good to be certain.

The clip opened on shaky night footage from the fence line, the Overaughs' skylight window in frame, their silhouettes moving in a slow, grim ballet on the landing. The edit then switched outside. A muffled voice. Seth's, no mistake, carried clean enough to cut skin. Not the fight, not the blood - the aftermath. The bit where decent men say indecent things and the night takes notes.

"This little bastard tried to harm you, he laid hands on your mother, he broke into our home, came upstairs into our space and for sorting him out we're the bad ones? I don't fucking think so. Life is not bubble-gum and wishes, Izzy!"

Nat, Seth and Izzy in shot, outside Moorside's front door. The perfect recorded confession implicating all of them. Moxy had cut the rest of the footage, stacked a clean subtitle across the bottom in stark white, and burned a date and time overlay he'd mocked up to look like CCTV.

He'd added two things he loved: a watermark in the corner - COPIES HELD - and a two-frame flash of a countdown in the last second, so whoever watched felt time pick up pace at the end. His final touch was naming the video "Fire pit Antics Scene 1".

He made sure he had deleted the main file from his new burner, just in case the phone was swiped, he couldn't risk anyone else getting wind of this. The original stayed on Brendan's burner nice and safe, back with the soft lad. If anyone was going to get nabbed with a video like that in its entirety it wasn't going to be him, he was too smart for that, Brendan could take the fall. This was his pension, his lifetime play, his shot at the big time and he wasn't going to let it slip.

"Beautiful," he muttered, voice half-smoke, half-satisfaction. "Little work of art."

A twig cracked behind him. Brendan stepped out from the trees, hoodie up, though it wasn't cold enough to earn it, eyes wet and jittering. He looked younger today. Smaller. He'd texted Moxy from the toilet, the new excuse at his Mum's whilst on the burner. He had to be quick; she'd started counting the kettle boils every time he left the house.

"You're late," Moxy said, not looking up.

"Couldn't get past her," Brendan replied, rubbing his forearms. "She's got eyes in the back of her head. Thought she was going to follow me to the bus stop."

"And yet," Moxy said, tapping the screen, "here you are."

Brendan swallowed. "What's this move you keep on about?"

Moxy angled the burner so Brendan could see the freeze-frame of the Overaugh skylight in long shot. He didn't hit play, instead he watched Brendan look at the thumbnail.

"We stop waiting and we start charging," Moxy said. "The quiet and polite phase is over."

Brendan's mouth pulled thin. "We were never polite."

"That's where you're wrong, sunshine, we've been saints."

Moxy finally thumbed the clip. Seth's voice bled through the tinny speaker. Clear words... followed by that heavy, awful silence that made his guilt sound louder. The subtitles mirrored it, simple as a slap.

Brendan flinched like he'd been touched. "You can't send that."

Moxy smiled without humour. "I'm not sending anything; I'll be showing it him in person. Isolating Seth, he's the money man. It will be his choice if he tells the rest of them or not. If he decides not to then that's even better, we can use that as leverage as well if we need to."

He killed the sound and pocketed his new burner. Brendan stared. "You're going to their house?"

"Kind of, just outside it on the lane, so I'm not on their CCTV." Moxy said. "I'm not stupid. I'll wait until he sets off to drive to work and then stand in front of his car on the lane.

He'll have to stop.

"I'll show him the video, arrange a meet in a nice public place on Saturday morning and explain how the dead drop is going to work each month. Two grand, every month, regular as clockwork and his nice little life carries on as normal."

"Two grand?" Brendan said, eyes widening.

"Peanuts for a man like him. They can afford it; you've seen their house." Moxy said, as if explaining something to a child. "He'll make the calculation in his head - family versus numbers. Two grand's cheaper than court. Cheaper than the girl hearing her dad say those words on a screen. Cheaper than them all spending twenty years in prison."

Brendan swallowed. "And the crowded place?"

Moxy's grin thinned. "Collection happens where he can't start swinging. The Mall, Blackburn. Food court under the big skylight where the doughnut stall is. Eleven a.m., first Saturday of every month. Envelope of twenties in a plastic bag. He'll walk past, put the bag down on the seat next to me. I'll finish my doughnuts, pick it up and walk off. No chat. No eye contact. No phones."

Brendan rubbed his forearms again. "And if he… doesn't?"

Moxy tapped the pocket with the burner. "Then the world gets to hear how a good father narrates a bad night. Twenty seconds to ruin an entire family. Police. Press. Socials."

Brendan's jaw clicked. "He's going to lamp you."

"No, he isn't," Moxy said, patient now. "He's a protector. He's already figured out his hands are expensive. He'll keep them in his pockets while his brain runs through the options. I'll show him the clip. I'll explain the terms. I'll give him thirty seconds to breathe. Then I'll leave. He can talk to himself for the rest of the night."

Brendan's gaze slid towards the distant line of roofs. "He'll call the police."

"Maybe," Moxy said. "But decent men don't like uniforms in their hall, not when their kids are watching. He'll make a spreadsheet in his head and he'll choose 'quiet'. He'll tell himself it's just for a month or two. Then he'll tell himself it's cheaper than therapy. Then he'll stop telling himself anything and just put the bag down on Saturdays."

Brendan looked at the ground. "What do you want me to do?"

"Nothing heroic," Moxy said. "Go home. Eat something with a fork so your mam stops counting kettle boils. Keep your burner on you. If I ring twice and hang up, that means he took the terms and kept his mouth shut. If I send you a full stop, that means we go to Plan B."

Brendan frowned. "What's Plan B?"

"Same deal, different buyer," Moxy said. "You think your Mr Overaugh is the only man who'd pay to own that little clip? Might be three or four who'd bid for the privilege of keeping it out of sight. But that's messy money. I prefer clean."

Brendan looked ill again. "He'll hate you."

"Good," Moxy said, pulling the cap low.

He checked the burner's battery, checked the backup power bank, then stood. He pointed with his chin down the towpath.

"Tomorrow morning at seven, I'll walk the Moor Road as if I'm heading to the shop. Twenty past I'll be near their gate on the lane. When he drives out, I'll simply stand in front of his car and beckon him to roll the window down."

Brendan hugged himself against a shiver that wasn't weather. "You sure about this?"

Moxy rolled the burner in his palm like a coin. "This is the easy bit, son. The hard bit is keeping two thousand coming on Saturdays without them getting brave. That's where you go back to being useful."

"How?"

"By staying alive and boring," Moxy said. "By being the ghost in their rear-view. You don't talk to them. You don't look at them. You just keep existing. They have no idea you recorded that footage. Over time you can befriend them again and be the man on the inside. Keep this money train going. That's the second lever."

Brendan nodded slowly, like someone learning a prayer in the wrong church.

Moxy flicked the ash from his roll-up and ground it into the damp earth. "Right then," he said. "Tomorrow morning I'll go and see the money. Here you go, I take it you need this..." He held out a small wrap of heroin which Brendan quickly snatched.

Chapter Twenty-Five

Friday, 11th April 2025 – 07:42

Moorside House, Altham

The mist lay low in the hedgerows, cold enough to make breath look like smoke. Seth eased the Audi out through the gates and onto the lane, tyres whispering on damp tarmac. He'd gone twenty yards when a man stepped from the verge and planted himself square in front of the grille.

Cap. Grey windcheater. Hands open, like a bloke asking directions.

Seth braked cleanly. No horn. He wound the window down two inches, then put both hands still on the wheel where the man could see them. He logged details without looking like that was his purpose.

Left pocket heavy; roll-up at the corner of the mouth; something bright and watchful in the eyes. White male, early twenties, skinny, scruffy, oily black with style disguised with a cap. Looks like a tramp.

The man bent a little, his voice pleasant. "Excuse me, pal, have you seen my friend, Steven?"

Seth met his eyes. Calm. "No. Sorry, I don't know a Steven."

"Yeah, you do, course you do" the man said, the smile not moving. "Steven, Steven Skeggs."

There was a momentary pause between them.

"Steven is the man you killed, sawed up, and buried in your fire pit a few weeks ago."

Seth let the words arrive. Let them settle. Finally, the adversary had made his move. This was now about intelligence gathering.

He calmed his breath and brought the window down another three inches as if to be courteous. "Can I help you with something," he said evenly. "or are we finished playing in the lane?"

The burner appeared - cheap, black, new case, older iPhone model. The man held it just far enough from the glass to be visible and not snatchable. His thumb tapped play.

Twenty seconds. The skylight glowing; figures moving on the landing. Then the front step. Three silhouettes and his own voice dropped back into the present with clarity that made the tinny speaker feel too big for the air. White subtitles. A mocked-up timestamp. A tiny mocked up watermark in the corner: COPIES HELD.

Seth watched it as if it were weather. In situations like this he was well versed in not reacting but waiting to respond. He noted the cheap resin sheen on the case, the bitten thumbnails, the man's habit of shielding the screen with his palm against glare - practised.

He let the clip end, watched the freeze-frame until the display dimmed, then looked back up. "Alright," Seth said softly. "So now what?"

"Now you listen," the man replied. His tone stayed friendly, almost helpful. "Tomorrow morning. You meet me at The Mall in Blackburn's food court, under the big skylight by the doughnut stall... alone. You bring five hundred in cash as a show of good faith. Plastic bag. You sit opposite me, we have a nice little chat about how all this is going to play out, then you keep walking, I finish my doughnuts, then I leave."

Seth didn't blink. "Time?"

"Eleven," was the reply. "And bring nothing clever. No phones, no police, no mates in sunglasses. If I see tails, if I see a uniform, if I see you try bravery..." he tapped the burner with a knuckle, light as rain "...then Monday, nine a.m. the world meets your little bedtime story. Police. Press. Socials."

Seth took him in. Blackburn accent; weight carried like someone who runs from trouble rather than at it. He shifted his hands on the wheel, slow and unthreatening, and repeated back what mattered like a man confirming a delivery slot.

"Tomorrow. Eleven. The Mall. Blackburn. Food court under the skylight. Alone. Five hundred in a plastic bag. No phones, no police, no tails."

"That's it," the man said, pleased. "And after tomorrow, we talk about the proper number. Two thousand. First Saturday. Same spot. Regular as clockwork. But you'll like it better if we ease you in with a small one. I'm a reasonable geezer."

Seth held his gaze, let himself be the version of himself the man wanted. Complicit, manageable, counting instead of

judging. "I understand."
"Good boy," the man said mockingly, stepping back from the bumper. "Enjoy work, Seth."
"Sorry I didn't catch your name?" Seth inquired.
"Moxy, but you can call me boss man."
Seth closed the window, let the car creep forward, and didn't look in the mirror until the bend. The grey windcheater had already slipped back into the hedgerow, shoulders loose, hands in pockets, the burner warm against his thigh.
He didn't go back home. He took the right by the post box, looped the back lanes, checked the glass for a tail - nothing - then swung onto the A-road towards the office. Four breaths in, six out, just like he'd taught the children.
He ran the details back in his head until it clicked into place as clean as fittings on a mount. Tomorrow, eleven, skylight, doughnuts, five hundred, alone.
At the lights by the garage, he let the engine idle and made two calculations, one on each front.
Dream front: pack discipline holds. Conduct the tests. Regroup and debrief in the kitchen.
Daylight front: log everything. Cameras checked. Burners quarantined. No deviation from routine. We do not improvise. He would not ring. He would not text. He would not tell the house until they were all in the kitchen and the kettle was on and the door was shut.
Seth gave a slight smile, finally he knew who he was fighting, and the treasure trove of information 'Moxy' had offered up voluntarily warmed his heart. This guy was clearly an amateur. The lights changed. He pulled away without

flourish, a man on his way to work with a meeting at eleven and nothing at all worth noticing in between.

Seth had the solemn thought that the adversary in the day was going to be a lot easier to deal with than the one in the night.

Chapter Twenty-Six

Friday, 11th April 2025 – 17:33

Moorside House, Kitchen

Seth came in with the weight of the day on his shoulders and put his keys on the side as if placing evidence. Natalia was already at the counter, mug down, eyes up. Izzy and Jonah drifted in on the air behind him, reading the way he stood before he'd said a word.

"Contact has been made," he said.

Natalia didn't flinch. "Today of all days," she replied, and they all had the same thought simultaneously: We've got the dream to contend with tonight as well.

Seth pulled out a chair but didn't sit. He rested his hands on the back of it and let the room settle around his voice.

"Lane," he began. "On the way to work. Stepped out in front of the car. Cap. Grey windcheater. White male, early twenties, skinny; hair black, oily, style hidden by the cap. Roll-up in his mouth. Blackburn accent. Left pocket heavy. Bitten thumbnails. Eyes too bright. Smelled of damp nylon and tobacco. Called himself Moxy. Told me I could call him 'boss man'."

Izzy's grip tightened on the edge of the island. Jonah folded his arms and looked at the floor.

Seth went on, even and exact. "Opened with: 'Excuse me, pal, have you seen my friend, Steven?' Then escalated to 'Steven Skeggs. The man you killed, sawed up and buried in your fire pit.' Immediate threat laid, no build up. Used a burner - cheap black case, older iPhone model. Showed a twenty-second edit. Skylight. Landing. Then the front step. My voice. White subs. Fake CCTV timestamp. Fake 'COPIES HELD' watermark. Practised shielding the screen with his palm to cut glare. Stood out of snatch range."

Natalia had already pulled a notebook and pencil across and was writing in clean, angled script. "Route in and out?"

"No vehicle on the lane. Likely on foot through the hedge or cut from the Moor Road. Two dog walkers in the distance. He timed it for witnesses without engagement. He's watched the house enough to know I leave around that time."

"Counter-surveillance?" she asked.

"None," Seth said. "No lookout, no reconnaissance sweep, no sense of a second. He volunteered his name. Gave me tomorrow's place and time. Changed his language mid-flow. First said 'sit opposite me and we'll have a nice chat,' before finishing with 'then you keep walking, I finish my doughnuts, then I leave.' Inconsistent instruction. That's nerves, not tradecraft. He wanted to look clever and couldn't hold the script."

Jonah glanced up. "How much did he ask for?"

"Five hundred tomorrow," Seth said. "Down payment. Alone... Eleven a.m. food court under the skylight by the doughnut stall at The Mall, Blackburn. 'No phones, no police, no mates in sunglasses.' Then he previewed the long game: two grand monthly, first Saturday. Plastic bag. Regular as clockwork. He thinks we'll fold and repeat."

Izzy's mouth tugged. "Will we?"

"No," Seth said. He let the word sit like weight. "We are far better than this clown."

Natalia's pencil paused. "What did he miss?"

"Dashcam," Seth said smiling. "He didn't clock it. No face mask. Voice and build now on record. Didn't check for tails, didn't check for static cameras on the lane. Didn't vary his threat... just one clip, he's a scrawny bully with a phone, not a professional." Seth pulled his phone out and showed them the small clip, more for facial recognition than anything else. He looked at the three of them in turn. "The enemy in daylight isn't this 'Moxy'. He'll be easy enough to handle. The real enemy is the footage on that handset and wherever he's backed it up to. That's the real threat."

Natalia nodded once and switching into military intelligence mode. "So, we treat him as a courier with a bomb he doesn't understand." She tapped the notebook. "Objectives: identify device model and OS; locate storage for the device and redundant data locations, if they exist; map his approach and exfiltration; establish his routine; find his hiding hole. We need his infrastructure. If we can map that out, we can take him down."

"Exactly," Seth agreed. "He said, 'Monday nine a.m. was his timing for release', so could be a library account or someone else going to send. Might be a bluff. Might be a scheduled upload he can stop with a password. We assume two redundancies: cloud plus physical. We need to find both, or at the very least deal with both. Tomorrow gives us the first look. I don't think he has anything set for timed release, he's not good enough. Calling him an amateur would be doing amateurs a disservice."

Izzy's eyes flicked between them. "You're not meeting him alone, are you?"

"I am," Seth said, and the calm of it made it sound like an appointment, not a risk. "The down payment is noise control and a show of compliance. We buy time with five hundred quid and spend that time intelligently. We don't want to trigger his internal alarm with a show-of-force if he's already primed himself to see one, we can't take that risk. We observe, gather intelligence and then respond accordingly, with the appropriate action when the time is right."

Natalia closed the notebook and slid it aside. "I'll be at The Mall from eight o'clock," she said. "Shopper's kit. Hair up and dull. Covid face mask and specs. New tote. I'll walk the concourse twice, map the cameras, check the sightlines, mark exit routes and where we can park without getting pinned in. "I'll sit where I can see the skylight and every exit from the food court. When he arrives, I'll clock his shoes, his gait, any tells; then I'll tail him out. No engagement. We want his method and direction of travel, any rendezvous. If he's on foot, I'll follow to his bus or taxi, then his street. If he's in a car, I'll get the plate and peel off. We don't spook him on day one."

Seth nodded. "Clean burners only. Scripted calls only. If you need me to pull out, text a single full stop and go to exit bravo – which is the exit onto the high street with the toy shop. Exit alpha is the main entrance, which I will be using on entry and exit. If you're burned, you go into Superdrug, ask for a refund and walk out the rear door. Make sure you buy something first thing on your sweep of the concourse when you get there, so you can make sure a legit refund request can be triggered."

Jonah shifted. "Err… where has all this come from?"

"What do you mean?" Nat said quizzically.

He raised his eyebrow "What do I mean? Mr and Mrs bloody Bond over here."

Seth looked at him "This was mine and your mum's day job for quite a long time before you were born, and we were very good at it."

Jonah shrugged. "Well, I'm a little freaked out by it, but cautiously glad to hear it. This is some next level shit right here."

"Good, then you'll understand why we need you and Izzy well away from this. It's not just keeping you safe, it's about keeping you out of the way whilst the trained professionals work," Seth said gently. It may have been firm, but it was fair. "You stick to your routines. College work. Rest. Phones in the biscuit tin overnight, burners quarantined. Be in the kitchen at six in the morning. That's your job. You can spend the day gaming or whatever it is you guys do during a

Saturday at home. Don't go anywhere and try not to contact anyone. If me or your mum gets in a bind, we may need you do something, so picking up and being ready to rock and roll is vital."

Izzy swallowed. "So, Mum goes alone?"

Natalia's eyes were steady. "I'm not walking into him love. I'm walking behind him. There's a difference."

"He could still..." Izzy started.

Seth cut in, soft but firm. "Your mother's an ex-intelligence professional. This is what she did for a living, long before you arrived. No panic. Two fronts. Two plans. That's all this is. Plan one is for the dream, plan two is for Mr Moxy Bossman."

Natalia's mouth softened, understanding her daughter's concern. "I'll be seen by a thousand people, and no one will remember me when they get home," she said. "That's the point. I'll be perfectly safe love, and I certainly know how to handle myself if things go wrong."

"You're not wrong there!" Seth spluttered, giving his wife a wry smile.

Silence held for a moment.

He went on. "Tonight, we do the dream as briefed. We arm ourselves early. Get a branch, stick, rock, anything. Rally at the tree line, we all confirm we can see each other. Then straight into your tasks. No deviation.

"We debrief and decant our learnings, then tomorrow I meet Moxy at eleven, alone, with five hundred quid visible in a plastic bag." He held up a finger. "Visible, not available. Bag will be double-skinned, large and taped. If he snatches and runs, he'll be running with a bag which should slow him slightly. If he sits, I stay sitting, we chat, we part. Meanwhile Nat has already made him and is away on the tail."

"Trackers?" Jonah asked.

"No active tags," Natalia said immediately. "He's got an iPhone. It will warn him if an AirTag or AirPods are following it. We keep it passive. Eyes, plate, direction, gait. And a discreet UV dust on the bag handle, in case we need to confirm contact with any other surfaces afterwards. That's it."

Izzy managed a thin smile. "Sloppy brains don't win," she said, throwing his own line back at him.

"Exactly," Seth said. "Our brains are sharp. We've been training for this." He took a breath, settled his shoulders, and the room seemed to settle with him. "We keep our heads. We keep each other safe. We hold the line on both fronts."

Natalia reached for his hand across the island and squeezed once, like a promise, then let go. "Boots at nineteen-thirty," she said. "Breathwork at twenty-thirty. Alarms set for five-fifty."

Jonah picked up his mug. "Aye."

Izzy nodded, eyes brighter than she wanted them to be. "Aye."

Outside, a thin rain thickened. The padlock on the shed caught a brief gleam and gave it back. Inside, they moved into their places, the way people do when they know the night is coming and the morning won't wait.

Chapter Twenty-Seven

Saturday, 12th April 2025 – 00:06

They were all sat in the snug waiting for what they were now calling the "witching hour" – a loose play on the Pendle Witches over the hill.

"Does anybody not find it weird that we don't struggle getting to sleep on Fridays?" Izzy mused.

Seth looked across at her. "What do you mean?"

"Well, we've been through quite a lot recently and we know we have to face Mr Dodgy Hat Silly Coat Psychopath every Friday, and yet we all seem to have no issues nodding off."

"Mm... That's an interesting point," Natalia said, already pulling the little reporter's notebook towards her and scribbling it down.

Seth was watching her hand. "It'll be tied to the statue. Everything is. We need a test."

Nat's pencil moved faster.

Jonah stood and stretched. "That's a simple test. One of us stays awake and watches the others. Like that old film with the guy with razor blades for hands and the dodgy black-and-red jumper."

"What? Edward Scissorhands?" Izzy frowned.

Seth, Nat and Jonah chuckled.

"What?" Izzy said, deadpan. "He wasn't dangerous, and I reckon he slept well in the film. He was rather nice actually."

Jonah checked his watch. "Speaking of which, it's time to get into positions. Or, as we used to call it, bedtime."

"It will be bedtime again before long pal," Seth said. "We're gathering intel every time. The side with the best intel always wins."

"I hope so Dad," Jonah muttered, shouldering the door.

They moved with a quiet economy now. Natalia flipped the biscuit tin, dropped the family mobiles in face-down, then set the burners beside it and snapped an elastic round the tin. Izzy chalked a tiny cross by the newel post - habit, not superstition - and put the chalk back in the canvas bag. Seth checked the latch on the back door, then the front, then touched the fuse drawer once like he was clocking in.

"Recap," he said. "Arm yourself early. Rally at the tree line. Confirm eyes-on. Then taskings. 'Three and out'. We wake and move to the kitchen and write first, then talk later. Those notes are vital."

"Test list logged," Natalia said, tapping the notebook. "Stay-awake trial can happen next week. Tonight, we need the clean task run for tomorrow's daylight job."

They climbed the stairs without the old fear chewing at their heels, the house breathing its slow, old breath around them. In the landing light their shadows kept pace and at the top they split to their rooms with a line each, like a ritual.

"See you at the lane," Seth said.

"See you at the lane," they echoed.

In her room, Izzy tied her hair back twice, then once more for luck, and lay flat, palms open on the duvet. Natalia wrote a single word at the top of her page... 'Observe' and then put the notebook on the bedside table where her hand would find it first. Jonah sat, counted four in, held, six out, twice, and let his shoulders drop. Seth stood a moment by the window and looked at the black of the garden until his mind was empty.

Lights clicked off. The house settled as if it had been waiting for this exact sound.

They didn't force sleep. They didn't have to.

The dream did not come fast.

It crept.

Folding them in, one by one. It took them.

One moment they were in their own rooms; beds creaking, the house settling, the slow drift of sleep beginning.

The next, they were standing together. Seth, Natalia, Izzy, and Jonah, side by side in the field beneath the black sky.

The grass was tall and wet with dew, cold against their bare feet. The house loomed in its usual terrible calm. The ha-ha cut its shadowed grin.

Seth didn't waste a second. Pack check.

"Here," Natalia said, eyes already scanning left to right.

In the dreamscape their mouths barely moved, and their words seemed to thread straight into one another, clean and without echo. It was a strange sensation, thought passing

like breath.
"Here," Jonah answered, setting his feet.
"Here," Izzy murmured, shoulders squaring.
"All present," Seth said. "Arm up. On me."
They turned as one, moving with the quiet competence of routine. Jonah stooped and lifted two fist-sized stones from the churned lip of earth near the treeline. He weighed them once, then handed one to Izzy.
Seth's palm closed over the same low branch as last time and he wrenched; fibres tore, then gave, the familiar jolt sent up his arms. Natalia crouched at the hedge and slid a crooked length of fallen limb from the grass, testing its weight with a quick roll of her wrist.
"Rally point," Seth said, and they loped towards the notch in the field where the line of trees kinked inward. The spot they'd chosen as their centre. From there, the terrain presented itself in its old, rehearsed geometry. House to the right; the lane a pale scar beyond the hedge; the ha-ha and the deeper dark of the trees where the child always broke cover.
"Tasks," Seth said. "Jonah – kitchen boundary. Izzy - women. Nat - the girl. I hold centre and go for him. Three and out. Rally if we lose sight. No heroes."
Four small nods. Then they were gone, the pack breaking and flowing into lanes they'd walked in their heads all day.
Izzy cut low across the dew, bare legs silvered, the stone tight in her palm. She reached the path where the mother would come barrelling down and planted herself in it; wide stance, chin lifted, heart hammering out its stubborn beat. The front

door flew with the same single slam.

Bang.

The woman burst through, calling "LOTTIE!" Izzy stood her ground, shoulders square, pulse blazing. The woman did not see her. She moved straight through Izzy's shoulder like fog through wire. It was cold and it tingled, there and gone in an instant, leaving nothing but a wet prickle on the skin and a furious, useless certainty.

"Negative," Izzy sent, jaw clenched. "No contact. Women passed straight through."

"Logged," Seth replied.

Jonah skimmed the edge of the ha-ha and struck for the rear of the house. The kitchen door shimmered in the moonlight, that same wrong stillness, like the glass was holding its breath. He didn't sprint this time. He counted; four in... hold... six out... and lengthened his stride to a steady, fast-paced run. The stone sat cool and heavy in his hand. The gravel path at the back felt more there than last week. He could feel individual pebbles under his feet. He reached for the handle - "Stand by," Seth pulsed across the field. "Hold. Don't touch."

Jonah froze, hand hovering a breath from the metal. "Copy. Holding."

Natalia was already moving, the curved stick tucked close, gaining yard after yard on the child. The girl burst from the trees - the white nightdress, the hair like blown straw. Her flight was as frantic and heedless as always. Natalia cut an angle, found balance in the wet grass, and pushed... closer now... closer... just three strides off...

"Stop," Seth thought, the word snapping through the four of them like a tug on a rope. "All of you. Hold position."

They obeyed without question. It felt wrong to stop. It felt like standing between falling glass and the floor and refusing to move your hand. The girl ran on, small feet flashing, the long hem catching at the grass. Natalia held herself back with a visible effort, breath flaring, eyes on the back of the child's knee where it would buckle if she mislaid a step. But she held.

Seth's gaze combed the treeline, the grass, the black angles of the house. "Where is he?" The timing was off. By now the figure should have been a moving density at the edge of vision, cutting across the field like a shadow with intent. The pattern had been the same every time: door slam, mother's cry, child's run, the tackle in the blind spot below the rise.

Not this time.

"He's late," Izzy sent, unsettled. "He's..."

"He's learning," Seth thought, and that realisation sat on him like a ton weight.

The child carried on, halfway across the field now, and Natalia had nearly caught her. Two strides, one... hand out, about to pass straight through again.

Then the air beside Seth changed.

It felt at first like a pressure drop, a small collapse in the space he occupied, the same type of sensation you get from an elevator that steals a fraction of your stomach when it starts and stops. The grass to his left lay down as if under a boot and rose again. Cold spread from his shoulder like spilt water. The figure was not where it should have been. It had not come gliding out from the trees. It simply was. Standing one pace to Seth's left, coat moving as if in a wind the rest of the field ignored. No footsteps. No approach. A dark cut-out with the wide-brimmed hat and the long black wool, the edges of it smudging the night. Closer than it had ever been. Seth didn't turn his head. He moved his eyes like he was checking a mirror.

"On me," he pulsed, calm and bright and sharp. "Rally centre. Now."

He felt them shift. Natalia breaking off the chase in a wrench, Izzy pulling back from the path, Jonah easing from the handle - all three vectors angling for him, fast and silent, like a flock changes direction without losing a feather.

The figure tilted its head. The hat's shadow erased whatever passed for a face. When it spoke, it was not voice, not exactly, but a shape pressed into the back of Seth's eyes. He could not have said what he heard; only what he understood.

The figure inclined its head, and when it spoke the sound arrived wrongly. Not through the ears, but somewhere behind the eyes. Old words pushed through a crack.

"Well now..." it said, the syllables drawn out like wire. "What divertissement do we have here. I had thought thee shades on a casement - no more than witnesses, bound to watch my sport and enjoy my endeavours."

A gloved forefinger lifted. It tapped Seth's shoulder once, neat as a maître d' announcing the next course.

Cold jolted his body. He shifted, not by choice. The grass scuffed under his heel.

The figure's mouth, or rather the place where a mouth should be, widened. A dry, delighted rattle came up from its chest.

"Ha!" it crowed, giddy as a child shown a new trick. "After all this time! I never dreamt I might lay so much as a finger upon the watchers. I have taken my fill of these little pageants, aye - the door, the wail, the fall, the silence, the mother's delicious aguish. But this…"

He leaned nearer, the brim a shadow over Seth's cheek. The voice dropped to something like intimacy.

"This is quite another prospect. New rules, good sir. New play."

Seth did not blink. "Logged," he sent, calm and bright. "Manifested at centre. No approach. Speech Victorian. Physical contact - confirmed."

"We shall have rare sport, you and I," the figure went on, almost tenderly. "Let's heed this well - if I may reach thee, thou may reach me. And if I may touch..." It tapped his shoulder again, soft as ash. "...then so may I take."

It laughed, a thin cackle that seemed to crease the night like scorched paper.

The field tore.

All four of them were upright in their beds at once, breath snapped in like rope. Lights banged on in order down the landing and feet hit floorboards in the same four-beat.

No one spoke.

They filed to the kitchen in their drill of silence, took their places at the table, and reached for pens. The kettle went on again with its small, sane click.

Seth wrote the header as if carving it into oak:

LOG: 12/04 - 00:24 DREAM EVENT (No. 8)

Natalia was already noting in her clear hand: Girl and women intangible. Figure absent until midfield. Manifested at Seth's left with no visible approach. Cold pressure before appearance. Speech - Victorian diction ('divertissement', 'thou', 'thee').

Izzy's started scrawling: Women passed through. No sound. Could not break their line. Figure spoke to dad as if he were… target? Called us 'watchers'.

Jonah flexed the shoulder he hadn't realised ached and wrote Handle not tested (held), Firm to touch. Halted on command. Rally time good. Then, beneath it: Figure's cackle felt like metal on teeth.

Seth rolled his shoulder once, the skin under his shirt tender where the tap had landed, and printed the words as close to verbatim as he could drag them up:

"Well now… I had thought thee shades at a casement… never dreamt I might lay a finger upon the watchers… after all this while… new rules."

He underlined new rules twice, then put the pencil down and finally looked up at the others.

"Tea," he said, voice steady.

Natalia glanced over Seth's scrawl, thumb already flicking at the burner. "What are shades on a casement?" she muttered, typing. The handset chewed for a second and spat up a cheerful home-improvement article.

She read, deadpan: "For casement windows, choose shades that don't interfere with the crank handle - outside-mount, reverse-roll roller shades, Roman shades, or no-drill, frame-fit blinds."

Izzy raised an eyebrow. "Helpful. We can fight him off with a pelmet."

Natalia huffed, scrolled, then killed the screen. "Wrong century. Shade as in spirit. Casement as in window. He's saying he took us for one thing only... watchers at the window. Present, but out of reach."

Seth tapped the note where he'd underlined the phrase twice. "Which tracks with how it's been. Observe, don't touch. We couldn't move the scene; it couldn't move us." He turned the page and wrote as he spoke. "What matters is the last line. 'And if I may touch - then so may I take.'"

The room thinned around the words. Natalia's mouth tightened. "He assumed we were fixed in place. Now he's testing the edges."

Seth nodded. "He's testing us now. He's realised it's not a diorama; it's a door. He's pleased, not alarmed. That's the bit that worries me."

Izzy leaned back in her chair, tapping her nails against the tabletop under her finger. "Brilliant," she said, dry as dust. "We've gone from ghosts at the window to audience participation. This just got a lot madder."

Seth closed the notebook and set the pen across it like a latch. "That's enough for tonight," he said, voice back to orders. "We've logged what we needed. Enemy number one is logged on paper. Now we sleep, and we meet enemy number two on our feet, we must be ready."

He moved through the drill without hurry: burners into the biscuit tin, lids on mugs, chairs pushed home. "Breathwork.

Phones stay off. Alarms five-fifty. Boots on at seven. We keep the shape."

He waited until each of them nodded. "Bed. We've dealt with the man in the field. In the morning, we deal with the man from the lane."

Chapter Twenty-Eight

Saturday, 12th April 2025 – 07:30

By half-past seven the house was already moving on rails. Natalia showered, hot then cold, tied her hair in a plain knot and took it down to a looser, forgettable ponytail. No perfume. Moisturiser, yes - shine kills a face faster than nerves. She stood at the wardrobe until the clothes stopped saying anything about her: stone-coloured mac, oatmeal knit, straight-leg jeans, flat-soled trainers that made no sound. A canvas shopping bag with a book spine poking out, a folded cotton tote inside it. A blue ballpoint, a pocket notebook, a pack of tissues, a lip balm, a covid mask, a bottle of water. Purse with a ten-pound note and three one-pound coins. No knives. No tools. No jewellery to snag.

On the dresser the biscuit tin sat open: four burners asleep. She took hers, powered it up just long enough to clear the queue - one test ping at 08:00, nothing else - and killed it again. The family phones remained stacked, screen-down on top of the freezer. She printed two emails for Izzy's coursework on the way out and left them under a magnet marked MAP.

"Back-channel's dead," she said. "No contact unless the building is on fire."

Seth nodded. The lane, the man, the voice. He had relayed it all with the slow, even cadence of someone counting teeth. Now he was all edges: flat, grey jacket, clean trainers, no logos. In the glovebox, the burner, powered off. He'd shaved and he looked like a man who would buy doughnuts for his kids and think about spreadsheets.

"Half-hour floats, one sweep each," he said. "We stick to the shape. You log; I sit. We're early."

Natalia checked her watch - 07:56 - and headed to the car. "It's good to be early," she said, and meant it.

08:19 - Jackson Street

She parked two streets away, not in the shopping centre's multi-storey. Never feed a later pattern. Before she locked the door she sat a minute, the mac still on her knees, and looked at the mirrors the way she'd been taught. Not for cars but for behaviour.

Who looks twice without a reason? Who slows in a way they haven't planned? A man in a hi-vis vest checked a parcel and moved on. A mother corrected a buggy's drift and a young man in a tracksuit walked past staring at his own reflection. Clean.

She took the long way in, past two cafés and a card shop, taking a left by the opticians then pausing in the doorway to read a poster. A glance up to mark the first dome camera. At the service corridor she counted the fire-door hinges and listened for radio chatter: security at low volume, half a sentence about a spill near Boots. And then she moved on.

08:31 - North Entrance

She entered through the glass doors with a small stream of bodies, turned immediately to her right, and let them pass her. First purchase: a paper from the newsagent. Many people in a shopping centre at eight-thirty on a Saturday have gone there to do something. The people who are simply there attract attention. She folded the newspaper at the page with the weather and walked to the mezzanine, her eyes doing the work and the rest of her pretending not to.

08:38 – 09:10 - Recon 1

Even this early the food court had a pulse: prams, three tables of teenagers plucking at hash browns, a pair of older men dunking digestives into too-hot tea. The doughnut stall was where Seth had said it would be, a glazed island under the light, pink boxes stacked like sugary bricks.

Two cleaners did a slow circuit with the wide mop, their radio earpieces blinking. Security did a lazy figure of eight, one leaning more than watching... one actually watching. Noted. Cameras: eight by sight, overlapping cones. Two blind spots. The far end of the banquette under the planter and the slice of shadow behind the handrail by the lifts.

She bought a tea she didn't want, sat at the second table from the skylight and turned the newspaper so that the crossword faced up. She didn't fill it in. She took a photo of the page for her own records and for something to do with her hands.

Her mac stayed on; the shopping bag on the chair to her left with the cotton tote invisible inside it. She timed how long it took for a cleaner's circuit. Seven minutes when uninterrupted; ten when interrupted. She noted who wiped tables and in which order. The woman with the bun had a system; the boy didn't.

She wrote SAT 08:49–09:10 / cams ×8 / two cones / cleaners 7–10 / guard 8-min loop in small, tight letters in her notebook.

09:17– 09:52 - Recon 2

Circulate. She got up and 'browsed' the doughnut menu, reading every absurd flavour as if she couldn't quite commit. She took a lap of the balcony, glanced down to the escalators and marked the sight lines. She checked signage for the nearest first-aid point and the quickest way to outside air - south doors, the ones that always stick when it rains. Then she bought a bottle of water from the vending machine, because people in crowds like to see you do things that crowds do.

Twice she stopped to tie an already-tied lace. Once she stepped aside to let a child run past and used the pause to look at who the child ran to. At 09:43 the regulars started arriving: the chess pair with the clipped voices, the women

with the hymn books, the lad who put his phone face-down before he met his mates. She waited for someone with no 'tell'. The absence of a tell was its own note.
At 10:07 she sent no message to no one and sat again.

10:29 – 10:44 - Pre-position

The food court found its mid-morning temperature. A queue coiled at the doughnut island. The fryer hissed and sugar dust hung in the air like static. She moved to the third table from the stall, the seat with the line of sight to both the north entrance and the lift bank. She placed the paper in front of her and opened it at the book reviews. Her eyes did the work. She was thinking about how the man in the lane had smiled without his eyes and how men who smile like that either want to sell you something or take something from you.
At 10:45 she stood and drifted to the edge of the court to free the chair at the exact table Seth had chosen earlier. She passed a bin, dropped her empty bottle, and marked two details in the corner of her mind without looking at them. The mother-of-pearl flicker of a CCTV dome over the lifts and the small clock on the wall above Greggs that had been three minutes slow all morning.
Then she saw him.
Not their man. Seth. Already in place.

10:48 - Skylight

He had chosen the seat with his back to the planter and the

skylight in his left eye. Grey jacket. Plain black T-shirt. Jeans. Clean shoes. No bag. No papers. He looked like a man who had bought doughnuts and regretted it but would eat them anyway because waste was worse than sugar. In front of him sat a cardboard tray with two glazed rings cooling and a tea going tannic. His hands were folded on the table, not because he'd thought about it, but because he'd decided to look as if he hadn't.

He checked the time only once - a glance at the wall clock, not his wrist – and then went still.

Natalia crossed the sightline behind him without pausing, then looped, and took a position at the table two rows over, facing the lifts. The shopping bag stayed on her lap, the book half-out like a marker. She looked down, not up. She let her peripheral vision do the work.

This was the shape they'd built between them: the watcher in plain sight and the shadow in daylight. She felt the rules settle round her like a second coat.

All that was left now was the part of the plan that was never loved. The bit where someone else arrived.

He arrived at 10:56 like a man who'd never queued in his life. Cap. Cheap specs. Grey windcheater zipped to the throat, collar greasy with old rain. He cut in ahead of a dad with a buggy and requested cheerfully, "Four of your finest - jam, glaze, chocolate, one with sprinkles - and he's paying." His thumb jerked towards Seth.

Seth didn't look up. He lifted the cardboard tray, slid a note across, calm as a tide table. The girl at the till flicked eyes between them, rang it through and changed the note.

Moxy turned with his box of sugar and planted himself opposite without asking, legs wide manspreading, elbows on the table as if he owned surfaces by sitting at them. Close up he smelled of damp nylon, stale smoke and the sour-sweet tang of burned vinegar. His pupils were pin-prick tight against the skylight; his lids heavy, fighting a friendly gravity. He scratched the crook of his elbow and then, catching himself, scratched the side of his neck instead. The performance was swagger, stitched over softness.

“Right then,” he said, clapping once, theatrically small. “You’re a man of means; I’m a man of solutions. We can be… what’s the word… mutually beneficial.”

Seth nodded as if he were being sold printer toner. “You’ve a turn of phrase.”

“I read,” Moxy said, pleased with himself. “I’m mercantile. Set up a nice little recurring revenue stream. Regardless of the moral components.” He opened the box, pushed one doughnut towards Seth and took a lurid pink thing for himself, biting in and talking round the mouthful. “Two grand a month is nothing in the grand economic paradigm. It’s the cost of doing business.”

Seth held the tray steady while Moxy shed sugar like weather. He watched the hands, the tremor absent, the slackness present, and filed it. Not wired; warm. Not buzzing; floating. Heroin, not coke. He tucked the conclusion where the other conclusions lived: junkie. Soft centres, hard edges.

“Your terms are clear,” he said. “Collection, first Saturday, eleven. Food court. Blue bag, no chat.” He lifted a finger, as if to make a list he didn’t need. “But if this is to be… mutually beneficial, as you say, I'll need to know who I'm in business with. You called yourself Mr…?"

"Bossman," Moxy said, delighted by his own nonsense. "Like I say: I facilitate. I know people. In Preston and down Blackburn Road. I can shift things. Gear, bits, merch. You need a thing gone, or you need a thing moved, I can tap lads. You'd be surprised how… nimble I can be."

"You've got reach," Seth said, neutral admiration, just enough grease to make it slide. "Useful. Could be other ventures down the track. Quiet ones. If you've truly got connections who can shift… product… without squeak."

Moxy sat back, glowing with borrowed light. "This is what I'm saying. We don't have to be adversarial. We can be… adjacent. You keep your end nice and clean; I keep mine." He wiped pink sugar on his jeans and seemed to realise the mark he'd left. He laughed, a small, damp bark. "I'm a professional, me."

Seth let the word sit. He didn't look at the doughnut; he tore a neat bite and chewed like a man thinking about a meeting. "Professional," he repeated mildly. "So professional that you don't need to see my phone, or hear me confirm anything, or watch me walk out. You'll know your bag is down by the skylight seat, and you'll stand up in your own time."

Moxy beamed. "Now you're learning. Discretion is the better part of valour. Next week's the pilot. You do next week and two grand's a stroll after. Irons itself out. After that we're just two blokes on standing orders."

Across the court, Natalia watched his mouth move and wrote, speech: misused phrases; giddy when mirrored; ego responsive. She timed his sits and stands (he fidgeted on the minute), noted the little nose-scratch-tap every few sentences (habit), and the way he repeatedly filed his thumb along his index-nail as if checking for a ridge (tell).

She clocked a faint brown stain at the cuff of his windcheater, a blister on the web of his hand where foil has burned a careless man, and a pale scab constellation along one forearm. She didn't need to write gear; the room already had.

Seth let his eyes soften, as if he were filing the edges of a future purchase. "Alright," he said. "Next week as you've set it. And if it continues without a hitch… we'll talk about scale. Other avenues. If you're as… nimble as you say."

Moxy sat taller, chest a fraction out. "See? We're aligned." He picked up another doughnut and held it as if offering communion. "You're a clever man when you're not panicking. Keep your little angels off the telly, keep your gob shut, and we'll be the best of mates."

Seth touched the side of the tray with one finger, a small acknowledgement. "We done here?"

"We are adjourned," Moxy corrected, mangling it and loving himself for it. He stood, the chair leg screeching an ugly inch across the tile. He left the pink-smeared napkin where it fell. He straightened, winked and swung off, swagger turned up a notch for the audience he believed he had. On his way past the counter, he tapped it twice and called, "Cheers, banker."

Natalia watched him go; head bent to the crossword. She counted five, ten, fifteen, then rose in time with the cleaner's next loop and ghosted after him. She passed a bin and dropped the folded paper she hadn't read. In her pocket, the burner stayed dark. In her head, the route drew itself as he made it.

At the table under the skylight, Seth broke a piece of glaze with his thumb and pressed it to the napkin as if completing a task that he'd promised himself. He didn't look up. He didn't call anyone. He finished his tea with a practised patience and, when the minute hand touched the number that he'd agreed with himself, he stood, put the tray in the bin, and walked out into the Saturday like a man who had errands and time to run them.

Chapter Twenty-Nine

Saturday, 12th April 2025 – 11:17

Natalia became someone else.
Head down, shopper, she slid into the cleaner's wake and let the radio's lazy hiss cover her first sixty seconds. Moxy didn't look back. He never did. He had the gait of a man who believed pavement unfurled for him. Heels first, slight sway in the shoulders, hands free until they remembered to check pockets.

11:19 - North Entrance

He didn't take the escalator. He bled past the optician, through the north doors with a little theatre, and hit the pavement like he'd been thrown there. Natalia let two bodies buffer between them and watched the glass swallow him whole.
Outside air had the hard shine of noon. She paused to pretend tuck something into the tote and used the reflection

in the smoked pane to drift left. Moxy went right, quick glance at nothing, then towards Northgate with pace, cutting across the flow of shoppers like he'd planned them, he hadn't.

11:26 - Cathedral Quarter

He took the direct route: kerb, bollard, a skip, a narrow slip between scaffolding boards that smelled of wet timber and old smoke. He didn't check for a tail. Twice he stopped dead, not to watch, just to re-lace a trainer and flick a lighter that wouldn't catch. The windcheater's hem was fretted with burn marks she hadn't seen in the mall.

Natalia let him get forty metres ahead and took her time. She read shop windows, counted floorboards in her head to keep her pace even. And she used the city's furniture - bus stops, café chalkboards, a delivery truck - to break sight lines without ever losing him.

11:34 - Back streets, Audley

He dropped out of the town centre and into the terraces as if he'd done it since he was twelve. He didn't use the main drag. He took the rat-runs: Duke Street, then a right, then an alley with a wheelie bin tipped and a mattress folded like a book. His phone never left his pocket. He didn't call anyone. He wasn't being brave. He had no one to call.

The dealer's house announced itself the way they always do if you know how to look. Curtains that never quite open; a door repainted three shades of the same gloss; two bells, neither labelled; a film of leaf-mould on the sill; stickers saying **'NO COLD CALLERS'** printed at home and taped inside a cracked pane. A bike wheel leaned against the wall without a bike attached to it. There was a CCTV dome above the door, dead to the world.

11:41 - Score

Moxy knocked once with the back of his knuckles. The door opened to the chain; hand, eye, the quick abacus of faces, and then the chain lifted. He slid in sideways, already patting pockets for a note. Natalia didn't slow. She crossed the street, lifted her phone to her ear as if she'd remembered something awful, and paced out a problem to no one. Eleven minutes exactly. Long enough to make a cup of tea and weigh something. Long enough to put a wrap on a saucer and teach a boy how to burn slowly if need be.

He came out brighter at the edges, lids heavier, walk looser. He didn't put anything in his mouth in view. He swallowed once, wiped his nose with the back of his hand and didn't realise he'd done it. He scratched the crook of his arm, thought better of it, and rubbed his earlobe with his thumb and forefinger instead. There were spots of foil ash on the cuff of his windcheater she hadn't clocked before.

She let him have the length of the street and set a pebble on her notebook with a thumbnail: **11:52 OUT - SCORE CONFIRMED (ten–twelve mins). House: back-to-back terrace off Audley. Door chain. Dummy cam.** She didn't write vinegar tang in the doorway; she didn't need to.

11:56 - Towpath

He cut for the canal like a homing bird, slipping past a betting shop and a shuttered barber, then down the embankment steps two at a time, not even bothering to check for cyclists. The towpath was damp and empty. The day had pulled itself into a grey yawn and most of Blackburn was buying chicken or petrol. Moxy tucked himself into the hedgerow and moved fast, head down, hands deep. He didn't look over his shoulder. He didn't need to. He had never had a reason to.

Natalia took the towpath in segments: sight, cover, sight. She practised the oldest trick - walk like you belong. Twice she paused to take a picture of the water, once to retie a lace that hadn't come undone. A spaniel dragged a man towards a scent under the bridge; the man apologised and was grateful when she smiled. He was the only person who passed her in the first half-hour.

12:15 - Altham, Scrubland

The place revealed itself the way it had in her head; the way she imagined it. A hollow of ground beside the railway embankment where uprights of elder and sodden hawthorn stitched a rag of shelter together. Two tents hunched against one another, one green gone grey, one a cheap orange that had bled in the rain. A pallet had been dragged close as a floor. Half a tyre lay like a black smile; a ring of stones held the memory of a fire. Carrier bags were knotted round a sapling; a saucepan hung from a branch on baler twine.

Moxy didn't hesitate. He ducked into the orange tent, tugged the zip behind him and disappeared. The fabric snapped against itself. There was a hush.

Natalia didn't break the line. She kept to the opposite bank where the hawthorn made a bower of shadow and crouched as if to look for something she'd dropped. She wrote without looking at the page: **12:17 IN - ORANGE TENT. No other bodies visible. No second man. No observers or sentries, no visible alarms or mobility triggers.** She drew a quick plan from memory: **rail line / hedge / two tents / pallet / tyre / fire ring / saucepan.** She marked sightlines, blind ground, three approaches, two exits, the place a camera might see without being seen. This would be perfect for a trail cam setup to observe.

12:28 A dog walker passed. A woman in her late fifties, blue fleece, headphone in one ear, Springer on a long line. The dog lifted its head, tasted the air, dismissed the world and trotted on. No one else. No bikes. A lone can fizzed and turned in the weeds when a gust took it. A train rolled over the cutting and made the hawthorn fizz back at her like a shaken wire.

12:55 No movement from the orange tent. No change in the seam of the door zip. No cough. No argument. She knew what that meant. He was either asleep or gone. Given the ten-minute stop at the terrace and the swallowed air on the way out, she didn't bother to argue with the data.

She picked up two small pebbles and launched one at the grey tent. She needed to make sure this was single occupancy. No movement. She waited five minutes and threw the second stone. Still no movement from either tent. This meant it was single occupancy, and the sole occupant was high enough not to notice small infractions. Good.

She let another ten minutes pass to make it look like a walk. She stood, stretched as if a calf had seized, and turned her face to the bit of sky that had finally opened. She left by the longer path, the one that would spit her out behind the retail park instead of back at the obvious steps and let the route dilute itself into shops and buses and other people's Saturdays.

13:06 - Jackson Street

Her car was where she'd left it. She didn't get in straight away. She walked past it, counted to twenty-five, and then returned from the other direction. Habit. Always give your own shadow a chance to show. Nothing moved but a plastic bag falling asleep against a kerb.

She slid behind the wheel, shut the door carefully, and sat with her hands at ten and two until the breath she'd been keeping went away by itself.

13:54 - Moorside House, Kitchen

Seth had a legal pad on the table and a pen already bleeding a neat header: **12/04 - TAIL**. He didn't ask if she wanted tea. He watched her go to the sink, rinse a glass, fill it, and take two mouthfuls like someone returning herself to her bones.

"Well?" he said.
Natalia set the glass down on a coaster as if it needed a place to live. "He's worse than we thought, in a good way." she said. "He walked out of the shopping centre like he was crossing a stage, scored on a back-to-back house just off Audley - ten to twelve minutes inside, door chained, dummy camera - then straight to the canal path. Led me straight to some scrubland. "Two tents, green and orange. Fire ring. Pallet. Only one dog walker in nearly an hour and they certainly didn't look like they wanted to be interfering with the camp. He went into the orange tent at twelve seventeen and didn't move. He's not using a car. He's not using a look-out. He's not looking at anything that isn't his next bag."
Seth's mouth tightened. "Junkie."
"Junkie," she agreed. "A total amateur. No transport. No counter-surveillance. No discipline. If he's got a lock-up, it isn't close. He can be contained. Two tents; I tested the second one by throwing stones, no movement. It may be a wild assumption, but the second tent might have belonged to our intruder, it would certainly explain the connection and the recording."
Seth wrote it as she spoke. **No vehicle. No second. Score 11:41–11:52. Canal route. Base: scrubland by rail cutting.** He drew a thin rectangle for the pallet and a circle for the fire pit and marked the two tents with an X. He underlined **no witnesses** and put a bracket by **dog walker (F, 50s, springer)** as if even that mattered.
"He thinks he's untouchable because he's never had a reason to be touched," Natalia said. "We couldn't have asked for a

more incompetent adversary if we'd put it on a form."

Seth tapped the pen against the margin and gave a slight chuckle. "Good. Then we set the board and make sure he walks where we want him."

She nodded, rubbing a thumbnail along the notebook's spine. "We'll have to be careful of one thing."

"What."

"He's high," she said. "High men are unpredictable. They don't behave to pattern; they behave to need. He may spook at air or sit under tarpaulin until Monday. If he changes his mind about anything, it won't be because of us. It'll be because something in him twitched."

Seth closed the pad and set the pen along it like a rule. "Then we plan for both," he said. "We keep boring. We keep our line. And next Saturday, we let him do exactly what he told us he would do, and we watch him learn what happens when his world includes adults."

Natalia managed the shadow of a smile. "You should see the state of that campsite," she said. "Lydia would have it tidied in twenty minutes."

Seth huffed, a dry sound that wasn't quite a laugh. "Let's not send the dog to do it."

She glanced at the clock: 14:02. The day had already started to slope towards evening. Upstairs, a floorboard clicked as someone crossed a room. The phones in the tin were still in rank and file, screens face down, quiet as slate.

Natalia picked up her glass and finished it. "I'll map the scrubland on a proper sheet and shoot it to your pad," she said. "Then I'm having a shower. The stench of that place is crawling all over me."

Seth nodded. "Boots at nineteen-thirty," he said. "Then breathwork. Then the field."

She was halfway to the door when she looked back. "He is not the worst thing we have to worry about."

"No," Seth said. "He's just the one who turns up on time."

"It's the recording that we have to deal with."

Seth nodded, "The longer we leave it, the worse the exposure is. We need a plan."

Chapter Thirty

Saturday, 12th April 2025 – 22:11

Moorside House, Snug

Izzy read her notes back once, pen ticking a margin: rally centre under ten seconds; women intangible; figure late-manifest, centre. Jonah's page had distances broken into numbers and arrows - terrace to ha-ha, lane to rear path - clean little ladders he could climb without thinking.

Seth had the legal pad open on the low table, He watched their heads bow and lift, and then he set the pad down and let his voice find its old, level weight.

"That's enough for tonight," he said. "We've logged the drill. It's good work."

They both looked up.

"You two go up," he went on. "Me and your mum need to plan. Daylight. You're not near it."

Jonah shifted, the half-protest already dying. "I can..."

"You can do what you've been doing," Seth said, gentler now.

"Six o'clock. Writing first, talking second. Eat. Sleep. Breathe. Keep the shape. The dream, that's your battle front."

Izzy's mouth tugged. "So, we stick to ghosts," she said, dryly. "And you two play with humans."

Natalia's smile was small and real. "Something like that. We need you focused on the field. Pack discipline wins the fight. The rest of it - Mr Bossman - is for us."

Jonah glanced at the biscuit tin on the dresser. "Phones?"

"In the tin. Burners quarantined," Seth said. "If anything happens you can't solve by writing it down and making tea, you wake us. Otherwise, bed."

Izzy rose, stuffed her notes into the pocket of her hoodie. "You do realise 'Bossman' is the least boss thing you can call yourself," she said, heading for the door. "It's like naming a cat Dog."

"Upstairs," Natalia said fondly, and got a sigh for her trouble. The good kind, the one that said the child was still a child long enough to be told off.

Jonah paused at the door. "You'll text a full stop if…?"

"If we need you to stay out of the way faster than usual," Seth said. "Yes. Now bed, both of you."

They went. The house took them with its usual soft noises. A tread on the stair, a door breathing shut, the old wood settling like a chest filled and emptied.

Seth waited until the landing was quiet, then turned the pad towards the light. Natalia moved to the dresser, dropped the family phones into the tin and elastic-banded the lid as if restraint could be a blessing, and then came back to the table with her own notebook already open to a clean page.

"Two fronts," he said. "Night is logged. Daylight is now."
Natalia clicked her pen. "We've got a route, a base, a profile, and a routine," she said. "He's a junkie. He's static. He's sloppy. The only adult in his world is that recording."
Seth nodded. "Which makes the recording the target. We plan the week." He wrote as he spoke. "Tomorrow: rest. Monday: download dashcam, back up to external, off-site copy to the safe. Tuesday: trail cam deployment at scrubland - approach from retail park; no prints, no fuss. Wednesday–Friday: route surveys, exits, camera cones, staff patterns. Saturday: first payment window - decoy bag prepped; visible-not-available; Nat on tail, me on sit. No improvisation."
Natalia put a small tick beside each. "Comms."
"Burner script only," Seth said. "No live calls. No unscheduled movement. We write what we intend to do, then we do only that."
"Paperwork."
"Everything in duplicate. Yours lives in the bottom of the flour bin, mine in the garage loft under the camping box and once this sorry mess is done we burn the lot."
Nat mused chewing on the edge of her pen.
"I know that look Nat, what's going on?"
She took a deep breath. "Well, I've been thinking."
"Oh Christ, here we go."
Nat shot him a stern glance. "As I was saying before I was rudely interrupted."
She didn't sit back; she leaned in. "You said it yourself: The daylight threat wants us busy and tired. The easiest way to end that front is to let nature take its course."

Seth stilled the reflex in his jaw. “Spell out ‘nature’ for me please.”

“Not with us there. Not with our hands on anything,” she said. “He’s already killing himself. If he gets hold of something stronger than the usual chalk he’s pumping into his veins, he’ll do what he always does. We wouldn’t have to push him. We’d just...” She broke off, to find words that would soften the impact. “...step out of the way and let nature take its course.”

Seth stared at the cold ash in the grate. “And the phone.”

“It’s an older iPhone,” she said briskly. "Almost certainly stolen, wiped, set up with a new Apple ID if at all. Those things lock hard. If it isn’t unlocked when he drops, and the battery runs flat wherever he is, it’s in what the labs call BFU.”

His eyes came back to her. “BFU?”

“Before First Unlock,” she explained. “If it hasn’t been unlocked since it last booted, or the last time it was unlocked was 48 hours ago, or if it dies, you can’t get past the lock screen without the code. Not with Face ID, not with a thumbprint. Those don’t even work again until someone puts the code in. And if there’s no proper iCloud backup? There are no back doors, not for a device like his. Time becomes… our friend.”

She swallowed. “They bag it. It sits in an evidence locker. It never wakes up, and they certainly can’t compel a dead person to open a phone or use his biometrics. iPhones require attention for Face ID, which looks for open eyes and uses the TrueDepth camera to confirm the user is alive and looking.”

He said nothing for a moment, then: “And the

toxicology report?"

"They will find what they find," she said. "The lab here is good. If it's one of the modern poisons, they'll name it. They'll write opioid toxicity. The coroner will say drug-related death. They'll follow the supply line, because that's their job. But without a live phone and with his history, it's a file, not a murder board."

Seth nodded slowly. "You are not wrong about where his road ends."

"And I am not asking us to put him there," she said, softer now. "I'm talking about a thing that's already in his world, the stuff that isn't chalk, isn't sugar. It's laboratory. A fleck no bigger than a crumb and you stop breathing. That's why crews carry the spray now. You know the briefings and so do I."

"Fentanyl," he said, and the name felt like a bruise in his mouth.

She met his eyes and gave a small, grave nod. "Yes, let's call it what it is so we don't dress it up."

He was quiet for a long time. In the hall, the regulator clock ticked like a metronome as the heating died down for the evening. "Even saying it drags us somewhere," he said. "I don't want the children anywhere near that."

"I don't either," she said. "So, we partition. Two fronts. They stay with the dream; breath, timing, notes. We deal with the man who is alive and choosing to try and harm us, and we do all this without becoming what we can't live with."

He let out a breath he hadn't realised he'd been holding. "How?"

"The drop off," she said. "If we can source a couple of wraps of Fent you can pass it to him as part of a much bigger deal you have in the pipeline, you've primed him for this already. Tell him to test it and if likes it then he can expect a kilo of the stuff to shift next month."

Seth's eyes narrowed. "That's really loose Nat, do you think he'll go for it?"

"Definitely," she said. "In fact, I think the only struggle we'll have is him waiting to get back get to his tent. This guy is a strung-out waster, he's light work, very easy to manipulate."

Seth watched her and the slow pulse in her throat. When he spoke, his voice had lost its bark. It was the one he used in briefing tents, when you asked men to do something they would have to live with for years afterwards.

"If we start talking like that," he said, "what does it make us?"

Natalia held his gaze. "It makes us honest about the landscape. Not architects of it."

"You just drew a line and then put your toe over it."

"I drew it," she said, "so we can see it. We are not handing him anything he must take, it's still his choice."

Seth rubbed his jaw, the old habit of checking himself before he spoke. "Intent matters."

"So does survival," she said, softer now. "We are not saints, Seth. We're parents. We've got two children asleep upstairs and a man out there who will happily burn our lives with a clip on a phone. We only do what we can live with, and I understand the trepidation. But this is different, he's doing it to himself."

He sat back, thumb working at a nick on his pen, the question he'd been skirting finally out in the air.

"And where exactly are we supposed to get something like that? We're not in Mexico, Nat. We don't know those types of people anymore."

She didn't blink. "We don't need to," she said. "We only need to know one person and he's the only person on the face of the Earth I would consider trusting with something like this."

She held his gaze while Seth's mouth curled into a half smile and then she said one word, a name.

"Tam."

Act VIII

IRAQ 2006

Chapter Thirty-One

Monday, 1st May 2006 – 11:28am

Shatt-Al-Arab Hotel, Basra

The Signals office had been a ballroom once. You could still see the ghost of a chandelier in the ceiling, a rusted rose of bolts and wire, and the parquet under the sandbags squeaked when you walked across it in boots. Someone had stencilled COMMCEN (Communications Centre) on an old gilt mirror and taped a frequency plan to the frame. The air was two parts heat and one part generator fumes.

Seth sat with a handset cradled to his shoulder, pencil behind his ear, annotating a contact matrix the way some men annotated novels. Across from him, Andrew 'Tam' Tamlin had his boots hooked round the legs of a chair and was coaxing a stubborn bit of kit to behave with the gentleness of a Scottish dwarven locksmith.

"Left it in the sun again?" Seth said, not looking up.

Tam didn't bother to deny it. "Aye. It sulks like me after a dry

Sunday. I'll give it ten minutes and a promise of some shade."

"You were meant to be a football prodigy," Seth said. "Did they not manage to teach you to keep your kit squared away?"

"They taught me to pick a lane and run around some cones pal," Tam replied, watching the LEDs blink back to life on the radio. "That's when I picked this lane and here I am, making radios feel special in a ballroom in Basra, with your stupid mug grinning at me daily." He tilted his head. "You'd have been a ball boy at best."

"That's Staff Sergeant ball boy to you!" Seth said, deadpan.

"You're insufferable as a SSgt," Tam said, not unkindly. "I should have elbowed you at the board and you know it."

"You didn't miss it by much pal," Seth replied. "You'll have your crown above them tapes by teatime."

Tam made a face. "Don't want it if it comes with your shite haircut."

He was Andrew Tamlin on the paperwork and 'Tam' to anyone who mattered. Five-ten, sixteen stone of compact power with jet-black hair that still wanted to be Elvis when he let it grow, and dark eyes that did their best work by watching. Edinburgh born, a youth football prodigy who could have gone all the way if the itch to serve hadn't got under his skin.

He and Seth had a friendship that didn't require much heat. They met in basic training in '98, then did selection together a lifetime later. Tam watched first, spoke second; Seth set the metronome for the room and expected everyone to hear it. And if you stepped out of line Tam would get you before Seth did.

A murmur of traffic came through the open window: horns, a motorcycle, a donkey braying like a knackered trumpet. The Shatt al-Arab, a smear of dull metal water, lay somewhere beyond the grit and the walls and the heat shimmer. The hotel, which was commandeered years before, served as the British Forces' node in the south: a comms and liaison hub, a place to park advisers, send patrols and drink tea until the sugar rotted your fillings. The ballroom was the beating heart of it: nets, burst traffic, message handling, the dead-eyed rhythm of shiftwork and heat.

"What's the parade at Rustamiyah this week?" Tam asked, scrolling through a situation report detailing the upcoming event.

"Sword to the honour graduates," Seth said. "Sandhurst music in a bin-fire breeze. The usual pass out parade."

"Tell them to teach breathwork," Tam said. "That's the only thing that gets you to lunch at IMAR, that place stinks worse than your boots."

IMAR wasn't so much a unit as a promise written in concrete and dust. The Iraqi Military Academy al-Rustamiyah, IMAR for short, sat on the east bank of the Diyala, six miles southeast of Sadar City in Baghdad. It had been a cradle for officers since the 1920s, when British instructors in Sam Brownes drilled a republic into existence on a parade square chalked under a sun that could flay you alive.

It had fallen quiet through coups and sanctions, the parade boards pitted, the drill shed turned to storage, the academy's colours bleached to nothing. Then, in the long aftermath of 2003, NATO's training mission in Iraq (NTMI) arrived under a UN mandate - no combat, all "advising and mentoring" - and shook the place awake, striving to make it the Iraqi equivalent of the British Sandhurst military academy.

By 2005–06 the academy was back on its feet. Platoons of cadets in sand-coloured combats on the square, Italian Carabinieri in neat black uniforms at Camp Dublin teaching federal police how not to lose their heads and Iraqi sergeants rediscovering the pleasure of a clean bed block and a working weapon. The brief was simple and seemingly impossible: build a professional officer corps with a non-commissioned spine to match; create an ethos that would stand when the foreign flags came down; teach ethics and orders with the same seriousness as marksmanship.

On good days, you could almost hear the place breathing again: a whistle, a shouted cadence, a bark of laughter in two languages. On bad days, the wind swung round and the shamal pushed a skein of dust across the square with the burning trash field on its left and the sewage treatment plant on its right letting off an aroma that could wake the dead.

Seth and Tam knew it like you know a favourite holiday destination: the way to the comms container by feel, which Iraqi captain would have his lesson plan squared away properly and where to get tea strong enough to trouble a spoon. It wasn't glamorous but it was better than the hotel. It made sense, it was working.

You could count it in lieutenants who no longer died because someone had bothered to teach them how radios worked properly, how to write an order you could actually follow in the heat, how to hold a line without becoming what you were fighting and ultimately how to engage and defeat an enemy that was adept at seeping into the civilian populace.

On a previous visit, Tam had drilled the recruits with a simple line: "Standards set to Western," dragging the word out and making it less foreign. "Not because they're Western but because they work." That always got the point across, and the recruits at Rustamiyah were all too familiar with what doing the wrong things could cost them. In this conflict there was no room for old school sentiment. Sentiment got you killed.

Seth capped his pen, slid the matrix into a folder. "Right," he said to Tam and to the rest of the room. "Let's go grab a tea."

A shadow flattened itself against the glass in the door and the handle went down. Lt Fletcher stuck his head in. He was lean, sunburnt and with eyes that never quite finished blinking. A young, yet professional officer that Seth respected.

"Gents," he said, breathless in the 'hotel way' that meant he'd jogged the short corridor in Body Armour Lite. "Boss man wants you. Both of you. Now would be good. Two minutes ago, would have been better."

Seth slid the pencil behind his ear, set the handset into its cradle and stood. "Fletch," he said. "What kind of want?"

"The smiling kind," Fletcher said, which wasn't as reassuring as it should have been. "Training team up at Baghdad. The Rustamiyah crowd. There's talk of us lending them some hands again."

Tam clicked the lid back onto the radio with the satisfaction of a man who had won a small argument with plastic. "And here was me thinking I'd get to finish my love letter to this frequency plan."

"You can write it from the boss's sofa," Fletcher said. "One minute and counting Overaugh, get a shuffle on."

Seth and Tam exchanged a look that adds ten years of shorthand to any sentence. Seth grabbed the folder he'd prepped that morning, Tam palmed a notebook that had seen four countries and an unsuccessful promotion board, and together they stepped out into the baked corridor where the air smelled of dust and diesel and tea.

"Race you," Tam said, already moving.

"Don't leave your comms in the sun again sport Billy!" Seth said, and followed, clearly trying to overtake Tam, who equally defended his lead.

Tam and Seth rounded the corner to Captain Sparks' office. They tapped the door. "Enter," came the order from inside.

Captain Sparks was head-down over a blotter, sleeves rolled, tie dragged loose, sunburnt nose already peeling. He looked up as they came in, grin wired in place.

"Ah," he said. "The Tweedledum and Tweedledee of the CommCen. How are my two favourite SFCs?"

Seth kept his face straight. "Flattery, sir? Let me guess, a random task awaits?"

"How could you possibly tell?" Sparks said, eyes bright. "Sit. Indulge me."

For the uninitiated, Special Forces Communicators are the ones who make other people's heroics possible. They're the quiet insert at the back of the patrol photo with a rucksack that looks like a wardrobe.

Before they ever touch a radio, they undergo a version of the same selection process as the special forces blokes they'll be glued to: hills that steal your lungs, jungle that rots your feet, navigation that doesn't end, and the gentle humiliation of being cold, wet and wrong until you aren't.

Then come the black arts:

HF/VHF/UHF radios, satellite communications, rebroadcast, cryptography fills, blue-force tracking, the darkly comic skill of fixing a dead node with black nasty, a combi tool, and a prayer.

They don't just pass messages between patrols. They set up, maintain and control the networks that the tip of the spear needs to operate in the harshest of situations, which means they are often side by side in those very same situations. Hence the necessity for passing special forces selection.

Sparks flicked a glance between the two men and allowed himself a small, satisfied huff. He liked having them in the room. "Right," he said. "Since you're both my gold-plated, cast-iron pains in the arse, congratulations."

Seth raised an eyebrow. Tam didn't.

"We need two bods up at IMAR," Sparks said. "Advising, mentoring, a bit of course design, a bit of handholding and reassurance, a lot of not letting things explode. Four weeks. Baghdad is screaming for actual grown-ups, and as you did such a bang-up job last time, you've been selected from a cast of thousands."

Tam made a show of looking behind him. "Where are the thousands?"

"Busy," Sparks said. "You two aren't."

Seth opened his mouth to argue on principle, closed it on discipline. "We leave when sir?"
Sparks checked his watch, then a scrawl on his blotter. "Tomorrow. Zero-five-thirty. Air Rhino up Route Irish. Pack light, pack twice. I want lesson outlines in my inbox before you steal my oxygen in the morning. And, Tam, try not to seduce any more of my radios or appropriate any more confiscated weaponry. They are not trophies!"
Tam put a hand on his heart. "No promises, sir."
Seth stood. "We'll square it, sir."
"Good," Sparks said, expression softening for a heartbeat. "It's a mentoring mission, not kinetic. But you know the ground. Keep your heads. Make them better than we found them. And for the love of God, leave the place with more sergeants than it had when you arrived."
"Aye, aye Captain." Tam said. "We'll teach them how to stay alive…"
"…and unalive the bad guys," Seth added.
"Good," Sparks said, waving them away. "Go on. Before I change my mind and send Fletch."
Fletcher made a noise in the doorway that might have been a laugh. Seth clapped him on the shoulder as they went past; Tam winked, then paused, turned back.
"Sir?"
"What now, Tamlin?"
"If you're borrowing our ballroom for a month," Tam said, "try not to let anyone dance on the parquet. It's the only thing keeping the sandbags off the floor and make sure the fridge is stocked with Coors for when we get back. You know how

Seth gets when he's been dry for too long."
"Out," Sparks said. "And tell someone to shut that generator up. It's murdering my soul, and NO STEALING!"
Back in the corridor, the heat reached up like a hand. Tam fell into step again. "Well, Staff," he said, "looks like we're off to teach the young how to not die again."
Seth grunted, already building a kit list in his head. "You can brief the ethics block on how to 'appropriate' equipment."
"Aye," Tam said. "And you can teach them how to get a shite haircut."

Chapter Thirty-Two

Tuesday, 2nd May 2006 – 05:30

Outside Shatt-Al-Arab Hotel, Basra

The Rhino runner armoured vehicle was idling in the parking area. Seth and Tam loaded their gear into the storage bins and then climbed aboard. Only one other person was on board, a civilian contractor who looked like he was about to be sent into the seventh circle of hell. If petrified was a person, it would be him.

They called it a Rhino with the same mix of affection and contempt soldiers reserve for anything that might save their life and jolt their spine. Not an elegant animal, more armoured shoebox than bus, welded from thick steel, hung with doors that shut like bank vaults, and studded with thumb-wide vision blocks of green-tinged ballistic glass. In another life it might have been a hotel shuttle with a coat of paint. In Iraq it was a rolling strongroom, built to soak up punishment that would turn a soft-skinned vehicle into confetti.

Inside, it was bench seats and harness points, a spine of grab handles overhead, the air-con doing its heroic best against 40-degree heat. The smell was its own cocktail: hot diesel, spilled oil, dust, a memory of last night's curry run, and the sharp, metallic tang of burnt electronics from the jammer racks that pulsed out over the convoy like an invisible force field.

You didn't so much ride a Rhino as put it on - pack, rifle, radio, and then body, wedged knee to knee with twenty other people trying not to tread on each other's toes.

From the outside it looked almost comical: slab-sided, square-jawed, sometimes painted white to look less like a target and somehow achieving the opposite. This one was desert-coloured, thankfully. Run-flat tyres sat under armoured arches; the floorpan was braced to shrug at small blasts; there were roof hatches for a gunner and for air when the A/C inevitably gave up.

They were never glamorous, never meant to be. Their job was simple and brutal: get people from A to B along roads everyone else called kill-boxes. In Baghdad it was used at midnight for the 'Rhino Run' up and down Route Irish between the airport and the Green Zone, a convoy of buses and gun trucks moving in tight formation, jammers ticking, speed up, lights off. In Basra and the south, it was hotel to airfield - Forward Operating Base (FOB) to port gate. A steel cocoon that let training teams, civil servants and junior officers make it to their briefings still breathing and come back the same way. They were crewed by drivers contracted from US private security companies who talked to their machines like old horses at the rodeo.

People joked about them. They were the "armoured kebab van," "Elvis's hearse," and a dozen other nicknames. Because joking was easier than saying what everyone knew: that the route from door to door was the most dangerous few miles on Earth, and the Rhino was all that stood between you being featured in a routine airport run or a newspaper headline.

A shadow crossed the windscreen, and a pair of dusty boots appeared, followed by the rest of a man in a sweat-salted Stetson hat and a grin you could hear before you saw it. He planted one boot on the Rhino's spine, like a rodeo rider surveying his bull, and pitched his voice over the diesel thrum.

"Ladies, gents, and assorted miscreants, thank you kindly for flyin' Air Rhino," he drawled, pure Texas over baked steel. "Name's Chip. I'll be your pilot today. We cruise at a luxurious six feet above angry gravel level, service is limited, and the in-flight movie ain't worth a dime."

Tam and Seth laughed. Chip tipped the hat brim, then got practical.

"Couple things before we go sightseein'." He tapped the kit slung and holstered across him, slowly and clearly, a safety brief that had learned to capture its audience. "This..." a gloved hand pointed to the carbine across his chest "...makes big noises. This..." palm to the pistol at his hip "...makes smaller, tidier noises. This..." he hitched a boot onto the front chair, revealing a stubby backup revolver tucked above his ankle "...is my 'you surprised me' noise maker. And this..." a knife winked a mean inch from a sheath on his vest "...is for birthdays and bad manners."

He let the smile flatten. "If we get a song and dance outside, you stay in the bus. I go out, I calm the noise. You keep your heads down and your mouths shut, and you do not open a door unless I make it real hard for you not to. If, by some cosmic clerical error, I go quiet, the rules get simple: you are now part of the band. These instruments," he patted each weapon in turn, "are community property. You point 'em away from our good people, and towards anybody auditionin' for the wrong side. You'll know the difference. Trust me."

He let the hat tip forward, broke the tension with the grin again. "Questions? Complaints? Marriage proposals?"

The civilian contractor leaned forwards and emptied the contents of his stomach into a sick bag.

Seth and Tam erupted in laughter.

"Attaboys," Chip said, thumping the roof. "Strap in. Keep your halo straight. Air Rhino is pushin' on."

Chip slid into the driver's seat and thumbed the ignition. The Rhino coughed, shrugged, and then settled into its familiar iron heartbeat. He reached up, flicked a battered head unit, and the speakers crackled into life with AC/DC's opening riff of 'Highway to Hell' sawing through the diesel hush with perfect, stupid bravado.

Seth felt Tam's elbow nudge his ribs. "Route Irish. Highway to Hell," Tam murmured, dry as sand. "Subtle."

Chip glanced back once, hat brim tilting. "A little on-the-nose for the Irish Run, I know," he said, grin back in place. "But it keeps everyone grounded."

And with that they were rolling north, Highway to Hell

rattling the eardrums and Route Irish unspooling ahead of them - a line on a map that would turn into a fuse. They told themselves it was just another lift, just another hot run between walls, but somewhere beyond the checkpoints and the heat haze lay the first of a hundred small decisions that would bind Seth, Natalia and Tam together forever.

Chapter Thirty-Three

Friday, 5th May 2006 – 04:25

Iraqi Military Academy al-Rustamiyah (IMAR), Baghdad

"This is fucking shite," Tam announced to the room at large. "First week in and we're on stag in the bloody COMMCEN. Absolutely outrageous."

"Stop whining," Seth said, not turning from the message wall. "You're like an old granny. Here... catch."

He side-armed a fruit pastille without warning. It thudded off Tam's temple and skittered under a bank of kit.

Tam stared at him. "You're a terrible person."

"Staff Sergeant, terrible person," Seth said, still marking timings on the log with a stub of pencil.

The first few days had slipped by without drama. They'd walked the wire, found the tea hut that didn't water it down, learned which generator needed a kick and which needed coaxing. IMAR hadn't changed much since they'd last been here: sand, square, sweat. Situation normal, just brighter.

Outside their dust-filmed window, the camp was a map of sodium orange and dark. North of them, the country was on the boil. Operation Iron Triangle had gone in, a U.S.–Iraqi sweep with the 101st and the 4th Division pushing into the Tharthar/Tikrit–Samarra belt to smother an Al-Qaeda in Iraq (AQI) training hub.

It meant that every spare pair of hands had been hoovered up by someone's priority. Which left the overnight COMMCEN to whoever wasn't glamorous enough to be in a brief.

Staying on watch through the small hours was called 'stag' or, if you wanted to make it sound less dignified, "stagging on." Tam loathed it with the focused purity of a man who loved a bed. Seth didn't mind. The lull between nets suited him; quiet made sense. Tam's hatred of it, like most of his opinions, was an inexhaustible source of entertainment for Seth.

The door knocked. Two quick, neat taps.

Seth, who had been standing with his back to it, turned. In the spill of corridor light stood a woman in dusty combats, braid tucked back, clipboard under one arm. For a breath too long, nobody moved. Her eyes found his; his found hers and he fell into them headfirst. In that two-second stillness the room seemed to narrow to nothing more than two people hypnotised.

Tam got there first, chair legs scraping as he stood. "Ma'am," he said, Edinburgh softening the edges. "What can we do for you?"

She blinked twice, as if waking. "Oh, oh - hello." The vowels were Lancastrian, rubbed down by heat and time. "Captain Natalia Jones, Intelligence Corps." She stepped in, handing over a sheet of timings to Tam, grids and names. Seth didn't move, his head merely followed her. "We've got a high-profile detainee coming in early doors. No facilities in the adjacent camp, so we're running the debrief from a container just outside your west wall with a little bit of theatrics. We'll have local actors rotating through to help with exercise before he lands. Make sure they're booked in and badged, no mobiles anywhere near my box, escorts know the drill."

Tam took the paper, scanned it, nodded. "Roger that. First serial?"

"Zero five thirty wheels-down. First run at zero six thirty." She turned to go, then paused in the doorway, something like mischief touching her mouth. "Come to think of it," she said, glancing back, "We're two bodies light. You fancy a turn at play-acting? Nothing complicated. Angry men in bad shirts stood in the background."

Tam started to protest.

"Done," Seth said, too quickly

Tam looked at him, then at her. "Err, aye," he said. "We can do a very convincing pair of angry men. He's been practising."

"Excellent," she said. "Leave the fruit sweets at the door." The faintest curve of a smile. "See you just after zero-six."

She was gone in three strides, boots ticking away down the corridor.

For a moment the COMMCEN was all fans and far-off traffic. Tam turned to Seth, delight already brewing and a devilish smile forming. "What was that?"

"What was what?"

"That." He pointed at the empty doorway, then at Seth. "You

and love's young dream. I've never seen you forget your own name before."

Seth flicked the pencil back behind his ear and went back to the log. "You're hallucinating. You need more tea."

Tam leaned on the edge of the table, grinning like a man who had found a new toy. "Captain Jones, eh? Seth and Jones sitting in a tree, K-I-S-S-I-N-G."

Seth didn't look up. "Get your head back in the game, Sergeant. And find that fruit pastille. Losing one of them is a war crime."

Seth shook his head slightly and focused on his notes… although he must admit the thought of kissing Captain Jones in a tree was not unpleasant.

Chapter Thirty-Four

Friday, 5th May 2006 – 06:24

Outside Iraqi Military Academy al-Rustamiyah (IMAR), Baghdad, storage container

The container sweated in the dawn, a twenty-foot ribbed oven that smelled of iodine and hot steel. Seth and Tam came up the beaten track in civvies that didn't fool anyone; trainers, battered ball caps and that particular economy of movement that men carry even when they're pretending not to. An Int Corps corporal in a sand-bleached beret clocked their cards at the door and shooed them inside with a flick of a clipboard. "Keep it tight, gents," she said, voice pitched to cut through the generator whine. "You're here, stand at the back wall, eyes out. You're background today, not main event, try and look as menacing as possible."

The space inside had been staged with a grim sort of theatre. Four camp beds ran down one side, each occupied by an Iraqi amputee playing patient, their shirts cut away, limbs bandaged in crisp white. A pair of medics worked down the line with quiet efficiency, laying fake saline cannulas and feeding tubes, taping sloshing bags to hooks welded to the roof ribs, dabbing theatrical blood with a painter's economy. A bloke with a camera on a strap around his neck was adjusting a cold light and a stack of clipboards. He looked up just long enough to nod at them, then went back to making sure the lens could see what it needed to see.

Tam raised an eyebrow at Seth as they steered their way to the rear. "I didnae sign up for the Royal Variety," he murmured.

Seth didn't answer. He took the spot he was given, back to corrugated steel, a view of the whole narrow shoebox: the door, the beds, the chair bolted to the deck in the centre of the space with ring bolts flashing at its feet.

The corporal - Barker according to her tape - ran through the motions with the same tidy authority that Tam reserved for a frequency plan. "Right. It's a showtime. Booking sheet at the door; banding is blue for role-players, green for med, red for us; no mobiles inside the box; any photography cleared by me. Questions?"

Tam opened his mouth. Seth elbowed him lightly.

"Grand," Barker said. She ran a practised eye over the beds, tugged a bandage here, smoothed a sheet there, nodded to one of the medics. "Looks great."

The temperature seemed to rise with the second hand. Somewhere beyond the walls a generator coughed and steadied, and then the container settled into the listening hush of a place about to matter. At zero-six-thirty on the dot,

Barker lifted a finger.
"Positions."
On the beds the amputees stilled, eyes sliding shut, a few well-timed groans thrown into the heat. The medics took a half-step back and went statue-still, hands folded, eyes down. Seth felt the air change the way it always did just before a door opened on something you hadn't rehearsed.
The bar lock clacked back. The main doors yawed a hand's breadth, then the rest of the way, flooding the box with a sheet of white light and a draught of dust and diesel.
Two soldiers in sweat-darkened combats muscled a figure through the gap: spit hooded, ear defenders clamped over the mesh, wrists cuffed to his spine. The man's steps were half-blind and half-resistant, the choreography of someone who'd been forced to move and told not to dare. They pivoted him into the chair, metal legs screeching on metal floor, and worked with the speed of men who'd practised this twenty times and meant to get it right: wrists to the armrest rings, ankles to the deck eyes, chain through, locks snapped.
Barker glanced at Seth and Tam as she checked each fastening with a tug, and nodded.
She straightened, checked her watch, and nodded once to the medic on the far end, who leaned into a bed and whispered in Arabic. The groans along the line rose and fell together, a ragged chorus. The hooded man's head jerked a fraction under the fabric; the ear defenders meant to box his world to breath and heartbeat and the scrape of his own cuffs.
Tam caught Seth's eye, mouth quirking for half a second. Seth didn't give it back. He was already in his notch, shoulders to

corrugations, gaze raked across the room and back again, a familiar weight settling between his shoulder blades.

Outside, the compound cleared its throat. Inside, the container became a stage, the lights harsh, the air thick, the props too real. And when Barker said, “Stand by,” the room held its breath.

The doors yawned open and the rhythm changed at once. No camera shuffle, no medic’s pantomime. Two of the patrol lads were backlit in the square of white and between them the figure sagged, hooded, the ear defenders bulbous over the mesh like absurd black fruit. Dust swirled in behind them and then settled with the door.

Captain Natalia Jones came in on her heels, the temperature of the room dropping a degree with her. She didn’t waste words on anyone else. She walked straight to the chair, setting the clipboard down on the folded blanket as if this were just another ward and this just another patient.

Her hands were steady and, for all the steel in her eyes, almost gentle. She cupped the ear defenders with her fingertips and lifted them away, folded them, set them on the floor out of reach. Then she found the edge of the spit hood and, with a professional’s care for Velcro and skin, peeled it back ever so carefully.

The man beneath was younger than the file photo, eyes wide, lashes caked with sweat and a week of beard spiking through the dust. The air hit him and so did the room. He jerked against the cuffs, breath coming high in his chest, a stream of Arabic tumbling out - denials, appeals, the litany of a thousand lies.

Jones leaned in until her face filled his world and put a finger to her lips. "Shhh."

The sound was soft, and it cut him off more cleanly than a shout. His eyes fixed on hers because there was nowhere else to put them.

"Hadi Karim al-Salman," she said, crisp, the vowels right. "Born in 'Eight One. Two sisters. A cousin in Al-Karma you stay with when the heat rises. You speak English well enough to haggle, well enough to listen. So, we'll use that. Because we know who you are. You know why you're here. If you're smart, you'll start by letting me hear your own voice, in your own words."

He swallowed, the dart of his throat visible above the collar. The first few English syllables came out hoarse and clumsy, as if he were relearning something abandoned a lifetime ago. "What is this place?" he stammered.

Jones nodded once, offering neither smile nor frown, and eased a fraction to one side so that he could see past her to the side wall and the beds.

Outside, a rotor thudded somewhere to the east. Inside, Barker's pen hovered over the log, and the container held its breath.

Jones didn't bother with a chair. She stepped into Hadi's eyeline and let him see only her and the neat line of her collar. When she spoke, it was in that same conversational register that made statements sound like simple facts.

"This place? I'm glad you asked."

"It's a secure containment facility," she went on, as if giving a tour. "It's been manned twenty-four seven, three six five since just after Vietnam. This is where we keep our prized possessions. Bad men. Professionals. People we can't afford to have out in the world. People just like you. We ship it from conflict to conflict picking up new members as we go. Completely outside of any jurisdiction."

Hadi's breath rasped loud under the hush of the generator. He tried to lift his hands, and the chain reminded him of where they were. Arabic flickered out of him again, a spill of a prayer and denial.

She didn't raise her voice. "You see, everyone breaks. Everyone. It's just a matter of time. Our job is to help time along."

She turned her head a fraction, included the whole container with a glance. "To facilitate that process, we make sure you're comfortable. We make sure you're secure. We wire you to the best medical kit money can buy. Because we want you to live as long as humanly possible."

She stepped aside an inch, enough for him to glimpse the line of beds, the men on them, the slung bags of salted water, the tapes and tubes. "We start at the edges; we call that part 'trimming'. We trim a bit here, a bit there," she said, as if reading from a manual. She lifted her hand and pointed.

"First your feet." A nod to the first bed; the man there kept his eyes shut, his stumps neat under crisp gauze.

"Then your legs." Another bed. Another white parcel where legs should have been.

"Then your hands." A set of bandaged forearms lay on a sheet, fingers gone to a careful puff of dressing.

"Then your arms." The third man's sleeves were pinned to his chest; he didn't have shoulders under the blanket to fill them. Hadi's breath had gone high again, thin, faster than a bird. His eyes kept trying to dart away and kept finding her instead.

"We leave the head for last," Jones said, conversational. "We take an eye." She tapped her own left temple with a fingernail. "Then the other. Then an eardrum. We like to go slow. You see how that works? We make sure you're still here with us, listening. We make sure you can hear every word through your one good ear."

She tipped her chin to the fourth bed. "And if, at that point, you still fancy being stubborn? We take your tongue. Just like Niall here."

The man on the end - older, half his body gone to blankets and tape, looking like a sealed-up torso - worked his jaw and made a sound that was mostly breath and hurt. It didn't take much imagination to turn it into a groan from a man with no tongue.

Jones stepped over, laid a hand on Niall's hair as if calming a child. "Shh... shhh." she cooed as if comforting a baby. "Forty-five years," she said, glancing back at Hadi. "He's our longest resident. There's plenty of life left in him yet though, but I'm sure you can give him a run for his money. You're a young man, I think we can get at least seventy, maybe even eighty years out of you."

Seth felt Tam shift a fraction beside him, that small unsettling he did when something in a room wasn't quite a joke anymore. The medics kept their faces empty. Barker's pen hovered, not writing now, just ready.

Jones came back to the chair; her hands loose at her sides. "Clinically, it's called enforced locked-in syndrome," she said. "But we like to call it the 'Jihadi Spud-U-Like.'" The line landed as if she'd used it before. "Would you like to be our next Spud, Hadi?"

She let the silence sit until it pressed against the ribs of the room. Then, from somewhere behind the beds, a high whine spun up. The unmistakable whirr of a dental saw testing its own anger.

Hadi went very still and then he was very not still, spasms of panic running through him. His shoulders bunched against the restraints; his knees tried to come up and couldn't; a dark stain spread under his thigh and the smell of human faeces hit the heat.

"Or..." Jones said, as if offering a menu, "You talk. Names. Places. Phones. Tonight's work plan. Speak, and the Jihadi Spud-U-Like is off the menu. We can even get you a nice little trip into Syria once your intel checks out. How does that sound?"

She looked him dead in the eye. Her face changed into a demonic incarnation of unimaginable terror as she walked forwards, leaning in so that her face was exactly four inches away from his and then she spoke in the most authoritarian voice Seth had ever heard:

"Hadi Karim al-Salman, either you start talking, or we start sawing!"

The dental saw buzzed to a defining crescendo.

He broke like a soggy KitKat. "I tell, I tell," he screamed the kind of serviceable English men learn in garages and ports.

"No more, no more, please. Hadi… Hadi tells. I tell everything!"
Jones didn't smile. She looked over his head at Barker. "Time on: admission begins." Then, back to Hadi, voice level and narrow as a blade. "Good boy Hadi. Now start with who pays you. Slowly. Properly. We've got all the time in the world, well you have at least."
The drill wound down to a purr and died. Outside, a lorry rattled past, its horn complaining. Inside, pens began to move again as Hadi spilled the beans while the container, for all its heat and iron, felt colder. Seth watched Jones work the thread she'd made, felt the familiar click of a room under control, and did what he always did when a plan was doing its job: he breathed, he listened, and he let the weight between his shoulders settle.
It was craft, not cruelty, she hadn't laid a finger on him just bent the air with words and used his own mind against him. Even Seth, who prided himself on being unflappable, felt the container shrink to the command of her voice and the tilt of her head. She was a magician in green braid, a master of her trade, and he found himself - against training, against caution and against all logic - absolutely spellbound!

Chapter Thirty-Five

Friday, 5th May 2006 – 10:45

The PX (Shop), Iraqi Military Academy al-Rustamiyah (IMAR), Baghdad

The PX was a concrete cupboard with pretensions, a humming bank of fridges. A wire-fronted counter, a sun-bleached poster of a Dallas Cowboys cheerleader curling at the corners. The air-con fought a losing battle with the heat and the smell of hot plastic and instant noodles. A bored third-country national in a faded AAFES polo shirt rang up the same three things on a loop: warm cans, salt, sugar.

Seth stood in the shadow of a stack of Mountain Dew, considering whether he could face it at this hour. He didn't see much point in pretending they were on an American base, but he had to admire the way the Americans built little bits of America wherever they went: PX, AFN burbling out of a tiny TV in the corner, shelves of jerky sitting companionably beside 'Chipsy' crisps with cartoon aubergines on the packet.

Tam arrived behind him with the gracelessness of a man who'd been robbed of sleep and intended to make everyone complicit. "Never seen anything like that," he said, reaching past to liberate two Snickers and a packet of Pringles the size of a mortar tube.

"I've seen some grim theatre in my time, but that?" He shook his head, half laugh, half shudder. "Whole thing wired like a telly studio and she..." he made a little helpless flap of his hand "She just walks in and turns the tap. No voice raised. No fuss. If she'd asked me my bank details, I'd have told her my PIN and my childhood nickname."

Seth found a bottle of water that was only half tepid and another packet of fruit pastilles for his ongoing campaign of harassment. He didn't look at Tam when he said it, voice lighter than it had any right to be. "I think I'm in love."

Tam stopped mid-stride, then grinned as if he'd been given yet another new toy. "Oh, are you now."

Seth shrugged, paid the man behind the till, thumped the pastilles against the counter to break them up. "I said think, not am. She's bloody awesome!"

"Aye," Tam said, trailing him out into the glare, tins under his arm like grenades. "You think you're in love. That's worse. That means ye've written the whole wedding speech in your head already. 'Ladies and gents, when I first saw her, she was elbow-deep in a set of ear defenders and a man in a hood..."

Seth let the door swing shut behind them. The heat hit like a wall. He cracked the water and poured a capful over the crown of his head, let it run down his neck. "You do realise you're a child."

Tam popped a Snickers like a pill. "A very mature, handsome child." He chewed, squinted. "Right, Staffy bobs. Tell your Uncle Tam what it is. The voice? The way she says shh and full names like swords? The way she touches people like they're bombs?"

"The way she knows the room," Seth said, before he could stop himself. "The way she knows what to do without looking at anyone. No theatre. Just… the right thing, right speed." He gave a half-laugh at himself. "And the way she said Hadi like she'd known him since school, then took him to bits with it. Mate, she is a pro, one of a kind."

Tam made a show of fanning himself with a phone card, Edinburgh creeping stronger into his tease. "Oh, we're away. Next, you'll be askin' me if your boots are too scruffy for courtin'. Wait till I tell the lads you fell for a bird who can make you admit your middle name wi' a raised eyebrow."

"Tell them," Seth said, dryly. "Tell them over the net while they're bouncing a rebro off the arse-end of nowhere. That'll go down well."

They cut along the edge of the square, past a stack of Hesco barriers and a row of Carabinieri in their immaculate blacks, cigarettes cupped like little secrets. A patrol trundled by. A Humvee bristling with antennas and an Iraqi MTLB - ex Russian armoured vehicle - that had been painted three different shades of sand and was pretending it had always meant to be that way. The day was already threatening the kind of heat that made metal feel like a living thing.

Tam shouldered the PX door with his foot to bin his wrappers. "So, what you going to do?

Seth stopped and decided there and then.
"I'm going to ask her out, and I'm going to do it right now!"
The office that the Int Corp had been given was two old guest rooms knocked into one, air-con chugging against the May heat and the smell of paper and bleach. Natalia had colonised the left-hand desk with military neatness: HUMINT (Human Intelligence) proformas fanned in precise stacks, a map of the Tharthar belt bristling with pins and Post-its, a battered Dictaphone asleep on a folder marked TQ – A.M. SERIALS. She had her hair twisted up with a ballpoint pen and a smear of dust on one cheekbone she hadn't noticed.
Across from her, Captain Jenny Rathbone had made a small civilisation out of chaos: mug of tea on a coaster fashioned from a ration-pack sleeve, three colour-coded folders like stepping stones, a stress-ball knot of rolled blue nitrile. She worked fast and quiet, pen skittering, pausing only to tilt her head and listen when a phone rang two doors down or a shout drifted from the corridor. When she did speak it was usually to land a joke, like a paper dart in the ribs of a long, hot day.
"Are you going to put him out of his misery?" she said now, without looking up.
Natalia didn't look away from the form she was signing. "Put who out of what misery?"
Jenny's pen paused. "Who?" she scoffed, scandalised. "The Signals Adonis who's walked past this door three times in thirty minutes carrying absolutely nothing of consequence, pretending he's got business with the photocopier, when all he's got is the world's emptiest clipboard trying desperately

to get your attention."

Natalia made a noise that could have been a laugh and could have been a faint. "Really? I hadn't noticed." She started to blush.

"Oh really," Jenny said. She looked up at last; one eyebrow deployed with surgical precision. "You want me to spell it out then? You didn't notice the gorgeously hot man-mountain of a Special Forces communicator floating about our corridor like he owns the oxygen? The one you've been side-eyeing while you pretend not to? The one whose file you have very definitely been snooping through all morning?" She tapped the open manila folder on Natalia's desk with her pen, where OVERAUGH, S.SGT, UKSF (COMMS) sat in neat caps, paper corners worn soft by somebody's thumbs.

'BUSTED!' Natalia thought.

Heat pricked Natalia's neck a beat before she could will it away. "I was… familiarising myself with attachments," she said, prim to the point of parody. "It's my job."

"Mm," Jenny said. "And my job is interrogation. You forget we're both very good at it."

A shadow drifted across the frosted pane in the door. Both women watched it pause, hesitate, move on. Jenny didn't take her eyes off Natalia's face. "Fourth time," she murmured. "We'll be into pattern-of-life analysis at this rate."

Natalia made a show of tidying a stack of papers that didn't need tidying. "We've got Iron Triangle in full swing and a serial at fourteen hundred. I don't have time for… corridor theatre."

"You have time to breathe, Nat," Jenny said, voice softer now.

"You have time to be a human as well as a rank slide. Go and bump into him. It's a corridor, not a minefield."

"It is a bit of a minefield," Natalia countered, but the protest had less steel in it than she meant. She found herself glancing at the door as if the man might obligingly provide the excuse by walking past again.

Jenny caught the look and grinned. "There she is. Tell you what. I'll come over all helpful and ask him to run this down to the S2 shop." She held up a sheaf of utterly generic J2 Summary sheets. "And then I'll realise, to my horror, that I've forgotten to initial something and pop back in here to do it. You will, tragically, have to go and retrieve the papers and thank him, because I'll be trapped in here with a live phone and a broken pen. It'll be awful. We'll all write stern memos to ourselves afterwards."

Natalia tried to glare at her and failed. "This is juvenile."

"This is human," Jenny said. "Also, he's a SSgt, not a gobby sapper, he has shoulders like a Hesco bastion, and I bet he's in proportion elsewhere if you know what I mean. What's the worst that can happen?"

Natalia opened her mouth to answer and found she couldn't name a single thing that wasn't either ridiculous or true. Beyond the door, that same shadow hesitated again, then moved on.

Jenny was already on her feet, straightening her sleeves. "Right. Operation Totally Innocent Paperwork is a go." She held up the stack and winked. "Breathe, Captain."

Natalia rolled her eyes despite herself and pushed her chair back, smoothing her blouse as if it mattered. "If this goes

sideways," she said, "I'm blaming you in writing."
"Wouldn't have it any other way," Jenny said, already halfway to the door. "And Nat?"
"What?"
"He's been outside that door five times in thirty minutes," Jenny said, in the tone of someone pointing out a fact on a map. "Don't make him come back for a sixth."
Natalia shook her head, felt the smallest, most inconvenient smile pulling at the edge of her mouth, and reached for the handle. She opened the door and stepped into it, heart steady, stride even, a captain with a sheaf of papers and, just for once, no plan at all.
She timed it like she hadn't, and there he was: Seth Overaugh coming the other way with an empty clipboard and that halfway-to-a-salute posture men wear in corridors they've walked too many times.
"Oh... hi, Ma'am," he said, almost tripping over the formality. "Fancy seeing you here. I, uh... just wanted to say… great work this morning."
They stopped, a metre apart, and stared at one another with the helpless politeness of people who could brief a battlegroup without blinking and yet could not, in that instant, remember how hands were meant to behave. The corridor hummed on without them. Seth's ears went pink. Natalia felt, to her utter irritation, like a sixth former who'd been handed back an essay with a gold star on it.
He cleared his throat. "I was err.. wondering if you'd like to get one of the err.. err.. those err.. nice coffees from the PX in the fancy cups."

Natalia fidgeted with the corner of her folder she didn't need to be holding. "Umm... are you asking me out on a date SSGT Overaugh?" she said, a shade too brisk.
Seth stared at the floor slightly and for some totally unknown reason he started to twist his boot on the floor like a schoolboy.
"Well, maybe I need a little bit of a caffeine boost after this morning's events. But don't read anything into this, Seth Overaugh. We're just having a coffee to discuss this morning's debrief."
His head snapped up and he blinked. The blush flickered into a grin he tried and failed to suppress, and his left eyebrow raised. "Right. And, not to read anything into anything Ma'am, but when you introduced yourself, you said your name was Captain Natalia Jones." He tipped his head, playful now. "You know I am SSgt Overaugh from today's register, but who told you my first name? I certainly haven't."
Her mouth opened, then shut.
'BUSTED!' Natalia thought - Again - twice in less than five minutes, what was happening to her!
He went on, with the forensic gentleness of a man laying out radio parts, "So, you either pulled my file, or you've been asking around about me. Either way, I'm going to take that as a positive demand signal." He made a small, triumphant face and his smile was uncontrollable. Good Lord! That smile, its intoxication, she thought, as her heart skipped.
Before she could marshal a counter-brief he stepped to one side, so they were walking level down the corridor.
She tried to look offended and failed, the corners of her

mouth treacherous. “You’re insufferable,” she said, falling into step with a girlish grin.

“That’s Staff Sergeant insufferable to you, Ma’am,” he said, as they set off towards the PX. Two very competent, lethal adults pretending they were going for a simple coffee and not, in fact, walking into a story they would be telling badly, together for the rest of their lives.

Chapter Thirty-Six

Tuesday, 30th May 2006 – 11:41

COMMCEN, Iraqi Military Academy al-Rustamiyah (IMAR), Baghdad

Four weeks went the way weeks do when the map is always hungry for battle plottings. The Iron Triangle operation had come up like heat under a door. The pins on the board crept north and west and back again and the morning brief grew every day.

With nearly the best part of 200 bad guys captured, Natalia was out more than she was in, serials at first light, container runs, liaison shuttles and when she wasn't in a convoy, she was in the COMMCEN sleeves rolled, voice steady, turning reporting into routes and names while the nets chattered. Somewhere between the first "ma'am" and a hundred cups of tea she and Seth had stopped orbiting and settled. No announcement, no nonsense, just the quiet arithmetic of two people who found each other's company intoxicating.

Tam folded himself into the shape of it without ceremony. The three of them became a rhythm. Seth setting the metronome as usual with Nat feeding the tune, Tam throwing in the backbeat and the joke at precisely the moment you needed to remember you were human. On paper they were SSgt Overaugh (UKSF Comms), Capt Jones (Int Corps) and Sgt Tamlin (UKSF Comms). In practice they were the small circle you drew around a long day and wrote 'We've got this' inside it.

The COMMCEN had learned their habits. Two mugs lived under the edge of the message wall; a fruit pastille ransom appeared without comment on the third shelf, a chair against the back bulkhead had taken to creaking only when Tam sat in it as if the room were in on the joke. The ballroom's ghost chandeliers in Basra were a memory. Here at Rustamiyah the light came hard through louvres and scratched glass. The high frequency radio sang that thin mosquito whine you stopped hearing until the generator coughed and you started to notice it again.

"Time hack?" Seth said, pencil ready.

"On your mark," Tam replied, eyes on the network schedule timing sheet (often referred to as a sked), voice casual in the way of men who had set watches side by side enough nights to do it in their sleep.

Natalia slid a fresh HUMINT report onto the spike, pin-cushioned another Post-it into the Tharthar belt region on the map and felt the odd, treacherous thing that had been happening more often lately: the sense that for all the dust, for all the noise, this made sense. You could make a list, strike through it, and something in the world went from untidy to almost right.

"Eleven forty-one… now," Tam said.

Seth marked it, neat as always. "Logged." He looked up, found Natalia already watching him and the exchange took all the time it needed. A flicker of what had been happening between long briefings and short sleeps, held just behind the business of the day.

"Summary at twelve," she said, turning the warmth down to professional heat. "And I want that grid for the last container debrief today before the interpreters go to lunch, or they'll forget and we'll have no idea where we're going."

"Aye aye, Ma'am," Tam said, and then: "How does it feel, Staff, being the junior partner in your own relationship?"

Seth didn't look up from the log. "I've always preferred competent leadership."

"Careful," Natalia said, dryly. "You can't blame me when your training team forms a queue to thank me for saving them from your handwriting."

Tam grinned, hooked his boots round the chair legs and the three of them bent to their lists as the nets buzzed and the heat climbed and another day of the longest month of the year rolled itself out, exactly as it should.

Seth checked the sked, for the first time in weeks let himself notice the line at the bottom in someone else's handwriting: 'RHINO - 0001, BIAP → BAS'. Last day. The four weeks Sparks had promised, had shrunk to their last handful of hours, and at midnight he and Tam would be back on the Rhino express, shoulder to shoulder with a crate of jerky and some terrified contractors, rattling south to Basra and the ballroom that awaited.

It should have felt like dislocation. Instead, it felt like a plan with an extra line added. He'd filed the paperwork two days earlier, a request for return to IMAR. The answer had come back quicker than he'd expected: approved, three-month extension. It was half logistics, half honesty.

The work made sense here; the academy breathed again when you listened properly between one serial and the next, he'd stopped telling himself he and Natalia were a temporary collision. They were an item, and they both knew it. Call it unromantic to put it in an email - 'RETURN TO IMAR – JUNE–AUG' - but it did the job. Life, for once, had the decency to line up.

Natalia capped her pen and pushed back from the desk, gathering the folder marked 'NJ - P.M. SERIALS'. "Right," she said, stretching the kink out of her neck. "I've got another pantomime to orchestrate. I'll be out till fifteen hundred."

She reached for the door, then turned back, the habit of a hundred briefings and let slip: "See you later, love."

It came out on the same breath as the order, and she didn't seem to hear it until Tam's eyebrows shot up like semaphore flags.

"Oh, we're there now, are we?" he said, delighted. "Love, is it? Staff, you'll be writing poetry by teatime."

Natalia's ears coloured half a shade. "Behave, Sergeant," she said, but there was no heat in it. She tapped the doorframe twice, a little ritual she'd never admit to, and was gone, boots ticking down the corridor, the folder tucked under her arm like a promise.

Tam watched the empty doorway for a beat, then tipped an imaginary hat in Seth's direction. "Enjoy your last day, love," he said, and dug an elbow into the log to hide the grin spreading across his face. Outside, a rotor spooled up; inside, the COMMCEN hummed as if nothing in the world could possibly go wrong. But unfortunately, war keeps its own calendar.

It waits until your shoulders drop, until someone says "Love" like it's guaranteed, and then it taps the glass to see if you're still awake. The tap was coming, and it wouldn't bother with manners. Within the hour, the room that felt like an office would remember it was a target, and all three of them would remember exactly where they were.

Chapter Thirty-Seven

Tuesday, 30th May 2006 – 13:58

COMMCEN, Iraqi Military Academy al-Rustamiyah (IMAR), Baghdad

BANG!

The first round landed like a door slammed by a god. The floor picked them up and put them somewhere else; air punched through the room and took the paperwork with it in a flurry of white birds. Seth felt the world go thin and bright, the strange, clean silence of a bell too close to your ear. Then the noise came roaring back: the wail of the IDF alarm, metal groaning, cups skittering their way off tables and shattering.

"Helmets!" Tam barked by reflex, already dragging his from the hook, shoving Seth's into his hands. They pulled straps with clumsy fingers while plaster dust fell like weather and the COMMCEN's old glass rattled in its frame.

Another explosion to the south, closer; the lights hiccupped. The nets, quiet a minute ago, went feral, every circuit alive at once, overlapping like a fistful of angry bees.

"Contact, contact-"

"IDF, grid-"

"SITREP follow-"

"multiple impacts East-"

"standby for counter-battery-"

Seth slammed a palm on the priority handset, voice already in the groove he kept for days like this. **"All stations, Net One - this is COMMCEN, IMAR. IDF in progress. Confirm impact grids and casualties, over."**

"Square three - dust off the parade -"

"Perimeter East - multiple -"

"Lob-bombs over the wall, likely -"

The third round hit short and sent a ripple through the sand outside that the building swallowed like a flinch. Tam dragged the wall map straight and started pinning grids in with vicious little stabs. "That's three, Staff - East, North-east, South-east - they're walking us in."

Seth's pencil was already carving a log; the lead digging grooves in the paper. "It's a pattern, not a tantrum," he said, half to Tam, half to the room. "Someone's decided today is a message."

Another net cut across them. Ops, breathless and too loud. **"Be advised - reporting of simultaneous IDF across MND - Tikrit, Samarra, Taji - this smells like a coordinated push. AQI are making a song and dance."**

Tam shot him a look that needed no translation. Iron Triangle had bitten, and the snake was biting back.

"Where's Jones?" Seth said, already knowing the answer.

"Out 'till fifteen hundred, She's literally just down the road at the one of the containers." Tam said, too fast, eyes on the board.

A fourth impact – closer- thumped the air from their lungs. A hairline crack chased itself across the COMMCEN's window like a lightning sketch. The old building held.

Seth pressed the transmit again, voice ironed flat. **"IMAR to all: implement IDF posture. Casualty collection at Med One. All non-essential movement ceased. Report only. No chatter. Out."** He dropped the handset to his shoulder and looked at Tam. "We keep the nets clean. We keep the picture. We don't let anyone down."

Tam nodded once, grin gone. "Aye."

Outside, the alarm wailed. Inside, the fruit pastilles lay scattered among the dust like ridiculous, bright shrapnel. The next round took a bite out of the parade square and the COMMCEN remembered, all at once and without romance, that it was not an office after all. It was a target with a desk in it. And somewhere beyond the wall, in a corridor she'd promised to walk back down by three, Natalia was in the open.

Seth's mind switched, now they were in the moment that saved lives or lost them. The nets were now a hornet's nest activity:

13:59:12 – NET 1 (Battle Group OPS): "All stations, Ops. IDF (Indirect Fire) across IMAR and adjacent camps.

Confirm impact GR. Counter-battery pending. Report only. Over."

13:59:18 – IMAR PERIM (EAST): "East Perim. Impacts just short of East Gate, likely lob-bombs (improvised mortars). Small arms now audible outside wire. No breach. Heavy contact. Over."

13:59:24 – MED 1: "Med One. Establishing CCP (Casualty Collection Point) inside clinic. Two Dead, two walking wounded, lacerations and blast ear. Awaiting further. Over."

13:59:30 – QRF 1 (Iraqi Army): "QRF (Quick Reaction Force) One set. Mounted, four-vehicle pax (People), moving to East Gate. ETA 2 mikes (Minutes). Over."

13:59:36 – QRF 2 (Carabinieri): "Dublin QRF rolling. Three vehicles, 12 pax. Covering North Spur. Over."

13:59:41 – NET 3 (Mortars): "Mort Platoon. Counter-battery laid on bearing 2-7-5-0. Await fire mission from higher. Over."

13:59:49 – IMAR NORTH TOWER: "North Tower. Spotters on rooftops beyond the water treatment plant. Two, maybe three MAMs (Military Aged Males). No obvious tubes (Mortars). Request ISR (Intelligence, Surveillance, and Reconnaissance). Over."

13:59:55 – AIR (ISR TASK): "Air Cell. Kiowas freed up in 10–12m mikes; Pred (Predator Drone) on other tasking. We can push a Raven (mini drone) in 5m. Over."

14:00:02 – IMAR COMMCEN (Seth): "COMMCEN. Raven priority: East Gate and North Spur. Call when airborne. Over."

14:00:08 – CAMP ADJ (Partner): "Adj Camp. Three

impacts inside their motor pool. One vehicle on fire. Firming perimeter. No breach. Over."
14:00:15 – OPS: "Copy all. All stations, maintain IDF posture. QRFs move on my count. Med One, prep for dust-off. Over."
14:00:22 – IMAR WEST GATE: "West Gate. Neg IDF this side; reporting movement at distance - possible recce-by-fire. Holding. Over."
14:00:34 – QRF 1 (IA): "QRF One at East Gate. Contact right! Small arms outside wire. Returning controlled fire. No breach. Over."
14:00:42 – IMAR PERIM (EAST): "Visual on two shooters behind the berm. No eyes on tubes. Request smoke along the canal track. Over."
14:00:49 – Mort Pl: "Smoke available. Need authorisation. Over."
14:00:53 – OPS: "Authorised. **Mort Pl, smoke** on **grid** [redacted]. QRF One, hold line. QRF Two, push north spur and anchor. Over."
14:01:01 – QRF 2 (Carabinieri): "Copy. Anchoring north. IFP dismounting to clear culverts. Heavy contact. Over."
14:01:08 – MED 1: "Med One. One litter (Recruits) inbound from parade-blast fragment, stable. Dust-off requested. Over."
14:01:15 – AIR: "Dust-off tentatively at **14:12. LZ parade** if secure; alternate car park bravo. Mark with smoke only. No flares. Over."
14:01:22 – North Tower: "Raven airborne. Feed in 90 seconds. Over."

14:01:29 – IMAR COMMCEN (Tam): "All stations, report only, short transmissions. Keep the net clean. Over."
14:01:36 – Adj Camp: "Adj Camp now in contact South fence - single AK. Likely probe. Returning minimum. Over."
14:01:42 – OPS: "Copy. This is coordinated. Maintain posture. No pursuit outside wire. I say again No pursuit outside wire. Over."
14:01:48 – East Gate / QRF 1: "East Gate - contact breaking. Smoke effective. One squirter north-east along canal. Holding. Over."
14:01:54 – Raven: "Raven on station. One **heat sig prone by pump** house; second moving low along berm. Pushing feed. Over."
14:02:01 – Mort Pl: "Counter-battery now **fire for effect** on suspected **launch arc** outside east. Splash in 30. Over."
14:02:07 – OPS: "All stations, stand by for splash. Med One, status?"
14:02:12 – MED 1: "Litter at clinic. **Triage green/amber** only. CCP holding. Over."
14:02:17 – IMAR COMMCEN (Seth): "COMMCEN to all: no comms chatter, report grids, no heroics. Hold the line, let the QRFs work. Over."
14:02:24 - East Gate: "Copy. East stable. **EOD** on site. Over."
14:02:30 – North Spur / QRF 2: "North stable. Two detains from culvert check. No tubes. Handing to **IFP.** Over."
14:02:36 – OPS: "Good work. Maintain posture. Counter-battery splash in 5… 4… 3…"
14:02:40 – (Background) distant concussions roll across the

nets; dust sifts from rafters; a chorus of "splash" and "on target" answers in turn.

14:02:47 - OPS: "All stations - continue stand-to. This looks like an AQI push-back across the belt. Expect follow-on attacks. We hold. Over."

Seth took his finger off the transmit and let the room breathe for half a second. Tam's pin-scarred map had steadied into a picture: smoke blooming at the canal track, The Raven feed came in clean over the pump house. Somewhere in all the chaos was a woman who'd said she'd be back by three and meant it. He tapped the log, met Tam's eye, and nodded once. "Keep it tidy," he said. "They're not done yet."

Tam could sense his unease. "She'll be fine pal."

Seth stared at him and for the first time in a long time, his internal monologue started to pray. 'Please Lord let her be safe'.

The nets had steadied into something like order when a familiar voice cut across NET 1- calm, clipped, a fraction breathless under engine noise.

14:03:11 – J2-ALPHA (Capt Jones): "COMMCEN, J2-Alpha. Departing west spur; returning via Service Route Bravo. ETA two mikes to gate. Traffic light, visibility moderate. Over."

Seth's head came up before he knew he'd moved. He marked the time, the route, the reflexive ease of that voice. She was close, real close – thank the Lord!

14:03:23 – COMMCEN (Seth): "J2-Alpha, Commcen. Copy your route and ETA. Report when through the gate. QRFs holding East/North, you have to enter from the West

gate over. Over."
14:03:30 – J2-ALPHA: "Roger. one-mike out. over."
Tam pinned the route SR Bravo with his thumb and forefinger on the western portion of the map, ran a neat arc to the gate. "If they're pokin' the compound, they'll poke the road too," he said, mostly to the map.
One minute later the net carried a significant step change. The engine noise in the background screeched, the breath under the words went tight.
14:05:44 – J2-ALPHA: "COMMCEN, J2 - heavy contact - " A loud judder, the rattle of loose kit. "Ambush left-five pax, AK-white Hilux barricade in front-" The voice flattened into muscle memory. "Road blocked, burning wasteland to right, canal berm left-grid 1 2 6 / 7 4 5- braking-braking-smoke-"
A burst of automatic fire came in over the transmitter. It was dry, too close, the ugly, tearing pop of 7.62mm rounds on sheet metal. Seth felt his ribs turn to ice.
14:05:51 – J2-ALPHA (shouting off-mic): "CONTACT LEFT, CONTACT FRONT! - driver, reverse - no, no, forward - get past -" Breath. Back on-mic, voice narrower. "Five plus one - pickup across lane -masked MAMs-closing-"
Another burst of fire let rip. Someone in her cab swore in Arabic; a window cracked, then agonised screaming with a mixed gurgle.
14:05:58 – J2-ALPHA: "COMMCEN, ambush SR Bravo, burning wasteland to right, canal berm left, five assailants, white Toyota blocking - request QRF."
Seth's hand hovered over the transmit, not moving. The room

had narrowed to his own pulse and the white rectangle of Tam's thumb on the map. For a second he heard nothing: not the nets, not the alarm, not Tam saying his name.

"Staff." Tam's voice, suddenly very close. "STAFF!"

Seth didn't answer. On the wall, the second hand walked past 14:06. On the net, Natalia drew a breath you could hear all the way to the corrugated steel and made her world an order again.

14:06:03 – J2-ALPHA: "Contact left and front, five, one vehicle blocking, grid as sent. Returning controlled fire." A sharp intake. "Requesting QRF."

Seth's finger still hadn't dropped. His body knew how. His head, just then, didn't. The COMMCEN, with its maps and mugs and fruit pastilles in the dust, tilted an inch, and he stood in the middle of it. Frozen.

He looked at Tam, they both knew the inevitable, it was etched on Tam's face. She was in that vehicle with Cpl Barker and an interpreter, who had clearly been hit. Against a Hilux truck roadblock and five terrorists with AK-47s and an RPG. Corporals carried standard SA80 assault rifles with iron sights, and 120 rounds in four magazines, but officers only carried 9mm Browning pistols and two magazines. Interpreters, being civilians, carried nothing.

But that wasn't the worst of it, He looked at Tam, who was still staring at him horrified. They were the map, eyes and ears of the battlefield. They knew that every QRF asset was deployed north and east of her position in heavy contacts and at least ten minutes away. There was no one coming to save her. She was on her own.

Chapter Thirty-Eight

Tuesday, 30th May 2006 – 14:07

COMMCEN, Iraqi Military Academy al-Rustamiyah (IMAR), Baghdad

Seth snapped left, took three long paces out of the door and bellowed down the corridor like a man possessed.

"AMMO!"

"OI - SETH!" Tam was half a stride behind him. "What the fuck are you doing? We're mid-battle."

Seth didn't even look back. "AMMO!", shell shocked faces started to peer from out of the other offices down the corridor.

A popular misconception about deployments is that everyone walks around bristling with ammunition. They don't. You hand your ammunition in at the armoury when you come off task; you sign it out before you go back on. Every bullet is accounted for, every empty case a line on a sheet, every discharge a small novel of post-incident forms, but that part is conveniently left out of Hollywood blockbusters. The armoury at IMAR sat up by the front gate, over a kilometre of blast walls and bad ground away. The only people fully tooled up inside the wire were the gate guard and the QRF.

Seth stopped just long enough to slam a palm flat on the ops desk, breath coming like he'd swallowed ice. “She's less than five hundred metres that side of the west wall Tam, out by the burning tip. QRF are ten minutes away at least. I can be there in four.”

He threw his head back and roared a third time, voice cracking on it. “AMMO! Does anybody have any FUCKING AMMO?” His hand hit the desk again, a sharp, helpless crack that turned three heads and achieved exactly nothing.

“Right then,” Tam said, the panic dropping out of his voice. “Good job your Uncle Tam packed for every occasion.” He yanked his bergen out from under the comms bench, flipped the lid, and came up with a metal boxy magazine like a magician producing a rabbit. “Merry Christmas.”

Seth snatched it, glanced and grimaced. “Mate, this is seven-six-two. It won't fit my gat-” he jabbed a thumb at the L85 rifle racked in the corner “-SA80s use five-five-six. It's useless, you know this!”

Tam's mouth did a thin, wolfish thing. “Aye. Which is why,” he said, digging again, “it's a good job I also... appropriated this.”

He hauled a bundled oilcloth free, peeled it back, and there it was: a scuffed, wood-furnished AK-47, one of the confiscates from last week's sweep, tags still tied to the sling. For the first time since the net had gone bad, Seth's face moved. He looked at the rifle, then at Tam. Somewhere beyond the walls the crackle of AK fire stitched the air; somewhere on the net a dust-choked voice was still talking.

"You're a terrible influence," he said, and the ice in his veins turned to heat.

"Aye, now go get the boss lady and I'll handle the nets."

Seth was moving before the nets caught up with what he'd decided. Three strides, five, and then he was out into the glare, hammering the parade square, a hundred metres of baked concrete that turned his breath metallic.

He cut left for the west wall, boots slapping, lungs razored by dust. A squat diesel generator sat chugging under the T-wall; he hit it at pace, planted, and went up in one hungry scramble. At six-one he could just get fingers over the lip; forearms burned, webbing bit; he hauled until his hips cleared the crown of the wall and the world beyond rolled up to meet him.

There it was: the Hilux slewed sideways in the road; the white 4×4 Natalia had taken, pinned in a V of concrete and flame. The crack and spit of AK fire came in sharp, impatient bursts, ricochets troubling the rubbish slope, smoke dragging low across the burning tip.

He threw himself forward and rolled over the razor wire, chest rig taking the full bite but not all of it; felt two clean kisses score his ribs and filed the promise of getting stitches later to a quiet part of his head marked 'If we get back'. He hooked a heel, swung, lowered until his arms sang, then dropped. The ground came up harder than he'd planned. Thank God for issue boots. He was up and running before the jolt had finished, legs finding the broken rhythm of clinker and rebar and sun-baked ruts. As he moved, he glanced at the rifle, working parts clear, magazine rocked home, bolt dragged and let go, selector flicked down.

The old, stolen gun settled itself against his shoulder like it remembered what men were for. He drove on, faster and flatter, a streak of kit and intent darting across the filthy wasteland, breath ragged in his ears, eyes locked on the white truck and the smear of figures around it, and the single thought in his head as clean and hard as glass. Get there.

Tuesday, 30th May 2006 – 14:08 pm

Route Bravo, Ambush Point, West of IMAR

The interpreter was slumped against the wheel, eyes glassed, blood slicking the dash. The white 4×4 juddered as rounds stitched the doors; glass pebbled and hissed. Corporal Barker had jammed herself tight behind the front offside wheel, the engine block and hub giving the only honest cover in Iraq. She leaned out, snapped a two-round burst, and ducked back as a curtain of 7.62 chewed at the mirror.

"Five MAMs left!" she shouted over the din. "White Hilux still across the road. Closing!"

"I see them." Natalia had flattened herself behind the nearside wheel, shoulders pressed to hot steel, pistol high by her cheek. "QRF?"

"Commcen says ten mikes," Barker gritted, thumbing her radio for a burst.

The only answer was more fire and the angry cough of a misfed magazine from somewhere beyond their cover.

Rounds slapped the arch inches above Natalia's forearm; she jerked back as grit sprayed her face. "We're about to be rolled," she said, calm as a clergy. "I'm going to try and thin them."

"Make it count," Barker said, feeding a fresh mag. "And keep your head down."

Natalia slid flat into the prone position, wormed right until her shoulder found daylight behind the bumper, and edged her pistol under the sill. From that low slit of world, the wasteland became a wedge of tyre and dust and boots - one pair, fifteen metres out, closing, trousers bloused, dirt-caked laces.

She drew a breath, let it out until the muzzle settled, and the sight picture drew over his ankle perfectly, she squeezed the trigger. The crack was swallowed by the rattle of the ambush; the boot jumped; the man went down with a curse that turned into a hoarse yell as he landed on his back. Natalia held the front sight picture steady, walked it up as he flailed, and sent three controlled shots - thigh, hip, centre mass - then snapped her arm back and rolled hard into the shadow of the wheel again.

The firing paused. Half a heartbeat, but enough. One of the gunmen shouted something urgent and the line hesitated, bunched. They had all the gear and some tactics, but they were amateur marksmen, probably restaurant workers and farmers not so long ago.

"One down," Natalia called, racking a fresh mag with the heel of her hand.

"Nice one," Barker said, risked a glance and another short burst to keep them honest. "They're panicking and thinking." A round smacked the bonnet and ricocheted off into the rubbish slope with a predator's whine. The Hilux's passenger door flew open; a man with a scarf over his face jumped to the flank, waving the others up. "They're going to push," Barker said. "We need to move, or they'll walk it in."

"Negative," Natalia said. "We hold. QRF will see the smoke and the jam. We need to stay vertical for nine minutes."

Barker's radio crackled; Tam's voice cut through, tight but even. "J2-Alpha, Commcen. QRF One is off the line, five mikes. Eagle One's lifting now. Report sits."

"Two green, one KIA, one enemy down, five enemy advancing, six enemy not five as reported, white Hilux blocking road still, no exit." Barker kept it spare. "Be advised, we are low on ammo."

"Copy, hold." A half-beat of silence, then Tam again, lower, just for her. "Nat... help is coming. Keep your head down."

Natalia didn't answer. She could feel the road through her palms, feel the thud of enemy boots in the dust. She caught Barker's eye, gave one hard nod, and slid flat again, hunting for another pair of ankles, but what she saw instead was a MAM (Military-Age Male) behind the rear of the Hilux aiming a Rocket-Propelled Grenade straight at them.

The cheer went up a heartbeat before the 'whoomp' - a hollow cough that didn't sound like small arms. Natalia risked a glance and saw it. A man bracing on a shoulder-fired tube, a smear of backblast kicking a fan of dust and paper behind him, the rocket already away in a dirty white corkscrew.

"RPG!" Barker screamed, and then the world ran out of air.

The warhead hit the front wing with a flat, obscene crack. Overpressure punched them both at once, a hand the size of a lorry swatting them off their wheels. Heat rolled under the 4×4 and through it as a sheet of orange that turned paint to boiling skin. The bonnet leapt, the windscreen atomised to glitter, tyres collapsing in black petals as the engine bay went up.

Natalia's ears went from noise to wool. The ground came and went. She found herself skidding on her back into the open, jacket smoking, the taste of coins in her mouth. Barker was a pale shape on hands and knees, coughing, already dragging herself for the ditch at the side of the road.

Sound came back in shards: the tick of cooling metal, the greedy roar of fire, and, closer than thought, the hooting triumph of men who believed the thing was finished. Boots crunched. A figure loomed through the heat-haze, less than ten metres, scarf up, rifle low, muzzle climbing. He spat a string of words that didn't need translating and levelled on Natalia's face.

The shot took him in the left temple and switched him off like a light. Another two cracks, spaced perfectly, and the nearest pair of shadows folded onto the ground with their legs tangled.

Seth burst out of the smoke at a run, AK high, dropping to a knee so fast the dust hadn't settled around him. He put himself between Natalia and the fire, body blocking, the black column from the wreck rolling past to blind the road.

"Got you," he said and their eyes briefly met, voice too steady for the hammering in his chest. He gave a slight smile. 'Good Lord, that smile,' Nat thought. His left hand hooked the strap of her rig and he hauled, dragging her into the shallow ditch that cut along the verge. Barker was already there, face grey and furious, slapping a fresh mag home with trembling fingers.

Rounds laced the smoke where their heads had been. Seth was breathing through the burn in his ribs. "QR will be at least five mikes," he said, more for himself than anyone. "We hold. This is going to be close."

Natalia blinked grit and heat from her eyes and found her pistol still in her hand. "Aye," she said, voice raw but there. "Let's make them work for our scalps."

The ditch was little more than a gouge in the rubbish-churn, knee-deep and rank with old rain and oil. Seth leaned over the lip and fired the AK in short, three-round bursts, sending rounds into the berm where a pair of shapes flitted between heap and tyre stack. One broke left. Barker caught him on the calf, and he went down cursing, rolled, came up firing blind. Two more bailed out from behind the Hilux, scarves up, rifles high, the lot of them yelling to keep their courage.

"Two new MAMs!" Barker barked, flat as a range voice.

"Seen," Natalia said. She fed her last magazine, counted herself down without looking: nine, eight, seven... She pushed out over the bank, took a clean shot. The nearest man's rifle jumped out of his hands as the 9mm round hit it. He clutched at it, confused, and Barker's follow-up took him in the ribs and folded him around himself.

Rounds raked their gutter. Clods of burned soil spattered their backs. The AK in Seth's hands hummed and heated. He felt the bolt bite, counted what was left in the tin box by instinct and years of training. He rolled to his other knee, sent his last two at the muzzle flash by the shredded tarpaulin and was rewarded with a grunt and a disappearing shape.

"I'm out!" Barker shouted, patting pouches that were suddenly nothing but canvas and grit.

"Same!" Seth snapped, the AK's bolt hanging back like a yawn, the chamber dry.

Natalia looked at the pistol, the locked slide, the empty ditch, the now three figures resetting their nerve in the heat-haze. She let out a breath she hadn't realised she'd been holding.

"Well," she said, almost conversational. "That's it then."

Seth glanced at her, eyes bright and very calm, soot making a map of his face. In the roar and reek and the cheering coming from the road, he found a voice that sounded like his own.

"There's nowhere else I'd rather be, Nat." he said. "Nowhere else I'd rather die."

He shifted, putting his shoulder to her, the dead rifle across his knees, and they watched the nearest man square up for the walk-in of a lifetime. His stride triumphant, his weapon rising, his eyes with the unmistakable gleam of a man about to make a couple of easy kills and increase his own legend.

"Me neither, I love you, Seth Overaugh." She squeezed his hand.

"I love you too darling."

And they simply stared at one another, about to meet their fate together, as one.

Chapter Thirty-Nine

Tuesday, 30th May 2006 – 14:09

Route Bravo, Ambush Point, West of IMAR

BANG!

The Rhino came out of the smoke like an immovable wall. One second the Hilux was a white barricade with men in front of it; the next it was a shrieking, twisting thing, shouldered aside by eight tonnes of armoured shoebox with a bad temper. The pickup spun half-about, nose snapping, rear axle torn sideways.

Two of the gunmen froze a heartbeat too long and vanished under the Rhino's snub bow and tyres, legs buckling, bodies mangled. Others in the adjacent building broke and ran, their courage finally keeping pace with common sense.

Brakes howled. The Rhino lurched to a stop, reverse lights flaring in the heat-haze. It slewed back toward the ditch, armour plates clanging, and settled broadside to the burning

4×4 in a shower of grit, shielding the ditch from the inferno. The big door popped its latches with a hydraulic hiss and swung wide.

"Room for three and a chaperone!" yelled the driver from behind the wheel, broad Scots and pure mischief. "Any lovebirds need a lift?"

Tam.

Seth didn't waste breath on an answer. He palmed Natalia's back and hauled her up and forward. Barker was already scrabbling, boots sliding on spilled gravel, face set in that empty, uncomplaining way medics wear when there's nothing left in the pouches. The heat off the wreck slapped them as they staggered the last few metres and folded into the cool, fume-thick belly of the bus.

"Go!" Barker barked, yanking the lever to throw the door shut. "Go, go!"

Tam dumped the clutch. The Rhino leapt backwards, straightened, then punched a three-point turn with all the grace of a kicked safe. The cabin filled with the stink of hot brakes and the blessed roar of the air con. Outside, the last futile rounds aimed at their departing tailgate rattled and died.

"Commcen, Rhino Two," Tam sang into the dash mic, half driver, half radio op. "We've got J2-Alpha plus two. Three green, one KIA left at scene. Returning to base, west gate now, sixty seconds. Over."

"Copy, Rhino Two," A voice came back faintly from the speaker. "Gate's clear. CCP ready."

Seth let himself sag into the bench as the Rhino thundered

up the service lane, the world reduced to steel and noise and the judder through his ribs. Natalia was beside him, helmet askew, soot streaked, eyes too wide and very, very alive.

She turned her head, found him. "Did you..." her voice was ragged, pitched low so only he could hear. "Did you mean it?"

He didn't make her spell it out, this was not the time for playful antics. "Yes," he said, the smile finding him even here. "Every single syllable. I love you, Natalia Jones."

For a second the bus was only the two of them and the space between their shoulders, the confession hanging in the air like a truce.

Natalia let her head thud back against the bulkhead, found his hand, squeezed. "Good, that's very reassuring." she said, almost laughing at how wrecked her voice sounded.

"Because I think I might be pregnant."

For a heartbeat, Seth stared only at her, grime cracking at the corners of his eyes as something softer pushed through. The grin that came up was wide and ridiculous and boyish as a boot camp photo. Up front, Tam processed the words on a half-second delay, then yelped, "Jesus wept!" and swerved accidentally.

The Rhino lurched, clipped a crater, banged down again; Barker clapped her hand over her mouth in shock. Tam coughed, found the lane, and muttered, "Right, well, no pressure at all then Tam," and the bus thundered towards the gaping gate and the waiting blue armbands.

Act IX

Collateral Damage

Chapter Forty

Sunday, 13th April 2025 – 09:04

Pristina, Kosovo

Pristina was all hard light and afterlives. UN-white Land Cruisers nosing past café awnings, blue-glass ministries reflecting old bullet scars, the Newborn Monument scuffed but still defiant.

Tam sat under a striped café canopy on Rruga UÇK street with a demitasse that could have taken a nail-head off, watching steam lift from the coffee cup and the city move in layers: students with a single battered rucksack between them, a pair of KFOR peace-keeping vets who'd never quite gone home and a toothpick-thin dealer in Ottoman sabres arguing, in three languages, about provenance.

He'd done well out here the honest way. Export licences immaculate, museum letters on headed paper, crates of walnut and oilcloth that smelt of attics and empire rather than cordite. He liked the straight edges of it.

His phone shivered twice on the table, screen dark, then stilled. A moment later it buzzed again: a text, a single letter - 'O' - and then another two clean rings from a number the handset pretended it had never met. Old, simple, and theirs. Tam didn't answer because answering wasn't part of it; he just looked at the phone until the shape of the day changed.

He dropped a few euros on the saucer, nodded thanks to the barista, and stood, the chair legs rasping the flagstones. "Right," he said to no one, shrugging the strap of his holdall higher on his shoulder. The years in between fell away like dust from a bayonet in a museum case. He stepped into the white glare, eyes already working the glass for tails, and let the city swallow him as he turned towards whatever fine mess the O's had got themselves into this time.

The code was simple; it meant to call either Seth or Nat from a pay phone. Inbound phone calls from pay phones are notoriously hard to trace. Getting to the phone box was easy enough but narrowing down who made the call and why was a nightmare. It still wasn't totally secure, but you could get enough conversation across in those types of calls to ensure you got the picture.

He reached a pay phone, scrawled for Seth's personal mobile number.

He fed a two-euro coin into the scarred aluminium mouth, dialled the number, and turned his shoulder to the street. The line rang twice. A click, a breath, the hiss of a cheap handset.

"Yeah?"

"Awright, ball bag!" Tam said.

A beat. Then Seth's voice, low and tight in that way Tam

remembered when the shit had hit the fan. "You picked up fast."

"Always," Tam said. "What's burning?"

"Everything," Seth said. No preamble, no pleasantries. "It's worse than Rusty ever was pal. More urgent. We're already in it. This is..." He stopped himself, found the steel again. "It's everything, Tam."

Tam watched a trolley bus rattle past, counted three and a half seconds, listening to the tone beneath the words. "You alone?"

"For now."

"Same number?"

"No. Don't use this again; it's my personal mobile. We're clean on our side but I don't trust the air."

"Good," Tam said. "Tell me what you can."

"Not over the air," Seth said. "We've got someone pulling on our house and we need something very specific that only someone very specific could get."

Tam closed his eyes a moment, saw a west wall, a burning tip, a Hilux. Different decade, same gravity. "Right. You've got the kids in the building."

"Yeah."

"And you're still playing clean."

"Cleaner than a chapel floor," Seth said. "We need your contacts. We needed them yesterday."

Tam looked up at the slice of blue over the rooftops, already building a route in his head. "I'll be there by afternoon."

"You sure?"

"Aye," Tam said.

"Copy. Thank you."

Another breath. Softer now. "We owe you."

"No, you don't," Tam said, and meant it. "Go dark. Kiss the bairns. I'll be there soon."

The line thumped once in his ear and went dead. Tam held the receiver to the dial tone until it annoyed him, then set it back.

Flights flickered across his mind like tracers: Vienna, Munich, Gatwick, hire car, the M6 motorway north. There is no way Seth would reach out like that if it wasn't life or death. Mentally Tam made a note of the severity.

He checked his watch and headed for the hotel at a pace that didn't look like a run.

Chapter Forty-One

Monday, 14th April 2025 – 17:20

Moorside House, Kitchen

They'd tidied the kitchen twice already. Izzy kept circling the table, straightening placemats that didn't need moving, peering down the hall every time tyres sighed on gravel. Seth rinsed clean mugs that were already clean. Natalia pretended to read an email and read the door instead.

The knock was a rap. Confident, spare, the way you'd tap a radio to make sure it was listening.

Natalia was moving before anyone else. She opened the door, and Tam filled the frame: travel-dust on his jacket, holdall strap creasing his shoulder, that familiar half-smile that made rooms feel smaller and steadier.

"Hi," she said, and the word caught somewhere warmer than she expected.

"Awright, hen," he said, voice soft Edinburgh with the edges scuffed by years abroad. "I'm here."

She hugged him. He didn't do showy embraces, never had, but he folded her in with both arms and a quiet, bracing pressure that said more than noise could. He could sense the anxiety in her. Somewhere behind her a chair scraped, then a rush of feet.

"Tam!"

Izzy cannoned into the hall, and he scooped her up, laughing, spun her once so the world blurred and set her down again upright with the solemn ceremony of a pilot placing a chopper on a pad. "Look at you," he said, mock indignant. "You were knee-high when I blinked."

"I'm sixteen now," she said, as if this were both a warning and a badge.

"Aye, and I'm twenty-one plus twenty-three with better knees," he said, then nodded past her as Seth met him at the kitchen threshold.

They didn't bother with handshakes. Two steps, one beat, the hug men keep in stock for the few people they trust without thinking. Tam clapped Seth's shoulder, stood back and gave him a once-over. "Still the junior partner in the room, Staff?"

"Always," Seth said, and the corner of his mouth moved.

"Good." Tam's gaze flicked to the biscuit tin on the side. He clocked the four phones asleep under an elastic band and didn't say a word. He clocked the new hasp on the door to the garden; the padlock key had been moved to a different hook. He noticed the slight whiff of bleach, the faint fire-smell that never quite left Moorside anymore and filed it all without showing. Something had happened. Definitely.

Jonah appeared in the doorway. Broad-shouldered now and

haunted around the eyes in a way Tam had seen before on other boys in other years, he froze for half a second as if unsure how to carry his arms.

"Good Lord," Tam said, delighted. "Look at the size of you." He opened both arms, no fuss, and Jonah stepped into them like he'd been waiting his turn and had finally heard his name called. The hold was brief and hard, a quick reset of something all four of them had needed.

"Alright, pal?" Tam said, stepping back. "Ye awright?"

Jonah managed a grin. "Awright."

"Right," Tam went on, business beginning to crowd the warmth now. "Let me fetch my kit from the hire car before the neighbours decide they need a rummage. Then we'll put a kettle on, and you can tell me what's got this house burnin' hotter than your oven."

"I'll give you a hand," Seth offered.

"Leave it," Tam said lightly. "One trip. I've still got a back worth braggin' about."

He disappeared down the hallway and out into evening air that was glowing the colour of weak tea again. Natalia watched him cross the car port in three long strides, pop the boot, lift a holdall and a flat, battered case. When he came back, the kitchen had put its shoulders down and started to feel warm again. The kettle was already grumbling. Izzy had found the good biscuits. Seth had moved the pad of paper from the end of the table to the centre as if that were all it took to turn it into a map.

Tam set the case and bag down by the dresser, no clatter, and took the mug Natalia handed him like a truce. "Ta." He

sipped, nodded at the taste. "Tea. Correct. We can proceed."
"You got here fast," Seth said.
"Aye," Tam replied. "Two rings and an 'O' tends to shorten my routes and ruined my weekly plans."
Izzy looked between them, eyebrows up. "Is that… spy code?"
"It's old friends' code," Tam said, with a half-wink that folded the years down to nothing. He turned to Natalia. "Right. Give me your headlines, hen. Just the bones. Then I'll tell you how we'll put meat on 'em."
Natalia found she'd already sorted her notes into three clean stacks - 'Daylight, Dream, Devices' - and felt briefly foolish about it. Then she remembered who she was speaking to and let the structure earn its keep.
"We've got a bully who thinks he's the only adult in the room," she began. "He's got a video and a timetable. He believes we'll pay forever to keep his hands off the fuse."
"A bully with a habit," Seth added. "Based on the canal scrubland. No counter-surveillance, no discipline. The phone is his power, or more accurately the footage on the phone. The person is noise. It's the footage that can do the damage."
"Exactly," Natalia said. "We've been trying to keep the kids off the board in this next phase, but that's easier said than done."
"Wise; it's exactly what any parent would do, how did they get involved in this in the first place? and pardon me for asking, but what is on this footage?"
Nat and Seth stared at each other and Jonah shifted nervously. Izzy, who had been vibrating quietly for several minutes, blurted, "You know when they say if you kill somebody, only

two people should know. You and the person you've buried?"
"Aye." Tam nodded.
"Well. Let's just say I don't think Dad read that memo!"
Seth shot her a glance.
Tam set his cup down. "Alright, I think I might need something a little stronger… Tell your Uncle Tam everything, and don't leave anything out."
The next two hours were spent downloading information for Tam to decant, all four Overaughs with their own woes and takes on proceedings.
Tam sat back, let out a long breath through his nose and looked at the ceiling as if it might offer a different version of events. It didn't. He brought his gaze down and found four faces watching him, looking for hope like they'd run out of their own.
"Right," he said at last. "I've heard some shite in my time, but that's… that's a banquet. The body is bad enough. The phone is worse. And the… dreams?" He gave a small, helpless tilt of his hand. "I don't even have a box to put that in, hen."
Natalia stared into her tea as if it might change colour. Seth's jaw had gone to granite. Jonah examined the grain of the table until it blurred. Izzy, who had been sitting on her hands because otherwise she'd chew her nails to the elbow, couldn't help herself.
"Can't we just… move him?" she said, small and fierce. "Somewhere no one will look? That way the footage is useless!"
Tam shook his head. Not unkind. "No. Listen to me." He leaned forward, forearms on his knees, voice dropping to the

tone he kept for frightened soldiers and stubborn friends. "Moving him crosses a line you don't want to cross. It's not telly. You drag him, you dig, you carry... you spread trace. Skin, fibres, fluids. The soil keeps grave scent for months. Cadaver dogs don't care if you've shifted the body; they'll sit on grave soil that looks clean to you and sing for their supper. And legally?" He tapped the table. "You're stacking charges on charges. One crime becomes three. And it still won't change the ending. The right thing is the fires, keep the scent down as much as possible until the body decomposes to nothing."

Izzy's bravado fell a notch. "So, we just… leave him?"

"We don't touch him," Tam said. "We don't make gravity or create waves, remember? We deal with the living problem. The phone, the footage, the timetable, the bully - and we don't add a sin we can't pray away."

Seth rubbed a hand across his face, then nodded once, slow. "Aye."

Tam glanced at Seth, then back to Natalia, and let some of the iron bleed out of his voice. "When you rang, you said you needed something. So, I'm assuming the boss lady has a plan, for the daylight threat at least. The dream bit…" He gave a small, apologetic tilt of his hand. "I've not got a box for that yet. I'll need a minute to let it land."

Izzy's scowl was quick and adolescent and very human. "Don't you believe us?"

"Hen," he said gently, "It's a stretch. I need processing time, aye?"

"Fair enough," she said, shoulders loosening.

Natalia looked between them, then fixed both kids with the same calm that had made rooms behave for twenty years. "This is where you leave us," she said. "Daytime is mine and your dad's battlefront. Go upstairs and do what you do. And Izzy," she held the girl's eye, "no sneaking onto the stairwell to listen. We need you both well clear of this."

Jonah nodded, grateful to be given something simple to obey. Izzy opened her mouth, shut it, and then surprised them all by just leaning in and kissing Natalia's cheek. "Fine," she said. "But if you need us, you shout."

"We will," Seth said. "Promise."

They went, the house swallowing their steps. Natalia waited until the last stair creaked, then turned back to Tam and slid the Daylight stack across the table. "Right," she said. "Do you still have contacts in the Narco world?"

Chapter Forty-Two

Monday, 14th April 2025 – 21:30

Moorside House, Kitchen

Tam turned the empty mug in his hands as if it were a compass and he was waiting for the needle to settle. The light outside had gone from weak tea to pewter; the garden was a single pane of dark. When he finally spoke, it wasn't to argue tactics but to weigh their souls.

"Before we get clever," he said, "tell me you've both looked this in the face. Not the mapping out of the plan, or the practicalities. The actual thing itself. Because what you've just asked for… that's not a nudge. That's a drop kick. Once you take that step, it doesn't un-happen. You don't get to be the folk you were last week, and when you shuffle off this mortal coil you will have your maker to answer to."

Natalia didn't look away. "If that video gets out, we don't get to be any kind of folk," she said. "Not for a very long time. Twenty-five, maybe more, for me and Seth. Minimum. Izzy is sixteen. She'll be in for years, even if a judge calls it 'misadventure'. Jonah knows enough to be complicit; he'll serve time he won't come back from. We lose the house. The company. Our names. We lose the children. Our reputation. Their futures. Our futures. Everything."

She flicked a glance at the ceiling; at the two sets of footsteps, she'd just sent upstairs. "All of it, because a scavenger came through our door and we survived him."

Silence settled. The clock above the cooker ticked as if it were proud of itself. Seth had his hands flat on the table; the veins stood out on the back of them.

Tam stared at those hands and then shut his eyes a moment. "You're askin' me to bless something I've spent a lifetime not blessing," he said. "I don't move that stuff nor anything like it. Not for money, not for mates. I don't put it in a chain of custody, and I don't put it in anybody's arm. That's a line I hold because once you let it go -" He opened his eyes, met theirs. "- there's no floor underneath you. It's just you and a one-way ticket to Hell."

Natalia was already nodding. "We're not asking you to pour it down his throat," she said, steady but tired. "We're telling you what he's already doing and what he'll do again tomorrow, and the day after, because that's what he is. We're asking whether you can help us make sure the only person in danger from his next bad choice is him."

Tam rubbed a thumb along a scorch mark in the wood. "Most men who are where he is at don't see forty," he said, and the admission tasted of iron. "That's not a judgement. That's a statistic. So, aye... if I put it in the book like a mathematician, I can make your numbers add up. His fifteen or twenty years against your sixty. Only… humans are not numbers, regardless of their habits."

Seth's voice was very quiet. "So, you won't help us."

Tam looked at him. "I didn't say that now did I?"

Seth held his gaze, something easing at the edges.

"I'll help you," Tam went on.

Natalia let out a held breath. "Thank God. I know it's a lot, but this type of collateral damage I can live with."

"Good," Tam said. "Because living with it is the point." He tapped the Daylight stack of notes with two fingers. "We start here. We keep the house boring, routines in place. We own Saturday. And if any part of this starts to look like a thing you can't look your bairns in the eye about, we bin it and take the hit."

Seth nodded. "Copy."

Tam stood, rolling his shoulders as if shrugging a bergen into place. "Right then." He glanced at the window, at the soft dark pressing its face to the glass and his own sallow reflection. "Tomorrow, I go see a man about a dog."

He reached for his coat. Natalia's hand covered his for a second, warm and grateful and shaking a little. "Thank you."

"Don't thank me yet hen," he said with a tired smile. "Save it for when you're in the clear." He picked up the battered case, paused at the door, and looked back at them shaking his head. "Bloody statues, bogeymen and dreams," he said. "You're all off your rockers!"

Chapter Forty-Three

Tuesday, 15th April 2025 – 10:45 am

Moorside Lane, Moorside House

Lydia clicked along at Natalia's knee with that self-important prance only opinionated dogs can manage. The air had that late-afternoon clearness that comes after rain. Somewhere over the hedgerow a blackbird was auditioning for spring, and the canal smelt of iron and nettles. Natalia took the slow way to the lane, counting her steps between landmarks because it gave her mind something to do. Fourteen slabs to the goose-neck bend, six to the old sycamore, three more to the red-painted post box that had swallowed her letters for a decade. She wasn't just walking a dog. She did the simple sweep she'd promised herself she would do every time she went to the gate now. Eyes for sightlines, ears for cars that idled too long, a glance for the tell-tales only the job teaches you to see. No unfamiliar vans. No phone raised just as she looked up. The world was wearing its best ordinary face.

The post box yielded three envelopes: one BT bill, machine franked and apologetic; one from HMRC with the broad-shouldered brown font that always managed to look like a summons even when it wasn't ('Confirmation Statement due – Companies House'); and a thin airmail with a blue-and-red border and a tidy hand she didn't recognise. The address was to The Occupiers. No name. No return address beyond San Francisco, CA and a postmark dated April 6. She turned it over in her fingers, felt the crisp paper and the faint buckling where a fountain pen had bitten.

"Come on then," she told Lydia, who had found a particularly offensive tuft of grass to threaten. "Interesting." Back in the hallway, she set the bills on the side table and slit the airmail with a thumbnail. The paper slid out: cream, watermarked, the type of paper you don't buy by accident. She read the salutation and felt the oddest flick of heat under her breastbone, like a match striking.

6 April 2025
From:
Charlotte Richardson
Richardson Occult Antiquarian
Jackson Square, San Francisco, CA 94111, USA
E: charlotte.richardson@richardson-occult.com
T: +1 (415) 555 0176
FB/IG: @RichardsonOccult

To:
The Occupiers
Moorside House
Altham, Lancashire
United Kingdom

Dear Sir or Madam,

I hope you won't mind a note out of the blue. My name is Charlotte Richardson. I live and work in California, but my family's history has long threads in Lancashire, and one of them leads - very particularly - to your front door.

My mother, Meredith Richardson (née Hawthorn), spent part of her girlhood in Moorside House during the 1940s. She is in her nineties now and too frail to travel unfortunately, but in recent years I have been helping her put her memories in order. In the process I have been tracing places that were important to her. Your house appears again and again in her stories. The sweep of the drive, the sound the stairs made in winter, a certain window that "kept more secrets than it let out". It clearly meant a great deal to her.

By trade I am an antiquarian researcher; I specialise in historic domestic objects and the ways houses hold their histories. I shall be in Lancashire next week on unrelated work and wondered, very tentatively, whether it might be possible to arrange a brief, quiet visit to see Moorside in real life. Five or ten minutes at most, and entirely at your convenience. I am acutely aware that it is your home; I would be grateful simply to stand at the gate and look, if that is what feels right to you. No photographs without permission, no posting, no fuss.

If you would prefer not to be disturbed, I completely understand. If you would consider it, I can be flexible with timing and am very happy to make a donation to a local charity of your choice. I can provide identification and references in advance if that is helpful.

You can reach me by email at charlotte.richards@richardson-occult.com, by telephone at +1 (415) 555 0176 (WhatsApp ok), or via Facebook: @RichardsonOccult. I'll be in the area from Tuesday 22nd to Friday 25th April, and can fit around your day.

Thank you for reading, and for taking care of a house that has clearly looked after more than one family. Whatever your decision, I send you my good wishes.

Yours sincerely,

Lottie Richards

(Charlotte Richardson)
Richardson Occult Antiquarian
Jackson Square, San Francisco, CA

She read it twice, then a third time, heartbeat ticking in her throat. The handwriting was firm, the tone precise and careful, a professional who knew how to come to a stranger's door and not spook them. That would have been enough to give her pause. It wasn't what snagged.

It was the signature. Lottie.

The name was a match thrown from the dreamscape.

For a second the hallway seemed to tilt. The last few Fridays unspooled at once, the white hem, the breathless panicked LOTTIE! ripped from a woman's throat as if it were her own skin. She put her palm flat on the sideboard to steady herself and felt the old wood cool under her skin.

Lydia made a questioning noise and nudged her calf, as if to check she was still there. Natalia folded the letter back along its tidy crease.

In the kitchen, Seth looked up from the kettle with that instant, quiet attention he saved for when something was wrong. "Post?"

"Bills," she said, and her voice came out normal. "And this."

She handed him the letter. He read it, mouth tightening, then paused, eyes catching on the last line. "Lottie," he said, and the syllables landed between them like a stone in a shallow pool. "You don't think-"

"I don't know what I think," she said. "It could be a coincidence. It could be a very polite… something else."

Izzy, who had drifted back in on the scent of biscuits like a cat, reached for the letter and read the signature. The colour seemed to drain from her cheeks and then come roaring back in two bright flags. "You're joking," she said, breathless.

"Mum..."
"I know," Natalia said, more sharply than she meant. "I know."
Seth turned the paper over, held it up to the light. "Jackson Square," he said, half to himself. "Antiquarian. Occult. That's not a Facebook scavenger hunt."
"We don't know what it is," Natalia said. She touched the edge of the envelope again; the postmark, the neatness of the script. "But she's not a spammer. And if her mother was here in the forties…"
"Which is when the girl was," Izzy said, more softly now. "In the dreams."
Natalia pressed her fingers to her temples, as if she could hold the timelines still by force. "This is ridiculous," she said. "We have a bully at the gate and a… visitor on a plane, and a… ghost in the middle. We can't hold all of it. Maybe the girl didn't disappear, maybe she's been in California all along?"
Seth folded the letter and slid it into his jacket. "We don't have to deal with it all right now," he said. "We do boring tonight. Stick to the plan. Tam's five minutes away. We tell him about the letter and ask him to vet Charlotte Richardson, and the Hawthorns while we're waiting for Saturday. That way we can keep up appearances - phone number, email, a soft pass from the edge. And we don't answer this from anything with our names on it. I don't believe in coincidences."
"Agreed," Natalia said.
Izzy tipped her head. "Do we… let her come?"
"We don't know enough yet," Natalia replied. "She could be

exactly who she says. She could be a journalist with a new hairdo and a polite pen or one of Mr Bossman's associates. She could be a woman with the same name as a dead girl and nothing to do with any of this, but I doubt it. We will be kind. We will be careful. And we will not give anyone the run of our house while we are under siege."

Jonah ghosted in, drawn by the voices, and leaned a shoulder against the doorjamb. "What's up?"

"A letter," Seth said, and handed it over. Jonah read it slowly, lips moving on Lottie, eyes flicking up, then down again. "Do you want me to Google her?"

"Not on the family Wi-Fi," Natalia said, "We'll get your Uncle Tam to do the research. We all stay well clear just in case."

Izzy took the letter back and ran a finger over the looping L. "It's pretty," she said, which was not what Natalia had expected her to say.

"It is," Natalia said, surprising herself by smiling. "That's half the problem."

A car door thumped on the gravel. Three heads turned as one. Seth set the letter on the dresser, half under the BT bill, as if camouflage could be courtesy. Natalia touched the edge of it once, a tiny absurd caress, then wiped her palms on her jeans and straightened.

"All right," she said. "That's for tomorrow. Tonight, we see what Tam has managed to rummage up."

Izzy was already halfway to the hall, hair flying. "I'll get the door," she called, and did, light on her feet, the house which had been holding itself tense for so long it had forgotten any other way to live, felt something ease in its joists.

In the brief silence before voices came back down the corridor, Seth reached across the table and squeezed Natalia's hand. "Lottie," he said again, softer this time.

"I know," she said, squeezing back. "I've got a bad feeling about this."

Chapter Forty-Four

Tuesday, 15th April 2025 – 21:07 pm

Moorside House, Kitchen

The door thudded a second time, softer than a knock, more like the heel of a palm against wood. Seth was halfway to it when Tam stepped in anyway, closing it behind him with his boot. Night clung to his jacket; the cold came with him in a ribbon. He set a battered Peli case on the flagstones as if it might argue and met Natalia's eyes.

"You've had your tea?" he asked.

"Yeah, earlier on," she said.

"Good. Mine's waitin' in the car."

He flicked the catches of the case and lifted the lid. Inside lay a smaller, clear pouch - heat-sealed and double-bagged, the sort of thing you'd expect to see on a charge sheet. Within it, four tight white twists sat like grubs on plastic. Even through two layers of polythene, Natalia thought she could smell something metallic and wrong. Maybe that was her mind filling in the gaps.

Tam didn't touch the inner bag. He kept his hands either side of the case. "This is the part I hate most," he said. "I don't carry this. I don't keep it. I don't do this. Tonight, I'm makin' an exception because you asked and because I know what you're carryin'. But we do this my rules, or we don't do it."

Seth nodded, jaw tight. "Understood."

Tam's voice dropped half a notch; all edges turned to instructions. "Rule one: No one opens this bag in this house. Not for curiosity, not for courage. It stays sealed. Rule two: No bare hands. If it must be handled, it's outside, gloved, mask on, wind at your back, and only as long as you must. Rule three: No testing, no cleverness, no 'just to see'. This isn't telly. It's chemistry that doesn't care what about your intent. Rule four: If anything goes wrong - headache, woozy, slow breathing - then phone 999, and you say the word. Opioid. Don't be a hero."

He slid a second item across the case. A flat cardboard sleeve with two nasal vials in a blister. "Naloxone," he said. "Legal to carry. If the worst happens, put it up your hooter, both barrels. Then the ambulance comes. Then it's me shoutin' at you for not listenin'."

Nat, white around the mouth and trying very hard to hold it together, stared at the twists. "Is that… all it is?"

"That is enough to kill every single person in this room and every paramedic that attends," Tam said, without looking at her, "Milligrams. That's the scale. Treat it like a wet electric main. You don't poke it to see if it's live; you just assume it is.

"You make sure you'r wearing see-through latex gloves when

you hand the wraps over. They are wrapped real tight. When he opens it, hopefully he just sticks it on the spoon or the foil before any effects start. But if he sniffs it, he'll knock himself out instantly and drop dead on the spot.

"Pray he puts them in his pocket and walks otherwise you'll be dealing with a casualty in the middle of a shopping centre."

Seth swallowed, forced his shoulders down and leaned in just long enough to lift the outer pouch by one corner with two fingers. The inner bag hardly weighed anything. He had shouldered packs heavier than schoolchildren and felt nothing. This little thing made his arms ache.

"Where should I keep it?" he asked.

"In the safe. Keep that shit as far away from me as possible." Tam said. "Bottom shelf. Double bag stays on until showtime. It doesn't leave that safe until it's time. Just drop the wraps into his hand and tell him to pocket them."

Seth looked to Natalia. She held his gaze, then gave the smallest nod. He disappeared down the cellar steps with the pouch and the naloxone, boots hollow on stone. The two of them listened to the hiss of the safe's door and the clack of the bolts. When he came back his hands were empty, and he scrubbed them at the sink for longer than the soap required.

Natalia's fingers worried the rim of her mug. "You've done this before," she said. It was not a question.

"I've watched men fall down the same hole for twenty years," Tam said. "I've learned how not to kick them into it. That's as far as I go." He looked at each of them in turn. "You asked me earlier what I believe. I believe in tidy work and fewer funerals. I believe in gettin' you to the far side of this with the least damage that a terrible situation will allow."

Nat found her voice again, thin but steady. "And if… if it all goes wrong?"

"Then we do what decent folk do, you can't run forever, and this is one hell of a climax," Tam said. "We tell the truth as best we can, and in the dock, we take it on the chin. We are through the looking glass now people."

Silence held for a moment. Outside, a fox barked somewhere up the lane.

Seth broke it. "Thank you," he said.

Tam waved it away with two fingers and the ghost of a grin. "Buy me a coffee when this is settled," he said. "The good stuff. Not whatever instant powdered sorrow that is." He tapped the jar by the hob. "I'll be staying in Preston for a week or so, just to make sure things don't get out of hand or in case you need your fairy Fent father again."

He turned and walked out the door into the night air. Natalia and Seth sat in silence. The rest of the week slipped past with lists, time trials and planning discussions. The enemy in the night had changed the game, so they were acutely aware that the unknown waited for them. They made a practice of boring and steady. Alarms at five thirty; lunches in Tupperware; emails answered in full sentences; college attended; burners into the biscuit tin; routes run and times checked. Everyone knew their jobs, and they were becoming a well-oiled machine. But in the back of Seth and Natalia's mind they knew the inevitable countdown to Saturday, and a path of no return was in-flight. It was unspoken and unnerving, but most of all it was terrifying.

Chapter Forty-Five

Friday, 18th April 2025 – 23:48

Moorside House, Snug

“Right then, it’s showtime.” Seth hit the light switch with the flat of his hand and the snug dropped into shadow, only the hall glow striping the doorway. For a second, they all just stood there in the dimness. Four silhouettes in mismatched joggers and pyjama bottoms, looking more like they were about to binge a box set than go and face down a nightmare. Then, as they’d done the last few Fridays, they formed an awkward little procession towards the stairs, slippers and socked feet scuffing on the boards.

“Goodnight, Jim Bob,” Natalia called, putting on a strange, sing-song American twang as she shepherded them out.

Jonah paused halfway to the bottom step and glanced back. Izzy blinked at her from the banister.

“Who’s Jim Bob?” Jonah asked.

"No idea," Izzy said. "He sounds like he owns a tractor."

Natalia sighed, already regretting opening her mouth. "It's from a TV show, all right? Used to be on when I was a kid. Big family. Corny as hell. They all said goodnight to each other at the end of every episode."

"Wow," Jonah said. "Gripping stuff."

"Shut up," she muttered, fighting a smile. "Some of us grew up with four channels and no internet, ungrateful little sods."

Seth gave her a nudge with his elbow as he passed. "You've lost them, Nat. You've officially crossed into 'vintage reference' territory."

"At least I had a childhood that didn't involve unboxing videos on YouTube," she shot back.

Seth snorted. "All right, Grandma Walton, come on. If we don't go to sleep soon, Lottie's going to start without us."

That earned a small, involuntary shiver from all of them, comedy skidding up against the edge of what waited. The moment of daftness thinned, but it didn't vanish. It stayed there like a buffer, something soft between them and the thing in the field.

They broke off to their separate rooms, doors clicking, taps running, the ordinary noises of a house shutting down for the night. Natalia lingered at the top of the stairs for a heartbeat, listening to it all – the swish of water, the creak of floorboards, Seth humming tunelessly in the bathroom – and let the faint ghost of the Walton joke settle over her like a thin blanket.

If they could still manage to take the piss, still find room for a stupid line about an old TV show, then they weren't beaten just yet.

The dream did not come fast.

It crept.

Folding them in, one by one. It took them.

Seth, Natalia, Izzy, and Jonah, side by side in the field beneath the black sky.

Seth didn't waste a second. Pack check.

"Here," Natalia said.

"Here," Jonah answered.

"Here," Izzy murmured.

"All present," Seth said. "Arm up and then form up on me."

They turned as one again, moving with the quiet competence of routine.

Once they had collected their weapons Seth called "Tasks," "Jonah – kitchen boundary, try and get in this time. Izzy – women, you'll be close to the statue, observe it and report back. Nat - the girl, this time try throwing objects at her. I hold centre and go for a nice little dance with him. Rally if we lose sight or you get in trouble. No heroes."

Four small nods. Then they were gone, the pack breaking and flowing into the routes they'd be running in their heads all week.

Izzy cut low across the dew, bare legs silvered, the stone tight in her palm. She reached the path where the mother would come barrelling down and went beyond it to the bottom left corner of the house where the oversized statue stood. It bristled, like it was alive.

Bang.

The woman burst through, calling "LOTTIE!" Izzy spun around to the women, and then back to the statue. It was growing. They always knew it was bigger in the dreams, but they had never noticed that it grew as the memory unfolded.

“The statue, it’s growing taller as the scene unfolds,” Izzy sent, jaw clenched. “It feels like it’s alive.”

“Logged,” Seth replied.

Jonah skimmed the edge of the ha-ha and struck for the rear of the house in record time. The kitchen door shimmered in the moonlight, that same wrong stillness, the glass was still holding its breath. He reached for the handle -

Natalia and Seth were both at breakneck speed.

Nat reached the girl first and went through her, turned and then threw the branch she’d collected, and it travelled straight through her.

“Branch went straight the girl, definitely a memory or apparition.”

“Logged,” Seth replied.

The dark figure emerged from the treeline, and he started to make his awkward, jerky run right on cue.

Seth saw him - Perfect!

Seth broke for him, branch low at his hip. The figure had barely cleared the first line of trees when Seth came in from the side and swung, all the coiled dread of the week poured into the blow. The branch connected with a crack that shuddered up his arm. The dark shape left the ground, rolled twice in the grass and came to rest in a heap, limbs knotted.

He didn’t get back up.

He curled up like a child.

The thing folded in on itself, hands over its head, shoulders hunching like a beaten dog. The great, looming presence they'd braced for wasn't there. What lay in the grass was smaller somehow, shrunken, dressed in the same shadow-clothes, but more frayed and tattered. It was shaking. A thin, high noise leaked out between its emaciated fingers that covered its face, half-laugh, half-sob.

"Please," it whimpered. The voice was wrong. Not the low, hollow growl Seth had heard before, but a cracked, raw sound, young and ruined. "I did what Master wanted, I did it, I did it…"

Seth stopped a pace away, breath sawing in his chest. The air around the thing shimmered like heat over tarmac. It twitched when he moved, flinching with each shift of his weight.

"Who are you? Where is he?" Seth demanded.

The figure didn't answer the question. It let out a rush of giggles that sounded like they hurt coming out, shoulders jerking. "He will be so happy," it hissed. "He'll be so happy you hurt me. He likes it when people are hurt. He said you would. He said you'd learn your place."

A chill went through him, colder than the field, colder than the sky.

"It's not him," Seth sent, hard and sharp, forcing the words across to the others. "This isn't him. It's someone else. Does anyone have eyes on him?"

"Negative," Natalia replied at once. "Girl loop still running. No change."

"Statue still -" Izzy's thought cut across itself, a static jolt of alarm. "It's taller again. It's looking at me, Dad, I swear it's -"

"Nothing here, about to go into the kitchen." Jonah threw out in a panic threading his thought.
"No Jonah, wait -" Seth sent.
The handle turned under his hand and the door opened inwards.
The figure leapt on him from a crouched position within the doorway from inside the kitchen knocking him backwards.
He went down hard, shoulder blades cracking the tiles, the breath punched out of him. The figure scrambled on all fours and hands as strong as clamps locked round his throat, thumbs digging deep just under his jaw line. Knees drove down over his upper arms, pinning them, grinding his shoulders into the floor, he couldn't move. The dark figure loomed above him now, brimmed hat and wicked smile reaching into his soul.
Jonah's mouth opened and spasmed in a silent howl. No sound came. Black dots burst across his vision.
"Contact!" he tried to send, panic flaring white, but the pressure on his windpipe turned the thought into static. His heels scrabbled against the tiles, looking for purchase that wasn't there. The figure leaned in, weight increasing, thumbs tightening with a sick, precise pleasure.
"JONAH! Someone get eyes on Jonah!" Seth sent across the link, already breaking from the tree line. "Does anyone have eyes on -"
Izzy interrupted, "The statue, it's taller than me, it looks like there is some kind of plate above it, on the house wall, it looks like it's going to touch it -"
"Not now Izzy, get to Jonah," Natalia sent.

Jonah's hands clawed at the wrists on his throat, it was futile. The hands felt like cold steel. The skin under his fingers felt wrong. Not flesh, not cloth, something in between, slick and unyielding, like pressing into cured leather over stone. His lungs burned. Eyes going black, throat throbbing.

Above him, the figure's head tilted as it throttled the life out of him, he leant closer to Jonah's face.

"...And if I may touch then so I may take…

…You're mine now!"

The dream snapped.

Not slowly, but like a cable whipping loose. Seth lurched, every nerve screaming that he was still running, still shouting, throat raw with a word he hadn't managed to get out. He came upright in his own bed with a hoarse bark, lungs heaving, heart already halfway down the corridor. Beside him, Natalia jolted so violently she slid off the edge, hit the carpet on her knees and was already grabbing for the door handle.

"Jonah!" she screamed.

They hit the landing almost together and tangled, Seth shoulder-barging the frame, Natalia bouncing off him with a curse as they scrambled for the same direction. The house had a strange, silent feel after a bad dream; Izzy's door flew open as they barrelled past. She clutched the frame with one hand, hair in her face, eyes huge and glassy.

"What's happening -?"

"Stay there," Seth snapped, not even looking back. "Iz, stay in your doorway."

He got to Jonah's room first.

The light from the landing threw a crooked band across the

bed. Jonah lay on top of the covers, twisted halfway onto his side as though he'd been ripped there and left. His eyes were open but clouded, staring at nothing. His mouth hung slack. His chest wasn't moving.

For a moment Seth's brain refused to acknowledge the scene. The only thing that made sense, absurdly, was that Jonah must still be in the field, and this was another layer of trickery.

Then he saw the marks.

Two ugly, perfect bands ringed Jonah's throat, darker than bruises, like someone had tried to thumbprint him all the way round his neck. The skin was mottled, angry red shading into a muddy blue, and in four places on each side you could see where the pressure had been worst, deep thumb-shaped dents punched into the flesh under his jaw.

Seth's knees went from under him. He caught the edge of the mattress, fingers digging in, and leaned over Jonah. Behind him, Natalia stopped in the doorway and made a sound he'd never heard her make before, one hand flying to her mouth, the other slamming against the frame as if she needed the wood to hold her up. Izzy was just behind her shell shocked.

For half a heartbeat, the three of them hung there. Seth bent over the bed, Natalia braced in the doorway, Izzy a pale outline in the hall.

All of them staring at Jonah's lifeless body.

Chapter Forty-Six

Saturday, 19th April 2025 – 00:34

The Dark Quarters

The Dark Quarters thrummed.

Not with sound but with the memory of it. Screams absorbed so often into the basalt that they had become a pulse. A low, delighted vibration just under the stone. The air was neither warm nor cold. It simply existed, dense and black, like ink rolled flat.

The figure stood with his gloved hands clasped behind his back, watching the new body cooling on the floor.

Jonah.

He lay on his back where the stone became not-quite-stone, the border where the dark quarters pressed closest to the waking world. His chest was still, his face slack with the last expression he'd worn when the fingers closed round his throat. Confusion folded into terror, then nothing at all. A faint colourless cord ran from his chest into the gloom, tethering him upwards, back towards the bright.

For the moment the cord was slack.

He admired his work. The marks were perfect. Each bruise around the boy's neck lay like an inked ring, his own hands etched in purples and black. It had taken effort to make them mirror what he had done in that other life – on that other bed, in that other room – a cheap iron frame in Miller's Court, the air thick with coal smoke and blood. He felt the echo of that night brushing his shoulders, like hands tugging at his coat.

One hundred and thirty-seven years since he had felt the last jolt of a soul leaving under his fingers.

He inhaled, though he did not need air. It was the habit of a man, he still liked the way it made his chest lift, the way it made him feel anchored inside his own shape.

"Mine," he murmured, savouring the word. His voice slid along the walls, stroked the stone, woke up the things that hung there. "Finally, mine again."

A wet sound broke the stillness. A kind of sucking rip, followed by a scream that started human and then went thin and high, like steam forced through a pinhole.

The figure turned.

Skeggs hung from the ceiling by his wrists; arms stretched so long his shoulders had torn twice and knitted twice and now trembled on the edge of tearing a third time. Hooks of stone had grown smoothly from the roof to hold him. The man's chest was open again; skin folded down like the front of a butcher's apron. Muscle shivered underneath, raw and glistening, a map of white lines where it had been sliced and re-sliced.

As the scream went on, the stone itself shifted.

Threads of black rose from the floor, sliding up over Skegg's ankles, his thighs, his belly. They wrapped him like bandages made of smoke. Wherever they passed, flesh closed. Torn muscle plumped and smoothed. Skin crept over the gaps, leaving him as he had been on the towpath years ago before the incident: soft, pale, thin as badly rolled pastry.

The scream cut off. Skeggs sagged in the hooks, his chest apparition heaving, what used to be real eyes rolling wildly in the dark.

He found the figure and tried to smile.

"Did..." His voice broke into a hoarse cough. He swallowed, "Did I do good, boss?"

The figure stepped closer. He liked to be near them when they were in the most pain. It was important to reward loyalty. Properly managed, even the most wretched animal could be made useful for centuries.

He reached up and took what would have been Skeggs' chin between thumb and forefinger. What used to be the man flinched but didn't pull away.

"Not boss," the figure said. "Never boss."

Skeggs' eyes darted sideways, searching the dark where the bulk of the dark loomed, just beyond sight. The weight of it pressed down on everything. Even here, where its main mass slept in the shed at Moorside, its presence filled every inch of this place.

"Master," Skeggs whispered quickly. "I meant Master. Did I do good for Master?"

The figure smiled. It did not quite reach his orbs for eyes. Those stayed bright and feverish, fixed on Skeggs' face like a doctor considering where to make the next incision.

"You did as you were told," he said. "You tricked the man. You played your part."

Skeggs' head bobbed weakly in the hooks. "I took the hiding. Took the blame. Kept the plan safe. Never told no one. Not even him."

"Hm." The figure let go of his chin and walked a slow circle around him, what would have been boots clicking on stone that was not really there.

Master felt plump again. Satisfied. What would have been air in the quarters had a that thick, syrupy quality it always took on after a kill. But this time there was something extra in it, a crackle, a sweetness on the back of the tongue.

"Master is pleased," he said.

Skeggs let out a shaky laugh that almost became a sob. "Thank fuck. Thought..." He broke off as the hooks shifted, biting deeper into the meat of his wrists. "Thought I'd messed it up."

Skeggs blinked. "So, I did good."

"For Master," the figure said again. "Not for you."

"Right." Relief and terror wrestled in what used to be Skeggs' face, leaving him with the fixed grin of a man at the wrong end of a joke he didn't understand. "Right, yeah. For Master."

The figure stepped back into his eyeline and smoothed an imaginary crease from his coat. He enjoyed coats. The weight over his shoulders. The way they moved when he walked. He had chosen this one carefully, copied from an old memory:

dark wool, high collar, a cut that would look equally at home in a Whitechapel alley or a modern street.

"This cycle," he said lightly, "you will be flayed nine hundred and ninety-nine times."

Skeggs stared. For a moment the words didn't land. Numbers were not his world; they had never paid his rent.

"Nine… hundred and…" He mused. "What?"

"Usually it is one thousand," the figure went on, as though explaining terms to a child. "One thousand unmaking's for each turn before the weekly theatre. It keeps you soft. Teaches you to hold your shape properly. Keeps Master amused. This turn, you will get one less."

The hooks squealed as Skeggs jerked in them. "You..." His eyes flooded suddenly, "You're... you're knocking one off?"

The figure's smile widened, teeth very white in the gloom.

"You have earned a reprieve," he said. "For your service. Only nine hundred and ninety-nine this time." He lifted one hand and pressed thumb and forefinger together, leaving a tiny gap. "A little mercy. See how generous Master is, when his dog does well?"

"Thank you," he gasped. "Thank you, Master. Thank you. That's… that's sound, that. That's really -"

His words dissolved into a raw, animal shriek as the first strip of skin peeled away from his chest.

The figure watched the strip unwind – long, pale, impossibly fine – and felt something like peace. The sound of Skegg's screaming stitched itself neatly over the silence that had followed Jonah's last breath. Familiar. Comforting.

He could have closed his eyes and been back in The Yard. The copper stink of Whitechapel. The swish of a blade through wet cloth. The way a whole city held its breath when they realised there was someone among them who could take and take and take and never be caught.

One hundred and thirty-seven years since he had felt this complete.

"Oh, this is going to be a wonderful millennium," he said, almost to himself. "A truly joyous cycle. New blood. New fears. New games."

Behind him, Skeggs' scream tore itself ragged, dropped into hoarse sobbing, rose again as another line of flesh came away. The figure smiled up into the dark as the memory of Jonah's corpse began to fade, the boy's outline thinning, the cord drawing him back towards the shouting and the desperate, hopeful hands.

"Run, little Overaugh," he murmured. "Run back to them. Show them I've learnt how to kill again by my own hand, and soon I'll be making them kill with theirs. I can smell the sorrow." He made to sniff the air like wolf looking for its next meal.

He turned away as Jonah vanished, the last echo of his presence snapping like a cut string.

Then he went back to his work. After all, he had nine hundred and ninety-eight flayings left this cycle, and such a lot of time to enjoy them.

Chapter Forty-Seven

Saturday, 19th April 2025 – 00:34

Moorside House, Upstairs

Seth moved first.

One second, he was on his knees beside the bed, the next he was hauling Jonah flat onto his back, clearing the pillow away, fingers scrabbling for a pulse at the side of his neck. Nothing. Or if there was something, it was buried so deep under the cold and the bruising he couldn't feel it.

"Nat." His voice came out strange, thin. "Nat, help me."

She was already crossing the room in a dazed stumble. Whatever sound she'd made in the doorway was gone now. Her face had snapped into something tight and serious; all noise shoved to the edges. She dropped to the other side of the bed, shoved Jonah's jaw up with one hand and pinched his nose with the other.

"Inferior airway, looks obstructed," she muttered, half to herself, half to him. "Right. We're going to breathe for you, son. Seth... compressions."

Seth locked his hands and started counting under his breath. Thirty hard pushes into his boy's chest, ribs creaking under his palms. Jonah's head lolled with each rise and fall, bruised neck tendons standing out like ropes. On "thirty" Natalia bent and sealed her mouth over his, giving two sharp breaths, watching for the rise that didn't come.

"Again," she snapped.

They fell into the rhythm. Press, press, press, press. Breathe. Press, press, press. Breathe. It wasn't working. The room shrank down to the sound of Seth's counting, Natalia's breaths and Izzy's ragged sobs from the doorway where she'd ignored her instruction and stepped inside anyway, hands jammed over her mouth.

Natalia opened his mouth and pinched his tongue forwards with her forefinger and thumb; she pressed her mouth around his nose in a perfect seal and started blowing through his sinuses.

On the third cycle Jonah jerked.

It was small at first, just a twitch under Seth's hands, then his whole body arched, like something had been ripped loose deep inside him. A horrible, tearing gasp tore its way out of his chest. He rolled onto his side, coughing without sound, throat spasming, chest heaving uselessly.

"That's it, that's it, come on," Seth said, voice breaking. He slid a hand behind Jonah's shoulders, trying to get him into the recovery position like the posters always showed. But Jonah fought him, clawing at his own neck with both hands. Natalia caught his wrists. "No. Leave it. You'll make it worse."

The noise coming out of him wasn't quite breathing. It was a high, whistling rasp, every inhale a fight, every exhale a dry bark. His face mottled a deeper purple; his lips edged with blue. His eyes rolled towards them, wild and unfocused, tears standing in the corners.

"His airway's compromised," Natalia said, and this time there was no space between the words. "Partially crushed or blocked. He can't move air properly."

She twisted, snapping her head towards the door.

"Izzy! Phone an ambulance. Now. 999. Tell them strangulation injury, eighteen-year-old male, breathing but struggling. Do it now, Izzy. GO!"

Izzy vanished, bare feet slapping down the landing. Seth could hear her in the hall, voice wavering as she rattled off the address to the call handler, stumbling over "Moorside House, Altham, yes, the big one near the industrial estate. My brother, he's... he can't breathe, he's..."

"Stay with me," Seth said, leaning so close his forehead almost touched Jonah's. "Jonah. Look at me. You're here. You're here, lad. Keep pulling it in, that's it, keep pulling it in. Stay calm, lower your heart rate."

Jonah wheezed, throat dragging in another shredded breath, then another. Each one sounded worse.

"How long to an ambulance?" Seth called, not looking away.

Izzy reappeared in the doorway, phone clamped to her ear, tears streaking down her face. "They're sending one," she said. "She says to keep him like that and keep talking to him and they'll be as fast as they -"

"How long?" Seth roared.

Izzy flinched, listened, then looked back at him, stricken. "They don't know. Ten minutes? Maybe more. They said you're rural and -"

"We haven't got ten minutes," Natalia cut in.

They both looked at Jonah. His breaths were getting shallower, the gap between each one stretching. The whistling noise had turned to a thin, horrible squeal. His fingers were starting to twitch, not with panic now but with something slower, more frightening.

Seth made the decision in the space between two of those sounds.

"Right," he said. His voice dropped into something flat and hard, an old, buried register. "We're not waiting."

"Seth..." Natalia began.

"If we sit here, he dies in this room," he said. "If he crashes in the car, at least he's moving towards oxygen and a full crash team. I am not standing here watching him choke while we wait for a bloody postcode check."

He was already moving as he spoke, sliding his arms under Jonah's shoulders and knees. Jonah was dead weight, head lolling, breath catching in little stuttering gasps as his neck shifted.

"Careful," Natalia snapped, hands hovering uselessly. "Mind his airway. Keep him slightly forward."

"I've got him."

Seth lifted his son. It was like lifting him out of the bath when he was small, except now there was eighteen years of bone and muscle and dead weight, and the guttural noise in his throat made something in Seth's chest feel like it was tearing.

He held Jonah against him in an awkward cradle, one arm under his thighs, one clamped across his back, trying to keep his chin tipped just so.

"Izzy, tell them we're going by car," he said, already backing towards the door. "Tell them Blackburn A&E. We're on our way now. Stay on the line with them and get them to ring ahead."

Izzy nodded frantically, phone pressed tighter to her ear. "He's taking him to hospital," she babbled to the unseen dispatcher. "Blackburn A&E, it's quicker, we're closer to the motorway, he says we can't wait, he can't breathe -"

Natalia was right behind Seth as he stumbled onto the landing. "I'm coming," she said. No argument in it, just fact. "Izzy, grab your hoodie and shoes, you're in the back with me. Bring the phone."

"I'm not leaving Jonah," Izzy said, as if that could ever have been an option.

They thundered down the stairs together, Seth feeling every step in his knees, in his spine, muscles screaming as he tried not to jolt Jonah more than he had to. Jonah's hand bunched weakly in the fabric of his T-shirt, clutching, then slackening, clutching again.

"Stay with me, lad," Seth muttered into his hair. "Stay with me. You do not get to check out now, you hear me?"

The front door flew open under Natalia's hand. Cold night air slammed into them, bringing with it the smell of damp earth and the faint tang of smoke from some distant garden. The Audi sat under the car port, black and solid and stupidly normal.

"Back seat. Lie him across," Natalia ordered. "Head on my lap, I'll manage his airway. Seth, you drive. Izzy, front seat. Keep that phone on speaker."

They wrestled Jonah in, half-dropping, half-guiding him onto the leather. He made a low, awful sound as his neck tilted, eyes rolling back for a second before Natalia got her hand under his jaw, lifting, angling, searching for the position where the air whistled a fraction easier.

"There, there, that's the least shit," she panted. "Go!"

Seth slammed the door, slid into the driver's seat and stabbed the key into the ignition. The engine turned over, dashboard flaring to life. He jammed the gearstick into reverse, one hand white-knuckled on the wheel, the other braced on the back of Jonah's seat as he shot out onto the lane, gravel spitting.

Hazards on. Headlights to full beam. The narrow, black ribbon of road ahead of them.

"Hold that angle, Nat," he said through his teeth as he took the first bend far too fast. "Izzy, what's she saying now?"

The phone on Izzy's knee crackled. The operator's voice was thin but steady in the dark. "You're doing well. We've alerted Blackburn A&E. Keep talking to him. If he stops breathing completely, your mum will need to start compressions again. Can you see if his chest is still moving for me?"

"It's moving," Natalia snapped. "Barely. Stridor, tracheal trauma, probable soft tissue crush. We'll be there in five if he doesn't arrest on me."

Seth swung them left at the end of the lane, tyres skidding for half a second on the damp tarmac before biting. The sign for the M65 loomed up, green and reflective.

"Come on, come on," he muttered, foot heavy on the accelerator. "Hold on, Jonah. Just hold on."

They hit the slip road hard, the Audi surging forward, engine howling as they shot up towards the motorway lights and the dark stretch of tarmac that led to Blackburn, and whatever waited for them there.

The sliding doors of Blackburn A&E yawned open before they'd even come to a full stop.

Seth barely had the handbrake on when a woman in navy scrubs and a yellow tabard was at his door, rapping her knuckles on the glass. Behind her, a porter hovered with an empty trolley, its metal sides rattling faintly, another nurse already pulling on gloves as she walked.

"Mr Overaugh?" the woman called, voice sharp over the engine. "You're coming in from Moorside House?"

Seth killed the ignition and flung the door open. "He can't breathe," he said, stumbling out. "My lad... he's eighteen, he's been strangled, his throat..."

"We've got you," she cut in. Her accent had that flattened East Lancashire music to it. "I'm Karen, I'm one of the nurses. Is he breathing at all?"

"Just," Natalia answered from the back seat. She was half-crouched, half-kneeling, one hand still under Jonah's jaw, the other braced on the door frame. "Severe airway compromise, stridor, likely soft tissue crush. He needs a controlled airway now."

Karen's eyebrows flicked, just for a second, at the precision. "Right. Let's get him inside."

The porter swung the trolley in alongside the car with

practised speed. The second nurse, young, her dark hair scraped back so tightly it shone, dropped the side rail with a clatter.

"On three," she said. "Dad, if you can take his shoulders? Mum, keep hold of his head if you can, same position. We'll take his hips and legs."

"We need to minimise movement in case of cervical -" Natalia began.

"We'll support his neck," the younger nurse said calmly. "Promise. Ready? One, two, three."

Jonah came out of the car in a limp, awkward bundle. For a heartbeat Seth thought he was going to slip straight through his arms. Then the trolley caught him, the thin mattress sighing under his weight. Jonah's head lolled, the awful purple rings on his throat stark under the strip lights.

"Jesus Christ," Karen muttered. "Okay. Straight to Resus. You lot, follow me. We'll talk as we go."

They hit the doors at a trot. The bright, chemical-lit chaos of the department opened: people in plastic chairs, a drunk shouting at someone behind reception, a child crying in hiccupping bursts. None of it touched them.

A green-clad Senior House Officer glanced up, clocked the trolley, and slapped a red button on the wall. A set of double doors buzzed and swung open, revealing a bay lined with machines that beeped in different keys.

"In here," Karen said. "Bay Two."

The room swallowed Jonah. In seconds there were six, then seven bodies around the trolley: blue and green scrubs, plastic aprons, gloved hands. Someone pulled a curtain partly across, shutting out the corridor. A woman with short grey hair and a stethoscope round her neck stepped to the head of the bed.

“I’m Emma, I’m the A&E consultant,” she said, already leaning in to look at Jonah’s neck. “Tell me what happened.”

“Strangulation,” Natalia said, breath still coming fast. “No ligature that we could see, looked like manual. He arrested briefly at home, we did CPR. He came back but with severe stridor and increasing respiratory distress. We drove in because we’re closer to the motorway than ambulance cover and they couldn’t give us a time.”

Emma’s eyes flicked to her, taking in the clipped sentences, the steadiness. “Any previous medical conditions? Allergies?”

“No,” Natalia said. “He’s fit. Healthy. Was.”

“Right. Thank you.” Emma’s voice softened. “We’ll take it from here for now.”

“BP’s low,” someone at the trolley said. “Ninety systolic and falling.”

“Sats seventy-two on room air,” another reported. “Tachy at one-fifty. Stridor present, severe inspiratory effort.”

“Get him on high-flow oxygen now,” Emma said, not looking away. “And I want anaesthetics down here NOW! Page ENT as well. Tell them probable laryngeal trauma. Let’s get a collar on him in case there’s any C-spine involvement.”

A mask descended over Jonah’s face, fogging with each ragged breath. A monitor started up with a flat, relentless beep-beep-beep that set Seth’s teeth on edge. He watched one of the nurses, her name badge flashing M. Hussain, slide a blood pressure cuff round Jonah’s arm and start tightening, lips moving as she counted under her breath.

"Dad."

Seth dragged his gaze away. Another nurse had appeared at his elbow, this one in a maroon tunic instead of scrubs, her hair in a loose plait. She had a clipboard tucked to her chest like a shield.

"I'm Rachel," she said. "I look after relatives. We're going to take really good care of your son. Right now, though, we need a bit of space round him to work. Would you be able to come with me for a few minutes? There's a quiet room just next door."

"I'm not leaving him," Seth said. The words came out harsh, ripped straight from somewhere deep.

"We're not asking you to leave the building," Rachel said gently. "Just the bay. You'll be a few steps away. We'll come and update you as soon as we stabilise him. At the moment there are too many of us and not enough room, and that makes it harder to -"

"Dad," Izzy whispered. She was pressed into the corner, one hand still clutching the mobile, the other wrapped round her own ribs. The whites of her eyes looked too big in her face. "We're in the way. Look."

He looked.

From where he stood, he could see only fragments of Jonah now: a bare foot, an elbow, the edge of his jaw. The rest was a blur of hands moving in fast, practised patterns. Someone drawing up drugs, someone snapping open a foil packet, someone fitting a rigid collar round his neck. Emma was talking about predicted difficult airway, about swelling, about not wanting to lose the window for a safe intubation. Words and phrases like "rapid sequence" and "crash" floated in the air.

Natalia's hand closed round his arm. He hadn't even noticed her move.

"Let them work," she said, her voice low. There was iron under the tremor. "We've done what we can do."

Seth swallowed. The taste of motorway tarmac and panic was still thick in his mouth.

"Don't you let him out of your sight," he said to Emma, the words half-plea, half-threat.

She glanced up, meeting his eyes properly for the first time. "I won't," she said simply. "We're on him. Go and breathe for a bit. We'll come and find you as soon as I've got a tube in and I know where we are."

Rachel took that as her cue. "This way," she murmured.

They were eased out of the bay like pieces being slid off a chess board. For a moment, as the curtain fell back into place, Seth caught one last clear glimpse of Jonah's throat with the oxygen mask lifted. The deep, brutal fingerprints stark against the mottled skin.

Then the curtain shut and he was in the corridor, the sudden emptiness around him almost worse than the crush had been.

Rachel led them a few doors down to a small room with no windows and a blue vinyl sofa. "If you sit in here, I'll bring you some tea," Rachel said. "I know it sounds daft, but hot drinks help. I'll be back with news as soon as I have any, all right?"

Natalia nodded for him. "Thank you," she said. Her voice had gone thin round the edges. "We'll stay here."

Rachel slipped out, closing the door with a soft click that sounded unnervingly final.

Izzy slid down the wall until she was sitting on the floor, arms round her knees. "He was breathing when we left," she said, as if that were a promise the universe had signed. "He was breathing. We got him here. That's supposed to be the hard bit."

Seth sank onto the edge of the sofa, elbows on his knees, hands hanging loose between them. His T-shirt was stiff where Jonah's fingers had bunched and released, bunched and released.

He stared at the scuffed lino and tried not to picture his son's throat under that oxygen mask, and the hands that had done it, and the voice in the field saying, If I may touch, then so I may take.

Chapter Forty-Eight

Saturday, 19th April 2025 – 02:13

Blackburn A&E

"This is on me."

Seth said it to the scuffed floor between his boots, but it hit the air like a verdict. The relatives' room hummed faintly with strip-light and vending machine noise. Somewhere out in the corridor a trolley squeaked past, then silence again.

Natalia looked up from the untouched tea Rachel had brought. "Seth -"

"If I hadn't laid into him with that branch, this doesn't happen," he went on, as if she hadn't spoken. "If I'd just… kept eyes on him, shadowed him, not provoked him… he doesn't know he can go for Jonah. He doesn't..." His throat closed. He pressed his fingers hard into his eye sockets, like he could force the images back in. "I poked the bastard. I kicked the hornets' nest, and now our baby boy is fighting for his life."

On the floor by the wall, Izzy flinched. Her knees were hugged tight to her chest, hoodie sleeves pulled down over her hands.

“We don’t know that.” Natalia said.

“Yes, we do,” Seth snapped. “He said it in the field. Clear as anything. ‘If I may touch, then so may I take.’ And I went swinging because I thought I’d found a weakness. Thought I was being clever. And who does he take? Jonah. Course he does.”

“You hit the decoy, not the main event,” she said. “You didn’t know he had layers and at least we know we can hit the decoy as well now.”

“That makes it worse, not better.”

He dropped his hands, staring at her. His eyes were bloodshot, his skin sallow in the harsh light. He looked ten years older than he had at midnight.

“That thing has been poking at us for weeks,” he said. “Every time, we’ve adapted. Tightened up. And this time I go full caveman on it, and it escalates. I gave him an excuse to change the fucking rules. I might as well have marked Jonah’s throat myself.”

“Don’t,” Izzy whispered.

They both glanced at her. She was pale, freckles standing out like someone had redrawn them with a pen.

“Don’t say it like that,” she added. “Please.”

Seth’s face crumpled for a heartbeat. He scrubbed a hand over his jaw, forcing his voice flatter before he spoke again.

“I should’ve been quicker,” he said. “Should’ve got to the kitchen faster. Should’ve pulled Jonah back or not sent him,

I should've stood in that door frame. I'm the one who started all this. I'm the one that picked up that statue. I'm the one who..."
"Enough." Natalia's voice cut across him like a blade.
He shut his mouth on the next self-inflicted blow.
She set the tea down on the low table with care, as if the mug were something fragile and important, then leaned forward, elbows on her knees, hands linked loosely between them. When she looked at him, the softness she'd used on Jonah was gone. This was the look he'd seen across briefing containers years ago, in places that had dental saws whirring in the background.
"You don't get to sit there and write poetry about your failings," she said. "Not tonight. You can do that in a decade when we're all still breathing."
"Nat -"
"No... You listen to me. This self-inflicted pity party stops, and it stops right fucking now Seth Overaugh!" She nodded towards the closed door, where the sounds of Resus came muffled and thin through the wall. "He's in the best place he can be. They've got a tube in, his sats are coming up, he's sedated, and for the first time in ninety minutes his airways are open. That is not nothing."
Seth swallowed, saying nothing.
"You want to blame yourself?" Natalia went on. "Fine. You swung at something that looked like a threat. That is what you've always done, that is the nature of the beast you are. Sometimes that saves people, sometimes it makes things worse. You don't get to know in advance. But right now, your

guilt is a vanity project we can't afford."

Izzy frowned. "Mum -"

"What?" Natalia turned her head. "You want him sat there paralysed, while the other one rolls that video out on Facebook from some scabby burner and lands us all in prison? Is that better?"

Izzy's mouth opened, then closed again. She shook her head, mute. She had never seen this side of her mother before, and it shook her.

Natalia looked back at Seth. "We have two fronts. We always knew that. Dream front and daylight front. Night-time bastard and junkie bastard. Tonight, the dream showed us exactly what he can do. Fine. Logged. We adapt. But daylight doesn't stop because we had a bad fucking night."

Seth let out a bitter laugh. "Bad night."

"You know what exactly what I mean."

He stared at his hands. The ones that had pounded Jonah's chest. His son's chest.

"I can't leave him Nat." he said quietly. "Not again."

"You won't be leaving him," Natalia replied. "You'll be doing something to protect him. And us. And whoever else that little shit decides to target once he realises how valuable that clip is. Do you think we are his first victims? Do you think we'll be his last?"

Izzy shifted.

Both parents paused. It was small, that beat, but it was enough to make the air feel different.

"Iz..." Seth began.

"No." She sat up straighter, hands uncurling. "You keep

talking about 'daylight front' and 'junkie bastard' like it's a football match and I'm too thick to follow. I'm not twelve. I know you're holding back. What are you planning?"

Natalia inhaled slowly through her nose, buying half a second.

"We've told you what you need to know," she said. "Your dad and I are dealing with that. Your job is Jonah, and the dreams. That's it. We need you well away from the daylight enemy."

"That's not an answer," Izzy said. "If this is about me as well..."

"It is about you," Seth cut in, more sharply than he meant to. "That's why you're not involved. Full stop."

Izzy's eyes shone. "You drag me into the field every week, make me log statue heights and loops and whether ghost-woman blinks, but I'm apparently too fragile to know what's going on in the daytime?"

"I didn't say -" Seth started.

"This isn't about fragile," Natalia said. "This is about plausible deniability."

Izzy frowned. "What?"

"If anyone ever comes knocking," Natalia said, "about anything me or your father has or hasn't done, I want you able to look them in the eye and tell the truth when they ask you what you knew."

There was a silence. The word anything sat between them like another person.

"You're going to do something," Izzy said slowly. "Something dodgy."

"Something necessary," Natalia corrected. "And arguably

long overdue."

Izzy looked from one parent to the other. "And I just… what, pretend I don't see it?"

"You don't see it," Seth said. "Because you won't. You won't be there, you won't be involved, you won't hear the details. You keep your head on your shoulders; you look after your brother when he wakes up. That's your lane. Stay in it."

She stared at him, jaw working, then finally nodded once, sharp as a salute. "Fine," she said. "But if this comes back and bites us, don't you dare tell me it was to protect me."

"I'll tell you it was to protect all of us," he said. "Because it is."

She huffed, scrubbed at her face with the heel of her hand, and shrank back into her corner, pulling the hoodie over her knees again.

Natalia waited until Izzy's gaze had dropped, then turned back to Seth.

"We have a window," she said quietly. "You know that. Today. After that, the story starts to spread. Nurses talk. Paramedics talk. Someone from the original arrest hears that the Overaugh lad's nearly been choked to death in his bed, and suddenly all the wrong people are looking at Moorside again."

Seth rubbed his eyes. "He's hardly going to know I've left," he said. "He's sedated."

"This isn't about him knowing," she said. "It's about you acting before this spirals. Jonah in hospital is the perfect cover. You at Blackburn tomorrow, everyone assumes you're where any dad would be. Sitting with your kid. Grabbing a brew. Talking to consultants. No one would ever think to check the mall CCTV."

He looked at her. "You mean do it as planned, today?"

"Yep, next scheduled meet is this morning," she said. "He'll be expecting you. If you don't show, he gets jumpy. If you show and try to postpone, he gets twitchy and starts thinking about backups.

"He's not clever, but he's paranoid and he's got something we can't allow to sit on a cheap handset for another month. That little shit is one shoplift away from getting that phone taken into police custody."

"That means you can't tail him this time," Seth said.

Her mouth tightened. "No. I can't. Jonah needs one of us here when he comes round, and between us I'm the one who sounds like I know what I'm talking about when someone says, 'laryngeal trauma'. They'll have questions. Police may turn up. Adult safeguarding perhaps. I'm staying. Hopefully we can get him home before anyone asks too many questions."

"So I go in blind," he said. "No eyes on where he goes afterwards, no confirmation."

"Yes," she said. "It means we have to wait for newsfeeds to be certain, but at least none of us are anywhere near that scrubland."

"It's not ideal," she said. "Ideally we wouldn't have a demon using our lad's trachea as a stress ball, but here we are."

"We roll the dice," Natalia said. "We must. Because the alternative is living another month knowing that somewhere, in some tent or back alley, there's a little glowing rectangle with you and me on it. And every second that passes is another chance for him to drop it, sell it, lose it or get nicked with it."

He could see it taking shape already, ugly and precise: the doughnuts, the bag, the four white twists. The way a junkie's eyes lit up when you said "sample" and "kilo" in the same sentence.

"I don't like you not being there," he said.

"I don't like our son being on a breathing machine," she replied. "We work with what's in front of us."

The door clicked softly and opened a fraction. Rachel poked her head round.

"Sorry," she said. "Didn't mean to interrupt. Just to let you know, Jonah's up in the High Dependency Unit now. Dr Emma managed to secure the airway nicely, swelling's already starting to respond to the steroids. It's still very serious, but he's stable. We'll let you see him in a bit."

"Thank you," Natalia said. The words came out on a long breath she hadn't realised she'd been holding.

Rachel nodded. Her eyes flicked between the three of them. "Try and get some rest if you can," she said, which was ridiculous and she knew it, but she offered it like a plaster. "I'll be back soon."

The door closed again.

Seth stood up slowly. His legs ached from the sprint down the landing, from the crouch to put him in the back seat, from the motorway. From everything.

"What time is it?" he asked.

Natalia checked the wall clock. "Two-fifteen."

He nodded. "If I go now, I can grab a couple of hours at

home to prepare properly. Shower. Change. Be at the Mall when it opens."

Izzy's head snapped up. "You're going now?"

He looked at her, heart twisting. "I'll be back later," he said. "You stay with Mum. When they let you up, you sit with Jonah. Tell him… tell him I'm sorting things."

"That's vague as hell," she said.

"Good," Natalia replied. "Vague is what we're aiming for."

Izzy stared at them both, then sighed, the sound too old for her face. "Fine," she said again. "Go do your… plausible deniability thing. Just come back, yeah? In one piece. Preferably without a crushed windpipe."

Seth crossed the room in two steps and crouched in front of her, ignoring the way his knees complained.

"I'll be back darling," he said. "I promise."

He kissed the top of her head, squeezed Natalia's shoulder, and straightened.

He opened the door. The corridor outside smelt of disinfectant and old coffee, the sounds of the hospital a low, constant murmur. For a moment he stood there, hand on the frame, looking back at his wife and daughter in the small, airless room.

Then he stepped out into the harsh strip-lit night, heading for the car and the half-built plan waiting for him in the dark.

Chapter Forty-Nine

Saturday, 19th April 2025 – 10:50

The Mall Shopping Centre, Blackburn

The shopping centre always smelt faintly of sugar and disinfectant. This morning it made Seth feel faintly sick.

He took his usual table under the skylight, back to the pillar, clear line of sight to the escalators and the entrance to the food court. The laminated surface of the table stuck slightly to his forearms when he leant on it. Above him, the steel beams criss-crossed the glass like a cage.

"Dozen assorted, love?" the doughnut woman asked, already reaching for the tongs.

"Aye," he said. "And a brew while I'm waiting, please."

He paid in cash, slipping an extra note across the counter. "There'll be a lad in a black hoodie in a bit," he added quietly. "Bit wired looking. When he comes up for the doughnuts, tell him they're already sorted and nod over to me, yeah?"

She gave him the look people reserved for anything even

slightly off script, then shrugged. "Whatever," she said. "As long as they're paid for."

"They are," Seth said. "Thanks."

He walked back to the table, tea in one hand, the plastic bag in the other. Four fresh twists sat on top of the packaged notes, easily visible if you peered inside. He rested his fingers lightly on it, feeling the tiny give of the wraps beneath the plastic.

The centre was waking up properly now. Prams, pensioners, two security guards doing slow loops pretending not to be bored. Seth checked his watch. 10:52. He pictured Jonah's neck: the rings, the swelling, the plastic. Pictured the monitor numbers Emma had rattled off. Stable. For now.

You could be sat by his bed holding his hand, a voice in his head said.

And doing what? he answered it. Watching numbers. Letting the other front run wild.

He sipped his tea. It tasted of metal and overboiled water.

Moxy was late.

Of course he was late.

It wasn't until the clock over the burger place ticked to 11:07 that Seth saw him: weaving out of the crowd rather than walking through it, shoulders loose, head bobbing slightly to some internal track. Black hoodie, grey joggers, trainers that used to be white. Eyes too wide, skin too slack.

He clocked the doughnut stand and changed direction like someone had pulled a lead.

Seth watched him go to the counter. The woman bagged up the box, nodded towards Seth's table. "He's already sorted it," she said.

Moxy turned, following her chin. When he saw Seth, his grin spread slow and lazy.

"Oh, we're living now," he said loudly, taking the bag like it was a trophy. He sauntered over, dropping onto the chair opposite without waiting to be invited.

So much for protocols, Seth thought. No sit-downs. No eye contact. No deviation. That had lasted exactly one meeting.

"All right, my guy?" Moxy tore into the bag with nicotine-stained fingers, already dunking a ring of sugar into his mouth. "Look at us. Perks 'o the job, innit." He chewed, talking around it, scattering sugar over the table. "You been here long?"

"Just got here," Seth lied.

Moxy nodded, pleased at the idea that he hadn't kept anyone waiting. "Sweet. Sweet, man. I like this set-up, you know. Civilised." He waved a bitten doughnut in a circle at the food court. "Classy environment. Pastries. My kinda business."

Seth let him enjoy the fantasy for a beat. Then he leant in slightly, lowering his voice.

"Listen," he said. "The timeline's moved up."

Moxy froze with his mouth open, then slowly lowered the doughnut. "What, for the… recurring arrangement?" He waggled his eyebrows. "My little pension plan?"

"For the bigger one we talked about," Seth said. "The one I said I might be able to cut you in on. Remember?"

A shadow of suspicion crossed Moxy's face, then was drowned under greed. "Right, yeah. Your… friends," he said. "Your people. The sellers."

"That's right."
"And what, they've… what, they've brought things forward?" He tried to sound like this was the sort of thing he'd heard a thousand times before, like supply chains and procurement were his day job.
Seth nodded. "We had it pencilled for next month. That's not going to work now. Circumstances have changed. So, here's me seeing if you're as useful as you say you are."
Moxy straightened in his chair, doughnut forgotten. "I'm always useful, mate. You know me. I've got reach. I've got channels. You name it, I can move it. Within reason, like." He laughed, a fraction too high. "So, what we talking?"
Seth tapped the plastic bag with one finger. "First, we're talking about you doing your homework properly."
Moxy frowned. "Eh?"
"There are four samples in there," Seth said. "Four little friends. You take those away with your management fee, you test them with your contacts. You tell me, honestly, if they're worth the risk. Because if you think they are, then next week there'll be a kilo in a similar bag, same time, same place. And I need someone who can distribute that quiet, without drawing attention."
The word kilo seemed to hit him physically. His pupils blew a fraction wider. Seth could almost see the numbers stacking up behind his eyes, the imaginary notes, the favours, the clout.
"A kilo," Moxy repeated, reverent. "Here? In the Mall?"
"Collection point's here," Seth said. "Where it goes after that is your problem. Bag, trolley, mate with a backpack, I don't

care. What I care about is that it doesn't come back to me and it doesn't get dropped on some Tesco forecourt because you've had a funny five minutes."

"Bruv," Moxy said, offended. "Come on. I'm professional, me."

Seth raised an eyebrow.

"I am!" Moxy insisted. "Look, I've been doing this a long time, yeah? You don't get to my level without knowing how to keep things… discreet." He said the last word like he'd only ever seen it written down.

"Your level," Seth echoed, letting a hint of amusement touch his mouth. "And what level's that, then?"

"Intermediate wholesaler," Moxy said promptly, as if he'd been waiting years for someone to ask. "I'm not some little street rat flogging bags outside the Spar. I'm… connected." He tapped the side of his nose. "You talk to me; you're talking to people."

"Good," Seth said. "That's very reassuring, because people are what I need and someone with your kind of reach is very useful to us."

Moxy couldn't help himself. He peered into the bag, fingers burrowing towards the wraps. His hand closed on the twists and his whole face lit up.

"Four," he said. "Four? For me?"

"For you, and whoever you want to test the merch, get people interested." Seth said. "Think of them as… due diligence. I don't want any arguments later about quality. You try it, you confirm it's as good as I say, then next week we talk about numbers and cuts. If you're here at eleven on Saturday, I'll know you're interested, and the kilo will be here with me."

Moxy rolled one of the wraps between his fingers, weighing impossible futures. "Looks decent," he said. "Nice tight twist. Proper. You sure your… mates... are all right with me getting a sniff first?"

"They trust my judgement," Seth said. "I tell them you're worth the punt, they'll listen. I tell them you're all mouth and no follow-through; they'll listen to that as well."

"Nah, nah, I'm solid, me." Moxy tucked the wraps deeper into the bag, suddenly possessive. "You won't regret it. I'll have proper feedback for you. Market intel, innit." He grinned. "You know what, I think this could be the start of a beautiful business relationship."

He said it like a line from a film he only half-remembered, leaning back as if he expected swelling violins and a crane shot.

Seth kept his expression neutral, almost indulgent. "That's what I'm hoping," he said. "So same time next week. Same doughnut stand. You come alone. You pick up the bag. You get it offsite fast. No loitering, no admirers, no victory laps."

"Easy," Moxy said. "Piece of piss. I'll bring my trolley man, like -"

"No," Seth said, too quickly.

Moxy blinked. "What?"

"No extras," Seth said, reining himself back. "I don't want some half-cut mate gobbing off about his big score. You want help moving it, you do that somewhere else, later. First leg, you're solo. That's the condition. You're the only person we trust to do this."

Moxy chewed that over positively glowing from the praise, then shrugged. "All right. Solo pick-up. Then we roll. I can work with that." He patted the bag. "This… this is good, man. This is proper. My people are going to wet themselves."

"I hope so, we have a lot more where that came from," Seth said giving a fake smile.

Moxy stood up, chair scraping. "I'd love to stay and chat, but, you know, I've got a busy schedule." He winked. "Clients to see. Samples to… look at."

"Of course," Seth said. "Don't keep them waiting."

He watched as Moxy swaggered away, bag swinging at his side, shoulders that little bit looser now he thought he'd levelled up. Halfway to the escalator he checked over his shoulder, just once, to see if anyone was watching the boss man at work.

Seth sat for another five minutes, finishing the tea even though it had gone cold, watching the space where Moxy had been. The whole thing was ridiculous. What type of person would willing take a Class A drug from someone he was trying to blackmail, let alone after only one week. Moxy hadn't even asked about where he should drop the money off for the drugs.

A strung-out junkie at the end of his rope would do anything for a free hit and logical questions always got in the way of a free score. He felt a small pang of guilt that quickly disappeared. He stood, dropped the empty cup in the bin, and walked out of the centre towards the car park, each step measured, the shape of what he'd just set in motion sitting cold and heavy in his heart.

Chapter Fifty

Saturday, 19th April 2025 – 12:32

Scrubland, Altham

By the time Moxy hit the scrubland he was sweating through his hoodie, more from the hurry than the weak midday sun. The two tents sagged in their usual place between the scruffy bushes, flysheet flapping where one of the pegs had given up. Brendan was pacing a narrow groove into the frozen-bog-turned-dried-mud between the fire pit and the orange tent. He kept rubbing his nose with the back of his hand, sniffing hard, eyes jittering. When he clocked Moxy coming down the track, he homed in like a missile.

“Where’ve you been man?” he blurted. “Mate, I’ve been waiting for hours.”

“It’s been ninety minutes,” Moxy said. “Chill your tits.”

Brendan ignored that. He grabbed a fistful of Moxy’s sleeve, then thought better of it and let go, fingers twitching. “You got owt on you? I’m rattlin’, man. Proper. I tried to kip, but

my legs kept going, I can't-"
"You got money?" Moxy cut in.
Brendan's face crumpled. "Not yet. I told you. Mum's on one. She's counting every quid now, right. Keeps asking where it's going. She's like, 'I'm not funding your little adventures, Brendan,'" he mimicked, voice going shrill. "If I even look at her purse she's staring."
"So that's a no, then," Moxy said.
"I'll get it," Brendan said quickly. "I swear. Dad's working nights tonight, yeah? I'll go through their room, I'll find summat. Or I'll nick his card, he leaves his wallet on the side like a knobhead."
"I'm not a charity," Moxy said. "This ain't Barnardo's. You can't just rock up empty handed and expect-"
He broke off because Brendan's hands were shaking so hard now it was distracting. Proper fine tremor, like he was cold down to the bone even though it wasn't that cold.
"Please," Brendan said. The word came out ragged. "Just sort me a bit to take the edge off, yeah? I'll pay double later. I'll do a run or summat. Whatever. I can't go home like this, she'll twig. She'll drag me to the doctors or some shit. I can't be doing with all that."
Moxy rolled his tongue against his teeth, thinking. The bag in his hoodie pocket felt suddenly heavy. Four tight twists. Four golden tickets. He wanted to get back in his tent and lay them out, look at them properly, savour the possibilities. He didn't need some gobby eighteen-year-old vibrating round the camp when he was trying to focus.
"You're doing my head in," he muttered.

Brendan's face flickered with something like hope. "So…?"

"So, lucky for you, I'm in a generous mood," Moxy said, sucking his teeth.

He fished inside his hoodie, careful to keep his body between the bag and the canal path, and brought the plastic out just enough to get his fingers in. The notes made a soft, satisfying crackle. His fingertips found the smooth, tight cylinder of one of the wraps and he pinched it out, palming it before Brendan could see how many were in there.

He held it up between thumb and forefinger. "One," he said. "On the house. Call it market research."

Brendan snatched at it, then seemed to remember etiquette and forced himself to slow, taking it more carefully. "Market research?"

"Yeah," Moxy said. "New supplier. Want to know if they're worth my time. You test it, give me your honest thoughts. Strength, burn, all that. If it's decent, maybe I can get more. Maybe your little drought ends. Sound fair?"

Brendan stared at the twist like it was a miracle. "Yeah," he breathed. "Yeah, that's… yeah. Course. Whatever you want. I'll give you a full review, TripAdvisor style, write you a fucking essay."

"Don't get clever," Moxy said, though he was faintly amused. "And don't neck it all at once like a dickhead, yeah? Treat it with respect. I want you alive enough to give feedback, not turning blue on me."

Brendan nodded so fast it was almost a twitch. "I'm not stupid."

Moxy raised an eyebrow.

"All right, I'm a bit stupid," Brendan admitted. "But I'm not that stupid. I'll just… a couple o' lines, yeah, see me through. She won't suspect a thing."

He said it with the earnestness of someone whose mum already suspected everything.

"You best had," Moxy said. "Last thing I need is your Ma storming up here with a rolling pin."

Brendan snorted, then sobered, glancing back towards the path that led out. "I should go," he said. "She'll be on my back soon, she always rings. If I miss it, she'll come looking."

"Go on, then," Moxy said, jerking his head. "Remember what I said. Take your time. Text me later, yeah? Market report for the board."

Brendan grinned weakly. "Aye, chairman," he said, backing away. "I'll let you know how your investment's performing."

He tucked the twist deep into his jeans pocket like he was hiding a diamond and trotted off towards the canal, shoulders hunched, hands jammed in his hoodie. Moxy watched him go until the scrub swallowed him.

"Soft arse," he muttered, but there was no heat in it. Junkies begging for freebies was just like the weather; always there, always a bit annoying. You worked round it, but they had their uses, and Brendan had proved his worth. Pension pot and a new supply, double jackpot!

He ducked into the orange tent, zipping the flap behind him. The faint smells of damp nylon, old smoke and sweat closed in. Inside, the light came through greenish, making everything look underwater. His kit was where he'd left it: spoon, lighter, bits of burnt foil, half a bottle of flat Coke.

He settled onto his sleeping bag cross-legged, hauled the plastic bag out proper and laid it reverently on his lap. The notes looked even better in this light, bundled neat with elastic bands. He laid out the three remaining twists, fat and promising.

“Hello, boys,” he murmured.

He took one, rolled it between his fingers, feeling the tightness of the pack, the weight. Different cut, maybe. Different smell, maybe. He held it to his nose and sniffed. There was no smell, damn these were wrapped good. The mark of a true craftsman.

“Fancy,” he said to no one.

He pinched the end and worked the paper open, careful not to spill anything. The powder inside was a little lighter than he was used to, less of the muddy brown, more a beige colour. It clung to the inside of the twist in a dense, fine layer.

“Proper gear,” he said approvingly. “None o’your baby formula shite.”

He tore a strip of foil from the crumpled roll, smoothing it with his thumb, then tipped a little of the powder onto the dull side and teased it into a neat, narrow line with the edge of his national insurance card.

His mouth was already watering, that anticipatory flood that came whenever he was this close. He felt the effects already. This stuff was amazing. His leg started to bounce.

“Market research,” he reminded himself, half-laughing. “Purely professional.”

He flicked the lighter, the flame licking blue under the foil. The metal warmed in his hand. As the powder started to darken and bubble, a rich, synthetic smell rose up, cutting straight through the damp and the tent funk, straight into the old, hungry part of his brain that didn't care about anything except the next ten seconds.

Moxy lowered his head, brought the tube of scorched foil to his lips, and chased half of the first line.

He fell backwards instantly.

Lee Moxon, 23, of no fixed abode, never regained consciousness and the burner with a 32% battery charge was slowly dying with him.

Brendan took the canal path at a half-run, half-stagger, his breath rasping in the cold air. His heart was going like a jackhammer, more from nerves than exertion. Every dog walker, every parked car, every curtain twitch felt like it had eyes.

Number twenty-four sat there in the neat row of semis, pebbledash and UPVC, same as ever. His mum's little blue Fiesta was on the drive. Net curtains in the front room, just high enough that she could see the path if she chose.

He didn't go to the front door.

He veered left on instinct, dropping into the crouch he'd used a dozen times before, squeezing into the shadow of the big overgrown bush by the bay window. It smelt of damp soil and cat piss. From here he could see the hallway if he leaned, the blur of the front room telly through the glass. He held his breath, listening.

No footsteps. No door. No "Brendan?" in that wary, sharp tone.

He let the breath out slowly and fumbled in his pocket for

the twist.

His fingers didn't want to work. They felt fat, clumsy, like someone had swapped them for gloves. For a horrible second, he thought he'd dropped it on the towpath, that it had shaken loose somewhere between the scrub and home. But then his thumb found the edge of paper and his stomach swooped with relief.

"Market research," he muttered under his breath, trying on Moxy's swagger. It came out thin. "Purely professional."

He glanced back at the house again, then hunched tighter into the hedge, shoulders brushing the branches. The twist was tighter than he expected; the paper didn't want to give. His nails worried at the end, tearing more than unravelling. A pinch of powder dusted his thumb.

A shiver ran through him that wasn't entirely from the cold.

"Come on, come on..." he whispered, forcing the paper to open. At last, it did, a little beige drift pooling in the crease of his palm. Lighter than he was used to. Looked… expensive, somehow. Premium.

His nose was streaming; he wiped it on his sleeve, sniffed hard, and bent over his hand. There was no space for ceremony behind the bush, no careful lines, no proper gear. Just urgency and the need to be level before he walked through that front door and looked his mother in the eye.

He brought his hand up and snorted a sharp, stinging breath, dragging as much of the powder in as he could. It hit the back of his nose like fire. He coughed, eyes watering.

"Fuck," he hissed, head tipping back against the brick. "That's… that's strong."

For a heartbeat nothing happened. Then his world tumbled, and he fell face first through the bush into the front garden which was suddenly very quiet.

Brendan Hughes, 18, from Blackburn, England, never regained consciousness.

Act X

The Silence We Share

Chapter Fifty-One

Saturday, 19th April 2025 – 18:45

Blackburn Hospital, HDU, High Dependency Unit

The monitors never shut up.

They didn't scream like in Resus, but they ticked and sighed and pinged in a constant low chorus, a reminder that every beat, every breath was being counted by something that didn't care who any of them were.

Jonah lay propped at forty-five degrees, neck braced, oxygen cannula looping under his nose. The bruising had come out ugly now, blooming from livid red into deep plum and sick yellow at the edges. Tape covered the puncture sites on the backs of his hands. Someone had wiped the worst of the dried blood from his lips, but there was still a rust-coloured shadow along the corner of his mouth.

His eyes were open.

That alone felt like a miracle.

Seth sat on the left side of the bed, Natalia on the right. Izzy had claimed the plastic chair by Jonah's feet and was half-curled in it, chin on her knees. All three of them were still in yesterday's clothes, yesterday's faces, yesterday's adrenaline.

Seth had come back just after four, smelling of shower gel and the outside world. He hadn't said much. He didn't need to. Natalia had met him by the lifts, searched his face, and he'd given her the only three words that mattered.

"It's done, Nat."

She'd nodded once, sharply, and that was that. Daylight front, shutdown. Night front, ongoing.

Now, under the harsh HDU strip light, they were back on the latter.

Jonah's voice was barely there, a dry rasp that sounded like it hurt every time it dragged up his throat. "So… it was him," he whispered, eyes moving from Seth to Natalia and back. "Not… not just a… dream thing. It was him."

Seth swallowed. "Yeah," he said. "It was him."

Jonah's fingers twitched against the blanket. The pulse-ox clipped to his index finger flashed green with every beat. "I could feel his hands," he croaked, voice rough and low. "Still can. It's like they're… inside my skin. Like they're still there if I think about it too hard."

Izzy hugged her knees tighter. "Don't," she said quickly. "Don't think about it too hard, then."

He tried for a smile and managed a ghost of one. "Sound medical advice. Cheers, Iz."

She rolled her eyes, but her mouth softened.

"What do you remember?" Seth asked. He kept his tone as even as he could, like he was taking a statement rather than interrogating his son. "From the field to… here."

Jonah stared past him for a moment, looking at a point somewhere in the middle distance.

"I got to the kitchen door and opened it," he said. "That was wrong straight away. It's never opened before. It felt… warm. Like the kitchen normally does. I thought…" He stopped, swallowed. The movement made him wince. "I thought if I could get in, I could… break it. Or at least see something we hadn't seen before."

"You did see something we hadn't," Natalia said. "You saw him properly, in a different location. Now we know he can move around the sequence."

"…and harm us…" Izzy mused.

Jonah's throat worked. "He was waiting," he murmured. "He was already there. I didn't even see him move. One second the door, next second… just… panic. He scrambled at me, like a dog. Hands on my neck." His own hand lifted to hover over the bruises, then dropped back. "It felt more real than real life. And then… and then I woke up here, with a tube down my throat and your faces hovering over me."

"You're welcome." Seth winked, but his attempt at humour landed heavy.

Izzy shifted, biting her lip. "I was still at the statue past the women. It was… it was massive by then, like it'd had a growth spurt just taller than me in the end. There was some kind of… plate above it on the wall? It looked like it was reaching for it, trying to grow to get to it. When the top of the statue touched it, the dream stopped."

"The statue was trying to touch the house," Seth said, mostly to himself.

"No," Izzy countered. "The plate on the house."

"But there is no plate on the house, just cornices," Nat said bemused.

"Well, there isn't a dark psychotic figure running around the house during the day trying to murder us all, but he's there in the dream, so here we are!"

"Fair point," Nat conceded.

For a moment they just listened to the room breathe for them. The soft hiss of oxygen, the elastic sigh of the blood pressure cuff inflating on the man in the next bay, the distant clatter of a bedpan somewhere out of sight.

"So, what does it mean?" Izzy asked. "The plate thing. The statue stretching. Him inside. The attack."

"We don't know yet," Seth said.

"We know some of it," Natalia countered. "We know he's not fixed. He can move around the sequence. He can wait behind doors. He can get your measure and adapt. He can interact and talk to us, as can his little helper. And we know the statue's interacting with the house in ways we haven't seen in waking life."

Jonah grimaced. "That's comforting."

"It's information," she said. "Comfort comes later."

Izzy chewed her thumbnail, frowning. "The plate," she said slowly. "It looked like some kind of metal. I'm sure it had something written on it."

Seth rubbed a hand over his jaw. "We don't have anything like that on the corner," he said. "We've got the stonework, the cornices, the guttering. No random plates stuck on for fun."

"Not that we've ever really looked," Natalia said. "Not with this in mind. Might just be in the dream. Might be something that was there in the Becker's time and isn't now."

"So… what, ghost masonry?" Jonah rasped. "We're dealing with retrofitted terror cornices now?"

"Don't make me laugh," Izzy said. "It hurts when you talk."

Jonah's eyes creased at the corners. "Hurts when I talk as well," he murmured. "We're all in this together."

Seth leaned back a little, the metal chair complaining. "Alright," he said. "Working theory for now: he's trying to link the statue fully into the house. Hardwire it. That corner piece might be… I don't know. A junction box. Power source. Whatever. We need to investigate that properly."

"Oh, don't worry, I'm sure we'll get an opportunity on Friday to go and have a good gander at it. Which isn't terrifying at all," Izzy shuddered.

"Which is why the statue stays in the shed," Natalia said. "And why, when we do bring it out, it doesn't go anywhere near that side of the house until we understand what it's reaching for and why."

"Until we understand?" Seth echoed. "I'm voting for 'we'll never understand' at this rate."

A rap sounded on the door. Three quick knuckles, familiar rhythm and it opened slightly.

"Permission to enter the war room?" Tam said.

He stood there in civvies: jeans, battered leather jacket, hair still damp from the rain outside. For once he didn't look like the loudest thing in the room. His gaze went straight to Jonah and stayed there.

"Christ, kid," he said quietly. "You look like you lost a fight with a python."

Jonah's mouth twitched. "You should see the other guy," he croaked.

Tam stepped in, crossing the narrow space in three strides. He squeezed Seth's shoulder, clasped Natalia's hand, then leaned over the bed as far as the rails allowed and very gently bumped his forehead against Jonah's.

He moved down to the end of the bed and bent to put an arm round Izzy's shoulders, hauling her into a brief, fierce hug that made her nose sting. "You alright, wee yin?" he asked.

"Define alright," she said into his jacket.

"Away wi' yer," he said, letting her go. "You're still gobby, so you're fine."

When he straightened, some of the softness went out of his face. He looked from Seth to Natalia again, that quick assessment he did when he was about to start a briefing.

"Can I grab you two for a minute?" he asked. "Outside. Won't be long."

Natalia glanced at Jonah. "We'll be just there," she said. "Shout if you need us."

Jonah nodded, eyes already drooping again.

They stepped out into the corridor with Tam. Out here the light was somehow harsher, the smell of disinfectant stronger. Tam walked a few paces down to a slightly wider bit near the fire door and turned on them.

"What the fuck are you playing at?" he said, low and flat.

Seth blinked. "Good to see you too, mate."

Tam ignored that. "When you told me about the dreams," he went on, "I thought – right. Classic. Military trauma, guilt, stress. You've dragged the whole clan into a nice, shared PTSD picnic, we calm that down, we manage your external threats, we get you through it. I did not think, 'In a week, the lad'll be sitting in HDU lookin' like somebody's tried to throttle him with their thumbs.'"

"We didn't do this to him," Seth said.

"Aye?" Tam's voice stayed quiet, but there was steel under it. "Because from where I'm standing, someone did and it was no fucking dream. Thumbs on the neck, four-point bruising, airway crushed. That's hands, Seth. Flesh and bone. Not night terrors."

"You think one of us, did it?" Natalia asked. There was no outrage in it, just a cold sort of curiosity.

Tam looked between them. "I think I've seen good people do some very stupid, very desperate things when they're pushed to the wall," he said. "I think I've just helped you put a very dangerous, very final plan into motion on the understanding that we were dealing with bad lads and bad evidence, not… this." He jerked his chin towards the room. "If there's anything you're not telling me..."

"There isn't," Seth cut in. "You know as much as we do."

Tam's eyes narrowed. "Do I, though?"

"We told you about the dream, the field. It's real Tam," Natalia said. "The girl. The women. The figure. The statue. The way it escalated. You thought we were being poetic about nightmares. We weren't."

"With respect, Nat, what you described sounded a lot like

trauma bleeding into sleep," Tam said. "Soldiers get it. Kids of soldiers get it. You get it." He tapped his own temple. "Brains love patterns. Brains love symbols. Statues and fields and running towards helpless wee lasses, that's… textbook."

"And textbook nearly crushed his windpipe?" Seth said. "Come on. You saw his neck."

"I can see the aftermath of an attack," Tam said. "What I didn't see is what happened between you four closing your eyes and him hitting the deck. You said you were going back in, week after week, poking the bear, trying to reconnaissance. You said you were conducting experiments."

"We are," Natalia said.

"So, you'll forgive me for asking if any of those experiments involved touchin', shakin', restraining him in the real world to see if it influenced the dream. Sleep paralysis games. Wake-training. That kind of shite. Because if it did, you need to tell me now, before some registrar with a safeguarding leaflet and half a clue decides this looks like non-accidental injury and flags it as domestic abuse."

"No," Seth said. "We didn't lay a hand on him. Not like that. We all went under at the same time. We all woke up at the same time. We all saw him go down. In there." He jabbed a finger towards his own chest. "In the field."

"Finger marks match," Natalia added. "He described the pressure in exactly the places the bruises are. And the timing. He stopped breathing at home at the same moment the figure choked him in the dream. We were there, Tam. We watched it."

Tam rubbed a hand over his face, exhaling slowly. "I am a

simple man, Nat," he said. "I like cause and effect. I like maths and physics. I can follow 'you lace the gear; a bad bastard dies'. I can follow 'you give a junkie a lifeline; he tries to blackmail you'. I cannot follow 'paranormal prick from your collective subconscious pops round and tries to murder your lad in his sleep'."

"Nor can we," Natalia said. "But that doesn't stop it happening."

He looked at her for a long moment. "You believe this," he said. It wasn't a question.

"Yes," she said.

"And you?" he asked Seth.

Seth thought of the hands, the sound Jonah hadn't made, the ugly bands round his throat. Of the line from the field that had followed them into the front bedroom at Moorside. If I may touch, then so may I take.

"I've believed in worse men than him," he said. "At least this one's honest about wanting us dead."

Tam snorted. "That's not actually reassuring."

"You asked," Seth said.

Tam braced one hand against the wall by the fire door and thumped his head lightly against his forearm, once, twice. When he straightened, his expression had shifted from angry to something like resigned.

"Right," he said. "For the sake of argument, let's say you're not mad and I'm not daft. Then this stops. The experiments. The nightmare reconnaissance missions. All of it."

"We're already thinking the same," Natalia replied. "We stand down. We sleep when we can and we treat whatever comes as defensive only. No more poking."

"Good," Tam said. "Because I swear, if you'd looked me in the eye just now and told me you were going back in next week for another look, I'd have dragged social services in here myself and let them adjudicate."

Seth's mouth twisted. "You love us really."

"I do," Tam said. "That's why I'm here instead of having a nice quiet pint somewhere that doesn't beep at me every three seconds.

"Look, I can mitigate what you've set in motion in the daylight. I can manage your wee extortionist and his tech. That's my playground. But I cannot shoot this thing in the face for you, because it doesnae have one. So, until we know more, I'll be staying with you at Moorside. Deal?"

"Deal," Natalia said, without looking at Seth.

Seth hesitated for the briefest fraction, then nodded. "Deal," he echoed.

"Good." Tam rolled his shoulders, like he usually does when he's decided. "Now let's go back in there and look like a normal, functional support network, aye? Before Nurse Clipboard decides I'm an inappropriate influence."

They walked back to the bay together. Tam let them go through the curtain first, then followed, his face rearranged into something closer to his usual sardonic calm.

As if on cue, a nurse in navy scrubs appeared, clutching a tablet. Different from before – this one had her hair in a plait and "A. Patel – Staff Nurse" on her badge.

"Evening," she said, keeping her voice low. "Sorry to disturb, just wanted to give you a bit of an update."

Seth straightened. "Good or bad?"
"Good," she said with a quick smile. "ENT are very pleased with how the airway's settling. The swelling's gone down a lot since this morning, his blood gases are much happier, and his observations have been nice and steady for the last few hours."
Natalia exhaled. "That's… good," she said, as if she didn't quite trust the word.
"If things carry on the way they are," Nurse Patel went on, "the plan is to step him down to a standard ward tomorrow or Monday, then look at sending him home on Tuesday. Obviously, that depends on him keeping well and being able to manage his pain and eating. But that's the trajectory we're on."
"Tuesday," Seth repeated, like he was testing the shape of the day in his mouth.
"Aye," Tam said softly. "Home in time for crap weekday telly."
Izzy's head lifted from her phone. "Home," she said, the syllable coming out half-relief, half-question.
"We'll give you written information before you go," the nurse added. "Signs to watch for, when to come back, follow-up with ENT. But yes. If he keeps going like this, Tuesday's realistic."
"Thank you," Natalia said. This time the word sounded like it belonged to her.
Nurse Patel smiled again. "You're welcome. I'll leave you to it. Just buzz if you need anything."
She slipped away, the door closing behind her.
For a few heartbeats they sat in a quiet that felt different. Not the brittle, waiting kind, but something looser, with a tiny

bit of air in it.
“Tuesday,” Izzy said again. “That’s… soon.”
“That’s awesome. We’ll be ready,” Seth said. “We’ll make it work.”
Jonah stirred a little, not quite waking, but his mouth moved. Natalia reached out automatically, resting her fingertips on the back of his hand.
“Hey,” she murmured. “You’re doing brilliantly. You hear me? We’ll get you home.”
Outside Nurse Patel made her way back to the nurses’ station. She logged into the terminal and opened the web browser. She navigated past the usual notifications and reminders and double clicked on the “Adult Safeguarding Report” icon and pressed ‘New Report’. She started to fill in the form.
Back in the room Izzy was hooked to her phone as usual, the habit too strong to fight, thumb resuming its slow, unconscious scroll with the beep of the monitors in the background. Notifications, reels, ads. A post about someone’s dog, another about a sale at Primark. A local group - Blackburn Community Chat - slid into view.
She almost flicked past it. Then a name snagged.
Brendan Hughes.
Her thumb froze. The post was a photo. Brendan pulling a stupid face at the camera, eyes half-closed in mock outrage. Underneath, a block of text. Her eyes raced over the first line, then the next.
Her stomach dropped.
“Oh my God,” she breathed.
Nobody looked up straight away; they’d heard that tone too

often in the last twenty-four hours. It was only when she made a kind of strangled, disbelieving noise and sat bolt upright that Seth turned.

"What?" he said sharply. "Izzy, what?"

She didn't answer. Her finger jabbed at the screen, scrolling frantically down the comment thread - crying-face emojis, broken hearts, "RIP lad", "can't believe this", "gone too soon". Her hand was shaking.

"Izzy," Natalia said, warning threading her voice. "What is it?"

Izzy swallowed, throat working. She turned the phone round with both hands and held it out so they could all see.

On the screen, above a flood of condolences, the post sat stark and simple:

RIP Brendan Hughes
18, Blackburn.
Taken from us far too soon.

Chapter Fifty-Two

Monday, 21st April 2025 – 09:14

Moorside House, Kitchen

Sunday hadn't really ended. It had just frayed at the edges and reformed into this: grey light over the car port and a sky the colour of milk.

They'd spent most of yesterday in transit. Moorside to Blackburn Hospital. Hospital back to Moorside. One run to pick up fresh clothes and phone chargers, another to drop off a bag for Jonah, another because someone had realised they'd not actually eaten since… whenever it had been.

The day blurred into corridors, the chimes of lifts and the rubber smell of hospital floors, punctured only by nurses' polite smiles and the watery coffee from vending machines that had never heard of the word 'strength'.

Tam had landed in the middle of it and simply folded himself into their pattern. He'd done the quiet walk round the house late afternoon, boots on the flagstones, gaze ticking over windows, doors, fence lines, as if he was back on patrol. By evening they'd cleared the last of the boxes out of the granny flat, dragged a second-hand chest of drawers into the corner, and given him a base: bed, desk, lamp, a tiny bathroom that steamed faster than the extractor fan could cope with. He'd plugged in his battered laptop, set his Peli case on the floor, and told them, in that calm, unarguable tone, that he was sorted.

"Go sit with your lad," he'd said. "I'm not the one wi' the crushed windpipe."

So, Sunday had disappeared into tasks. Practicalities. Drop offs. Check ins. A nurse gently explaining oxygen sats. Jonah drifting in and out with the dull, bruised-apple look of someone whose body hadn't quite decided if it trusted the world again. They'd skirted the edges of 'the post', the one Izzy had shown them on her phone in HDU, the words "RIP Brendan Hughes" burned into all their retinas.

They'd not had space to feel much of anything about it. Not properly.

This morning there was nowhere else to put it.

Seth sat at the table with his hands wrapped round a mug that had gone lukewarm a while ago. He'd shaved badly; a pale line of missed stubble traced his jaw. His eyes kept flicking towards the back door, like he half-expected someone to walk through it and call his bluff.

Natalia sat opposite, elbows on the table, fingers laced into her hair. Her phone lay face-down between them, screen buzzing every now and then against the wood. Condolences. Comments. News alerts. She didn't flip it over.

Steam feathered the kitchen window, blurring the view of the car port. The air still smelled faintly of bleach and yesterday's garlic from the pan left to soak in the sink.

"He was just a kid," Seth said finally, voice low.

Natalia let out a humourless breath. "He was eighteen, Seth."

"Yeah." He stared at the swirl of tea leaves at the bottom of his mug. "That's what everyone'll say. Eighteen, knew better, made his choices."

"And we'll say?" Natalia asked.

Seth's mouth twisted. "We'll say we've known him since he was nine and turned up here with shoes on the wrong feet and a lunchbox with Power Rangers on it."

She could see the scene as he said it. Brendan on the step, too small for his oversize school jumper, hair sticking up like he'd slept on it damp. Jonah at his shoulder, solemn and proud, introducing his "new mate" as if he'd personally discovered him.

"They spent that whole summer in the paddling pool," she murmured. "Do you remember? Jonah's lips were blue half the time but neither of them would come in."

"You bribed them with choc ices," Seth said. "Didn't work."

"I had to drag Brendan home by his backpack more than once." A small smile ghosted at the corner of her mouth then slipped away. "Jane used to say we were running a crèche."

"Yeah, well." He shifted, shoulders bunching. "Feels like we've done a piss-poor job of it."

Natalia looked up sharply. "Don't. Don't you dare start that."

He met her eyes, defensive, then let his gaze drop again. "Tell me you don't feel it."

"Of course I feel it," she said. "Of course I do. I feel sick when I think about it. That's not the same as it being our fault."

"His mum's going to need someone to blame." Seth rubbed his thumb over the handle of the mug, the ceramic squeaking faintly.

All the lies. The rehearsed scripts. Jonah's charge sheet, the court dates, the way Brendan's name had threaded through every conversation like a knot. They'd built their survival on keeping distance between their family and his, on telling themselves it was necessary to stay away.

Now he was dead.

"Look," Seth said after a moment. "Bottom line? He didn't die here. He didn't die because of us."

"We don't know how he died Seth," Natalia replied quietly.

Seth flinched. "Aye. Could have been anything."

"You should reach out to Jane, see how she is." Seth said again, softer this time. "She would do the same if it was you."

Natalia's phone buzzed against the table. Once. Twice. A third time.

She stared at it for a heartbeat, then reached for it, thumb swiping the screen awake. The notifications flickered past: local news headlines, a Facebook group post, WhatsApp messages in the family chat they shared with Jonah and Izzy. One stood out. "Jane Hughes".

Natalia opened it.

'Hi Nat. I'm so sorry you had to find out like that. The police said they'd be in touch with you anyway because of before. I didn't want you hearing it from some stranger in a uniform.'

Her throat tightened. She swallowed and typed back carefully.

'Jane, we're so, so sorry. We only saw the post last night at the hospital. How are you?'

Three dots appeared, vanished, reappeared. Natalia could almost see Jane pacing her small hallway, phone clenched in one hand, the other worrying at the hem of her jumper.

'How am I? I don't know. I can't think straight. Everything's a blur. He went out for fresh air and never came in the front door. Police said it might be drugs. Alan's just staring at the telly. I don't know what to do.'

Natalia exhaled slowly. "She says they think it might be drugs… What if…" she said aloud.

Seth's jaw clenched and he looked her in shock. "No, there's no link Nat, whatever it was it was nothing to do with Saturday."

"There is a link Seth, Brendan planned the robbery. Bossman and 'Steven' clearly had access to Brendan." Natalia's thumbs hovered over the keyboard.

Seth's face drained of blood, and he went drip white.

"We need to find out, I'll ask." She typed: 'Have they said anything else? Are you alone? Do you want me to come over?'

The reply came faster this time.

'They'll be back later. The policewoman from before. Sarah. I can't even remember what she said last night. I'm not on my own, Alan's here, but it feels… I don't know. A friendly face would be nice. If you're not too busy.'

Natalia didn't realise she'd started to nod until Seth spoke.

"Are you going?" he asked.

She looked up. "Is that alright with you?"

"Of course it's bloody alright." He pushed his mug away and

scraped a hand back through his hair. "Jane shouldn't be sat over there on her own thinking we're hiding from her."

"We have been hiding from her; Jonah isn't allowed anywhere near," Natalia said.

He grimaced. "Yeah. Well. Maybe today's the day we stop."

The back door clicked and swung inward. Tam stepped in, stooping slightly as if the frame was lower than it was. He'd changed into clean jeans and a dark T-shirt, bare feet in someone's old slippers. His hair stuck up on one side where he'd clearly dragged a hand through it instead of bothering with a comb.

"Alright?" he said, taking in the set of their faces, the phone between them, the untouched tea.

"Not really," Seth said.

"Aye, well. It'd be suspicious if you were." Tam moved to the kettle, lifted it, judged the weight, and flicked it on. "How's Jonah?"

"Stable," Natalia replied. "No change yet. They're keeping him on the ward for observation. We're going back in this afternoon."

Tam nodded, his expression tightening briefly at the word 'stable'. "Good. Boring's what we want."

He reached up into the cupboard for mugs, the movement easy and practised already. It was unsettling, how quickly he'd slotted into their kitchen, like a piece of furniture that had always been there.

Natalia stood, chair scraping. "Jane... Brendan's mum asked if I could go round," she said. "She… found out officially last night. She's struggling."

Tam's hand stilled on the cupboard door. "Understandable."

Seth glanced at him. "You think it's wise?"

Tam frowned. "Going to see the mother of a dead lad you've known since he was knee-high? Aye. On balance, I'd say that qualifies as wise."

"I meant with…" Seth gestured vaguely. "Everything. Police. History."

"History is there whether you visit or not," Tam said. "Better she sees your faces now, when it's fresh, then she listens to the neighbours fill in the blanks for her." He gave a small shrug, "Besides, his death is nothing to do with you." His gaze softened. "Go Nat, comfort your friend."

Natalia grabbed her keys from the hook by the door and shrugged into her coat. The sleeves still smelled faintly of whatever disinfectant the hospital used.

"Text me when you get there," Seth said.

She nodded, thumb already sliding over the screen to tap out a quick reply to Jane.

On my way. Ten minutes x

Outside, the April air hit her with a chill she hadn't been expecting. The sky was bright without being cheerful, that flat Lancashire kind of blue that made everything look slightly washed out. She crossed the gravel, the crunch underfoot oddly loud, and dropped into the driver's seat of the car.

For a moment she just sat, fingers on the steering wheel, breath fogging the inside of the windscreen. A flicker of memory rose unbidden: Brendan at twelve, gangly and sunburnt, holding up a bent bike wheel in the driveway and asking if Seth could "have a go" at fixing it. His grin when

Seth produced a spare inner tube from the shed like a magician.

"Fucking hell," she whispered, and swallowed hard.

She started the engine.

The drive to Blackburn felt shorter than it had any right to. Familiar landmarks slid past in a blur: the petrol station with the permanently broken air machine, the row of takeaways, the mini roundabout where Jonah had stalled the car during one of his first driving lessons and sworn never to show his face again.

She turned into the Hughes' crescent. The drizzle had left everything damp edged. The pavements shone, and bins huddled in little plastic clusters by garden gates. Number twenty-four looked the same as it had on the night Brendan had reappeared weeks earlier, yet completely different. Curtains half-drawn in the front room. A lamp burning in the hallway even though it was daytime. A police car wasn't outside, but she could almost see the ghost of one, tyre tracks imprinted on her memory.

Natalia parked a few doors down and walked the rest of the way, heart thumping unexpectedly hard. Her hand hesitated for a second before she knocked.

The door opened quicker than she'd braced for, as if Jane had been standing just behind it.

She looked smaller. That was Natalia's first thought. Smaller and somehow hollowed out, like someone had reached in and scooped a handful from her middle. Her hair was scraped back in a messy knot, streaks of grey more visible than they'd been last time. She wore a fleece with pyjama bottoms and her feet shoved into old trainers with the laces undone.

"Nat." Jane's voice broke on the second syllable.

"Hi, love," Natalia said softly. "Can I come in?"

Jane nodded, stepping back automatically. "Course. Sorry. I've not… tidied. Or anything."

The hallway smelled of stale cooking and something chemical. Disinfectant, maybe, or one of those plug-in air fresheners trying and failing to mask it all. A pile of post lay on the console table, untouched. The living room door stood half-open and from inside came the low murmur of the television, someone on the news talking about something that suddenly didn't matter at all.

"Alan's in there," Jane said, following Natalia's glance. "He hasn't moved since… I don't even know what time it is."

"It's just after nine thirty," Natalia said. "In the morning."

Jane blinked, as if that information didn't quite connect. "Right. Morning." She hugged herself, fingers digging into her own forearms. "Do you want a brew? Everyone keeps offering me tea. I've made about twelve and drunk none of them."

"Let me make it," Natalia said gently. "You sit down."

Jane hesitated, then shook her head. "If I sit, I won't get up again." Her lips twitched in something that might once have been a joke. "I feel like if I stop moving, that's it. It'll… land."

Natalia reached out and took her hand. It was cold, the knuckles rough and chapped. Jane gripped back like a drowning woman.

"Then don't sit," Natalia said. "Not yet. Come and stand in the kitchen with me. You can tell me what's happened while

I badly operate your kettle."

Something in Jane's face crumpled at the word "tell". The tears that had clearly been threatening for hours finally pushed through, spilling over. She pressed her free hand to her mouth, shoulders shaking.

Natalia stepped forward and pulled her into a hug.

Jane's body was full of tension at first, then collapsed, arms winding around Natalia's waist, fingers clawing at the back of her coat. She made a small, animal sound against Natalia's shoulder. Natalia held onto her and would do for as long as Jane needed.

"He's gone," she sobbed. "My boy's gone, Nat."

"I know," Natalia whispered into her hair. "I'm so, so sorry."

"Police said it was drugs… But not the 'normal' kind, some kind of super strong stuff, apparently the paramedic was affected as well when he got here."

Natalia froze, eyes widening, thanking the Lord that her face was over Jane's shoulder. She felt weak at the knees and sick to the stomach. She started to squeeze Jane tighter.

They stood there in the narrow hallway, two women clinging to each other while the television murmured rubbish in the background and the world outside continued as if nothing had shifted.

For the first time since Izzy had turned that phone screen round in HDU, Natalia let herself feel the full weight of it. Deep down she'd known. Coincidences like this don't happen. She remembered Brendan laughing in her kitchen. Brendan sulking at the bottom of the stairs when Jonah was grounded. Brendan's trainers dumped by the back door, toe to toe with Jonah's.

She closed her eyes, holding Jane tighter and sobbed, the grim reality of their plans and actions coming home to roost.

This was the type of collateral damage she never envisioned, and deep down knew she could not live with, but would have to.

Chapter Fifty-Three

Tuesday, 22nd April 2025 – 10:36

Blackburn Hospital

Seth had not slept so much as blacked out in short, useless bursts, each one ending the same way: Jane's voice in Natalia's retelling, saying "super strong stuff" and "apparently the paramedic was affected". Every time he surfaced he saw Brendan on the path, grey and still, the bags, the neat white twists Tam had set out like bullets on plastic.

By the time they reached the hospital car park his stomach felt lined with gravel as they made the way to Jonah's ward.

"We don't know it's us for certain," Natalia quietly lied as they walked in, subconsciously wringing her hands. "It could be something else. The toxicology will be at least two weeks."

"Yeah," Seth muttered in a dishevelled voice. "Right. 'Super strong stuff' that also affects paramedics attending the scene is doing the rounds in Blackburn."

On the ward Jonah was already dressed, perched on the edge

of the bed in a hoodie and joggers that seemed to hang looser than they had on Saturday. The bruising along his throat had gone from violent red to a sick yellow brown, mottled at the edges. The cannula had gone but the tape marks remained like ghosts.

"You look rough," Seth said, because anything softer might crack him.

Jonah managed a crooked grin. "Must be like looking in the mirror!"

Natalia rolled her eyes and kissed his forehead, careful of the bruises. "Don't make me tell your sister you've run off with all the good jokes."

A nurse appeared with a clipboard and a practised smile. There was a little flurry of signatures, discharge notes, leaflets about follow-up appointments and warning signs. "If he feels short of breath or dizzy, or if the pain gets worse, ring straight away," she said, eyes flicking from Jonah to Natalia, then to Seth. "He's young. That's in his favour. But this was… close."

"We know," Seth said, the words sticking.

Jonah slid off the bed. He moved stiffly but under his own steam, one hand pressed to his ribs. Natalia took his bag while Seth hovered at his shoulder, ready to grab him if he swayed. They made their way down the corridor at a slow, shuffling pace, past other beds, other families, other small catastrophes.

Outside, the air tasted different. Less filtered, more real. The car park shimmered slightly in the thin sun. Seth unlocked the car and eased Jonah into the front passenger seat, adjusting the belt so it didn't bite across his chest.

"Home sweet home," Jonah said as they pulled out, voice soft.

"Something like that," Seth replied.

The drive back to Moorside ran on muscle memory. Roundabouts, traffic lights, the familiar smear of retail parks and terraced rows. Jonah watched it all go past as if he'd never seen any of it before. Natalia sat in the back, phone in her hand, eyes on the back of Jonah's head as though she could keep him alive by sheer attention.

Halfway up the bypass Jonah cleared his throat. "Mum… Brendan. Is it true?"

Natalia met Seth's gaze in the rear-view mirror. There was no good angle.

"It's true," she said. "We can talk about it when you're settled, love. One thing at a time."

Jonah nodded once, jaw working, and turned back to the window.

The last few weeks had been highly intense, but the last five days had been almost unbearable. The stress, the strain, the drain on the conscious and subconscious mind was unrelenting and both Seth and Natalia were at their very limits.

That's why neither of them noticed the black Range Rover Velar that had been following them to and from the hospital since Monday afternoon.

Chapter Fifty-Four

Tuesday, 22nd April 2025 – 15:59

Moorside House

The knock came just as the kettle clicked off.

Natalia froze with her hand on the teabag caddy. Three short raps, polite but definite. Not the postman. Not Izzy's friends. Too late in the day for deliveries.

Through the kitchen window she could see part of it: sleek black paint, high bonnet, a flash of alloy. A black Range Rover.

Seth caught her eye. "Expecting anyone?"

"No."

They both listened for a second knock. It came. Same rhythm.

"I'll get it," Natalia said, wiping her palms on her jeans.

The hallway felt cooler than the kitchen. She opened the door on the chain first, then slid it free.

The woman on the step had a poise that suggested she was

used to walking into rooms that didn't belong to her and taking charge anyway. Dark blonde hair twisted up off her collar, a camel wool coat open over a navy blouse and tailored trousers. She looked in her forties but was clearly a lot older, with fine lines at the eyes that spoke more of laughter than stress. This woman clearly took care of herself.

"Mrs Overaugh?" she asked, American vowels softened by something older. "I'm so sorry to turn up unannounced."

"Yes…" Natalia said slowly. "Can I help you?"

The woman's smile flickered, contrite. "I hope so. My name's Charlotte Richardson. I mailed last month about the house and the… family connection. I was in Europe for work and there was a gap in my schedule, so I flew in earlier than planned. I should have called first, I know, but I didn't have a contact number." She lifted a hand, helpless.

Natalia's stomach dipped. The airmail. The one she'd half-thought a crank message at first, then filed away, meaning to deal with it after Jonah's next court date. Or after the incident with the statue. Or after Brendan.

"Right. Yes. Of course..." She forced her mouth into something like a welcome. "You caught us at a busy time but… come in, please."

Charlotte's relief looked genuine. Natalia caught the faint scent of expensive perfume, citrus and something darker underneath.

"In here," Natalia said, leading her through to the kitchen. "We were just making tea."

Sleeves pushed up; Tam had shifted to the island. A row of metal skewers was laid out on a chopping board. He worked methodically, sliding chunks of marinated chicken on to the skewers one by one, then tucking in discs of red onion and fat pieces of pepper, nudging them down the skewer with his thumb, so the colours sat snug together. The air was thick with garlic and lemon and the faint sweetness of paprika.

Seth sat at the table scrolling mindlessly through his phone, looking transfixed. He looked up as Natalia came in.

"This is Charlotte," Natalia began. "Charlotte Richardson. Her family used to live here."

Tam turned.

For a moment the room narrowed to the space between them. Charlotte's eyebrows lifted a fraction, something like amusement or interest flickering in her eyes. Tam straightened a little, shoulders squaring, the easy slouch gone. Seth noticed he'd sucked his stomach in.

"Charlotte, this is..." Natalia started.

Tam cut across and in front of her, the Edinburgh in his voice sharpening like he'd taken it out of storage and polished it. "Andrew Tamlin," he said, offering his hand. "But my friends call me Tam."

Her handshake was firm and cool. "Pleasure to meet you, Mr Tamlin."

"Oh, Tam please, and likewise," he replied, holding her gaze a heartbeat longer than politeness demanded.

Seth watched the exchange and bit down on a smile. Andrew now, was it? That was going in the vault for later.

Natalia cleared her throat. "And this is my husband, Seth."

Seth rose, wiping his palm on his jeans before taking Charlotte's hand. "Welcome to Moorside House," he said.

"Sorry about the mess. It's been… a week."

Jonah appeared in the doorway from the snug, hoodie hanging loose over his bruised throat, Izzy hovering behind him halfway down the stairs.

"Mum? Who's -"

"This is Charlotte," Natalia said. "Charlotte Richardson. Charlotte, this is Jonah and our daughter, Izzy."

"Hi," Jonah croaked.

"Alright," Izzy echoed.

"Hello," Charlotte said, smiling at them both. "My goodness, you look like you've been in the wars." She looked at the marks a shade longer than average person would.

"Err yeah, I had a nasty run in with some battle ropes whilst working out at the gym."

She nodded politely. "Well, thank you for letting me intrude like this. And please, call me Lottie. All my friends do."

The name hit the room like a dropped glass.

Jonah's head snapped round to Seth. Izzy's fingers tightened on the banister. Natalia felt the hairs rise on her arms.

Charlotte's smile faltered. "That's… odd?" she said lightly. "You all just looked at each other like I'd sworn."

"It's nothing," Seth said too quickly. "Just… a familiar name."

"Interesting." she retorted.

Tam broke the moment. "So, Lottie," he said, leaning back against the counter with what he clearly thought was casual charm. "What line of work brings you gallivanting across the Atlantic to our wee corner of Lancashire?"

Her mouth quirked. "I run a consultancy. Richardson-Occult out of Russian Hill, California."

Izzy blinked. "Occult?"

Charlotte nodded, elaborating on the truth slightly to suit her needs. "Yes, we investigate anomalous events, legacy sites, that sort of thing. Old houses with long memories, families that think they're cursed, objects that don't behave the way objects ought to.

"I'm a historian by training, and my business partner is a physicist. Between us, we try to separate folklore from… whatever's left over."

Natalia felt the hairs on the back of her neck stand on end. "And people pay you for that?"

"Quite handsomely, yes," Charlotte said lightly. "Mostly they pay for reassurance. We audit the stories they've been telling themselves for generations and see which ones stand up to scrutiny. If there's a rational explanation, we find it. If there isn't, we help them manage and cope with the effects."

Tam snorted, impressed despite himself. "So, you're a ghostbuster with a balance sheet."

"I prefer 'specialist consultant in occult antiquities'," she replied. "But sure. 'Antique Ghostbuster' works, if you must."

"And you're not scared handling all those objects?" Jonah asked. His voice came out scratchier than he intended.

"Oh, I'm scared all the time," Charlotte said, as if that was the most natural thing in the world. "That's why I've lived long enough to bore you with it."

Tam seized the opening. "My remit's not dissimilar," he said, straightening. "Former military. Tours here and there, mostly places you wouldn't choose for your summer holidays. I now provide bespoke risk solutions and export management to high-net-worth individuals and corporations operating in hostile territories. Extraction, convoy management, counter-surveillance, training. I've been shot at on four continents and stabbed three times, and that's just by people who liked me."

Charlotte's eyebrows rose. "Impressive." She nodded.

Seth coughed into his fist to hide a grin. Natalia narrowed her eyes at the "stabbed three times" portion but let it go.

"Well," Charlotte said, smiling at Tam. "It's good to know there's someone on site with a practical head. Between you and me, I've spent too many nights in old houses with nothing but a nervous caretaker and a dodgy lock for company."

"Any time you need a proper survey done, madam, you let me know," Tam said, the Edinburgh rolled out to its fullest.

"Alright, Rambo," Seth cut in mildly. "Give the woman a chance to sit down before you sign her up for a fire fight."

Natalia reached for a mug, then stopped, turning the conversation with a small pivot. "You said in your letter that your family lived here. Your mother. How is she?"

A shadow passed behind Charlotte's expression. "She's ninety-one now," she said. "In a nursing home in the States. Sharp as a tack some days, away with the fairies on others."

"Oh," Natalia said softly. "I'm sorry. That must be hard."

"It is," Charlotte admitted, then gave a small shrug, as if realigning herself. "But she talks about this house the same way she always has. Like it's a person she had to leave behind rather than a place. I promised her I'd see it properly one day. Not just from the gate."

"When did she live here?" Seth asked.

"From 1938 to 1942," Charlotte said. "Her name's Meredith Hawthorn. My aunt, her twin, was also called Charlotte, I'm named after her. Everyone called her Lottie, so I suppose I was always destined to inherit the nickname." She gave a small, wry smile. "They moved into the house with their parents, Patricia and James, my grandparents. Patricia Hawthorn, née Thompson. James flew Spitfires in the RAF."

"The war," Seth said softly.

"Yes. He was shot down over France in 1942. They got word he was missing, presumed dead. My mother was eight." Charlotte's gaze drifted past them, to the window, as if she could see younger versions of her family moving about in the garden. "My grandmother, Patricia… didn't cope very well. My mother said the house changed. No laughter. No music. Just waiting."

"What happened to your aunt?" Izzy asked, voice small.

Charlotte's fingers traced the rim of her mug. "She went missing in 1942 as well. Vanished without a trace. No one knows what happened to her."

Izzy's hand crept to the back of Jonah's chair.

"My grandmother died later that year," Charlotte went on. "In her sleep, according to the doctor. Grief, if you ask anyone who knew her. The War Office finally confirmed in 1944 that my grandfather wasn't dead after all. He'd been in occupied territory, trying to make his way back."

"By the time he did… his wife was gone, one daughter missing, the other had been sent to America to live with my great-grandparents in California. He came back to this house for a few months but… he died here as well."

"Did Meredith ever come back here?" Natalia asked.

"Not to live here," Charlotte said. "She always said it would break her to see it without them. She came close a couple of times when we were over visiting England, but she never quite made it." Her mouth tightened. "These days she can't travel at all. So, I'm the one with the boarding passes.

"She kept clippings," Charlotte added, the words coming a little faster now, as if they'd learned their route long ago. "Old photographs. Floor plans my grandfather drew on the back of envelopes. She'd point to rooms and tell me which corner the piano sat in, where the Christmas tree went, which step on the stairs creaked if you stepped on it wrong." She smiled, then let it fade. "When it became clear she'd never leave the nursing home, she made me promise I'd come and stand on the land for both of us. Make sure someone was looking after it."

Seth and Natalia exchanged a look that was part horror, part deep, bone-level understanding.

"That's a very tragic story," Seth said, because the silence felt too dense. "I'm sorry your family went through that."

"Thank you," Charlotte said. "My mother has always insisted the house wasn't to blame. That something else holds on to what you give it, for better or worse. She never explained what she thought that was."

Natalia set her mug down a little too firmly. "Well," she said briskly. "If you've come all this way to see it, we should do more than keep you in the kitchen. Would you like to see the grounds? The estate?"

Charlotte's face lit, despite the heaviness of what she'd just shared. “I’d love that.”

“Come on then,” Natalia said, reaching for her coat. “I’ll show you the garden and the field. It’s better from the back.”

Charlotte picked up her handbag. “Will you all be joining us?”

“Jonah’s only just out of hospital,” Seth said. “He needs to rest. I’ll catch up in a minute.”

“I’ll make a start,” Natalia said. “Before the clouds change their mind.” She glanced at Seth, a quick, loaded look that said later. “Come on, Lottie.”

Charlotte followed her to the back door. As she passed Tam, she gave him a small nod. “Don’t let them drink all the tea without us.”

“I’ll ration it,” he said. “Old habits.”

The back door closed behind them with a soft click. The noise of their footsteps on the flagstones faded towards the garden.

For a moment the kitchen was very quiet.

“Christ,” Seth breathed. “Shot down, missing, one twin vanishes, the other shipped off, everyone dead or scattered within a couple of years. That’s… a lot. Even for this place.”

“Poor Meredith,” Izzy said. “Imagine being that age and just getting… exported. Ending up in a different country with strangers.”

“Lottie,” Jonah murmured. He rubbed his thumb over the edge of the table, jaw tight. “They never found her. She could be anywhere.”

Seth glanced at him. “You mean in terms of…” He hesitated, searching for a safer word than ghosts. “Stories.”

"In terms of us," Jonah said. "In the field. The dreams. We've seen her, Dad. Over and over. If there was no body, no grave… where did she go? We know what happened to her in the field when she was snatched, but what happened after that?"

Tam, who had been standing by the counter with his arms folded, spoke for the first time since the door had shut. "Missing folk in wartime isn't exactly rare," he said. "Blackout, no streetlights, people moving through who shouldn't be there. Bad types flourish when everything else is chaos. People abducting children was not as uncommon as you think."

"This isn't just 'bad types'," Jonah said. "We've been watching her get taken, over and over. Same van parked outside the house, same statue. Same figure. It's like someone is pressing replay on a memory and is making us sit through it every single week, only now the lead actor is on a rampage."

"Ah, the bogeyman in the weird dreams again," Tam snorted lifting his mug to drink.

"The bogeyman doesn't strangle nearly fully grown adults in their sleep Tam." Seth snarled.

Tam did not press the issue.

The only person that was quiet was Izzy. Seth realised she looked disturbed. He held out his hand to touch Izzy's. "What's wrong love, are you okay?"

She looked him dead in the eye, everyone else was silent.

"Dad," Izzy said, voice quieter now but firm. "What was in that crate you found?"

Chapter Fifty-Five

Tuesday, 22nd April 2025 – 16:24

Moorside House, Grounds

The air felt different outside. Thinner, somehow. The kind that made you aware of every lungful.

Natalia led Charlotte down the flagstone path, past the herb beds and the weathered bench that Seth kept promising to sand. The lawn rolled gently away towards the ha-ha and the dip of the field beyond. April hadn't quite committed to being spring yet. The trees were in that awkward in-between stage, their buds fat but not fully burst.

"This is beautiful," Charlotte said. "Photographs don't do it justice."

"It's a lot of mowing," Natalia replied. "Less romantic when you're the one wrestling with the ride-on."

Charlotte smiled. "My mother used to talk about that line of trees there." She pointed towards the far boundary, where a row of beeches marched along the hedge. "She said in summer they made a green tunnel. She and Lottie would race to see who could get to the last one before the other caught them."

Natalia could picture them without trying. Two girls in cotton dresses, scuffed knees, ribbons coming loose. It made her throat pinch.

Charlotte fell into step beside her. "Do you use the field much?" she asked. "For anything? Picnics, gatherings… rituals?" She added the last word with a faint lift of a brow, like a joke she could withdraw if it landed badly.

"Bonfires," Natalia said. "The odd barbecue. Mostly it just sits there being muddy."

"Sometimes that's when places are noisiest," Charlotte said lightly. "When you think nothing's happening."

They walked a few more paces. Gravel popped underfoot where the path gave way to rougher ground.

"So," Charlotte went on, her tone casual, "how long have you been here? The Overaughs, I mean."

"Ten years," Natalia said. "Give or take."

"And before that?" Charlotte's gaze flicked to the house, measuring. "No one lived here for a while, right? It was on and off the market. There was some mention in the local archives about structural work, a fire in the sixties…"

Natalia felt it now: the shape of the questions, the way they curved. Open enough to sound harmless, precise enough to leave very little room to wriggle.

She stopped walking.

Charlotte took another two steps before she realised and turned back, boots scuffing in the damp grass. "Sorry," she said. "Too much, too soon?"

Natalia studied her. "You probe like this with everyone you meet?" she asked. "Or am I a special case because my house ticks every box on your haunted-mansion bingo card?"

Charlotte held her gaze, the wind teasing a strand of hair loose from its twist. "I'm just trying to understand the place," she said. "It's what I do."

"Mm." Natalia folded her arms. "No, no it isn't. I forgot to introduce my profession earlier. I spent a very long time in rooms with people who didn't want to tell me things," she said.

"Interrogator by trade. I know when someone's working round to the question they care about." She tipped her head. "So, let's skip the foreplay. It's been a very long week. What do you really want, Charlotte?"

For a heartbeat Charlotte looked almost wrong-footed. Then something softened in her shoulders, like she'd decided to change gears.

"Alright," she said quietly. "No more dancing."

She glanced back at the house, as if checking the windows for watching faces, then took a half-step closer.

"My mother has dreams," she said. "Has had them, since she was eight years old. They started after Lottie went missing. At first, she thought they were just nightmares. Grief, shock, all of that. But they never stopped."

"What kind of dreams?" Natalia asked, though part of her already knew, in the way you know a punch is coming a second before it lands.

"Always here," Charlotte said. "Always in this house.

Sometimes rooms she didn't recognise as a child, but years later she matched them to old photographs. She'd see people she didn't know, in clothes that were wrong for the forties. Names would float up - Becker, Lydia, Elias, Gideon."

Natalia's heart gave a single, heavy thud. "The Beckers built the house," she said slowly.

Charlotte nodded. "Ernest Hannibal Becker, commissioned in 1824. My mother used to sit in her bed in California, thousands of miles away, and dream about a man she'd never met walking these corridors with a lamp. About a girl with dark hair. About a... statue." Her eyes went to the slope of the land. "Always the statue."

Cold crept up Natalia's spine like spilled water. Her fingers had curled into fists without her noticing.

"She learned to live with it," Charlotte went on. "Sometimes the dreams were weeks apart, sometimes they came every night for a month and left her wrung out. Eventually they equalised and they happened every Friday night, regular as clockwork. Like being handed someone else's memories to carry for them."

"And you think that has something to do with us?" Natalia asked. She meant it to come out brisk, sceptical. It sounded thin.

"I think my mother has gone ninety-one years with one foot in this house whether she wanted to or not," Charlotte said. "And I think she would have carried on like that until she died. Only... they stopped."

Natalia wet her lips. "Stopped?"

Charlotte nodded once. "Nineteenth of March this year," she

said. "Your time. I was in Boston; I got a call from the nursing home at stupid o'clock their time because she was shouting my name. By the time I got them to hand her the phone she was calm. She said – and I'm quoting – 'It's gone quiet, Lot. The house. Something has changed. Your aunt's closer than she's ever been.'"

The date landed in Natalia's chest like a stone.

The Incident. The intruder. The statue.

"I looked at the news feeds the next morning," Charlotte said. "Moorside House is not exactly anonymous. There was nothing apart from a missing boy who turned up nearly two weeks later."

Natalia realised she'd stopped breathing. She pulled in air that felt too cold.

"Mother is convinced," Charlotte said softly. "She says something has shifted here. That whatever happened to Lottie, whatever tethered her and all those… impressions… to this place, has been disturbed. Maybe resolved. Maybe not. She begged me to come. To make sure the house is alright. To make sure you are."

Silence stretched between them. A gull wheeled overhead, its cry too bright, too ordinary for the conversation.

"And now the part where you tell me I'm insane," Charlotte said, attempting a faint smile. "Or selling you a line for my consultancy."

Natalia shook her head once, sharp. "No."

Charlotte's eyes searched her face. "Then I'll ask you the thing I've been circling around since I walked through your door," she said. "Is anyone in your family having dreams? About this place. About a statue that shouldn't feel… alive. About a dark figure?"

It was like being slapped.

Natalia's laugh came out ragged. "You need to go."

Charlotte didn't flinch. "Alright," she said. "If that's what you want, I'll leave."

"I mean it," Natalia said. "This… whatever this is... we can't... I can't have you interfering. Not now."

"I'm not here to interfere," Charlotte said. "I'm here because my ninety-one-year-old mother thinks of a place she hasn't seen in eighty-plus years and cries. She doesn't know you, Mrs Overaugh. But she knows this place, and she knows what happens to the families that live here, and she knows about the dreams and so do I. You don't have to tackle this alone."

Natalia felt that like a physical blow. She folded her arms tighter, as if she could hold herself together by brute force.

"Go," she said again, softer now. "Please."

Charlotte inclined her head. "Alright."

They stood there for a moment, the wind tugging at their coats.

"I'm staying at the Hilton in Blackburn," Charlotte said, breaking the silence. "Two weeks, maybe longer. If you, or your husband, or your children want to talk… about anything… you can leave a message at the desk. I won't come back up that lane unless you ask me to. You don't have to suffer in silence."

Natalia didn't trust herself to speak, so she nodded once.

Charlotte's gaze lingered on her face, something like pity and something like respect tangled together, then she turned and began to walk back towards the house.

Halfway to the terrace she paused and looked out over the field, eyes narrowed against the pale light, as if trying to pick out a figure only she could see. Then she got back into the Range Rover and left.

Natalia stood on the drive staring at where the car used to be for a long moment. The heavens opened and as the rain started to pour, she finally turned and made a solemn walk back to the kitchen.

Chapter Fifty-Six

Tuesday, 22nd April 2025 – 16:45

The Hughes residence, Blackburn

The light in Brendan's room always felt wrong at that time of day.

It pushed in through the single small window high on the garage wall, thin and watery, catching in the dust that never seemed to settle. The rest of the room lurked in soft gloom - the half-made bed against the far wall, the leaning tower of trainers in the corner, the TV still bolted to the bracket he'd insisted on putting up himself. Cables hung like stripped nerves down the plasterboard.

Jane sat on the edge of the bed with one of his photos in her hands. It was the print he'd made at college, the one he'd been oddly proud of. A black-and-white shot of the canal at dusk, water like poured lead, reeds jagged and sharp in the foreground. A bird caught mid-flight was just a blur of darker grey against the sky.

"It looks miserable," she'd told him, the first time he'd shown her.

"That's the point, Mum," he'd said, rolling his eyes.

Now her thumbs traced the white border repeatedly, smudging it. Her own face stared back at her faintly in the reflective surface, layered over the canal and the blur of wings. For a second she couldn't tell where she ended, and the picture began. Just a woman, a river, a smear of something taking off and leaving.

The door to the garage opened with its familiar sticky clunk.

"Janey?" Alan's voice drifted in before he did, tired and cautious, like he was testing the air. "I'm setting off for work."

She didn't look round. She knew the shape he'd be, hi-vis jacket half-zipped, work boots already laced, keys looped through his finger. Ready to vanish into fluorescent light and forklift beeping for another twelve hours where nobody would say Brendan's name unless he brought it up first.

"You're on nights again," she said, still staring at the photograph. It wasn't quite a question.

Alan stepped fully into the room, the smell of cold air coming in with him. "Short on staff." He gave a little shrug she could feel rather than see. "They've asked me to cover. You know what it's like."

"You said that last week," Jane replied, the words thin. "And the week before."

He didn't answer straight away. She heard the faint rustle of his jacket as he glanced around the room, taking in the bed, the consoles, the poster still pinned slightly wonky above the headboard. He never stayed in here long. She'd noticed that.

He'd get as far as the doorway, crane his head in as if checking a meter, then retreat.

"Gotta keep busy," he said at last. "Sitting around… doesn't help. Not me."

"Doesn't help you," she echoed softly.

He shifted his weight. "Have you eaten?"

"No."

"You should have something. I've done you a sandwich, it's in the fridge. I'll, uh…" Another pause. The air between them filled with the sound of passing cars from the street, distant and indifferent.

She still didn't look at him. If she did, she knew she'd see it – that flicker of fear in his eyes when she cried, like her grief was a fire he might catch if he got too close.

"Drive safe," she said, because that was what wives were meant to say.

He hesitated, then took two steps into the room after all. His hand landed on the top of the door frame, fingers spreading there as if he needed to hold something solid.

"I miss him too, you know," he said quietly.

She pressed her lips together. The photograph blurred. "Do you?"

A sharp breath from him, in through his nose. "Don't do that, Jane."

"Do what?"

"Like I'm… like I've forgotten him, just because I'm not…" He stopped, searching for a word that wasn't falling apart. "Not how you are."

She swallowed. Her throat felt raw, as if she'd been screaming

in her sleep.
"He was our son," she whispered.
"I know." His voice broke on it. The sound made her chest twist. For a moment she thought he might cross the room and sit beside her; might take the photo, or her hand, or both. Instead, he let go of the door frame.
"I'll see you in the morning," he said. "Try and get some rest."
The door closed. The sound echoed round the little room once, then went very quiet.
Jane sat there with the photograph until the sound of his van starting filtered in – the choke of the engine, the grind of gears, the reversing beep. Then even that faded, leaving only the ticking of the old electric heater on the wall and the light, thin and cold, creeping away another half inch.
She lowered her head.
The sob hit her from nowhere, a hard punch to the chest. One second, she was sitting, breathing, existing; the next she was folded over on herself, the photo dropping into her lap as her hands flew to her face. The sound that came out of her didn't feel like hers, but thick and ugly and too loud for the small space.
"Oh, Bren," she choked. "Oh, baby. Where are you? Where did you go?"
He hadn't been a baby in years, not really, but her body remembered the weight of him at three in the morning burning with a fever, his small hand tangled in her hair so tight she'd had to cut a chunk of it off. It remembered wiping mud from his knees, blood from his lip, sick from his shirt after that first party. It remembered hugging him the last time

he'd gone out the door.

"Back soon, Mum."

Liar, she thought now, a fresh sob shaking her. You liar, you bloody liar, you were meant to come back.

She needed something of him. Something that wasn't a framed school photo or a college print, something warm and soft that still smelt like him.

Jane pushed herself upright and wiped her face with the heel of her hand. Her eyes felt swollen and gritty. She stood and crossed to the free-standing wardrobe they'd squeezed against one wall when they'd converted the garage, the one he'd moaned about because it wasn't "proper fitted wardrobes like Jonah's".

The doors gave a little shudder as she opened them. Inside, his clothes sagged on mismatched hangers, colours dimmed in the half-light. Hoodies, T-shirts, a couple of shirts he'd worn for job interviews, jeans folded badly on the bottom shelf.

She reached straight for one of his hoodies, the black one with the cracked band logo on the front. The cotton was worn thin at the cuffs, faintly bobbled. She dragged it off the hanger and hugged it into her chest, burying her face in the fabric.

For a second there it was: that mix of washing powder, cheap aftershave and something uniquely Brendan, like cigarettes and crisps and late nights. The smell hit her like a hand round the throat. Her knees wobbled.

"Oh Brendan.." She sobbed.

Something thudded at her feet.

She stepped back automatically, heart lurching. A small

rectangle of black plastic lay on the carpet, half under the hanging clothes. For one wild heartbeat she thought it was a rat, or a spider the size of her palm, some lurking horror shaken loose from the dark.

She blinked, pulled the hoodie tighter round herself and crouched.

It was a phone.

Not the one the police had handed back in an evidence bag after they'd decided they didn't need it - his usual cracked Samsung.

This was smaller, older. Different make altogether. Scuffed along the edges, a faint smear of dried mud across the back. No case. No stickers. Anonymous, in a way that turned her stomach.

She picked it up carefully, as if it might explode. The screen stayed black.

"Jesus, Bren," she murmured. "What have you been doing?"

Her first thought was that it was some old spare he'd forgotten about. But Brendan kept his life on his phone. There was no way he'd have a second one without telling her. Not unless...

Not unless it was for the life that he didn't want to her see.

Her skin prickled under the hoodie. She carried the phone to the bedside table and rummaged blindly through the knot of wires until she found a charger that looked like it might fit. The metal tongue slid in with a tiny, satisfying click.

For a moment nothing happened. Then, slowly, a faint grey icon bloomed on the dark screen: a flat battery, deep in the red, and a tiny lightning bolt underneath.

"Typical," she muttered, swallowing. "Running on empty as

always."

It felt like hours before it had enough charge to wake. In reality, it was maybe two minutes. Long enough for her brain to run through every scenario it could find. Burner phone. Dealer's phone. Some girl's phone he'd nicked or borrowed. Evidence of something she didn't understand and didn't want to. She should unplug it, march it round to the police station, hand it over and walk away.

Her fingers didn't move. She was his mother; it was her right to know.

The screen flashed. A logo slid in, then out. The device vibrated once in her hand like something alive, then cleared to the lock screen.

Enter PIN.

She stared at the empty squares, heart thumping.

Her fingers shook as she tapped it in his date of birth.

The phone paused.

Then the screen slid aside.

The home screen was bare. No photo of him and Jonah gurning at the camera, no wallpaper of some footballer or a car he'd never afford. Just the default blue swirl. Four icons at the bottom. Call. Contacts. Camera. Gallery.

No Facebook. No Instagram. No Snapchat logo leering up at her.

Her mouth went dry. She opened Contacts.

There was only one.

'M'.

Just that. One letter. No surname. No picture. No number labels saying "work" or "home". Just the single initial of someone who'd clearly never needed more than that to be recognised.

Her chest tightened. Dealer, she thought. Must be. Who else would he hide like this?

The anger came in sharp and clean, cutting through the grief for the first time in days. Not at Brendan, never at her baby, not really, but at whoever this was. Whoever had taken her boy away from her.

Before she could talk herself out of it, she pressed the little green handset icon.

The call screen leapt up. There was a tiny pause, a faint hiss of a dialling tone.

Far away, in a place Jane would never see, something buzzed in a tent that would never be lived in again.

Moxy's phone lit his dead face in a pale, ghostly wash beneath the trees. The screen flashed 'B' across it in white and green, insistently cheerful. The sound was muffled – a standard ringtone, tinny and bright. A fly crawled lazily across his collarbone, undisturbed.

The battery icon, already slivered to almost nothing, winked once.

1%.

The phone rang on. The corpse didn't move.

Then the screen went black. The sound cut off mid-tone.

Deep in the circuitry, what tiny life was left had finally been extinguished.

Back in Brendan's room, Jane pressed the handset harder to her ear.

"Come on," she muttered. "Pick up. Pick up, you coward."

Nothing. No connection tone, no voicemail greeting. Just the flat, hollow silence of a line that had gone nowhere.

After a few moments the call cut itself. A message flashed up: Call failed.

Jane stared at it, breathing hard. Her reflection hovered faintly in the dark glass – pale face, red eyes.

Coward, she thought again, the word sticking like grit in her teeth. Hiding behind a number and a single letter. Hiding behind her dead son.

Her thumb hovered over the screen, then slid to the gallery icon almost of its own accord.

The camera roll opened.

There were no selfies. No screenshots. No photos of nights out or takeaway boxes or notes to himself. Just a grid of short, rectangular thumbnails, each marked with a tiny white camcorder symbol.

Videos. A dozen of them.

Her pulse spiked, a cold rush behind her eyes. She scrolled to the top. Date stamps blurred past. All taken on the same day, early in the morning after midnight. The oldest was near the bottom. Grainier, darker, time-stamped in a format she had to squint at.

She tapped it with a trembling finger.

The screen went black for a second, then flickered. Sound came first: footsteps on gravel, breath puffing close to the microphone. A low, excited swear she recognised before the picture cleared.

Brendan's face filled the frame, too close, all nose and grin and lit-up eyes.

"Is it on?" he said, laughing. "Testing, you better not be mugging me off, Moxy..."

The camera lurched as he turned. It was the end of the video. The next video automatically started.

It was Brendan again, looking briefly into the camera from behind some kind of tree or bush. Under the shaky movement, Jane saw it: a dark bulk against the sky, windows glowing faintly, the outline familiar from a hundred previous drop offs and pickups.

Moorside House.

Nat's house.

Jane's hand flew to her mouth. The phone wobbled in her grip; she tightened it, knuckles whitening. On the screen, her son turned the camera back to the looming house and the faintly lit skylight.

The videos rolled on.

Chapter Fifty-Seven

Tuesday, 22nd April 2025 – 16:43

Moorside House, Kitchen

Natalia came back into the kitchen soaked to the skin.

The back door gave its usual reluctant noise as she shouldered it shut behind her. Rainwater ran down the back of her neck, cold fingers between her shoulder blades. Her jeans clung to her thighs, heavy, and her trainers squelched faintly on the tiles as she stepped out of them.

Nobody spoke.

Tam stood by the hob with his hand on the grill handle, the oven door cracked open an inch so the heat could seep out. A roasting tray sat cooling on the wooden board beside him, metal skewers lined up in a neat row, chicken and vegetables glistening under charred edges. The smell of garlic and lemon and singed pepper filled the room, thick and homely and completely at odds with the airless silence.

Seth sat at the table with his forearms resting on the wood, fingers linked so tightly the knuckles looked bloodless. Jonah and Izzy faced him from the other side, their plates already laid with a couple of skewers each, rice mounded beside them. Nobody had moved their cutlery. The steam had bled away from the food. Oil had started to congeal in little cloudy moons along the edge of the tray.

Four sets of eyes turned to her.

"How'd it go?" Tam asked at last, voice softer than she expected it to be. "With Charlotte."

Natalia peeled her hood back with fingers that didn't feel quite attached to her. Her hair was plastered to her cheeks and forehead in dark ropes, rainwater dripping off the ends. She could feel the chill of it settling into her bones already.

"She knows something," Nat said. Her voice came out hoarse. "Or she thinks she does. She was… probing."

Izzy frowned. "What do you mean, probing?"

Nat shrugged off her coat. She slung it over the back of a chair and stayed standing.

"She kept skirting round the edges, she knows something is wrong with this place. She just doesn't know what."

Seth's gaze flicked to Jonah, then back to her. "Did she mention anything about the intruder?"

"No." Nat's answer was instant. "She doesn't know about the incident. She was focused on Lottie and asked whether we were having strange dreams."

The girl's name and the gravity of the whole statement sat on the table like another plate, an invisible weight between them.

Tam cleared his throat. "She say anything about a crate?"

"What's that got to do with anything?" Nat snapped. "It's an old box, Tam."

"Oh, I don't know," he said, eyebrows up. "An occult specialist rocks up at your door looking for a long-lost little girl who vanished in the war, and you lot have dug up a bloody chest from World War Two in the exact spot you buried a body. Might be nothing. Might be a Tuesday." He tapped the worktop with two fingers. "Or it might be something someone should have opened long before now, hen."

Jonah's chair creaked. Izzy sat very still.

Tam went on: "The question is, why nobody's looked inside it yet?"

"Because we forgot about it," Seth cut in. "Alright? We've had a lot on. It doesn't weigh anything, it's empty."

Tam stared at him. "You forgot about a small coffin-sized crate you hauled out of the ground with your bare hands on the night you hid a corpse?"

"We didn't forget," Nat said, before Seth could answer. Her voice had gone thin. "We… parked it. There's a difference. We put it on the list marked 'deal with later' and then later kept getting…" She gestured helplessly at Jonah. At Izzy. At the house. "Louder."

Tam's mouth tightened, but he said nothing.

Nat could feel it all piling on top of her, layer after layer. The rain still cold in her clothes. Charlotte's careful questions. Lottie's name in every other sentence. Brendan's face. The plan for Bossman. The crate, now sitting there in her mind like a second grave, squatting in the shed where the statue was stood. The sorrow was destroying her.

"I can't," she said suddenly. The word came out like a cough.

Jonah looked up. "Mum?"

"I can't be dealing with another thing right now, Tam." Her throat burned and she started to sob, something Tam had never seen before.

"I can't think about mystery boxes and missing girls and what's buried were. I am at capacity. Do you understand? I am…" She broke off, breath hitching. "We have Brendan dead and Jonah nearly dead and Bossman dead and that thing in the shed and the dreams and now Charlotte Richardson sniffing around with her questions and I am hanging on by my fingernails. I can't take one more… twist."

Her vision blurred. She pressed her fingers to the bridge of her nose, but the tears flowed anyway, hot and humiliating.

Seth pushed his chair back a little, as if to come round to her, then froze, caught between not wanting to crowd her and not wanting to stay put.

Tam watched for a beat, the muscle in his jaw twitching.

"Right," he said, suddenly brisk. "That'll do."

Izzy blinked. "What?"

He slapped his palms lightly on his thighs and straightened. "Show's over. You two, shoes on."

Jonah frowned. "What for?"

"We're going to the cinema," Tam said. "The pictures. The moving flicker show. Whatever you children are calling it these days."

"We can't just go to the cinema," Jonah said, bewildered.

"Watch me," Tam replied. "I'm going to remortgage my soul for popcorn and some godawful superhero sequel so that your mum and dad can have a couple of hours where they're not discussing murder, bogeymen or boxes."

Izzy glanced between Nat and Seth. "Mum?"

Nat wiped her face with the heel of her hand, eyes red. "Go," she managed. "Please. Just… go with him."

Seth cleared his throat. "Tam, you don't have to -"

"Yes, I do," Tam said, not looking at him. "Because if we sit here much longer, we're all going to start saying things we can't unsay, and nobody needs that on a Tuesday." He crooked a finger at Jonah. "Up. Trainers. Coat. You look like a hostage."

Jonah pushed his chair back slowly. "What are we even going to watch?"

"Something with explosions," Tam said. "Or a cartoon pig. I don't care. We're going to sit in the dark and let someone else's disaster take the weight for ninety minutes."

Izzy stood too, scraping her chair. "Shotgun aisle seat," she muttered, because it was easier than saying thank you.

Tam gave her a quick, fond look. "You can have whatever seat you want, princess, as long as you're not in this kitchen for a bit."

They disappeared in a flurry of hunting for phones and wallets and thrown on coats. The front door banged, then clicked. Their voices slid away down the path.

The house settled, ever so slightly.

Nat realised she was still standing in the exact same spot, rainwater drying cold on her skin, the smell of grilled chicken thick in the air. Her legs felt hollow.

Seth rose, walked round the table and pulled out the chair

opposite his, nodding towards it.
"Sit down, darling." he said quietly. "Before you fall down."
She let out a breath that was almost a laugh, almost a sob, and did as she was told. The chicken skewers on their plates sat untouched between them, cooling fast as she sobbed uncontrollably.

Chapter Fifty-Eight

Tuesday, 22nd April 2025 – 18:14

Moorside House

Out in the garden, the shed shook under the weather.

Rain came at it sideways now, not falling so much as being driven, needling the wooden walls, drumming on the roof until it sounded like a thousand fingers tapping to be let in. Wind worried at the padlock, rattling it in its hasp. Water crept under the warped boards and ran in thin threads along the concrete floor.

The statue did not move.

It stood where Seth had left it, cloaked and hooded, a silhouette carved out of something blacker than the dark around it. The plastic sheet he'd thrown over its shoulders had slipped halfway, pooling at its feet, rainwater gathered in cloudy puddles in the folds.

Something in the air shifted.

It wasn't the wind. That was tired and old, a big blunt thing that rolled over the house and went on. This was finer. A shiver, like the space itself had remembered it was not empty. Deep inside the basalt statue, the dark figure could sense the sorrow outside at fever pitch. It was his turn to conduct an experiment; all it would take is a little nudge and the sorrow would do the rest. He woke the sorrow inside the statue and giddied it outwards.

A slow stream of blue, so dark it was almost black, unfurled in the stone's core. It could sense something, its kinship – sorrow. It seeped outwards like dye in water, threading through microscopic cracks, filling old channels that had never properly dried. Every place sorrow had touched the statue, every hand that had clutched it and wept, every moment of grief that had fed it left a trace, a route. The blue ran along them all and now it sensed more was available.

It tasted the storm. The pressure. The weight of low cloud and soaked earth and a house full of people who had run out of ways to hold themselves together.

The line of blue pushed further.

It slipped through the base where rock met concrete, out into the damp, up through hairline fractures in the slab Seth had laid himself. It slid along the old paths the statue had always used. Up the wall, through the brick, into the cavity.

It found timbers and copper pipes, electrical cable humming faintly with the life of the house. It passed through them seamlessly, following the warmth, following the offering.

Inside, where the light burned yellow and the air smelled of cooling food and tears, it found her.

The blue spread thin as mist as it reached Natalia. It settled over her shoulders, sank through her jumper, sank into her skin. No glow, no flare, nothing a human eye could catch. Just a tightening of the chest, the sense of being dipped in something cold and dark that wasn't quite hers.

Neither of them noticed.

The house sighed in concern and the storm hammered on.

Natalia had stopped sobbing in great heaves. She'd run out of sound twenty minutes ago. Now everything felt scraped out. Her throat was raw, her eyes swollen.

Seth had parked her at the end of the table and slung her wet hoodie over the radiator.

Her hands lay on the tabletop, palms flat, fingers slightly curved as if she needed to feel something solid.

"I can't shake it," she said, finally. Her voice sounded wrong to her own ears. Too flat. "It's not just being sad. I know what sad is. This is… like someone's poured something into me and it's just sitting there. Like concrete. It's in my bones."

Seth sat opposite, a mug cooling between his hands. He'd made her tea and pushed it across to her earlier. She'd drunk half of it without tasting a drop.

He watched her as she talked, eyes steady.

"It's going to sound mad," Nat went on, "but it feels… foreign. Not all of it. Part of it is mine, obviously. Brendan, Jonah, everything. But there's this… extra bit. This… weight. Like I've swallowed somebody else's grief as well and I can't get it back out."

Seth turned the mug in his hands, thumb running round the chipped rim.

"You've had a lot thrown at you in a short space of time," he said. "Shock does that. Trauma. It layers. Sometimes you don't even realise what's sitting on top of what."

She shook her head. "This is different. When my dad died, it hurt, but it was… sharp. Clean." A faint, humourless smile tugged at her mouth. "If grief can be clean. This isn't. This is like… sludge. Like being stuck at the bottom of a canal with a tyre round your waist and mud up to your chest. Every time I think I've got a bit of feeling back in my legs, something else drags me down again."

He let her talk. He'd learnt that much. If he jumped in too soon, she shut down, folded everything back into herself.

She stared past him at the window. Rain chased itself down the glass in crooked lines, the outside light already going dim. "I feel guilty about everything. Brendan, Bossman, Lottie... all of it. I feel guilty for just existing."

She let out a breath. "I know it's not all mine to carry, but it doesn't matter what I tell myself, my body and brain haven't got the memo."

Seth took a slow sip of tea before answering.

"You've taken responsibility for everything since the night it happened," he said. "Way more than your share. You do that. You hoover up everyone else's feelings and stack them on top of your own."

"That's not what this is," she said, quietly stubborn. "This isn't just me being a martyr. I… since that night, since the intruder, I've felt… contaminated." She groped for words, frustrated by how clumsy they felt. "There was so much… noise. So much fear, and anger and… other things. It feels like it has all stuck to me. Like I walked through a spill and now I'm tracking it everywhere."

"You had blood on you," he said. "Literally. We all did. It's not surprising your brain's filed that whole night under 'contamination.'"

"It's not the blood." She rubbed her chest, as if something itched under the bone. "It's… deeper. I feel like… like I've been dyed. This horrible deep colour. And now everything I do, everything I think, comes out tinged with it."

"How much sleep have you had in the last week?" he asked.

She snorted. "Is that a trick question?"

"Roughly."

"I don't know. A few hours at a time. Sometimes less. Sometimes not at all."

"How many hot meals have you eaten that weren't made in a microwave or shoved into you by someone else?"

She opened her mouth, then closed it again.

"Your brain is knackered, Nat," he said. "Your body is running on fumes. You've gone from normal life to murder to cover-up to arrest to Wetherby to… whatever the hell that thing did to Jonah last week. You're not just grieving. You're running a marathon on broken legs."

"You feel it too," she shot back. "Don't pretend you don't. I see it on you. The… drag. The heaviness."

"Of course I feel it," he said. "I'm not made of stone."

"Then why aren't you drowning like I am?"

He hesitated.

"Different people sink at different speeds," he said. "And I haven't had…" He gestured at his chest. "That. Not like you describe. My guilt sits… other places."

She looked back at the window. Another gust of wind rattled the glass in its frame. The kitchen light flickered once, then steadied. The rain poured.

They sat in silence, together watching the rain.

A sudden pounding on the front door shattered the silence, hard enough to vibrate the hinges.

They both froze.

The rain on the windows, the hum of the fridge, the ticking of the clock – all of it dropped behind the sound of that hammering.

"Who the hell?" Seth began.

Another volley of blows cut him off. Closer together this time. Desperate.

Nat pushed her chair back, heart jerking into her throat.

They looked at each other for half a second.

"You stay here, I'll get it," he said.

The storm bellowed outside. The pounding came again, relentless, like whoever was on the step had run out of patience with the whole world at once.

Seth squared his shoulders and headed for the hall.

Nat stayed seated, staring at the table.

Chapter Fifty-Nine

Tuesday, 22nd April 2025 – 18:18

Moorside House

Seth flicked the chain off out of habit and pulled the front door open half an inch.

A figure in a duffle coat shoved in the rest of the way with rain and wind howling.

He stumbled back as she barged past him, wet wool slamming against his chest, the smell of rain and cold air filling the hallway. The hood was up, soaked dark, dripping onto the floor. She moved like someone who'd been held back all day and had finally snapped the lead.

"You," she spat, jabbing a finger into his shoulder as she forced her way inside. "You… fucking monster!"

"Hey -" Seth caught the edge of the door before it hit the wall. "Hang on a second -"

"Where is she?" the woman demanded, marching down the hall without waiting for an answer. Her voice cracked with fury. "Where is that fucking demon wife of yours?"

It took him a heartbeat too long to place her. The coat, the hood, the way she barrelled past.

Then she turned her head just enough for the light from the lounge to catch her face.

"Oh, Christ," Seth breathed. "Jane."

Jane Hughes didn't stop. She ricocheted off the console table, sending the bowl of keys skittering, and headed straight for the kitchen like she'd lived there for years.

"Jane, wait," he said, going after her. "You can't just..."

She shouldered the kitchen door open so hard it bounced off the stopper.

Natalia flinched at the bang, hand flying to her chest. She'd been staring at the grain of the table, lost in the rain and the ticking clock. The sudden intrusion made her chair scrape.

Jane took the room in with a glance. The empty places where the kids should have been. The plates in the sink. Nat's blotched face.

"You," she said again, voice lowering into something almost hoarse. "You have got some fucking front."

"Jane?" Nat blinked, trying to make sense of her. "What -?"

"You came to my house," Jane shouted, jabbing a hand towards her. Drops of rain flew from her cuff. "You stood in my kitchen. You looked me in the eye, and you told me how sorry you were. You held my hand, you comforted me, and you lied."

Nat's stomach dropped. "I -"

"Don't," Jane snapped. "Don't you dare. Don't you fucking dare try and do that soft voice bullshit with me again. I know." She ripped her hood back with a sharp, angry movement. Her hair was plastered to her skull, the skin round her eyes raw. "I know what you did to him. What you dragged him into. All of you. This whole… sick little set-up."

Seth reached the doorway, breath tight. "Jane, you need to slow down. Tell us what's happening."

She whirled on him.

"Oh, I'll tell you what's happened," she hissed. "I found his phone. His other phone." Her hand dove into her pocket and came out with a small black handset, cable still trailing behind it like an umbilical cord that had been ripped out a charger in hurry. She slapped it down on the table so hard it bounced. "This is what's happening."

Nat stared at it. For a second her brain wouldn't connect the object with anything. Then her mind caught up.

"Jane," she said, carefully, "I don't know what that is."

"Shut up," Jane said. The word cracked like a whip. "Just shut your mouth. You know exactly what it is. You know exactly what's on it. You and him and that precious bloody daughter of yours."

The blue in Natalia's chest tightened, cold fingers digging in.

Seth held his hands out, palms up, the way he'd done with angry suspects years ago. "Look, let's all just take a breath. If you've seen something that concerns you, we can talk about it. Nobody's trying to..."

"Oh, there'll be talking," Jane cut in. Her eyes were bright with furious tears. "There'll be talking when the police see this. When they see my Brendan outside your house in the middle of the night. When they see your nice big driveway and your nice big front door and work out exactly what kind of people live behind it."

Natalia's skin went cold.

"It's all on video!" she hissed.

"You've watched some videos," Nat said, barely above a whisper.

Jane's gaze snapped back to her. "All of them," she snarled. "Every single one. Him creeping round your garden. Him ducking down behind that bloody hedge out there while your husband..." She jabbed a finger at Seth. "...sawed a man up! it's all on here. Every second. You people have been lying to me from day one, you're sick."

Seth swallowed. "We didn't -"

"Don't." Jane's face crumpled, then hardened again. "You let me think he'd just… wandered off. That he'd got high or drunk or… whatever. You let me stand there at that canal and listen to all those speeches about how no one knew where he'd gone, while you..." Her voice broke. "While you knew what he'd been through on the night he disappeared. What he'd seen you do!"

Nat's heart pounded so hard she could feel it in her throat.

"We didn't know, Jane," she whispered. "Not like that. We didn't know about-"

"Liar," Jane spat. "You're all liars. You knew enough to come playing Florence Nightingale in my kitchen. You knew enough to sit there staring at your hands and pretending you were just 'worried about Jonah'." She mimicked the phrase in a cruel soprano, shoulders hunched. "It was all just a snooping exercise wasn't it!" It was a statement, not a question.

Seth took a step closer to her, slow, measured.

"Jane, you're soaked," he said. "You're grieving. You've just seen something horrible. Let us make you a drink. We'll explain what we can. Then you can decide what you want to do."

She laughed manically.

"Look at this! Look at what you are!" She thumbed at the phone and started playing a video. The audio screeched into life like a whining death sentence. Seth was still in the doorway; she turned to him and held the phone up sideways, her back to Natalia.

"Oh, I know exactly what I'm going to do, you fucking monster," she said. "I'm going to walk straight out of here, I'm going to drive to the station, and I'm going to hand this over to DC McIntyre and tell her everything. Every look. Every lie. When you turned up with that wounded little act and those big sorry eyes. MY SON IS DEAD BECAUSE OF YOU!"

Something in Nat's chest tore.

"I know," she said. "Jane, I know, I am so -"

"Don't say sorry, you fucking bitch!" Jane's voice climbed again, thin with rage. "

"This is the truth," she said, shaking the phone. "And it's going to save me from going mad. Because now I know. I know he was here. I know you knew. And I know you're all going away for a very, very long time." She was transfixed on Seth, leaning closer, spittle frothing from the sides of her mouth.

The blue inside Natalia flared.

"*Do it...*"

The voice wasn't a sound, not exactly. It was a pressure behind the eyes. A word pressed directly into the meat of her thoughts. It came with the cold, with the weight, with the sense of some enormous attention turning, just for a moment, fully onto her.

"*Do it...*"

Her fingers curled against the table.

Jane was still talking. Something about prison, about Jonah in handcuffs, about "rotting behind bars where you belong". But the words blurred. Nat's vision narrowed. The real threat, the footage had emerged and now it was time to deal with it once and for all.

The kitchen seemed to tilt, the edges of the room drawing in. All she could see was the phone in Jane's fist, her other hand poking her husband in the chest. The thin rectangle of plastic that could end everything. The image of Jonah in a cell again. Of Izzy on some stranger's sofa. Of Seth in a glass box in Crown Court.

"*Do it...*"

Her hand moved before she'd consciously decided to move it.

The roasting tray was still on the counter, pushed back out of the way. One skewer lay across the lip, abandoned when Tam had dished up. The metal was cool to touch now, the food on it half-eaten.

Nat's fingers closed round the handle.

She stood up.

Seth saw the movement out of the corner of his eye over Jane's shoulder.
Jane still had the phone in her left hand and her right-hand poking into his chest
"*Do it...*"
Natalia inched forward.
She drove the skewer forward into the top of Jane Hughes' spine, just below the skull with inch perfect precision towards the medulla oblongata - the connection between the brainstem and the spinal cord.
The sound was small. A wet, resisting pop, nothing like the movie crunch you'd half-expect. Her hand jolted as metal met bone and continued onwards with speed, force and accuracy. She could feel Jane juddering, no longer talking. She could see Seth's horrified face.
Jane's eyes went huge. For the split second they locked with Seth's, full of shock and disbelief, as if this was the one outcome she hadn't planned for.
The phone dropped to the floor.
Natalia gave the skewer a sharp, sickening twist.
Jane's knees went next. She made a noise; not a scream, not really, more a thick, startled gurgle, and crumpled sideways her shoulder slamming into the tiles, legs folding under her, twitching as the last brainwaves stopped.
Nat let go. She watched, numb, as Jane lay on the floor.
The blue inside her pulsed once, satisfied, then retreated back into its cold, deep place.
Jane Hughes, 45, from Blackburn, England, never regained consciousness.

Epilogue

Moorside House - 1829

Tuesday, 10th November - 13:10

The carter dropped him at the bottom of the path and left him to walk the rest with the plate wrapped in sacking under his arm.

Elias Haworth climbed slowly, boots slipping a little in the churned mud where horses and barrows had chewed the new road to paste. The house rose ahead of him, half-finished and already too big for the hill. A shell of pale stone and empty windows, chimneys standing with no pots yet, like bare teeth. He liked a building at this stage. You could still see its bones.

Men were packing up for the day as he reached the front. A couple of lads were carrying hods back to the yard, shoulders hunched, caps pulled low against what was blown in from the moor. Someone shouted something about ale, someone else laughed. Nobody paid much attention to the small, wiry mason with the bundle under his arm.

"Last job, Elias?" one of them called.

"Last of the corner-watching plates," he said. "Then I'll leave you lot to your draughts."

The lad rolled his eyes, but there was no real malice in it. "Mind the boggarts don't get you."

Elias just smiled and kept walking.

The first plate had gone up that morning on the high front right corner, the stone still new enough to drink in the strike of his chisel. He'd unwrapped it like something precious: a round of old bell-metal, hand-cast in the yard, the surface chased with the simple outline of a lark lifting from stylised hills. Hope was inscribed on that one.

The second, on the rear right, bore a leaping wolf with its teeth bared and its tail streaming. Courage. He'd liked the feel of that one under his hand. All motion and intent.

The third, on the rear left, was the lion. Strength. He'd had to stand on the very top rung of the ladder to set it, hammer swinging level with the jackdaws. The lion's mane had caught the weak sun for a moment, metal flaring bright against the pale stone, before the cloud swallowed it.

Now only the last remained, wrapped tight in its burlap shroud protecting it from knocks and bumps.

He skirted the side of the house, past stacks of slate and a tipped barrow, until he came to the left-hand elevation. From here you could see straight down over the rough fall of the grounds towards the line of the old path and, beyond that, the glint of the river. They said corpses had gone that way once, borne on shoulders to the church in the bottom of the valley during the Crusades. He didn't know if it was true. He

knew the land felt… used. That was enough.
Elias set the ladder against the corner stone and tested the rungs with his weight. Satisfied, he tucked the bundle under his arm and climbed, humming under his breath to steady his breathing.
"Four corners watching, four corners wake," he murmured, half-song, half-habit. "Keep the house standing, keep out what takes."
Mary Becker had watched him wrap the plates that morning, brow furrowed, fingers worrying the edge of her shawl. "If it eases the men," she'd said quietly, when her husband had scoffed at the expense. "And if it eases you, Mr Haworth. There's no harm in a house being well watched."
She'd said, "no harm," though her fingers had tightened white-knuckled on her shawl. At the top of the ladder, he wedged his hip against the stone and unwrapped the last plate.
Integrity.
This one was the simplest of the set. No roaring beasts, no motion. Just an owl, wings folded tight, perched on a straight horizontal bar that cut clean across the disc. The bird's head was turned as if listening, eyes picked out as two small hollows. Its stillness suggested vigilance, a metal sentry waiting for the world to misbehave.
"Now then," he said to it, quietly. "Let's see you earn your keep."
He held the plate up to the corner, gauging the line, and marked the fixing points with the tip of his chisel. The wind tugged at his cap. Down on the rough lawn, a couple of

labourers were already heading for the gate, their voices thin in the damp air.

He set the first nail and struck.

The noise rang out sharp along the stonework, carrying further than he'd expected. The owl quivered under his hand, then settled. He set the second nail, and the third, working round the edge until the plate sat flush with the corner. Metal cool and stubborn beneath his palm.

When it was done, he left his hand resting there for a moment.

"Four corners watching," he said softly.

"Four corners wake."

A draught slid round the edge of the house and under his collar. It smelled of wet earth and something older, a faint sour tang that made the hairs on his arms rise. Elias frowned, glancing down at the ground far below, but there was nothing to see - just mud, and piles of stone.

He patted the plate - a reassurance for the metal, or perhaps for himself.

"Keep the house standing," he finished under his breath. "Keep out what takes."

The owl stared out over the slope towards the old path, unblinking.

Down in the unfinished cellar, where the stone met the raw clay of the hill, something cold and buried shifted very slightly in its sleep.

Elias didn't feel it. He climbed down the ladder, joints protesting, and shouldered it up to carry back to the yard. Another job done. Another big house for someone

else's name.
Behind him, high on the left-hand corner of Moorside, the last of the four watching plates caught a scrap of grey light and held it.
The four wards of Moorside were now firmly in place.

Moorside House - 1954

Wednesday, 14th April - 11:15

The wind had not changed in 125 years. It still came off the moor with the same cold, wet teeth, chewing at the mortar and worrying the slates.
Lilith Thompson stood on the gravel drive, the hem of her emerald swing coat snapping against her calves. She was twenty-four, possessed of a face that could stop a room and eyes that could empty one. She watched the stonemason descend the ladder with the impatience of a woman who had waited a lifetime for a door to open and was done with waiting.
At her feet lay three plates of dull metal. The Lark. The Wolf. The Lion. They looked smaller off the wall, stripped of their height and their dignity, reduced to dirty scrap on the wet stones.
The mason, a man named Arkwright with hands like spades and a face carved from the same gritstone he worked, hit the bottom rung and wiped his forehead with a rag. He didn't look happy.
"Well?" Lilith asked. Her voice was glass. Smooth, clear, and

liable to cut.
Arkwright shook his head, looking up at the front left corner of the house where the ladder still leaned. “It won’t shift, Miss. I’ve broken two chisels on it already. The stone holds it like a fist. I strike it, and the house rings like a bell, but the metal don’t give an inch."
Lilith narrowed her eyes, looking up at the dark outline of the Owl against the grey stone. Integrity. The stubborn, silent watcher. She should have known that one would be the problem. The house was trying to reject her, holding onto its last scrap of protection like a child clutching a blanket.
"I didn’t hire you to ring bells, Mr Arkwright." she said coldly. “I hired you to strip this place of its old… superstitions. My fiancé has purchased a home, not a museum.”
“I’m telling you," Arkwright grunted, packing his tools with angry, jerky movements. "It’s not natural. The other three popped off with a bit of leverage. That one? It’s fused. If I go at it any harder, I’ll crack the corner stone and bring the guttering down with it."
Lilith tapped a high heel against The Lion plate at her feet, a small, vicious kick. She understood perfectly well why the plate wouldn’t move. The house knew what she was. It knew she was a cuckoo in the nest. A Thompson wearing the skin of a lady, come to take what the Hawthorns had squandered. But stone and metal could be outwitted. If you couldn’t remove a thing, you simply made it disappear.
“Fine,” she said, making the decision instantly. “If it won't come down, cover it up.”
Arkwright blinked, pausing with a hammer in his hand.

"Cover it?"

"Render over it," she commanded, gesturing with a gloved hand. "Roughcast the corner. Heavy dash. Then paint it. I want it buried so deep under stone and lime that no one will ever know it's there. If it cannot see out, it cannot watch."

The mason scratched his chin, looking doubtful. "That's a fair bit of work, Miss. Mixing, rendering, waiting for it to cure. It'll cost extra."

Lilith smiled. It was not a nice smile. It was the smile of a fox that had found the hen coop unlocked.

"Money is hardly an objection, Mr Arkwright. Do it. Today. I want that bird blinded before the sun goes down."

Arkwright shrugged, defeated by her certainty. "Right you are. I'll add it to the bill. Send it to the usual address? Mrs Thompson, care of Mr Blackwood?"

Lilith turned her gaze to the house - her house now. She thought of the twins, those precious, golden Hawthorn girls she had watched from the shadows for so long, hating them for their happiness, despising them for the ease of their lives. They were gone now. And she was here.

"Send the bill to this house, Mr Arkwright," she said softly. "But change the name."

"Change it?"

She turned to him, her eyes bright with a triumph that tasted like wine.

"Yes. Make it out to Lilith Hawthorn. My name will be changing very soon."

She didn't wait for his reaction. She looked down at the three plates on the gravel - Hope, Courage, Strength. Useless virtues. They hadn't saved the family before, and they wouldn't stop her now. But she couldn't leave them lying about. They still hummed with a faint, annoying resonance that made her teeth ache.

“Leave these,” she said, gesturing to the metal discs. “I have the perfect place for them.”

Arkwright hefted his bag. “Whatever you say, Mrs… Miss.”

As the mason trudged off to mix his render, Lilith looked towards the old shed at the bottom of the garden where the crate sat.

She would put the plates in there, give her some company. They could all rot together. That thought pleased her immensely.

She would wrap them tight, seal the lid, and bury the box deep in the fire pit as planned. Where the earth was scorched and dead.

“Let's see how well you protect the house from six feet under,” she whispered to the metal plates.

Lilith Thompson – soon to be Hawthorn - turned back to the front door, her heels clicking a conquering rhythm on the stone, ready to start a new era of silence.

Reading Group Guide

Moorside House: The Series of Silence – Book 2

Thank you for taking the time to read the Silence We Share – the Second Book in the Series of Silence (@SeriesOfSilence). It's important to understand that The Silence We Share is the fallout and escalation volume of the first Moorside trilogy – The House of Overaugh.

- In Book One – The Silence We Hide the Overaugh family commit an unthinkable act, bury the truth, and learn how far love will stretch to protect a secret.

- In Book Two – The Silence We Share that secret begins to leak: through blackmail, addiction, dreams, and the growing pull of Moorside's darker history.

- In Book Three – The Silence We Reveal the long-buried truth will finally be dragged into the light with shocking consequences.

Across the first trilogy, each book title describes what readers will experience during their journey:

- Hide – Secrets are hidden
- Share – Secrets are shared
- Reveal – Secrets are revealed

You might want to open your discussion by asking:

Which secrets do you think are truly “hidden”?

Which secrets are “shared” and who with?

What, exactly, will need to be “revealed” in book 3.

Most importantly – the main question for you to consider is:

“What’s in the box?”

Finally, the silence is revealed in the explosion conclusion to the House of Overaugh. Questions are answered and secrets are revealed with devastating consequences.

The following is an extract from Moorside House: The Series of **Silence Book 3: The Silence We Reveal**

The hinges screamed one last time and then the lid rolled back, revealing what lay inside.

Seth's mind tried to place its contents - but the first thing that came was not a word but a feeling, a weight dropping through him, as if the gravity in that little box were suddenly much stronger than the gravity in the rest of the shed.

The air thickened.

The light over their heads flickered.

Seth heard his own voice before he knew he'd spoken.

"Jesus Christ."

Natalia's hand crushed his.

"Oh my God," she breathed.

Tam stared down through the rising breath of that old, wrong smell, every line in his face pulled tight.

"Christ almighty," he said quietly. "What the fuck have you two got me into?"

THE SILENCE WE SHARE

THE HOUSE OF OVERAUGH

THE
SILENCE
WE SHARE